Veil of Shadows II

Omnibus Special Edition

M. R. Pritchard

Third Edition
October 2024
Midnight Ledger
Paperback ISBN: 978-1-957709-54-3

VEIL OF SHADOWS II

ENTER THE VEIL OF SHADOWS II

Haunted by Sparrow's shocking betrayal, Meg faces a breaking point. Caring for an amputee Angel and two refugees from the Earthen plane adds to her mounting pressure. With King Gabriel imprisoned and a kidnapped baby Thrush in her care, time is running out to prevent Thrush from sharing the Nightjar's fate.

Revenge and redemption collide, forcing Meg to confront her inner demons and desires. Will her quest for vengeance consume her, or can she find the strength to protect those she holds dear? In a race against time and her own turbulent emotions, Meg's choices will determine the fate of those she loves.

As Meg grapples with the heartbeat in her womb and the constant threat to her friends, she decides it's best to disappear. Fleeing to the Earthen plane to hide and plan her next move, she encounters mysterious help amid thunderstorms and insatiable hungers. Will Meg destroy the one man who would follow her through hell and high water?

Discover a world where love battles darkness, destinies entwine, and wickedness knows no rest.

———

"I was hooked from the get-go..." -ABNA Expert Reviewer

"It's unfortunate that one can't predict or be a part of aiding which books go viral, as Sparrow Man by M.R. Pritchard is certainly worthy of such reward ... this novel took me by complete surprise. What I thought was a simple zombie story morphed into something wild and completely unforeseen. Yet it fit perfectly within the world Pritchard has created, mysteries unfolding into fantastical developments. The eclectic characters were a joy to follow and the romance unfolded without being forced."-TheBehrg, KindleScout winning author of Housebroken

"Whoever thought a trip to Hell could be so interesting! Pritchard does a good job balancing humor and thrills—hell, it's mostly funny —and delivering the reader a cast of characters so unbelievable that you can't help but love them." - Charles, Vine Voice

"Another great fantasy ... with humor, edginess, childlike joy, and the frailty of love. Pritchard reminds us to nurture those we hold dear as we root for her characters to have a happily ever after." - Muddy Rose Reviews

"This is the story of being there for someone who is going through a tough time, of love and trauma with strong characters that you can't help but like. Meg, and Sparrow, stand out in a well told tale. I am not normally into fantasy but this one grabbed me as it is so much more." -Misfits Reviewer

Part One
Raven King

Dumb Ways to Die

Have you ever tried to fly? Takeoff is a bitch. Sparrow made it look easy—heck seagulls make it look easy. Nothing prepares you for the lack of strength in your back, the choking feeling in your throat, the uselessness of your legs, the feeling of purely sucking at life.

"Go!" Skeele shouts. "Launch yourself. Jump! Like this." He catapults himself into the air; his wings whip out and then he's heading toward the Hellsky. Effortless. Like a damned eagle on the coast. Of course, he's big and muscular and has had a lot of time to perfect flying. I flex my bicep and the smallest muscle bulges. Maybe I should do some push-ups. Skeele lands nearby, the dust of Hell swirling around his boots as he stomps down. "Now," he motions with the swoop of his arm, "it's your turn."

"I'm tired." I cross my arms and tip my head, trying to loosen tense neck muscles.

"You've been sleeping all day." He steps closer. "You shouldn't be tired. You sleep more than a baby." He keeps stepping closer.

Skeele is one big son-of-a-bitch and there was one point in time that he terrified the fuck out of me, but not anymore. He doesn't scare the ruler of Hell. I went through too much to fear anyone anymore, even this giant Hellion with horns and sharp teeth.

"Do it, Meg." He's too close. "Fly!" he roars. I jump and take two steps away. "What are you afraid of?" he asks.

I hold out my arms, directing him to stay away. "I just need some space."

"Don't be afraid of failing. None of us came out of the womb with wings. We all had to learn." He's so calm and encouraging, not like the Hellions of the past. He's not like the ones who would rather kill first and ask questions later. Sparrow taught him better.

"I've already failed enough." I roll my shoulders, loosening my back muscles. There's nothing there. It doesn't even feel like anything is thinking of being there. No wings. Nothing.

"Why?" Skeele scoffs. "Because you lost Sparrow?"

"Shut up." I glare at him.

He moves closer. "You're just hangry." Skeele frowns. "I could help you."

I have eaten nearly every Twinkie in Hell, every bag of chips, every orange soda, everything that might send a middle-aged man on a quick trip to cardiac arrest. Nothing will fill my stomach like a little bit of fresh blood would. Like a little sip of Sparrow's blood. But Skeele's blood. No thanks. Not on my life would I drink from him. That's crossing the line. Fresh blood brings the lust. I'm saving that for one man in my life.

Skeele's holding out his forearm, the blood pulsing through his thick veins. I can hear it; *whoosh-whoosh-whoosh* thundering in my ears. My mouth fills with saliva, anticipating the sweet flush of fresh blood. My eyes flick to his face. He's not Sparrow. Not even close. There are no green eyes, no mussed brown hair, no tick of insanity.

"Fucker," I mutter as I stomp away.

"It's not going to go away," Skeele shouts in my direction. "The hunger will never go away. If you don't do something about it, you're going to do something you regret."

Overgrown grass sweeps my legs as I walk to the nearby Jeep Wrangler. I didn't want to practice near the castle, didn't want the others to see that a loser who couldn't fly ruled them. They quivered in the presence of my grandfather. They must do the same for me.

A Northern Flicker whistles a trill from the hood of the Jeep. I stop. These birds keep haunting me. With Sparrow and the others around it was kinda endearing, now every flutter is a sign, every chirp a warning.

"They'll never grow out your back if you don't try," Skeele shouts from the field behind me. "They need an urge to sprout!"

I pick up a rock and throw it at the hood of the Jeep, scaring away the songbird. I gotta get out of here. I need to shake this feeling of defeat.

The thud of heavy footsteps is suddenly behind me. Large hands grip the waistband of my leather pants and under my arm.

"What the—" I kick, trying to escape but my feet are lifted off the ground.

The fucker doesn't know when to stop. "They'll never appear unless you try," he grumbles in my ear as he tosses me in the air.

My stomach remains on land as I pedal my arms and legs as my eyes scan the treetops.

"No!" I shout as gravity pulls me down.

Skeele is in the air; he grabs the back of my pants again and tosses me higher. "Fly!" he shouts.

My stomach flops like that day Noah and me skipped our exams, stole a car, and spent the day at Seabreeze. We rode the Jack Rabbit so many times I puked. I'm ready to puke again. Each time I fall, Skeele tosses me higher and it gets harder and harder to breathe. The air is thin this high up in Hellsky.

He lets me fall over and over again.

"You piece of shit!" I swallow back bile. "I will throw you in the pit for this," I shout.

It's hard to stop your arms and legs from churning in the air. I don't have time to reach maximum velocity like in that movie. I twist, my back facing the ground, and flip him off.

He's coming at me from above, just far enough away to induce panic. He laughs after glancing at my hands. I wonder for a split second if this is how my grandfather felt as his body fell to the ground. He was gone though. I'd sucked every drop of life out of him.

Skeele grabs me just before I hit the ground. He settles me on my feet and his wings fold against his back.

Fired up, I grab my blade, kick him in the shin, and drop him to kneeling. I slam my foot into the center of his chest and kick him back. Standing on his chest, I set the tip of my blade under his chin.

"I could kill you for that." I swallow down the thickness in my throat. I move the tip of the blade to his chest and press harder, until it pierces the first layer of his gear. "I still might kill you for that."

He shrugs thick shoulders. "I'm just trying to help." He twists his neck to the side, just ever so slightly, so I can see the pulse of his jugular.

Whoosh-whoosh-whoosh. It's hypnotic. I find myself leaning closer, tempted. The closer I get, the more I can smell him. It's not bad. Not repulsive. He's clean. Different than the Hellions of my past. I involuntarily lick my lips.

He smiles.

"I fucking hate Hellions," I remind Skeele before I stand up straight and step off his chest. I walk away, around the Jeep and toward the empty, crumbling road.

"Don't you want a ride back to the castle?" he shouts from the ground.

"Go fuck yourself." I wave with my middle fingers.

"Don't run away, Meg," Skeele grumbles.

But I'm good at running. It's really the only thing I've ever been good at. The only thing that's ever really saved me. Why not run away? Running away sounds like fun right now. I could ignore all my duties. No longer have this weight of being inept on my shoulders. Running away could be just what I need. Running away could be the best thing ever.

The walk back to the castle isn't long. I could *poof* and be there in an instant, but I need to walk off what just happened. I've got to burn that energy. I've traveled the trail more than a few times after a failed flying lesson. The only worries are the dead, schlepping it along and moaning like cows. They stay away from me now that I have a real title down here. It took me a long time not to run when I see them. Still, their shadows and moaning make me uneasy.

I take a deep breath and remind myself of who I am. "My name is Meg Clark. I killed my mother the day I was born. My father is the Archangel Gabriel. My grandfather was Lucifer, until I killed him. I've done some very bad things. I even own a blade that was forged in the fires of Hell. Oh, and I slid my blade into my boyfriend's heart releasing his last bit of grace and now he's lost to me." Can't forget that last bit. Icing on the fruitcake of shit-fuckery.

It sounds so impressive and depressing. But what I wouldn't give to escape to a beach or a bar and drown my sorrows in sunlight and liquor. But I can't escape to the Earthen plane. Or at least I haven't figured out how to–yet–without getting caught.

The smell of woodsmoke and pine gets stronger the closer I get to the castle nestled in the burning caves. I step foot inside. Creatures scurry to the shadows and still as I walk by. It's a far cry from my little white house with picket fence in Gouverneur. That was a life I was never meant to live, Sparrow once told me. How different my life has become now. I wouldn't say I've fully embraced taking Lucifer's place, but I'm getting there.

There is someone missing here. A large, lurking Angel turned Hellion known as Sparrow. He is mine and I am his, and I must figure out where the heck he went. I tap my fingers over the tattoo on my chest, a watercolor of a sparrow in flight, wishing it would bring him back to me. I whistle a light trill in remembrance. I miss my monster something terrible. He is the only one who has ever shown me love and caring and truth. He may be a monster, but he's mine. Most days, I'm pretty sure that I'm the bigger monster.

My stomach growls. The bloodlust doesn't want to wait for him. I can't cure it. There's only remission and relapse. Fuck it all. I make my way to the kitchen, my footsteps angry and hollow on ages old stone floors. The kitchen staff hear me coming. They run, which is good. I'm losing all control just like Skeele warned. The pressure builds as I near the door and slam it open, then slam it closed. My stomach growls so loud I'm sure all of Hell hears it. Nothing is sacred in this kitchen, in this moment. There's cake in the fridge, decadent and sugar filled. Someone spent hours decorating it with black roses made of buttercream. I dip my hand into it, grab a giant piece, and shove it in my mouth. I open a container of milk and pour it down my throat. This continues. Cheese, pepperoni, steak, chicken soup, ancient wines and spirits, sugar-baked carrots and loaded fries, chips, dips, Twinkies, and Hostess cakes. Everything I've asked the staff of the castle to stock for me, I tear through it all in record time. I pause, only to look around the kitchen and see my work. The place is wrecked, and my stomach is so full I might vomit. I slump to the floor, my back against the fridge that's covered in sugary fingerprints and splatters of food. I slide to the side and lay on my back, my stomach bloated, my throat bursting. I should weigh five-hundred pounds with the things I've eaten down here trying to fill the void. I just want one thing. One thing would stop this hunger. Biting into Sparrow's neck. And if we were both naked, that would help. That would fill another need.

I close my eyes in disgust and focus on the feeling of the cold, stone floor under my head. There was a time when my cupboards were empty. When I was more often hungry than full. I wrestled a dog for a peanut butter and jelly and won. That was a highlight in my life in childhood. Some would cry at the memory. It wasn't worse than trading my freedom to live with Jim for all those months. At least my stomach is full of food, my womb is empty, and I've got a handful of Hellions who will protect me until the end. Things aren't all bad. My life is kinda like those posters in elementary school of the kitten hanging on a branch. I've just got to hang on there until I can figure all this out.

"You know, you're kind of a slob." Noah looks down at me.

"If I say 'I couldn't help myself' would it matter?" I ask. The bloodlust is calmer but still there, threatening to explode under my skin. Noah can't help me. He's a ghost. A soul of the Astral plane and tied to me. Still, he's the best friend a girl could ever have.

"You are the ruler of this place, so I guess you can do whatever you want." Noah shrugs.

"Why does it have to be like this?" I ask.

"How would you like it to be, Meg? Or should I call you Lucifer?"

"Never call me that." I glare at him.

Noah spins on one foot, stomps down with his legs straddling my knees, and reaches for my hands. "Come on. You look pathetic. Get up."

I nod and sniff away the tears threatening the corners of my eyes. "Why are you always so nice to me?" I ask.

Noah smiles and everything is better. You'd know if you'd ever seen Noah or Jack smile, handsome isn't enough to describe it. "I got you into plenty of trouble when I was alive. I guess this is my penance." He pulls me to my feet. "Gosh, Meg, you look like crap." He looks me up and down. "And those leathers are looking a little tight on your ass. Since you've already scared the kitchen staff to death, how about you go clean yourself up and I'll take care of this."

I nod and rub my face with filthy, food covered hands.

"Go." Noah prods my rib, pushing me away.

"Do not tell anyone about this," I threaten as I walk away.

"Wouldn't think of it."

I head to my room, down long hallways and rooms I have yet to explore. I should probably learn what lies within my own castle, but I don't have the mindset for it today. I close the heavy wooden door to my room and move a chair in front of the door handle. There's a

Northern Flicker on my balcony, could be the same one from my flying lesson. I whistle but it's nothing like the wonderful way the others do it. I blame my sucking at whistling on the sugar and salt swelling my tongue and make my way to the bathroom. I start the shower and turn the handle until it's nice and hot. Hot enough to melt off my shame and the sugar crusted under my fingernails. Maybe if I melt off the top layer of my skin those wings will show up. I unstrap my blade and set it on the counter before stripping down. I don't bother to look at the tattoos and scars before I get in the blasting water. Maybe another day; I don't want to remember all of that right now. I wash and then stand in the stream of water and let it massage my neck and shoulders. Closing my eyes, I remember Sparrow touching my neck, the sides of my waist. The deep ebb of his voice, the roughness of his fingertips, the swipe of his shaggy brown hair against my skin. I shiver and slam my hand over the knob, turning the water off. Damn it. I wrap myself in a towel and step out onto a plush bathmat. I should be grateful for all I have down here. I didn't grow up with fluffy bath towels and bathmats. My feet didn't dry instantly as they hit a plush terrycloth mat. No, all I had for a long, long time was a single, threadbare towel that got washed when I remembered and barely soaked up the water on my skin, let alone the floor. The amount of time I've been on the plane of Hell can't erase the memory of bathwater airdrying off my skin and causing a chill in the dead of winter, bone deep. That could be why I turn the water so hot: it's a memory chilled in my bones that I can't warm.

As I brush my teeth, I swipe my hand across the mirror. My hair is too long, brushing my shoulders. I can't stand it. I search the bathroom drawers until I find a pair of scissors and go to town. Snip, snip, snip, until my hair is a chin-length bob, just like I like it. I stare at my reflection. I count to ten before I cut bangs. Bangs cure a lot. Plenty of women going through a personal crisis get bangs. I shake the short pieces loose. Bangs will do just fine right now.

I clean up the pieces of my black hair in the sink and throw them in the trash. The mess I left in the kitchen was bad enough. I need a little redemption in this place. I guess I'll start by not making Noah clean up my mess in the bathroom.

I make my way to the closet, open the door, and flick the light on. There are rows of clothes that Clea gave me; leather pants and skimpy tops, jackets and flimsy undergarments, stuff I could have never afforded on the Earthen plane. Couldn't get this stuff at Wal-Mart. Heck, I'd have to go to the mall four hours away from home. I chose dark jeans, a bright blue T-shirt, a leather jacket, matching black undergarments, and a pair of sturdy boots. Always dress for travel and ready to flee, that's one thing life has taught me. Be ready to run. Be ready to fight and then run. I get dressed in the closet and when I step out, Noah's back.

"Funny, you don't look like you gorged in full fat-ass mode." His eyes scan me head to toe. "Bangs?"

I shrug. "Better than some things I could have done."

"They look good." He sits at the table near the balcony and tosses seeds onto the railing, making a game of it as some bounce and fall to the yard below.

I sit next to him. We watch the songbirds fly from treetop to railing and back again. There's not as many as when Sparrow and Nightingale were here. Those days the railing was lined with colorful birds.

"I guess I should bring some seeds," Noah says as he stands. "What do you want me to get you?" Noah asks.

"A vial of Sparrow's blood so I can stop this craving." I settle my hands over my stomach.

Noah laughs and whistles a gloomy trill. "You'll have to go get that yourself."

"How about fried chicken and buttermilk biscuits?" I ask.

"You want something to drink? Or are you going to choke those down dry so you can remember what it's like to have Sparrow wrapping his hands round your neck?"

"Go fuck yourself, Noah." I wouldn't be so mad if he weren't the least bit right.

"Would if I could. Actually, it's all I have left to do now that someone married off my girlfriend to my brother. And now he gets to raise my child." He glares at me.

"Sorry 'bout that." It was a pretty shitty thing that happened. But the fate of the world was at stake. I don't apologize further, instead I say, "I'd like an orange Crush Big Gulp. No ice."

"Fine." He disappears to go wherever he goes to get me food.

I stare out into Hellsky and contemplate what the heck I need to do first. I don't get far with my thoughts before there's a knock on my door. Well, more of a slamming fist pounding relentlessly like the cops on a hot lead.

"Go away," I shout.

"Open the door," Skeele's rough voice says.

"Nope."

He tries the handle. "Meg. Open the door."

I close my eyes. "I never get a moment of goddamned peace in this place."

"You spend plenty of time having a pity party in your room." The door rumbles again. "Open the door."

"Open it yourself."

Wood creaks and snaps. The chair I had propped against the door goes flying across the room with splinters of aged wood. "Your wish is my command." Skeele bows and steps into my room.

I grip the blade that's strapped to my thigh. "I'm not a fan of Hellions who act like that."

Skeele crosses the room and drops himself into a leather club chair near the far wall. "Look, I came to apologize. I shouldn't have thrown you."

"Ya think?"

"I'm just trying to help." He crosses his legs, an ankle resting on his knee. "You need to learn to fly. It will help you travel faster, and it could save you one day." He pauses. "It just, it took you a very long time to recover from your fall. I sat here for months watching you."

"Thanks for that," I mutter.

Skeele drops his foot and leans forward. "No, Meg, I don't think you understand. Hell was unruled for months while you were out of it. And now you won't commit. The Hellion leader is MIA. Souls are dropping into Hell at record pace." He rubs his bald, horned head. "The Safe Houses and Deacons are overrun."

"Good. I haven't forgotten what they did to me. They're lucky I don't strike every one of them down." My fingers smooth over the blade strapped to my thigh as I imagine chopping their heads off. I'd love to kill a Deacon or a hundred of them, but they are one of those strange beings that help organize the realms. I can't kill them. I just have to stand back and watch them meddle.

"Then who would greet your new souls?" Skeele asks. "Who would collect the sins of the dead and offer their last chance to repent? There is organization down here, whether you understand it or not. Whether you like it or not. The dead need to learn their place, they still have a life after death. Would you like them to wake like you did when you were in that coma and oscillating between realms without knowing it? You were lucky to find Sparrow right away. Can't you at least hope for better for the ones you rule over?"

I stare him down. The fuck. Hitting me in the feels.

"I know you're bad, Meg," Skeele keeps talking. "Bad to the bone like Sparrow always said. But you have an ounce of compassion for these souls. I know it. Stop playing tough."

I move my hand off the blade and cross my arms. "I might. But it doesn't help me dislike the Deacons any less."

"They've learned their place. You won." He throws up his hands. "You literally sucked the life out of Lucifer mid-air for all of Hell to see."

"I did do that." I nod.

There is a moment of silence as I contemplate the future. I can't go on without Sparrow. The way it's going these days we've spent more time apart than together. He's spent more time trapped in the abject recesses of his mind than remembering who I am and who we are together.

"What are you going to do?" Skeele asks.

"Find Sparrow."

Skeele smirks, showing sharp teeth. "Excellent. It's about time you move forward on that."

I'm gonna try to move on but I won't forget my grandfather, Lucifer's, last warning. "An Archangel who's lost all of his grace now tattooed tailbone to scalp, unrecognizable to many. He's out there on the Earthen plane, collecting souls for *me*." Not anymore. He's collecting souls for me. Hell is my realm. I am Lucifer. But I prefer to be called Meg.

Wayward Son

Sparrow

Dark looked good on Sparrow. So good it didn't even scare away the people of the Earthen plane when they saw him coming. *If* they saw him coming. Without his grace, he didn't need shadows to hide; he is a shadow. Six and a half feet tall and Ireland-grass green eyes turned smokey hazel, the walking dead kept their distance and a few thought that meant he was safe.

———

Sparrow walked down Redwood Highway headed north. The crashing of Pacific waves on sharp rock quieted his mind and muffled the sound of shuffling feet that were following him from a mile back. Stars sparkled from high above, ready to give their last light before the sun rose.

He'd be in Crescent City soon. Not that Crescent City was a special place, it was just one more town on a long path he'd been walking for months and months; a path without a purpose. Sparrow walked, and killed, and did whatever he wanted.

Sparrow paused, hearing hushed voices. There were signs for DeMartin Campsite. He turned and entered the forest. Boots crunched over sticks and dry pine needles. Sparrow weaved between the redwoods and Douglas-fir. He could smell fire. He could hear the pulsations of twenty carotid arteries filled with blood. Sparrow's mouth watered and his stomach pinched. He slowed, stepped lighter, became a thing of the forest in the night. Invisible. Threatening. A raptor perched ready to attack.

Sparrow lowered to a crouch. There were two men sitting in folding chairs by the fire, shotguns set across their laps. Firelight reflected off a dozen or so tents. Sparrow's mouth watered. One of the men stood and went to relieve himself in the high ferns. Sparrow shifted his weight to drop a knee. A stick broke under him sounding like a firecracker. The other man stood and pointed his shotgun. The second man came back, zipping his pants and gripping his weapon.

"What did you hear?" one asked.

"Stick broke," the other replied.

They moved closer.

Sparrow crouched lower; a panther ready to pounce. There were a few hundred feet between them but the men would have to come into the forest to find him.

"Morning is coming," the one said. "It could be an animal."

"I can't see anything," the other replied.

They moved closer, both hesitating.

Sparrow focused on their throats. The blood was pumping at a fast rate. They were scared. He licked his lips. It had been a long time since he'd had fresh blood. It had been—he stopped thinking, didn't want to remember how good it felt to let go and release the monster inside him.

The men went back to their seats, both keeping a close eye on the shadows in front of them. The fire crackled and drowned out the small sounds of Sparrow shifting his weight. He waited and watched until the sun breached the horizon, and the forest woke.

A woodpecker knocked high in the trees. Sparrow turned to find the bird and observed as it pecked at insects before hopping off to drill another hole. Sparrow enjoyed the noise; it wasn't the usual chirp or chatter but a hollowed knock like bones on a solid door. The noise was comforting, it sounded like home.

The bird flew off, away from the camp toward the thick cropping of trees near the road. Sparrow followed until he stood at the base of a giant redwood, focused on the bird, a tugging deep in his chest. Memories he couldn't pull forth lingered in the back of his mind. It was agitating. The woodpecker knocked a handful of times on the trunk before flitting off. A small black and white striped feather drifted down from the branches.

Sparrow caught it between two fingers, agitation gone.

"It's a pileated woodpecker, you weirdo."

Sparrow turned to find a woman watching him from a few feet away. Her blowtorch-blue hair was a startling contrast to the shadows of the forest and the rising fog. She held a small baseball bat in one hand, her other resting on a handgun secured at her hip.

Sparrow tucked the feather in his pocket and moved on, unimpressed.

He didn't bother to be quiet as he walked out of the forest. Twigs crunched under his big boots as he broke the tree line and headed north. He never looked back to see if anyone was following him. He didn't care. He'd eat them if he had to. Heck, he'd eat them if he *wanted* to.

Sweet Dreams

Meg

It is all happening so fast: traveling between realms, being hunted in that tiny church, Basilica of St. Mary Star of the Sea in Key West, stabbing Sparrow, and taking the last bit of his grace. I will never forget the look on his face, the way his leathery Hellion wings rise to cover him, the speck of light that rises into the clear tropical night.

"They warned me that you'd break my heart. I should've seen it coming when the roses died." Sparrow said those words as I slid the sharp end of my blade past his breastbone and into his heart. I watched in horror as a tiny spec of light escaped his right cocoon of wings and smoldered to nothing. It was a trick, the Scarecrow, Reuben, tricked me. He told me I had to do it to reset the balance.

Everything moves in fast-forward. The Scarecrow made me do it, said Sparrow's grace was disrupting the fiber between Hell and the

Earthen plane. He was wrong. I upset the balance and let a monster loose on the Earthen plane.

I sit up in bed, grip my sweating head, and scream. I can't control it. I rock, silk sheets sticking to my sweating body. What have I done?

The room cools and a wavering figure appears. "Hush, child," Clea sits on the end of my bed. "It's not all doom and torment." Her chilled fingers touch mine. I pull away. "You killed the basilisk and freed me." She shivers. "I'll never be banished to that thing's gut again."

My answer is silence for the first time in my life. Jim would be so proud if he were here to see it. He could never get me to shut up. My mother and I seem to have a curse of our own. Dangerous men and even more dangerous situations. What would one expect from the daughter of Lucifer and a forbidden child.

"If you're feeling badly about the basilisk, you can get another one. You'd just have to hunt it." Clea inspects her fingernails. "They do come in handy, sometimes."

"I'm not sure what I'd need a basilisk for." I throw myself back onto the pillows and pull the damp sheets up to my chin.

While Sparrow was always the one to marinate in shame, now it is my turn. We were supposed to be invincible together. I've ruined that, much like I ruin most things. Still, cutting off Reuben's head felt pretty damn good, the bastard. Ripping open the basilisk's gut to free Clea felt pretty damn good too. And don't get me started on how good draining my grandfather of his blood felt because I'd tell you in a heartbeat that it was better than draining Remiel.

I scoot to the edge of the bed and set my feet on the floor. "I need to get out of here."

Clea rises and moves to the balcony. "Where would you like to go?"

"I need to find Sparrow." I toss the blankets aside and head for the bathroom. I wash my face and brush my teeth, then I head to the closet to find clothes for the day. Through it all, I try to still my mind. I try to focus on my tasks.

Clea is still sitting at the balcony table, Noah sits with her. I sense the presence of Skeele sitting behind me. "I guess it's a party then?"

I glance at the door. It was fixed after Skeele broke it to pieces the other day, but it seems it still does not work at keeping extra people out of my room.

Skeele folds his newspaper and sets it in the chair next to him. "Going somewhere?"

"Yes. I'm going to find Sparrow," I say.

"That's great and all," Skeele says, "but you can't leave."

"What?" I ask.

"You can't leave your realm for the Earthen one. That is God's land." Skeele drops his chin and stares at me. "We have to find another way."

"Oh no. No." I tighten the leather strap of the blade on my thigh. "I'm going. Now." I close my eyes to *poof* the heck out of here, but I don't go anywhere.

"It won't work," Clea warns me.

My eyes flash open. "Why?"

"You took Lucifer's place. You can't go to the Earthen plane on a whim. It's not like before. You must wait for the right time," Clea says.

"This is bullshit," I growl.

Noah smirks, waiting for my temper to come out full blast.

Skeele stands. "It might be. But, there are other things we can do." He motions for me to follow him.

I don't miss the worried look of Clea as I leave the room.

"Where are we going?" I ask.

"The lair," Skeele warns. "The Hellions have a plan."

"Fine." I grip my blade tight. "But no funny business."

"Wouldn't think of it," Skeele promises.

"Toodaloo," Noah says with a wave as I head toward the door.

Skeele leads me down the hall with ages old handspun rugs and down the wide rock stairway. We turn away from the kitchen and head to the lair. My stomach grumbles.

"We have blood," Skeele says.

"It's not the same." I press my hand over my stomach to make it stop.

"It's neutral and will stop you from doing something unexpected. You must be at the top of your game now, Meg."

"I'm always at the top of my game," I lie.

"Uh huh." He mocks and slides a hand down my neck and across my shoulder blade.

"Don't touch me." I shove him as hard as I can. He barely moves.

"I didn't feel any wings. And you're strung tighter than a yo-yo. You're not at the top of your game." Skeele's expression is placid.

There's music blaring from behind the carved door of the lair. A moment of panic passes through me–it always does at this threshold. Bad things happened in here. Next level bullshit went on. I push away the memories of my former fiancée, Jim, stringing me up and stabbing me in the chest. He was the reason I hated the Hellions. I remind myself. I also remind myself that he's dead now. I don't have to worry about Jim or his group of Hellions any longer. Trepidation still lingers though. Hellions are terrible creatures who take on the traits of their leader. The only thing keeping me safe is the fact that Sparrow is still their leader. Skeele is second in command, first now that Sparrow's gone. If this crew falls in line, I don't have a thing to worry about.

Skeele pauses with the door just cracked open. "They know you hate them. They're different than before. Sparrow retrained all of them. He replaced everyone. We have rules now."

I nod. Good ol' Sparrow. My worst fears came true the moment he became a Hellion to escape his family's curse of turning crazy. My Sparrow. An Archangel turned Hellion.

I straighten my back. "It's fine." I reach past Skeele's arm and push the door open further. The music inside stops and the Hellion's stand as I enter. It's strange, how the memories of before and the reality of now contrast.

"Sit." I wave at them.

"Meg, this is Tukka," Skeele points to a huge Hellion with skin as dark red as a kidney bean. "This is Chel." Chel waves from the shadowed corner of the couch. "And this is Klaus." The last one has a long white beard and white horns on the side of his head.

"Aren't there more?" I ask.

"Yes, they're out," Skeele replies. "They'll be back in a few days once they're done with checking the Safe Houses."

I take this time to try my hand at being the actual leader of Hell. "How's that going?"

Chel speaks first. "There's too many souls arriving daily."

"Too many people dying on the Earthen plane," Skeele clarifies. "But not all of them are arriving here. Some are getting lost."

"They're stuck on the Earthen plane," Chel says.

"There are walking dead there?" I ask.

Skeele nods.

"The demons don't want to stay in line," Klaus says with the cracking of his knuckles. "They want Lucifer."

"Well. I killed him," I reply.

"We are getting that point across, slowly," Klaus says.

Skeele moves across the room and picks up a handful of darts. He starts tossing them at a dart board as we're talking, motioning for the rest of us to join. The others let me go first. Skeele drops five darts in my palm as they tell me about the lesser demons they've had to take care of.

"The one thing to celebrate is that Hell grows stronger with each soul," Skeele says. "You've got to be stronger than your father by now. Damn near stronger than those dicks roaming around the Seven Kingdoms of Heaven."

I shrug. "I don't feel any stronger."

There's a beat of silence.

"Making the demons behave has been a big undertaking," Klaus says as he sends a dart toward the board and hits the center circle.

Tukka shoots next, and his darts hit just off center. He walks forward to pull them out of the board then hands them to me as he walks by.

I haven't played darts in a long time. Not since high school or maybe a little later when I should've been in college. I step up, steady a dart between my fingers. Skeele is talking loudly to Klaus. I throw. The dart hits off to the side of the board. Outside of the circles.

"Boo," Skeele howls.

I get ready to toss the next one. "Didn't know this was a sporting event." I toss the dart, it hits inside the outermost circle.

Someone claps.

"Come on," I sigh. "This is pathetic."

"You can do it," Klaus claps louder.

I toss another dart, and another. They get closer to bullseye each time. I have the final dart pinched between my fingers.

"If she gets this one, first round is on Tukka!" Klaus laughs and slaps Tukka hard on the back.

"And if I miss?" I ask.

There is a pause. "First round is still on Tukka!" Chel shouts. The Hellions bust out in deep laughter.

I smile and toss the dart. It hits the bullseye.

We play five more rounds and I lose every single one. Skeele, Chel, and Klaus prod Tukka.

When the game is over, Klaus says, "Sparrow would be proud."

My shoulders tense.

"That you're here," Skeele clarifies.

I nod as the Hellions lead me to the bar. I sit at the last leather stool at the end of the slab of aged wood. Tukka crouches down and opens the dented refrigerator. When he stands, he has five bags of blood in his hand. Playing bartender, he cuts the bags and pours the blood into glasses. He slides the glasses down to Skeele, Chel, and Klaus. He saves one for himself and sets the last one on the bar top just out of my reach.

I hold my breath, try not to breath in the scent. The others drink, their swallows loud and gulping. I close my eyes for a moment and open them just in time to see Tukka exhale, take the glass away from his mouth, and flash red tinted fangs. He slams his glass down, sending a few drops of blood splattering onto my arm.

The tiny hair on the back of my neck rise. I close my eyes, cross my legs, my back arches, and there's an ache low in my stomach.

Someone growls. It's an animalistic sound but as I try to control myself, I can't discern if it's the Hellion's hunger, a warning, or something else.

My eyes flash open. Uh oh. I scramble down from my seat and run for the door.

The Hellions watch, muscles twitching, never moving.

"I gotta go, boys." I swing the door open with force and slam it closed.

In the hallway, I press my back to the wall and slide down to sitting. My blood splattered arm resting on my knees, I stare at the drops. My stomach growls. I lick the blood drops off.

The low rumble of the Hellions' voices fills the lair.

They're talking about me. They must be. The way I just ran out of there was pathetic. I should have controlled myself. I should have asked for a Shirley Temple and filled my gut with sugar and maybe a few beers. I should have, but I didn't.

I sit on the cold, hard floor until my ass goes numb. No one disturbs me and the Hellion lair goes quiet.

I get back to my room with the sunrise.

"It's not like you to stay out all night with the Hellions." Noah is looking unimpressed as he scans me from head to toe. "Ho."

"Shut up." I throw my jacket at him.

"Is this … blood?" He inhales with an exaggerated shocked expression. "I hope it's not fresh blood. I'll have to tell Sparrow you've been cheating on him."

"I said shut up." I pull off my shirt and kick off my boots as I walk to the bathroom.

"I'd leave some money on the nightstand but since you rule down here now, I guess it's not necessary." Noah's smiling wide, really loving teasing me.

"Why don't you make yourself useful and go get me some spaghetti and meatballs."

"Heavy on the balls, huh?"

I grab a boot off the floor and throw it at him.

Noah laughs loud before disappearing.

"Asshole," I mutter to myself as I turn on the shower.

———

There's spaghetti waiting on the table near the balcony. I glance at it, then the bed.

Noah tsks. "I went through a lot to get you that."

"I went through a lot to get you here," I reply.

"We don't need to get so serious." Noah holds up his hands. "I just saw you contemplating sleeping over eating and that's not the Meg I've grown to love. Are you sick?"

"No."

"Sad?"

"Maybe."

"What did those Hellions say to you?" He stands like he's going to go to the lair and set them straight. Good ol' Noah.

"Nothing." I rub my eyes. "They were fine. Spending time with them just made me uneasy," I confess.

"Oh?" he asks. I don't want to explain the blood and the urges.

"Do you think we'll find Sparrow?" I change the subject.

"I don't think *we'll* find him." Noah clasps his hands together. "*You* will find him. You always do, Meg. You'll find him when the time is right. Just like you found me and you found Jack and you found Nightingale. You're good at finding people."

I shrug and head for the bed.

"Oh no. Get over here and choke this spaghetti down. I don't care if you rule down here. Noah doesn't get hot spaghetti dinner from VFW post 5885 for it to rot and grow maggots."

"I'll explode if I eat that now."

"I saw that happen in a Monty Python movie once. Can't wait to see it happen to you." He laughs as I sit and eat. "I didn't bring mints. You'll be fine."

"You're lucky I like you," I say between bites.

"Next time you're going to party in the lair all night, feel free to invite me. Not many parties going on in the Astral realm. Nightingale's been too busy lately to meet me."

"Sure," I say.

———

I DREAM of my old house. White fence, green roof. My eyes snap open in the master bedroom. I am reminded of leaks I couldn't afford to fix, a roof threatening to tear off during storm bursts, paint bubbling during the winter thaw when the ice on the roof backed up with melted water. I will be forever stuck in this place. Forever remembering when I'd rather not. Panic sets in. The urge to be elsewhere takes over. I am not meant to be in this place. I run down the stairs and touch the heavy brass doorknob to the front door. It's cool on my fingertips. He'll be home soon. I rip open the door and step onto the entryway. My footsteps sound all the familiar creaks and groans from hundreds of years old wood underneath. My heart beats faster. Panic rises. I'm supposed to be somewhere else. I know it. This can only be one person's doing. I push the screen door open, run across the front porch and down the steps, the solid concrete of the sidewalk pressing into the soles of my feet. I look up at the midnight sky, the full moon, the feathers floating on the wind.

"Night!" I shout into the darkness.

My eyes flash open.

Nightingale is here. Thrush in her arms, she purses her lips and delivers a cheerful trill. "He'd like to see his father." She motions to the baby.

"Jack isn't here," I say. "He can't be here."

"Noah." Her eyes turn dark.

"I really hate it when you control my dreams." I change the subject.

"It was better than what you were dreaming of before." She made a face. "I saved you from that. Would you rather be hating on that old house or hot-ass cell in Heaven?"

At least she chose the lesser of two evils. "Thanks," I say.

Noah materializes. "Nightingale?" He glances at the baby. "What's wrong?"

"We need to talk." Nightingale looks at me and then the open balcony door.

"Be my guest," I motion to the door. "But I'm going back to sleep." I flop back and pull the blanket over my head. My pillow is damp with sweat. As I flip it over, I hear the murmurings of Night and Noah as they talk on the balcony. They're interrupted by the soft coos of Thrush as he joins in the conversation. Noah laughs, the baby squeals. I force my eyes to close and try not to think how hard it must be for him to watch his son grow from afar. To watch the woman that he loves carry on with his brother. Noah got me in plenty of trouble when we were kids but I'm not sure anything will ever compete with the tangled relationship he's in with Nightingale.

At least they have each other. Sometimes.

I roll and tuck the blanket under my chin. Squeezing my eyes shut, I try to picture Sparrow in my mind. It's been months since I've seen him. I never had a picture, and the memories of him are turning into dark, blurry images. I tell myself that his eyes are as green as Ireland grass, his hair dark and shaggy, his stature tall and strong...

Damn.

LOST

Sparrow

Sparrow continued his walk down Redwood Highway. The Pacific waves had quieted, and Sparrow could hear the screams from the campsite as the walking sacks of dead flesh feasted. The morning chill was thick with fog. So much so that he couldn't even see the ocean anymore, only hear its gentle lapping against the rocky shoreline.

Footsteps followed him from the tree line. He ignored them. Someone had been following him for a long time. It wasn't the dead who had infested the Earthen plane. No, this was someone else, something else.

There was an empty car on the side of the highway. Thirsty, Sparrow tried the doorhandles. The passenger side opened. He dug through the car only to find empty water bottles and garbage. In the back there was an empty car seat. If Sparrow was of his right mind, he might've said a prayer for the child. Instead he walked away, leaving the car door open.

There were signs for a diner in two miles. He patted his pocket

"

for the wad of cash he'd come across in his travels. His fingers brushed over the feather and the small hairs on the back of his neck rose. He rubbed his skin until they went away. He was hungry and he wasn't sure if food would fill the void. He wasn't sure if he could behave in the daylight.

Sparrow followed the signs and winding road. Footstep after footstep. Until he came to the diner.

Dan's Diner was an old building just off the highway, up on a slanted hillside with a wall of windows that overlooked the Pacific. Sparrow followed the incline of the crumbling driveway. The open sign was lit. He made his way to the door and went inside.

"Seat yourself," a voice shouted from the back.

The diner was empty. He chose a corner booth, where he could watch the door and the road.

A tattooed guy came out from the kitchen holding a menu. "Hey," he said, dropping the menu. "Can I get you a drink?"

Sparrow nodded. "Sure."

There was a long pause.

"What would you like?" the man asked.

"Anything."

"Water. Coffee. Soda?"

"Water," Sparrow said.

"No problem." The man reached forward and flipped the menu open. "There's no specials. Deliveries are too infrequent. Um. Hm. No steak or chicken. I've got a few eggs if you're looking for breakfast foods. No bacon though." He tapped on the menu. "We have fresh fish from the Pacific, some crab." He eyed Sparrow. "We have wonton soup but you're a big guy, you'll probably want something more filling than that."

Sparrow looked at the menu. Then the man's neck. His nametag said: Jed. He blinked and shook his head. He knew a Jed once. The name caused a buzzing in the back of his skull.

Jed took a step back. "How about this? I can whip you up a deep-fried grilled cheese and some eggs. Half price."

"Sure." Sparrow agreed and slid the menu in the man's direction. "I'll take an orange soda too if you have it." Orange soda reminded him of sweet lips and soft thighs.

"Coming right up," Jed said.

Sparrow watched out the window. There were no vehicles, no other people out walking on this misty morning. Well, besides whoever was waiting at the tree line. Only the shadow in the trees. For the first time in a long time it wasn't Sparrow.

Jed came back with a tall glass of orange soda and a water. "Ice machine is jammed."

"I don't need any." Sparrow drank the water first as Jed returned to the kitchen. He watched the trees and saw more of the woodpeckers with their bright red crests flitting back and forth. He had a desire to rip their wing feathers out, one by one, and rub them between his fingers. He could line his pockets with them. He could...

Jed set a plate in front of Sparrow. A steaming fried grilled cheese and large pile of eggs. Sparrow devoured the meal and drained both drinks, eager to get out of diner and move on. Eager to avoid the shadow in the trees and the pretty flitting songbirds. Eager to fill the void in his gut that the meal didn't touch. He needed more than food. But that would have to wait. He had no desire to drain Jed of his blood. Something about the guy was unappetizing.

Jed came back, a white slip of paper in his hand. Sparrow had his cash ready.

"I have a deal for you." Jed waved the paper. "Money is pretty useless these days. I need help with something, and we'll call the meal even."

Sparrow wiped his mouth with a napkin. "What is it?"

"I'll show you. Follow me."

Sparrow stood and followed Jed behind the counter, through the diner kitchen and to a silver door. Thuds were echoing from inside.

"I noticed your weapon." Jed motioned to Sparrow's blade. "I need them killed. I can't do it." Jed put his hand on the walk-in freezer door. "There's three of them."

Sparrow gripped his blade. "Why can't you do it?"

Jed pointed to a picture on the wall. "They owned this place. It just seems wrong. I can't."

Sparrow nodded and motioned for Jed to get out of the way. He took the handle to the door and pulled. There were three of the walking flesh-bags just like Jed said there'd be. They moved when they noticed him. Sparrow blocked the door so Jed couldn't see. The dead knew his darkness; they were just as lost as he was on the Earthen plane. Both didn't belong. Both were in limbo. But only one would stay. He'd send them away. For a free meal it was a decent trade.

Sparrow reached for his blade and in one swift movement relieved the dead of their heads. The smell was terrible: rotting flesh and rotting food. Sparrow stepped back and slammed the door closed. He walked to the sink to wash his hands and clean off his blade.

When Sparrow looked up, Jed was holding a butcher knife and standing near the back door to the diner. "Thank you for your help. Just go now." He pointed the butcher knife in the direction of the front door. "You're not one of those zombies, but you're something else. I remember. But you're worse than before. You've become something I've worked hard to avoid."

"Thanks for the meal." Sparrow turned and walked out the front door of the diner and continued on his way. He could have warned Jed about the swarm that would follow but he didn't.

No More Rest for the Wicked

I dreamed of woodchucks, burrowing into the corner foundations of my house, gnawing away at the cement and wood and drywall. I filled their holes, sprinkled my foundation in fresh garlic. They still got in the house and scurried across the floorboards. I woke in my dream, a pinching feeling on my fingers and the blankets moving. I raised my hand to see a woodchuck bit me, teeth clamped in the soft spot between my thumb and index fingers. It dangled on the end of my hand, pinching my flesh. I gripped it under the arm with my free hand and the creature wiggled like a dachshund dog wanting to be put down. I ran to the slider door, kicked it open, and threw the woodchuck into the nearby pond. Fucking woodchucks.

I wake to a dark room, sweat soaking the satin sheets. Rubbing my face dry, I get up to use the bathroom.

I had a friend who once said, "I can't trust anyone. Not even a girl who can flash between realms and slay the walking dead like she was born and bred to take on the apocalypse single handedly." That was Jed. I'm not sure if he was truly a friend but he was a forbidden creature much like me. But damn him, he's the one who tattooed the runes into Sparrow's back with my own blood. He's the reason I can't find Sparrow.

I should find Jed. He should have warned me what a stupid idea it was to tattoo Sparrow so I'd never find him. It wasn't that long ago that I was *poofing* to his parlor, locking the doors in a desperate attempt to hide and asking him to help me.

"What are you thinking about, child?" Clea appears and the air turns chilled.

"Things," I reply. "Old things. Memories I can't seem to move on from."

Clea fidgets and paces, her image blurring to transparent and then returning solid again. Her dark flowing hair and ruby red lips are a stark contrast between her ghostly-white skin.

"What's wrong?" I ask.

"Have you thought any more about the basilisk?" she asks.

"Not really."

Skeele makes a noise from the corner of the room.

"What?" I ask.

"They come in handy," he says. "A basilisk is a powerful creature."

"So is a door. And I don't need a pet." I move to the balcony and set a row of seed out. "Besides, I wouldn't even know how to find one or catch it."

"Oh, there's a whole nest of them in the mountain streams," Clea says. "You just have to go hunt one."

"A nest of them." I shiver. "I'm not a fan of snakes, let alone giant snakes with teeth. I have no desire to hunt one. I'm trying to get out of here."

"You should have your house set before you venture out to the Earthen plane," Skeele warns.

"The Hellions are of no use while I'm gone?" I ask.

"A creature like the basilisk would give us a stronger edge," Skeele says.

"My grandfather's didn't. I sliced the guts out of that thing in an instant."

Skeele shrugs before leaving the room and muttering, "Think about it."

"Surround yourself with monsters," Clea warns before disappearing.

There are plenty of monsters in my life. I sit on the bed and glance at the jar of snowy owl feathers on my nightstand. They are all that remains of my daughter, Elise. There was a time in my life, before shit got real fucked up, when I was pregnant with a child. I didn't know my fiancée was the son of a demon, living on the Earthen plane. Heck, I didn't know what I was truly a product of. But Jim seduced me, knocked me up, and forever changed my life. Hellions made sure of this. Elise's soul rests now. She was two-thirds darkness and one-third light, the brightest light in the darkest of places. She was not meant for the Earthen plane, nor Hell. She was not meant for the slice of Lucifer's blade as she tried to defend me.

I pick up the jar and twist it to the side. The feathers fall softly. I don't want a basilisk. I want Sparrow. I want to get the heck out of Hell and roam the Earthen plane free as a bird.

Night Moves

Sparrow

Crescent City was quiet. The morning fog had cleared. Sparrow walked the main road toward the coast. People were out on boats and kayaks fishing. He took note of the houses. Many were boarded up. Sparrow needed to find someplace to hide until nightfall. He slowed his pace, listened to the hearts beating inside until he found a house that was empty and didn't look like anyone was coming back to it. Sparrow walked around the back, his boots disturbing dead leaves that had collected along the driveway. He found a back door, knocked. No one answered, just as he'd expected. He twisted the doorknob slowly; he met resistance but forced the knob until the mechanism inside broke with a snap. Sparrow let himself inside.

The house had been empty a long time. Probably before the dead started walking. There were holes in the wooden floorboards and a thick layer of dust coating everything. Sparrow found an old blanket next to the couch. He sat down, covered his knees and closed his eyes, ignoring the smell. He slept through the evening.

Sparrow left his hiding spot as soon as the sun went down. Only half the streetlights were working and after spending so much time walking the unlit Redwood Highway, he was finding their brightness annoying. The few people still living in Crescent City avoided him, running into their houses and locking the doors or driving in another direction.

The breakfast he'd eaten at sunrise was doing nothing to stop the ache in his gut. Something else would stop it. Only one thing. He made his way toward the sound of loud music and the smell of stale beer.

The sign of the bar was unlit, bulbs had been shot out ages ago and these days there was no point in replacing them. Most of the people still living in Crescent City knew they were on borrowed time. There was no rhyme or reason when or where the swarm of the dead would show up–reports had shown destruction headed north up the California coast.

Sparrow hit the door and pushed it open. The bar quieted for a moment as he crossed the room and sat in a corner. Most soon forgot him but a leery eye was quick to judge.

"What can I get you?" a woman wearing a Crescent City Dodgeball T-shirt asked.

"Whatever you have on tap," Sparrow replied.

"Uh huh." The woman stared at him. "You look new to town. Don't try any funny business. These boys don't have much of a reason not to shoot you." She thrust her thumb toward a group of men playing pool.

The corner of Sparrow's mouth rose as the woman turned to get his beer. When she came back, she slid a mug of the house special on tap slowly. Sparrow let his fingers touch hers as he took the mug. That was all he needed to do. It didn't take much for women to bend to his needs.

The woman in the dodgeball shirt kept his mug full and the people of the bar kept Sparrow entertained. Music played, got louder as the night went on, then migrated from classic rock to body swaying rave music. Sparrow got up to use the bathroom. Walking past the sweaty bodies with their heartbeats thundering was almost too much. Almost. He used the stall, washed his hands, and splashed cold water on his face and neck. He was lost, fighting an urge that was only quelled by walking away from everyone he came across. It was that or give in. Walk away or give in? Which was more dangerous? Which would put an end to the ache? He had a void that needed filled. Now.

Sparrow left the bathroom. His heavy footsteps were drowned out by the loud music. He watched a young woman in a low-cut blue shirt dancing. She had short dark hair, fair skin, ink decorating her shoulder blades. She caught him watching, spun and grabbed his arm.

"Dance," she shouted with a wide smile.

A pang of memories hit. Memories of a dark-haired woman covered with tattoos of him. A woman with blue eyes who only saw him. Sparrow could bury it and dance. He closed his eyes, felt the music loosen his muscles. The woman was close to him, touching him, her small hand resting on his hip as she rubbed her body on his. Sparrow looked down at her with half-lidded eyes. She smiled, tipped her head to the side and bared her neck. Someone knocked into his back and pushed them closer together. She reached out, took his hand and placed it on her hip as one song merged into another that was just as loud and upbeat. He squeezed her waist. He couldn't hear the words, couldn't focus on anything other than the pulse in her neck. He tipped his head, pressed his lips to the vee of her neck.

"Yes," she whispered in his ear.

Teeth bared, he settled them over her carotid. She kept dancing, her arms circling his waist, pulling them closer together.

Sparrow bit down and tasted blood for the first time in days. He wrapped his arms around the woman, held her up while he drained her. She never struggled. Her blood was heavy with alcohol, and something else. Drugs, maybe? The bloodlust was too strong to ignore. It didn't bother him that she was inebriated. He let go and she dropped to the ground, an empty sack of skin. The dark, crowded room barely noticed. Sparrow moved like a shadow across the room, feeding on one and then the next until someone finally realized what he was doing. There were screams. Gun shots fired but barely nicked him. What did, healed in an instant. The room filled with panic. A few screams echoed but fell upon a closed door. It was soon locked and covered in bloody handprints.

When Sparrow left the bar, there were no hearts beating. He let the door to the bar close behind him, wiped his mouth on the back of his hand, and walked away. The streetlights near the bar went out.

The hoard of the dead echoed from nearby. After they passed, they'd clean up his mess. No one on the Earthen plane would know what he'd done here.

Fishin' in the Dark

MEG

"Find the basilisk." My father is suddenly in the room. He is the brightest light in this place, shining through all the shadows. I wonder if this is what Clea meant when she described my child's light. My child that never was.

"Jesus Christ." I hold a hand over my heart. "You scared the shit out of me."

"That's no way to greet good 'ol dad." He smiles wide.

"How did you get here?" I ask.

He throws his hands in the air. "Magic."

"We both know it's not magic."

He pauses at the doors to the balcony. "True." His fingers fall on the doorhandle. "Only a few of us have the gift to travel between realms on a whim."

"They'll see you," I warn him. "And I'm pretty sure that you're not supposed to be here right now."

He clears his throat. "I was sent. The Seven Kingdoms of Heaven sent me to speak with you."

"How nice of them. No one else wanted to come down here?" I flash a mocking smile and bat my eyes innocently. "I've got my own cages now." I don't need to remind him of how they treated me in Heaven; locked me in a cage in the hot burning sun and let the angels judge me. My blood boils with the memory.

Heavy footsteps pound down the hall outside my door.

My father's brows rise in interest. "This could get fun after all."

"Not today, you celestial punk." I dash toward the door and pull it open just in time, before six giant Hellions bust it down. "Stop," I warn them. "I just got this door fixed. Do not enter here."

"Meg," Skeele argues. He's gripping a club. I glance over the Hellions; they've all got weapons.

"No." My hand grips the door handle. "You can stay out here, but do not enter this room."

Klaus sniffs the air. "It doesn't belong here," he growls.

Skeele raises a hand to stop the others. "We'll wait here."

"Of course you will." I retreat to my room and close the door.

"I figured you'd have more... protection." My father wanders the room before sitting on the bed.

"There's enough." I wave toward the door.

"You should have more." His fingers smooth over the dark bedspread. "Is your mother here?"

"Yes. Is that who you came to see?" I ask.

He pauses. "I suppose it's not the best idea to rip open old wounds."

"Probs not." I sit in a chair and glance at the door. The powerful aura of the Hellions is spilling into the room. We'd have to be dead not to feel it. Their heated rage could melt a statue.

"Are you aware of the missing souls?" my father asks.

"I'm not sure what you mean. There are a lot coming here and we've had backup in productivity at the Safe Houses."

He's shaking his head. "No. There's something more than that. They aren't even leaving the Earthen plane. They're walking around it. Dead."

"Oh." I remember those days, escaping the stinking flesh bags while I was hiding in Key West. "Heaven didn't seem to give a crap before when the Scarecrow was dropping zombies on the Earthen plane to toy with me."

"This is much different. The balance is so far out of whack..." he shakes his head. "They want to hold you responsible."

"Don't they always." I sigh, bored with the same old conversation. *It's Meg's fault. Punish Meg. Lock Meg up in some shitty dungeon and make her pay.* You'd think a group of Archangels would have a real strategy.

"I told them to fuck off." He laughs. "You should have seen the look on Raguel's face." Large hands clap. "Once in a lifetime. But, probably not."

"Sounds like a real great time."

He catches his breath. "You have to go to the Earthen plane and fix it."

"I know but I can't leave here. The Veil prevents me from leaving."

"Everyone knows about the solstice." He blurts out as though he's read my mind. "That's your time to go."

"You make it sound so easy." I mock.

"There's another way to go."

"Oh?" Now he's got my interest.

"Unless you relinquish the throne."

"Nah." I shake my head. "I won't be doing that." After all I've gone through why would I stand down now?

"Good. The solstice is a better choice. But, you need this." He reaches in his shirt pocket and pulls out a small vial of red liquid.

"What is that?" My mouth salivates. I already know. Blood.

"Consider it a gift."

I step back, afraid I won't keep it together around the blood. My veins sing at the sight, vibrating with anticipation. I thoroughly enjoyed the tang of Remiel's and Lucifer's blood.

He holds up the vial. "The blood of your father. It will mask you on the Earthen plane. But not for long. With this and the solstice you should get a good start." He stands. "Well, I guess that's enough chit-chat. Will you be coming with me?" He frowns. "I'd hate to see you locked up in the burning sun again." He pats a large hand over his heart. "Really made me want to kick some ass like never before."

"No." I shake my head. "I'm not ever going back there."

"Good, kid. I'll tell Raguel he can go fuck himself."

"Please do."

Gabriel laughs loudly, reaches across the table, and slaps me on the shoulder. "You've done good kid. Made a name for yourself and all." He surveys the room and the balcony. "Better than where you started off. I'm glad we found you."

"Thanks... Dad. Do I call you dad or father or something more?" I ask.

"Don't be a stranger." He waves before *poofing* back to Heaven.

I grab my jacket off the back of the chair, hide the jar of blood in a drawer, and cross the room. When I open the door, the Hellions are a wall of energy, barely holding back. Skeele looks ready to kill.

"He's gone," I say. "Calm down."

"What did he want?" Tukka asks, sniffing the room like a guard dog.

"To pass along information," I reply.

The Hellions push their way into my room and begin searching.

"I told you all he's gone." I wave toward the sky. "He went back to where he lives." I open and close the door to make sure it's really there and really works and isn't a figment of my imagination. "Do you all know what this thing is?" I wiggle the door, annoyed.

Skeele crosses his arms. "You shouldn't lock us out when one of his kind are here."

"He's my father," I say.

Skeele tips his head and narrows his eyes. "Family are the most likely to do harm."

I pause. Sure as shit they are. Memories of the man who raised me flood my mind. I put my jacket on and rest my hand on the door-knob. "We ready boys?"

"For what?" Skeele asks.

"Hunting basilisk," I say.

———

ONLY SKEELE and Tukka came with me. The others said since I killed one basilisk, collecting another will be a piece of cake. We walk out of the front door and load into the Jeep Wrangler. Skeele drives, Tukka crams himself in the back with a large reed basket.

Skeele heads north, toward what would be the Adirondack mountains on the Earthen plane. I guess they're the Adirondack mountains here too, just a darkened reflection.

"What do you think Sparrow is doing?" I ask Skeele.

"Something... weird."

I smile. "He's like that. Worse when he forgets who he is."

Skeele grunts in agreement.

"I have to go to him," I say. "I must do this. Then I'll go. Finally."

"Making a list." Skeele gets a tick in his cheek. "It's about time."

"What do you think he's surviving on?" I ask.

"Blood." Skeele is frank in the reply.

"Not mine."

"Nope."

Of course, he's feeding off others. He has too. I can't hold it against him, can I? I can't expect him to be traipsing across the United States without a spec of grace on an empty stomach. Who does that? What creature of Hell could have the strength to do that? I doubt I could.

"Stop thinking so hard about it," Skeele warns.

"Okay." I gaze at the passing forest.

"Maybe this is a good time to try flying again," Skeele says.

I hold my hands up and lean against the back of my seat. "I don't think this is a good time."

"Come on, Meg. Maybe just, jump off a big rock or out of a tree. Scare yourself a little." Tukka chuckles.

"You're something special, aren't you?" I ask.

Tukka shrugs. "I'm just a Hellion doing his job."

"No more from the peanut gallery," I warn Tukka.

"I'm not a peanut."

I turn and look out the passenger side window again. "You're definitely not." My stomach growls and I think about the vial of my father's blood that I left in my room.

"You want to stop and eat?" Skeele asks.

"Not right now. Just keep going," I reply. "I'll eat something later."

I can't deal with my stomach right now. I'll do what I've been doing for months. Binge on snacks, feel like crap, and in a moment of weakness give in to the bagged blood. It's a vicious cycle.

Skeele drives from Scranton to Old Forge via Interstate-81. There's no traffic, and we are the only vehicle on the highway. We pass herds of the walking dead. As we get close, they move away. It's a nice change from them coming after me and trying to eat my face. We pass pine forests and rocky cutouts. The further north we get, the more I remember my travels with Sparrow before we knew who we were. Although, the guy has so many issues with his brain I'm sure he's forgotten everything again. I long for the days in which we can just be ourselves. I'll take him either way though, a Sparrow who knows who I am is just as good as a Sparrow who has no clue. He's fun either way, and nice to look at.

Skeele pulls off the exit toward Interstate-481 north then Interstate-90 east. We pass forests and farmland. A few people run and hide as we pass. There's a man at the mailbox. He opens it and looks a few times. There's no mail delivery in Hell, must be a habit that stuck. He runs down the driveway when he sees us coming. There's a woman in an open field. She's picking black-eyed-susans and looking up at the sky. As we pass she drops below the tall field grass. It seems most of the souls here act slightly confused and reminiscent of their lives on the Earthen plane. I remember when that was me.

"They haven't figured it out yet," Skeele says.

"I've been there," I reply.

Skeele nods. "We all have. If you're dropped in a dead zone with no signs, it can take a long time to figure things out."

"How many people do you think are down here and dead without knowing it?" I ask.

"Plenty," Skeele says. "Basilisk den isn't far from here. There's a cave near the Black River."

"Wonderful." I shift in my seat, trying not to act anxious.

Skeele merges onto 365 E and veers off onto Eastern Rock Rd. "Avoiding the locals," he says as I reach for the door to steady myself on the bumpy road.

The road ends behind an old Tops grocery store. Skeele jerks the wheel to the left to avoid a walking sack of flesh, rounds a garbage dumpster, and takes a right. He drives for a block before turning right again onto Moose River Road.

"What's wrong?" Skeele asks.

"I'm fine." I don't care to tell him that this place reminds me of Gouverneur where I grew up. The busted roads, dingy old houses, and grocery stores barely held together bring back the sadness of life in a small northern town. Defeat hits a person early, around elementary school age when you know you'll probably never get out unless a miracle happens. You hunker down and prep yourself for a hard life of minimum wage jobs, high taxes, a shitload of snow in the winter and frozen water pipes. You'll be cold and angry and sad and settle for the subpar.

I can see the Black River from the road. Skeele points to the slick serpentine backs of the basilisk swimming in the river. I shiver.

"How many of them are here?" I ask.

"Plenty," Skeele replies. "They spawn here throughout the year."

"Remember, you only need one," Tukka says.

"One is more than I'd like." I settle my hand over the blade at my thigh. "The last basilisk I met I killed. Somehow, I have to get one of these back to my castle alive and train it."

"It can be done," Skeele says. "Lucifer did it."

The road turns winding, with the riverbank just a few feet away. Skeele pulls over and parks on an outcropping of sand.

"Let's get this over with," I say as I open the door and step out.

Tukka jumps out from the rear passenger side and reaches over the door to get the basket as Skeele rounds the front of the Jeep. We walk through the row of pine trees and out onto a giant boulder. The river is filled with basilisk, large and small, serpentine bodies wavering under the current of cold water. If I didn't know better, I'd simply think the water was dark black and filled with current.

"There are small ones?" I point upstream to a shallow area with about ten basilisk that are no longer than five or six foot long. "I can just take a small one."

"It's not that easy," Skeele says. "Those are babies. You can take a baby, but you'll have to face the mother. She'll come after you."

"Oh?" I move closer to the shallow pool of the river.

"There," Tukka says as he points to the center of the river.

I look up to see a giant head has risen from the surface of the river. Rows of sharp teeth hiss in my direction.

"Do you think that's the mother?" I shout back to the guys as I jump down from the boulder.

"I'm going to guess it is," Skeele says.

I run toward the pool of babies. The mother starts to swim closer, teeth bared.

"Wait for us, Meg," Skeele shouts.

Footsteps follow behind me. I grip my blade and stop at the edge of the pool. The mother is directly across from me.

"Toss me the basket," I order Tukka.

He throws it and it plops into the pool. The baby basilisk barely flinch.

"They don't seem scared," I say as I secure my blade, crouch down, and reach into the cold water.

"Just remember, a baby basilisk won't protect your castle until it's older," Skeele says.

I want the mother. Mothers follow one thing, their children. Looks like I'm about to get a basilisk family.

"I guess we'll take them all." I reach further into the water and scoop up a baby basilisk and put it in the reed basket. The mother's head and body start to come out of the water.

"What's your plan, Meg?" Skeele asks.

"We take them all, and she follows."

Boots thud behind me as Skeele hops down from his perch on the rock and starts helping me collect the babies.

"These things are gross," I say as I rinse the slimy ruminants off my hand with the river water.

"Don't think about it," Skeele says.

We get all the babies but three that are further back. I take off my jacket and toss it on the riverbank before I slip into the water, sliding my feet across the rocky pool, scoop them up and put them in the basket.

When I look up again, the mother is a foot from my face. A hundred tiny, sharp teeth greet me. I scramble back, grab the basket, and toss it up on the riverbank. Tukka grabs the basket as it tips to the side, slams the lid closed and locks it. The babies shriek and it is ear piercing. Skeele grabs the back of my jeans and tugs me out of the water. "What's your plan?" he asks as I stumble and grab my jacket off the ground.

"A mother follows her babies. So, we better run home as fast as we can," I say, out of breath.

We run toward the Jeep. The baby basilisk writhe and screech and Tukka's muscles bulge as he does his best to keep ahold of the basket as it shifts with their movement.

I turn and find the mother following us. "I hope you can drive faster than she slithers," I shout to Skeele.

He jumps behind the wheel just as Tukka loads the basket and jumps over the rear gate to get into the back of the Jeep. I scramble inside and lock the door.

"Go go go!" we all shout in unison.

"She won't just slither," Skeele says as he slams his foot down on the gas. "She can kinda fly."

"Like with wings?" I ask.

"Not really. It kinda floats in the air and water," Tukka says.

"Why in the hell does everything down here fly except me?" I ask.

Tukka breaks out in laughter from the back seat.

"What?" I ask.

"The dead don't fly," he says.

"Give it time. I'm sure they will eventually." I glance behind us and sure as shit the basilisk is floating above the asphalt.

"See, that wasn't so bad, was it?" Skeele asks.

"When you all told me I had to capture a basilisk, I figured I was going to have to fight it or play the flute to hypnotize it," I say.

Skeele drives fast as heck to get us back to the castle, the mother about half a mile behind us the entire time. Always watching. Always moving. She never stops pursuing us.

"What are you going to do with the babies?" Tukka asks. "Kill them now that you'll have the mother?"

"No," I say. That would be cruel. And while I am many things, I don't think I could live with myself for being cruel to a mother. The jar of feathers on my nightstand is a testament to that.

"Noah!" I shout.

It takes a few minutes for him to appear.

"Yes, your highness," he asks as he bows.

"I need a big fish tank."

"Please don't tell me you want live fish fry." Noah makes a disgusted face.

"No, I need a giant tank set up in Lucifers office for the basket 'o basilisk babies." I point.

Noah looks to my Hellions and the babies in the basket screech on que.

"Oh, of all the bullshit you get me into. Okay. Give me a minute." Noah disappears.

As we head to the front door, the mother turns down the curve in the road.

"Leave the door open," I say.

We make our way to the office. Doors slam as the basilisk mother enters the building. There's a few growls and the scattering sound of small shadow creatures running away.

Noah is already setting up a huge tank when we get there. It's already filled with water. Noah plugs a cord into the wall and a small octopus decoration emits bubbles from inside the tank.

"Let's get the babies in," I say.

Tukka sets the basket down and we take turns grabbing the slimy babies and getting them into the tank. It's a struggle with their long bodies and writhing.

"Oh lord," Noah whispers. "Those are nasty."

We turn to see the mother's head peeking through the door, large beady eyes and knife sharp teeth. She stares at me as she enters the room, sizing me up. I point to the dark ceiling where my grandfather kept his basilisk. Knowing, she slithers through the air and coils herself against the ceiling.

"Don't forget to feed the babies," Tukka whispers.

"What do they eat?" I ask as we walk out of the room.

"I am not in charge of that chore," Noah complains. "Feeding Meg is hard enough."

"Spinach and crawfish," Skeele says as we leave the room and close the door.

"I'm not sure I'll ever go back in there," I say. "It's all you, Noah."

"You have to train them all," Skeele reminds me.

I shudder. "I need a drink."

We walk down to the Hellions lair. I run to the sink and wash the slime off my hands. When I turn around, the whole crew is watching me.

"What?" I ask.

"You went to get one basilisk and come back with an entire family," Klaus says. "Never seen the ruler of Hell do that before."

I shrug. "What can I say?"

Keep On

Sparrow

Sparrow headed north, again. He was moving so fast he was nearly flying. The urge was there, the memory, but he didn't have wings on the Earthen plane. What he wouldn't give to spread them out and stretch with a gut full of blood. It would have been exhilarating.

Sparrow left Crescent City quick enough for the dead to clean up his mess. No one would suspect much at the bar after they see the rest of the town. Sometimes having a horde of the dead trailing you is a good thing. Well, good for Sparrow in the sense it hid his tracks from the unsuspecting.

The Redwood Highway swayed inland and took Sparrow's view of the ocean, the clash of the waves, and without them he could hear the garbled sounds of the walking dead taking over Crescent City. He moved faster, eager to escape the noise, knowing they'd be following him as soon as they were done.

When the moon was directly overhead, headlights lit the highway from behind him. A caravan of those who were lucky enough to escape were coming. They honked as they passed.

"Get out of the road!" someone shouted. Trucks spilling with people passed. Cars weighed down with families and supplies sped by. Their eyes were wide as they passed Sparrow, their heads turning in awe that he was merely walking alone and not running like them.

A vehicle lingered behind. Sparrow moved to the other lane and slowed. A Jeep Wrangler, with the top off turned in front of him and stopped.

Sparrow grabbed his blade, holding it out at arm's length. He was met with the rounded end of a baseball bat. He looked past it and recognized the woman from the forest with blue hair.

"You going to slice me up with that?" she asked.

"If I need to," Sparrow replied. "You going to bludgeon me with that?" he nodded toward the bat.

"If I need to," she replied with a smirk. "You want a ride?"

Sparrow looked past her and recognized Jed from the diner in the passenger seat.

"I like to walk." Sparrow secured his blade.

"There's blood on you." She motioned to his hand and face.

Sparrow wiped at his mouth with an open palm. "Got in a fight."

Her eyes narrowed and Jed whispered something. "I bet you won. Seem the type."

Sparrow smiled; it was arrogant and dark. "I always do."

Something fell out of the sky and landed at Sparrow's feet with a thud.

"What the heck?" the blue haired woman made a face.

Sparrow bent and picked up the dead bird. "It's a raven." Sparrow stroked the feathers. His fingers petted the thick flight feathers at the base of its wings. He gripped two and tugged hard, pulling them out. He tucked them in his pocket before gently setting down the carcass off the side of the road. He dug a small hole in the dirt with his hands and buried the creature. The eerie sound of a dozen crows cawing from the power lines filled the night.

"I'd get a move on. The dead are following." The chick in the Jeep pressed down on the gas pedal and began driving away.

"They always do," Sparrow said as he stood and looked up. There were more dead ravens, more feathers went into his pockets–some he didn't have the urgency to bury.

An unkindness of ravens above him cawed louder.

Nightmares

MEG

I'M FLYING, REALLY FLYING. MY WINGS SPREAD AND SOAK up the sepia light of Hellsky. Something hits me from behind, wraps its arms and legs around me. I fight. I bite. I tear whatever it is to pieces. My wings are suddenly gone. I drop from the sky like a sack of shit. Just like the night after draining Lucifer dry and I fell to the ground and broke every bone in my body.

———

I WAKE in a pool of sweat. I rub my arms and legs, making sure it was just a dream. It was just a dream. Damn you, Nightingale. I need these dreams to end. I wake more tired than the night before.

"It wasn't me," a familiar voice says.

In the darkness of the room, I see nothing.

"Where are you?" I ask.

"In between the Astral and your land." The sound of a baby cooing interrupts her.

"Are you…"

"Don't ask." Her voice is firm. "I just stopped by to remind you that the winter solstice is upon us. The extended hours of darkness will part the veil. It's how I used to sneak out of Heaven."

"You used to sneak out?" I ask.

"Sparrow was the only good one." There is a long pause. "I miss him, Meg. You must go find him."

"I'll find him," I promise. I hope it's not a lie. I have to find him.

"We only had him back for a short time." The sorrow in her voice is thick. "I'd like him to meet his nephew."

"He's a Hellion now," I remind her.

"It doesn't matter. He's still my brother. He's still doing his best to be a curse breaker."

"Okay, Night," I promise again. "I'm going to find him, even if it kills me."

"Be safe, Meg. We love you."

She's gone and I'm left with the echo of her words. Never has anyone said that to me. Besides Sparrow, but he must. He's required to say things like that. But not Nightingale. Not anyone else in my life. I throw the covers back and move to get out of bed. If the winter solstice is here, then I'm not waiting one second longer. I got the Basilisk. I glance at the nightstand drawer. I've got the blood of an Archangel.

I head to the bathroom to shower, knowing it might be a very long time until I get to shower again. I scrub and shave like I'm getting ready for prom. When Sparrow sees me again, I'd like to be all shiny and clean for him. I towel off, realizing that I'm going to miss the luxuries I have here. It didn't take long to get used to them, even though I lived without for most of my life.

I get dressed in the closet, selecting jeans, a T-shirt with a wide neck and a dark blue canvas jacket. I dig around until I find my old backpack with the single strap. I fill it with a change of clothes and clean underwear.

"Noah," I beckon. "Noah, I need you to get me some things."

The room chills as Noah arrives. "Are we taking a trip?"

"I am. Hey, I need you to get me a big canteen with fresh water, some granola bars and protein bars. Maybe some survival gear if you can find it."

"Sounds like you're going camping."

"Not camping. But if the Earthen plane is anything like it was last time the dead were walking around there, I need to prepare myself to walk into some apocalyptic bullshit."

"Look at you having all the fun. I'm jealous."

I pause, feeling guilty. Noah died; his soul is trapped in the Astral plane. At least that is an unruled plane, at least he and Nightingale can see each other there. I'd love nothing more than for him to come with me. "Sorry," I say.

"No biggie." He waves it off. "I'll go get your survival crap."

After he leaves, I dig out a pair of thick socks, add a second pair to my bag. I put on my leather hiking boots. There's still mud caked to them from mine and Sparrow's previous travels. It feels weird gearing up to walk into Hell. Well, not my Hell; a different type of Hell. America being torn apart by the dead as they eat their way across the continent. This sounds like the crappiest trip I've ever planned. The only bright side is finding Sparrow and bringing him home.

Home. There was a time when home was all I wanted. When I traipsed across upstate NY in search of a home nothing felt right, no matter where I landed. It didn't matter if I was going back to that white house with a green door and picket fence. I did my best to make that my home but it never stuck. I learned why in the worst way possible. I learned who I was and what I'd come from. But now, being here in Hell and knowing the rules and who makes them, knowing the flow of Heaven and Hell and the Earthen plane; now I finally feel at home. I will feel even more at home with Sparrow here. Just like Nightingale said, we miss him.

There's a noise in my bedroom. I step out of the closet and find Noah piling what he found onto my bed.

"Hey," he nods as he stacks protein bars and sets the canteen upright.

"Look at this." I toss my backpack on the bed and unzip it.

"You might have to remove some clothes to make this fit."

"I only packed one outfit."

"Maybe a bigger pack?"

"No." I shake my head. "I get the feeling I'm going to be running, a lot, and I can't be doing that with a huge pack on my back."

Noah whistles a trill as he scratches his head. I guess he picked that up from Nightingale. I've only seen Night and Sparrow communicate with birdsong.

I stack the bars and snacks and tuck them into my bag. "They'll be eaten before I know it," I say. "There's no point in leaving food behind. I'll be starving. Half of it will be gone in twenty-four hours."

Noah chuckles. "Hey, my girl likes to eat."

"I'm not your girl."

Noah raises his arms in defense. "Used to be." His brow rises and he smirks.

"Shut up."

Noah rubs his pinched fingers over his lips like he's zipping them closed.

I open the nightstand and take out the vial of my father's blood.

"What's that?" Noah asks.

"Nothing." I push it into my pocket, my mouth salivating at the thought of drinking it.

I pick up the canteen and weigh it in my hand. There's a strap to hold it or a clip. It's too heavy to clip to my pack. I've been on the road with nothing before. Just a nearly empty bag and scavenging from house to house. This packing session feels very hoity-toity and I'm ready to toss the bag and walk through the veil with nothing more than my blade and a prayer to Bon Jovi.

"You're right," Noah says.

"You read minds now too?" I ask.

"I can read you. You don't need all this stuff. I get the feeling you'll be tossing it all on the side of the road before you get very far."

"I might." I agree with him. "But I guess I should put forth the effort to pack for once in my life."

"If that's a goal of yours, I'd say you're there."

I smile. "Thanks, Noah."

He sits and stretches his arms behind his head. "I'm so ready for this vacation. No more running for food. It will be just me and this balcony and the birds."

"Boring." I toss a pillow at him. "You punk."

Noah catches the pillow. "I know you'll miss me."

I adjust the backpack strap and put it over my shoulder. "Don't forget to feed the Basilisk and its babies."

A groan of disapproval erupts from Noah. "Dear God, no."

"Hey, they're our pets now."

"I did not agree to this."

"Neither did I." I laugh as I leave the room.

———

The Hellion's lair is humming with wild energy. I knock on the door, warning them that I'm about to enter.

"You're up early," Skeele says as I enter.

"I should have never gone to sleep," I say.

"Where are you going?" Klaus asks, smoothing his beard with both hands. I notice all their batlike wings are folded taut behind their backs.

"It's time for me to go," I say.

Skeele is behind the bar, pouring packet blood into glasses. "One for the road?" he asks, his curled horns reflecting the overhead lights.

I pause, close my eyes, and nod. There's no denying that I'll need it for what I'm about to walk into.

"One of us should go with you," Tukka says. "From what I've heard it's absolute chaos on the Earthen plane right now."

"I don't think that's necessary." I pat the blade at my leg. "I'll be just fine."

"You still can't fly," Skeele points out.

"That doesn't matter. None of us can fly on the Earthen plane." I take the few steps to the bar and pick up the glass Skeele slides toward me.

"If the conditions are right, we can," Tukka says. "There's stories about it."

Skeele shushes Tukka. "Those are stories. That's it. The rules between realms are clear."

I down the blood, my body sings with relief. It's been weeks since I last gave in. I quell the lust and direct my brain elsewhere.

"I need a ride to the portal before the sun rises." I lick my lips, not wasting a drop.

"We'll take you," Skeele says as he waves for Tukka to follow.

"Good luck," Chel says from the shadows of the room.

We leave the dark castle built into the burning caves and walk toward the Jeep. A shadow covers the dull moonglow, I look up to see Clea as the argentavis flying above us. Skeele drives and Clea follows from overhead. The ride to the field with the portal is quick. As Skeele parks I notice the wavering shadows around the portal. Creatures slither back and forth.

"What are they doing?" I ask.

"Collecting things. Escaping." Skeele gets out and grips his blade. It glows and hums. The shadowed things scatter, and I see the extent of the parted veil around the portal.

"When you pass, it will rip further," Tukka says. "It won't be closed completely until you return. Or time runs out."

"So those creatures and souls can still leak out?" I ask.

"Yup." Skeele slaps a fancy cellphone into my hand.

"For the love of all that is holy, I do not want this thing," I complain as I press a button and check the battery.

"All the cool kids are carrying one, and it might come in handy while you're looking for bird boy." Skeele says.

"You're not coming?" I ask, testing.

Skeele smirks. "When have you ever needed help? Especially from a Hellion?"

I weight the phone in my palm. "I need a navigator for this pile of crap." With each year I age technology seems to escape me a little more.

"You'll figure it out." Skeele chuckles as he walks away.

I fully expected one of them to come with me, but I don't need them. I don't really want them. They are a distraction. I need to focus on one thing. Finding Sparrow.

I stand in front of the portal, Clea flying overhead, my Hellions waiting in the darkness. I take a deep breath.

I accept that I am bred of monsters. I am a monster, bloodthirsty and damned. The blood of the Archangel Michael and Lucifer pumps through my veins, and soon the pureblood of Gabriel. I remove the vial from my pocket and down it. Power rushes through my veins. I will miss the smell of woodsmoke and pine.

"I'm coming for you, Sparrow," I whisper into the night.

Snow Ash

MEG

I EXIT THE PORTAL AT A CHURCH IN PENNSYLVANIA. Prince of Peace Roman Catholic Church, the sign states. Its peaks are five stories tall. The windows are dark but I notice the gothic decorations in the early morning light. Gargoyles stare down at me.

I pull my coat tighter and kick at the snow that's built up on the cement steps. It didn't take me long to forget about winters of the Earthen plane. I grip the strap of my bag and walk down the steps. The early morning is eerie. There are no cars on the street and no one walking to work or school. Down the road I see a convenience store and walk toward it. The heavy canteen knocks against the back of my leg. That's going to have to go. I stop in front of a newspaper machine, pull down the handle and take out a fresh paper.

I didn't think I'd been gone from the Earthen plane for long, but it appears everything here has fallen apart.

"Oh God," I mutter to myself as I read the front-page story about a hoard of zombies eating their way up the coast of California. There's a picture of a highway by the sea and a burning sign. I keep reading. There's been outbreaks in every state. I turn the page and read about safe areas, how to stock up on weapons and food, and how to kill a sack of walking flesh. It seems they're taking this seriously. Too bad it won't stop until I get Sparrow in the correct realm.

The Scarecrow told us that Sparrow's last bit of grace was disrupting the fiber between Hell and the Earthen plane. But this seems extreme. Not long ago the Coast Guard and Military were able to secure the dead outbreaks. Now, it seems it's all gone to hell.

Shuffling feet interrupt my reading. I turn and find myself face to face with a dead man. He growls and decaying jaws snap open and closed.

I drop the paper, grab my blade and slice his head off. It rolls to the ground and his body drops, jaws still snapping for a few more seconds. His teeth are clanking together, hoping for a bite of fresh flesh.

"Gross." I clean my blade on the corpses clothes and secure it again.

I need to find shelter and think. I grab the newspaper off the melting snow and look toward the door of the convenience store. A woman inside is watching me. The doors are chained closed. She shakes her head no. I'm shit out of luck here in PA.

I pull the phone out of my pocket. Tap, tap, tap the screen but nothing happens. I hold it up in the air. There's no service. Damn. I told Skeele I didn't need this piece of junk.

I start walking and thinking. I grip the newspaper tighter in my hand. As I walk through the valley of the shadow of death, I realize that I can't always trust in Google maps. There's nothing here. Sparrow isn't here. Even though he's tattooed skull to tailbone in runes to hide him, I'd know. I'd have to know. That newspaper was a sign from... someone. I glance at the sky. This is God's land, but he's never helped me before. Maybe he's truly tired of us mucking it up? I no longer teeter on the fringes of belonging here. All I can figure is he wants us out. I don't have much time.

Poof.

I go to California.

———

I TRAVEL to the picture from the newspaper. The waves crashing drown out all sound. It's still dark here, the only light coming from the glow of the moon. I grip my blade, crouch, and take in my surroundings. Maybe I *should* have brought a Hellion with me. I've never been to California. Who knows the kind of horrors that lurk here?

I start walking.

California is just like every TV show from 2010. Tall pines, sea salt spray from the ocean, fancy cars. I focus on the abandoned Mercedes in front of me. There's a corpse behind the wheel. I blink a few times until my eyes adjust and remember Sparrow's rule from so long ago: cars make noise, noise brings the dead, we walk. Sure that there's no one nearby, I head north. I tuck the newspaper into the side pocket of my bag and release the canteen. I can't stand it whacking against my leg for one more minute.

I stay close to the guardrail of the road so I can see anything coming out of the forest on the other side. I weave around abandoned and broken cars. My stomach growls. That didn't take long. I tell myself that I'll have a snack when I get to the next road sign that tells me where I am. As I walk, the sky lightens and the chilled night air warms. A few crows lift from the nearby trees. I know one thing. Where there are birds, there is Sparrow. I pick up my pace, walking for a good hour before I come to a sign letting me know I'm on Redwood Highway. I pull out my phone and try to get it to work. There's another sign for DeMartin Campsite, and nearby Crescent City. The power icon circles on the screen. I give up too easily. I got by for plenty of years without a cell phone. I tuck it in my pocket, my finger swiping over the empty vial of blood. Later I'll eat something, I tell myself. Save the energy bars for later. I can do this without them. It's just walking. No fighting.

No drama. I tap the empty vial and remove my hand from my pocket.

———

THERE'S noise in the forest. Boots crunching over dried sticks and pine needles interrupts the early morning hours. And… a pulsing sound. I can smell blood that's unspilled. I can hear the pulsing of a handful of people. My mouth waters. I guess this is what I get for stepping into my grandfather's boots. Bloodlust and all the rest. At least I get a heads up that I'm not alone. Someone is watching me from the tree line.

"Are you alive?" a man's voice whispers.

"Mostly," I reply.

"Do you need help?" he asks.

"Nope." I keep walking and consider walking faster.

A guy steps out into the road.

"I'm just traveling through," I say.

"We have food."

If only he knew, he's food to me. "I'm fine." I grip my blade. "I'm just crossing thru these parts."

"You talk different." His eyes narrow on me.

"At least I talk."

The guy motions to the road ahead. "A whole heard of the dead came by these parts not too long ago. You won't find anyone alive."

I stare.

"Can I come with you?" he asks.

There's a bite mark on his neck. The teeth marks are black, the blackness spreading away from the wound like ice cracks.

"No," I reply as I think to relieve him of his head before he turns.

"Please." The desperation in his voice is terrible. He walks closer.

I point my blade in his direction. "Go live out the last of your days. Leave me alone."

That guy will be a walking sack of flesh in no time. I pick up my pace. He stands still and watches me go. I walk faster than I'd like too, glad that I stuck to my guns and kept the small pack and didn't switch to a bigger one like Noah suggested.

A good long time goes by before I see a sign that tells me I'm still on Redwood Highway. Crescent City is a few miles ahead and Demartin Campground is the next exit.

I never was much of a camping person. Sleeping on the hard ground in a nylon tent never sounded appealing to me. I can imagine there's plenty of people on the run these days. But a tent, no, you couldn't drag me into a tent to sleep for the night. I'd rather sleep on a floating door in the ocean.

———

CRESCENT CITY IS EMPTY. There's barely any cars and the ones I walk by are wrecked or abandoned with the doors open. There's blood everywhere. I consider stealing one of the cars, but I don't need any more dead on my trail, no more than the single guy from the woods who's been following me and slowly succumbing to his wounds. His pulse slows and slows and... slows. It's going to stop completely soon. And I really don't want to be around him when it does.

I can smell something familiar in the air. Someone was here. Sparrow was here. I follow the smell of him and thank my lucky stars that those runes didn't take away his scent.

I follow the trail to an empty house. Around back, I kick open the door and let myself in. The place is a dump with holes in the floor and filled with dust. He was here. I walk through the kitchen and find a couch with blankets. He slept here. There are footprints on the floor, a fresh indent in the couch. I take my time looking around to see if he left anything. Sparrow's not in his right mind and might've left something behind. It's a lie I tell myself. Even when he was the most cracked in the head, he never left anything behind.

I sit in the indent on the couch. The back door of the house creaks. I wait. Maybe it's him? Could it really be this easy? A figure lumbers through the door and crashes into the kitchen chairs. Damn. It's my dead friend from the highway.

Gripping my blade, I step aside and give him room to schlep on over.

"I told you to stay away from me." I'm not sure why I'm bothering to talk to the walking bag of flesh.

Jaws snap.

These dead are nothing like the ones down in Hell. At least down there they give me space.

I brace myself for the lurch that comes next. Sidestepping, I swing my arm out and cut off the dead man's head. His body drops to the ground. I walk toward the kitchen and get my bearings.

I leave the house without any more clues about Sparrow. I follow his scent mixed with the sea salt spray of the nearby Pacific ocean. It's not a scent of Hell. No, this is something different. Danger and freshness and energy linger around the smell of him. I follow the empty streets. The dead are upright here, meandering and moaning, but they keep their distance for now.

I stop at a bar near the town limits. The neon lights still blink in the window. Why would Sparrow go to a bar? I can only think of one reason. He was hungry. A shiver runs up my spine and my arms tingle. The thought of Sparrow seeking out blood from another woman... I know better. Skeele warned me. I don't go into the bar. I don't want to know the details. I don't want to see the corpses. I turn to the right and follow the road out of town.

The sign points to Redwood highway again. North. I notice a lump of something on the ground. As I get closer, I recognize the dead crow. I touch it with my toe and notice it's missing two flight feathers. If I had anyone to bet money with, I'd bet those two feathers are in Sparrow's pocket right now. I'd rather it was me.

———

I STOP at a small house just past the edge of town. The day didn't last long and as the sun started to set, the noises in the woods started. Now, I'm a creature of Hell, but I still have fear of the horrors of the Earthen plane. I lived through enough of them growing up. I'll catch up to Sparrow eventually. I'll take my time; don't want to roll up on him like some crazy ex-girlfriend and scare him off. Who knows what his mental state is like right now. I need to be careful because I need to take him back with me.

Feathered friends bring gifts

Sparrow

Sparrow is a shadow in the night, a pale giant in the morning light. Shay and Jed have been waiting for him. Every few miles he walks, there they are, waiting. Expecting. Watching. Anticipating for a sign. Waiting for him to show them what he really is.

"You might want to hurry up," Shay says, tucking blue hair behind her ear. "Something is following us."

"It's me," Sparrow says.

"No," Jed finally speaks up. "Something worse than you. Something darker than you." He raises his forearm and the tattooed runes glow blue. "They aren't supposed to find us." Jed's forehead wrinkles.

Sparrow blinks and then holds up his arms. His runes are dark. There's no blue glow. Just an ethereal iridescence.

"They were supposed to hide us," Jed says.

"We need more weapons," Shay says.

"So, who is it?" Sparrow asks.

"We aren't sure," Shay says. "But if we have any chance of surviving, it's with you."

"We know each other?" Sparrow asks.

"Yes," Jed says. "We've met twice in this lifetime. And each time our paths cross, chaos follows."

A shadow passes over them before landing behind Sparrow. Another follows. Then another.

They're crows. One drops a stick. Another drops a pocket knife. The third drops a small handgun.

"Don't touch it," Shay warns.

Sparrow kicks it away. "Don't need it."

Shay bends and picks up the gun, inspecting it. "Smart birds. I've never seen them drop something like this from the sky though."

Sparrow picks up the knife and tucks it in his pocket.

Unbroken Curses

Meg

I peek out the cracked window as the sun starts to rise. It's been three days. I'm out of time. The solstice is over. Heaven and Hell will be looking for me. That's okay. I've seen enough Jason Bourne movies to know what to do. I trace the runes on my arms. They're supposed to hide me, like Sparrow's do. I'm hoping it will take very long for someone to recognize me.

I toss the dusty blanket off me onto the floor and stretch. Sleeping in a chair wasn't the best idea but I couldn't bring myself to sleep in someone else's bed. Never could. I'd flipped all the pictures down in the room before falling asleep, unable to tolerate the stares from the people who lived here before. I wonder if they're dead now. I wonder if they packed their shit and ran to Canada with the hopes that the walking corpses would freeze in the snow, and they'd be safe from death by zombie bite?

I shrug in self contemplation. Sounds like a good idea. I'm sure someone has thought of it.

I reach for my bag and grab two of the protein bars Noah packed for me. The canteen is nearly empty, just enough to rinse my mouth out from the chalky taste. My stomach growls.

"Yeah. Yeah." I tell myself. "We'll find more food." I zip up my bag and sling it over my shoulder as I get a hard look at the street. From the second story, everything looks empty and quiet. What would Andy Dufresne do? I escaped. He escaped. I dream for a moment about sunny beaches and swaying palm trees, about treasure and white speed boats...

A loud clang from downstairs startles me. Crap. The place looked empty last night and I didn't notice anyone alive or dead when I walked through. Maybe they came in while I was asleep? I glance out the second-story window again. Wings would help right now. I could just fly away and avoid whatever shit-fuckery is going on downstairs.

There are slow footsteps, shuffling, furniture falling over and grunts.

I step toward the stairs and see shadows in the early morning light. I tighten my bag and grip my blade, ready. I walk down the steps slowly, staying near the wall. There's less of a chance of them creaking near the wall. I walk down a few more until I can see figures in a far mirror along the wall. The dead got in. And so did someone else.

I glance at the front door at the bottom of the stairs. I could run down and out. Or go back up and out a window and hope I don't break a leg jumping down. I catch a glimpse of blonde hair escape from under the cloak.

Wait a minute...

I run down the stairs to get a closer look.

One of the dead notices me and staggers closer. They're coming in through the back door, one after another. I take a few steps forward and chop off its head.

The person in the cloak turns at the sound, the hood falling back.

"Teari?" I ask.

She slices two heads off and backs up, kicking over a chair to block the deads path.

"I was trying to sneak up on you," Teari says.

"You failed at that," I say backing toward the front door.

"Your father sent me. You were supposed to be gone by morning." Teari moves toward me, unlocks the front door and opens it.

She pauses. "Bangs?"

I push my hair out of my eyes. "Shut up."

"Let's get out of here." She tips her head at the doorway.

She doesn't have to ask me twice. We run through the door and slam it closed.

As soon as we clear the house that's under siege, I ask, "How on God's green earth did you find me so fast?"

Teari smiles. "Being a healer, I have gifts of my own." She wags a finger. "You should know better than to think you could hide from me."

We jog down the street, ducking behind cars to catch our breath. The morning fog is thick.

"I think we've lost them," I say.

Teari nods in agreement. "So, where are we headed?"

"You're not going back, now that you found me being bad on the Earthen plane?"

"Nope," Teari smiles. "Go back and let you have all the fun? No way." She stands and stretches. "I'm guessing you're walking. You always walk. Which direction?"

I point toward the highway. "That way."

We scan the town and make sure none of the dead are following.

We walk the highway as the sun clears the sea mist.

Teari moves toward the edge of the road. "You think this was him?" she nudges a dead raven.

"Are there feathers missing?" I ask. "If there are, he was here."

Teari crouches down to inspect the bird. "Yup. Flight feathers are gone."

"Figures."

We walk US-101 north. There are signs for campgrounds and the Redwood forest. Teari nods toward the campground sign. "Guaranteed trouble there."

"I avoided the trouble at the last one."

"Speaking of trouble," Teari says. "Have you seen baby Thrush lately? Poor Nightingale never gets much sleep anymore. She always looks completely exhausted. I guess a baby will do that. Soon he'll be walking and tearing the place up." Teari smiles, thinking about Sparrow's nephew. "Oh sorry. I'm sure she hasn't brought him to see your realm. You'll spend lots of time with him when he's older."

"Why's that?" I ask.

Teari pauses before saying, "He's cursed just like the rest of them. He'll spend his time as a Hellion eventually."

Crap.

Friends of a Feather

Sparrow

Shay waited at the exit to Elk Valley Cross Rd. She turned off the Jeep to save gas and propped her feet up on the dashboard.

"He walks pretty fast," Jed said, digging in his backpack for something to eat.

"Then we shouldn't have to wait long." Shay shivered. She didn't like to be a sitting duck on the highway. The only solace was that Sparrow would be there soon and he'd scare away anything threatening.

"Why didn't you just ask him to ride?" Shay asked Jed.

Jed chuckled. "Not so sure I want to be sitting in the same vehicle as him. Last time I was in the same room as Sparrow, his girlfriend nearly killed me. I have little trust for creatures of Heaven and Hell combined."

Shay nodded. "Understandable."

A few of the dead ambled by. Shay and Jed held their breath and sat still as stone until they passed.

"I haven't seen them move ahead of Sparrow before," Shay whispered.

Jed nodded in agreement. "There must be something going on up ahead drawing them."

It was just a few hours until Sparrow caught up with them. Shay rolled down the window as he headed toward the exit to Elk Valley Cross Rd. "Where you headed, Sparrow?" Jed asked.

He didn't answer. Shay followed, her foot barely pressing the gas pedal.

They followed him past Sunset High School and turned right on Lake Earl Drive. They passed a pub and a T-shirt shop before Sparrow turned left onto Buzzini Road.

Shay and Jed saw what drew Sparrow. There was a giant house in front of them set on a lake and surrounded by a stone wall. Music thumped from inside.

Shay and Jed made eye contact. They'd seen what he did to the bar in Crescent City.

"We have to shut this down," Shay said.

Jed shook his head and made a face. "We aren't the police. What those people are doing is a death sentence."

Shay kept driving, looking for a parking spot that was both hidden but close. "They're probably just stupid kids." She thumbed to the road behind them. "Did you see the high school we passed?"

Jed leaned forward to open his bag and take out weapons. "Just so you are aware, I am not a fan of this."

Shay found a spot under the overhang of a large tree and near the stone wall that surrounded the mansion. They could get in and out easily and avoid most of the zombies that were currently knocking on the gate.

———

SPARROW WALKED UP to the house, around the horde, and jumped up on the stone wall. He watched the house for a few minutes. The music pulsing wasn't much different from the pulsing of blood through veins.

He jumped down and walked toward the front door of the house. It was unlocked. He let himself in.

More Dumb Ways to Die

MEG

AT THE END OF THE WORLD THERE ARE ALWAYS PARTIES.
The young people never fail in that aspect. I started off by following
Sparrow's scent. It let me to a gated mansion near a lake.

The dead are clawing against the brick wall and leaning into the
thick, iron gate. It must be cheap iron since it bends under their
weight. Or maybe they've been pining for what's inside for some
time now.

I used to do a lot of dumb things, but I don't think I was ever
dumb enough to throw a rager in the middle of the zombie
apocalypse.

A night breeze rustles the dead leaves on a nearby tree. It brings
the pungent smell of the dead. I gag a little and cover my mouth.

Teari's head snaps in my direction and she holds a finger to her
lips, effectively telling me to swallow the puke and not cause a scene. I
pull my shirt over my nose and take a few breaths. When the breeze
stops, I let it fall back into place. Teari walks closer, blade in hand.
Ready.

I can smell him. Faintly. He could be here.

Teari makes a questioning face and tips her head in expectation.

I nod.

Teari walks away and surveys the place. I notice a few trees and consider climbing one and jumping across the brick wall into the yard.

"Are you sure he's here?" Teari asks.

"Yes."

"How do you know? I have no sense of him anymore," Teari says.

"I can smell him."

"Like his cologne?" Teari asks.

"Like his blood," I reply.

"Oh." Teari reaches for her blade. "I could carry you over the wall."

"No." I shake my head. "That's too humiliating."

"Why do you never take the help that's offered?" she asks.

"I don't want to owe you anything," I say.

"I don't keep a tally."

I can't hide my expression of surprised disbelief. "Everyone keeps a tally," I say. "Everyone."

"Do you?" Teari asks.

"Of course."

"Then what do I owe you?"

I press my lips together, holding it in.

"Tell me." She urges.

"There was that one time when I was stabbed, and we were trying to escape, and you told Sparrow I wasn't worth the risk."

"And I owe you something for that?" She paces and watches the crowd of the dead. Teari is full of arrogant pride. She's always been that way. Can't hate on her for it.

"An apology," I say.

Teari sighs before turning to face me directly and saying, "I'm sorry. You were worth the risk."

"Thanks." I step to the side. "I think I'm going to climb that tree and drop down." I point to the giant oak tree near the wall.

"Just let me help you."

"No." I hold up my hand to stop her. "You can't be flashing around all your glory." I circle my hands around her. "It will bring questions." I tighten my bag and run for the tree. "The few left alive could see. They'll be spreading your image in newspapers and what news channels and social media platforms are still up and running."

"I just don't want us to fuck this up." Teari rests her hands on her hips. "There's enough turmoil in the Seven Kingdoms of Heaven that I must go back to. If I don't help you fix this, who knows what they'll blame on me."

"Are they threatening you?" I step toward her, raising my voice. It's hard not to. You see, I have this problem with wanting to put jerks in their place. Especially righteous jerks from Heaven. They've caused Sparrow's family enough grief. "Did they?" I ask again, louder.

Oops. Too loud. The dead notice us.

"Run," Teari takes to the air.

I race the dead to the tree trunk. I run and focus on a low branch. The dead start moving toward me. I dash the last few feet, jump, and grab the lowest branch to pull myself up. As my feet dangle, one of the walking sacks of flesh grabs at my boot.

"Get up there, Meg," Teari shouts from above me.

I pull my body up then climb to standing. I secure my foot in the vee of the trunk and climb up a few large branches. "You cheat," I say, out of breath.

She climbs down, balances on the branch that stretches over the wall, walks it like a circus girl on a tightrope, and jumps down.

I follow her, although I'm not as graceful, stopping to secure my bag in one of the vee's of the tree trunk. I don't want to bring a back-pack to a party. Those kids will probably be looking to score anything for a high. I know I did at their age.

I drop to the ground and roll before moving back to my feet. "See?" I say. "Easy."

"Uh-huh." She's staring at the mansion. "Should we just march in the front door?"

"Why not?" I shrug. "It's the apocalypse as far as these people know. Locks don't matter anymore."

"Hopefully not for much longer."

I skip to keep up with Teari's long stride as she heads for the door. The metal driveway gates clang behind us. I turn to see the horde there, reaching, growling, teeth clanking. For the first time in my life, I wish I were back in Hell. At least there the dead stay away.

Teari raises her hand to knock, but realizes the door is cracked open. She pushes it open further and we walk inside. The music is blaring classic rock. I smell beer and sweat and sex. I follow the noise, walking away from Teari. She's an adult and can handle herself. I've got one thing on my mind and that's to find Sparrow.

There are people on couches, eating at the giant dinner table, and sitting on the floor on pillows. They barely notice me, probably due to their inebriation. I'd love to be inebriated right now. I cross the threshold into a huge open living room. All the furniture is gone, there's a DJ booth set up in front of the wall of windows that leads to a pool area. The room is packed and everyone is dancing.

I search the crowd for a millisecond before I find who I'm looking for; the tall, dark-haired man in the center of the room.

Sweet goddamn. He's surrounded by a bunch of hussies all rubbing up on him and shit. Oh Hell no. I enter the crowd and dance my way to the center. There's lots of groping, lots of stares. Sparrow pauses when he sees me. I get closer and nudge a blonde out of the way.

Ah, there he is. My Sparrow. Tall, dark. So dark. I don't ever remember him being like this. Shadows grace the hallows of his face and neck. There is some type of energy surrounding him. It's intoxicating.

"You..." He whispers.

"You," I reply. "I've come a long way to find you."

Another blonde chick starts rubbing up on him. I shove her away with a one-armed thrust to the side.

"Hey!" the chick shouts.

I hiss at her. "Fuck off."

Sparrow touches my shoulder. He's dancing, slender hips moving with the heavy beat of the music.

It's been too long since he last touched me. Sparrow moves his leg between mine and starts dancing like we are in a dirty movie. Classic Meg and Sparrow. If I allow this to go on for one more second, one more heartbeat, there's no going back. This feels too good. I give up, give in, let the darkness consume me and touch him. Oh…

Sweat drips down my spine. His hands are touching my body. Touching me in places where there's ink hidden under my clothes.

"Why are we like this?" he asks. "Who are you?" He tips his head, birdlike and perfectly Sparrow. I wait for him to whistle a trill that never comes.

I spin and grind against him. Sparrow's large hands are on my shoulders, they slide down my arms to my hips. I press harder against his crotch.

He groans.

"Yes." I press my head to his chest and grind harder.

His hands slide under my top and across my stomach. I spin to face him.

"Who are you?" he repeats.

"You don't remember me?" I ask. The old Meg would be pissed. She'd kick him in the crotch and cross the dance floor to find someone else. Not the Meg I am now. He's mine. I'm his. He'll remember soon enough. I'll make him remember.

I reach up, my hands sliding across his chest, his shoulders, his neck. I stop and feel the steady pulse there. His eyes look different.

"You don't remember me, Sparrow. But I remember you. I crave you."

The music pulses. He glances down the wide neck of my shirt and notices the watercolor tattoo of a sparrow in flight.

"I like that," he says.

"I know you do. There's more." I lift the hem of my shirt as I dance and move in a tight circle.

Someone growls.

I spin to look at Sparrow.

He's searching the room.

"That wasn't you?" I ask.

"No," he replies.

There are screams from the corner of the room. Bodies start shoving back. A few revelers trip and fall.

Teari walks into the room. I catch her gaze and point to the corner where the growling came from. She looks to me and slides her finger across her throat.

Crap. Someone died and my guess is now they're biting.

"Get him out," Teari shouts over the crowd.

The music stops suddenly and screams start near the corner of the room where Teari pointed. Oh no. Shit is about to get real.

"Come with me," I say as I grab onto Sparrow's shirt and tug. He doesn't move. "Come on!"

"I'm hungry," he mutters, his eyes on the panicking people who are shoving their way out the doors.

"I'll feed you. Come with me, Sparrow. Now!"

Sparrow's head twists quick as his eyes settle on mine. "Feed me?"

"Yes." I tug harder at his shirt until he starts moving. "Come with me now." I lead him toward the slider doors to the pool. There's a bottleneck of people trying to get out. I shove my way through. Sparrow's stronger, he shoves harder. Dude must be starving.

We get out the door and break free from the crowd. I grip his hand and run toward the side of the house. I need to get back to the tree where I left my bag. And I need to find Teari.

"Teari!" I shout as we round the side of the house. "Meet us at the tree!" I don't know where she is, so I shout blindly.

We round the side yard only to be met with the horde.

"Shit," I mutter, gripping my blade and pulling it off my leg.

Sparrow makes a growling sound. A few of the dead back off but a handful make their way toward us. I put my blade to work, heads roll. It's been a while since I've had to use it. Feels kinda good.

"You're not going to help?" I ask Sparrow.

He has his blade ready. They're both glowing. I'm sure we're breaking a heck of a lot of rules between realms right now, but this is life or death. And there's no way I'm going out by being bitten by a dead thing.

We slice, dice, and run for it. I shout to Sparrow to head toward the tree. Thankfully he obeys.

"Meg?" Teari yells from the backyard.

"The tree!" I shout back.

Teari runs, leaps and —something grabs her. Gray arms tug at her. She screams and struggles until she finds her weapon and frees herself by hacking wildly, then launches herself into the air again.

I dash for the tree. Sparrow follows. So do the dead. They move faster than I remember. Their speed is like a bad dream. Maybe it's the drugs from the party?

"Help me reach," I say, motioning to Sparrow. He lifts me and tosses me up like I weigh nothing. I grab a branch and swing my leg over the side, straddling it. "Come up." I motion for Sparrow to follow. He assesses the brick wall and backs up. The dead are getting closer. Too close. Sparrow runs a few steps and leaps to the top of the wall but one of the dead grab his leg, then another, and another. He groans as they tug, jaws snapping.

"No!" I scream. This isn't supposed to happen. How could this happen? "Teari!" I shout.

I glance back. Teari is on her way, flying at warp speed. She's going to slam into us.

"Slow down!" I shout.

She's gripping her injured arm, her blade glowing in her opposite hand. She lands shakily on the top of the wall next to Sparrow. She grabs his arm and pulls him up the wall. Sparrow kicks off the dead and stands, gripping a branch above his head to steady himself.

"What the fuck just happened?" I ask.

Teari holds up her hand and I notice the rotting teeth marks. Blood drips out of the wound and down to her elbow in dark red rivulets.

"Oh no," I say.

Blackness starts going up her arm, following the outline of her veins.

"Can you heal yourself?" I ask.

Teari's a healer, that's what she's always done; used her angel magic to heal me and others.

"I've never tried on something like this," Teari says as she closes her eyes and holds her uninjured hand over the wound. She shakes her head, defeated. "I can't."

"You have to," I urge.

"It won't work on this," she says, giving up. "Do you have an extra shirt?"

"Yeah." I move to standing on the giant branch and wobble to my bag that's stuck in the vee of the tree. I never thought to bring a med kit. I unzip the bag and pull out my spare T-shirt.

Teari moves closer to me. "Are you ready?" Sweat is dripping down her perfect face.

"For what?"

In a quick movement she holds out her injured arm and slices it off above the elbow with her blade.

"What in the hell?" I scream.

"Wrap it!" Teari shouts back. "Don't let me bleed out! Hurry up!"

Blood is spurting out, drawing the dead closer to us. They collect along the brick wall. I look to Sparrow. His eyes are on blood. I've seen that look before.

"Can't you stop it?" I ask.

"You know how you can't poof when you're injured? Similar thing here. Too much energy being used. Forget about my healing powers, we're running on pure science and bog witchcraft until this heals."

"Well this sucks." My fingers fumble with wrapping her stump. My stomach growls. I pause to focus and control the bloodlust.

"Wrap it tighter!" Teari shouts. "You must stop the bleeding. You have to squeeze the arteries."

I wrap my T-shirt around the remaining half of her arm and stretch it, tying the sleeves. Blood soaks through and drips down the wall.

The dead scramble, licking the bricks and rubbing their faces on it.

"Umm..." a strange thought crosses my mind, probably from too many horror movies and supernatural TV shows. "Teari, what is your blood going to do to them?"

"Huh?" she asks. She's looking really pale.

"Your angel blood," I specify. "What does angel blood do to walking corpses on the Earthen plane?"

"Never had the pleasure of coming across that problem," she mutters, her voice weak. "Do you think you could fly us out of here?" Teari asks.

"I can't fly," I say.

Teari makes a face.

We both look at Sparrow. He's watching the dead corpses lick the bricks. I scan the trickles of blood and notice one coming from under his boot.

Shit. Shit. Shit.

I move across the wall, steadying myself by gripping a tree branch overhead.

I bend down and pull up Sparrow's pant leg. There's a large chunk of flesh missing and blood streaming down his leg.

I want to puke. I want to *poof* the fuck back to Hell so I can be safe in my little castle with my group of Hellions to protect me.

"What's wrong?" Teari asks.

We've been in some whacked out situations, but this is by far the worst.

"He's bit," I say.

"Cut it off," Teari says. "Cut off the bitten limb."

"It's his leg!" I shout. "You want me to cut his leg off?"

"Yes!" Teari screams back at me. "Get us the hell out of here or cut his leg off!" She leans into the tree, breathing heavy.

Sparrow growls. "You will not cut off my leg," he says.

"What did he say?" Teari asks.

"He said I can't cut off his fucking leg," I reply. "So what would you like me to do now?"

"Get us out of here, Meg!" Teari says.

BIRD ON A WIRE

More of the dead cluster around the wall, shoving to lick the blood off the bricks.

"Now, Meg!" Teari holds out her stump of an arm, fresh blood dripping.

Jesus Christ. I can't fly them. We can't run. I scan the roads and nearby houses. I can *poof*. I look at Sparrow and Teari. I've never tried it with two in tow.

I have to try something.

I reach for Teari's hand and grip it tight. Then Sparrow's. I close my eyes and–*poof*–I bring them back to the Roman Catholic church in Pennsylvania where I first landed.

"Snow?" Teari scoffs and shudders.

"It's all I could think of," I say.

Fresh blood drips from Teari's stump.

Sparrow turns in a circle, palms out, catching snowflakes in his hands like a child. He leaves bloody footprints in the fresh powder.

I point to the front doors of the church. "Sanctuary?" I offer.

"Sanctuary from the cold and nothing else." Teari starts climbing the stairs to the front door. "Can you even enter here?" she asks me.

There was a time when my daddy told me I'd burn to a cinder if I ever stepped foot in a church. I never have. But now... things are different. I'm different. I'm also cold. It's worth the risk.

I climb the steps. "We'll see what happens." I wave my arm. "Come on, Sparrow. Let's get moving."

Teari gets to the front door first. She presses on the handle and shoves hard. The door opens. She stops for a moment and listens.

Silence greets our ears. We stumble inside and close the door, sealing out the cold and snowy weather.

I pause for a second, waiting to feel myself go up in flames. It never comes. "I guess I can enter," I say.

"At least one thing can go right on this mission," Teari says as she walks toward the middle isle of the church.

Tall windows at the altar and toward the ceilings provide ample light for us to see. I wait and let Teari bait anything out of the rows of pews.

Sparrow is staring at my neck and making growling noises.

"Don't," Teari warns from the distance.

"Why?" I ask.

There's nothing I'd love more in this world right now than feeding off each other. It's been a long time since I've felt Sparrow's teeth on my neck. A long time since I've done the same to him. There's a wanting throb in my lower abdomen after dancing with him and being close. It took me so long to get him back again.

"Because you didn't cut off his damn leg." Teari points to Sparrow's bloody boot. "You want to turn into a walking corpse?"

Not really. For the first time in my life, I rather like my status. Turning into a walking corpse would really fuck that right up. So, no. I prefer not to turn into a walking corpse.

"Is he going to turn?" I ask.

Teari shrugs. "Probably. Nightingale is going to be pissed."

"Shit." I mutter. I don't want to feel Nightingale's rage.

"Not just Nightingale either," Teari warns. "All of Heaven is going to rain down their wrath upon us."

"We didn't do this," I remind her.

"We didn't prevent it." Teari touches the hilt of her blade as she stares at Sparrow's leg.

"Can't you heal him?" I ask. "You've healed us before."

"I don't know." Teari rubs her hand on her pantleg and makes a pained face. "I've never tried with something like this before. It could go terribly wrong." She presses her lips together in thought. "I don't trust myself to mess with it. Not like this." She moves her nub arm. "But, I can't even heal myself right now. I need to rest."

I step closer. "Sleep? Now? I don't think that's a good idea. We need to get the frick out of dodge."

"Now is not the time," Teari warns as she sits in the nearest pew. "I must rest. I've lost too much blood."

She does look considerably pale. Paler than I've ever seen her. She's always been tall and strong but right now she looks feeble and weak.

"Okay," I give in. "Okay, you rest." I glance to Sparrow.

"Don't you two do anything with each other," Teari warns.

I nod to myself and scan the room. The portal from Hell kicked me out here. I wonder if there's a portal back. Or maybe I could just poof between realms. Does it even matter if the other planes can tell I've left Hell? The balance is broken, fractured. God must be pissed. Not that I've cared much about how he feels. I glance around the church looking for anything obscure or out of place or glowing.

"Where are my friends?" Sparrow asks.

"What friends?" In all the time I've known Sparrow, he's never mentioned friends before.

"The girl with the blue hair and the tattoo guy." Sparrow motions to the tattoos on his arms.

There's only one tattoo guy.

"Jed?" I ask.

Sparrow nods.

Of all the fucks I've come across. I can't wait to find him and knock some sense into him for covering Sparrow in runes.

"Who is the girl with blue hair?" I ask, trying not to sound jealous.

He shrugs.

"Where did you leave them?" I ask.

"At the party," Sparrow replies.

"They're probably dead now," I say.

We barely made it out alive. And only time will tell how alive we really are by morning.

"I need them," Sparrow says.

"Why?" I ask.

"They need us," he replies. "There's no one else for them." He waves in the direction of California. "They don't belong out there."

Jed is from central New York, I doubt he has much to go back to. His shop was nearly ruined last time we were there, and he told me he's spent his life on the run because he doesn't belong. He's a hybrid and he's been hunted since childhood. Always hiding. Always on the run. He knows spells and magic I've never come across before. Maybe I shouldn't hate on Jed too much.

"I'll go get them," Sparrow says as he moves toward the door.

I grab his sleeve to stop him. "No. I'll go."

Poof. I return to the stone wall.

The dead still lick at the blood, they've almost cleaned the stone. I crouch and think of a game plan. I don't want to wander around on foot searching, I want to get back to the church ASAP. I have to find Jed and this other woman.

The daylight is starting to takeover. I squint and focus on the windows of the mansion where the rave was held. Survivors are rare after a shit show like that. If I were trapped inside, I'd go up. I've done it before and survived. I watch the windows, scanning them for movement. Poof. I flash to the porch overhang, getting my footing on the pitch. I look in the windows. The first one is a hallway of the dead. I ease away from that window, hoping they didn't see me. The next is an empty bathroom. The next is a room with the door barricaded shut. I crouch and watch. After a few moments I notice the barrel of a handgun pointing out of the closet door. Shit.

Bang!

I duck to the side as the bullet breaks glass.

The noise calls the dead. The ones from the hall start pushing on the window. I peer through broken glass, and the barricade is heaving. *Poof.* I flash inside to the closet door and kick it open. It's Jed and a woman with blue hair.

"Jed, nice to see you again," I say as I motion for them to come with me. "Would you like to get the fuck out of here?"

The chick nods and picks up a bag off the floor. I hold out my hands. "Let's go."

It wasn't so long ago that I despised being touched. This is different.

Jed looks at the chick and nods.

They both grip my hands.

We *poof* into the church where I left Teari and Sparrow. Jed turns to the side and vomits.

"Sorry," Jed mutters as he wipes his mouth on his sleeve.

Shay makes a face of disgust.

There's a strange gurgling sound that echoes throughout the church.

"Sparrow?" I ask, looking around. I notice Sparrow hunched over the pew where I left Teari.

"Oh my god!" I shout. "Sparrow, no!" I run toward him, grab the back of his jacket, and tug him backward with all my strength.

When the Blood Runs Out

I glance down at the pew. Teari is still asleep but she has a new bite mark on her remaining hand.

"What in the holy fuck, Sparrow?" He snaps at me. Teeth snapping and eager. "Ah!" I shove him in the chest as hard as I can. He stumbles back and falls. That's strange. Either I gained some magnificent strength, or something is seriously wrong with him. Sparrow is nearly three times my size.

I take a closer look. He turned while I was gone. He's sickly and gray and his darkness is something different now.

I feel sick. Why can't I just have my Sparrow? Why is he always transitioning to something else? He's never been just Sparrow; always fluttering between planes and curses and duty. It changes him so drastically. Still, I know one day I'll finally see Sparrow without all of that, one day it will just be him. Until then, I've been enjoying the pieces of him that shine through. I'm not sure how much will shine through this version of Sparrow though. My father once told me, *time as a Hellion spares no Angel's original form or mindset.* Still, I never dreamt I'd see him as a walking dead man.

Teari moans. I turn and shake her awake.

"What's going on?" she mutters.

"Ah" how do you tell someone they've been bit? In their only remaining hand?

"Kill her!" Shay shouts, unsheathing a gun from her hip holster. "Kill her before she turns!"

My fingers hover over my blade.

"Who turns?" Teari asks as she rubs her face. Pauses. "What the…"

She sees it. The black marks in the shape of Sparrow's bite. Perfect black ovals embedded in her hand.

"No." Teari says with an exasperated whisper.

"Kill her now," Shay says.

I hold out a hand. "Stop."

Teari holds out her hand. "Cut it off. Now, Meg." She waves her hand as the black starts to spread. "Cut it off now!"

"You'll have no hands," I say.

"I don't care. Cut! Now!" she screams at me.

I grip my blade. It glows in the fading light. Teari holds out her arm. Whack. The bitten hand falls. Long, delicate fingers curling in on themselves. Her hands had healed so much.

"Wrap it," Teari reminds me.

Blood is pouring out of the fresh wound. I reach for my bag and pull out my last clean shirt. Never thought I only packed to bandage wounds with my clean clothes and never wear them.

Sparrow is growling and moving to his feet. Clumsy. I've never seen him clumsy before. Only limber and strong. Something is very wrong.

"Secure him," I order Shay and Jed. "But don't kill him."

"What are you going to do with a dead man?" Jed asks.

"Whatever the fuck I want," I reply as I wrap Teari's wound. I have to do something with him. I have to get him to safety so I can figure out how to fix him.

Cloth rips and as I'm tightening Teari's bandage, I catch a glimpse of Shay standing on the pew and wrapping fabric around

Sparrow's lower face. Smart. Now he can't bite anyone else. Jed is wrestling with Sparrow's arms, doing his best to tie them behind his back.

"You should have cut his leg off. You're going to need to help them," Teari warns. "I'm going to pass out now."

Her head thumps against the wooden pew. I take in the sad figure. Teari was once formidable. A warrior, a healer. She went head-to-head with Hellions and my father and those asshole Archangels in Heaven. She doesn't deserve this.

Should I have cut his leg off? He told me not to. What would a one-legged Sparrow have gotten us? Getting him mobile with one leg would have been a bitch. He'd be starving after the blood loss. I swallow hard. He'd drain a whole town to fill himself again.

I scramble across the aisle, grab Sparrow's free arm, and twist it to meet the other arm that Jed is wrapping thin rope around.

"Where'd you get that?" I ask.

"Bugout bag," Shay replies. "Never unprepared. My parents trained me for times like this."

A memory of Jim taking me on long hikes pings to the forefront of my mind.

I scan her closer and notice the sneaker-like hiking boots, rip proof pants, and bracelet made of paracord. The girl has it all. I notice the bag on the floor is similar to mine with one shoulder strap that clips.

"Nice bag," I say.

Shay just stares at me.

I point at mine so she can see we have something in common. Well, something in common besides my boyfriend and tattoo parlor friend.

Shay nods in understanding. "What are you?" she asks.

Jed makes a noise as he struggles with Sparrow.

"Just let him go," Shay says to Jed. "He can't hurt anyone now. And he can't go far in this church."

I watch Sparrow meander down the aisle.

"Hey," Shay says to get my attention. "What are you?" she asks again.

"He didn't tell you?" I point to Sparrow.

"He never mentioned you," she says.

Ouch. I knew it, but it burns coming out of her mouth. "He didn't?" I ask pointing to Jed. "Jed and I go way back. He saved my ass a few times." I point to the tattoos on my arms. "Runed me up real good. Sparrow too."

"Nah," Shay shakes her head. "None of them mentioned you."

"Damn," I say, rubbing the spot over my heart. I hold out my hand to shake with her. "My name is Meg."

Shay doesn't move. Her eyes narrow on me. "You are something." She moves her hands in the air around me. "Dark. It's very dark around you. I don't trust you."

Jed elbows Shay.

"What?" Shay asks, annoyed. "You're just Meg?" she asks. "Nothing more than Meg?"

"She's much more," Jed warns, looking a bit more frightened of me than the last time we were standing in a room together.

"Look," I raise my hands. "Sparrow asked me to get his friends, so here we are. I didn't bring you both here for any other reason." I cross my arms over my chest. "But now I have a busted ass healer Angel and a zombie for a boyfriend." My stomach growls loudly. "And I'm hungry. So, we need to get the fuck out of dodge before Heaven sends some shitheads down here to screw things up more."

Jed makes a noise. "I knew that getting mixed up with you was going to send me on the run." He points, accusingly. "I told you that I can't trust anyone. Not even a girl who can flash between realms and slay the walking dead like she was born and bred to take of the apocalypse single handedly."

"You've said that before," I remind him.

"I repeated it to remind myself." He runs both hands through grown-out shaggy blonde hair.

Sparrow tasted Jed's blood last time we were together. He told me that Jed's is Nephilim of the Archangel Michael. He's been on the run his entire life.

"We need to get out of here," Jed says. "There's too many forbidden creatures in one room."

I nod in agreement. "I went through a portal that dropped me here." I start searching the room for anything resembling a portal or conduit to Hell. "Look for arches with inscription," I tell Jed and Shay. "I can't get everyone out of here at the same time."

We search the room. Every pew, every devotional space, every statue on display.

"There's nothing here," Jed says.

We meet at the altar. "I have to check on Teari," I say as I make my way back to the pew where she's resting.

Sparrow shuffles around the open space, knocking into things. His head tips to the side as he hears my footsteps.

Teari is ghost-white and blood drips from both her arms. Less than before but it's still enough to cause concern. My mouth waters. I clear my throat and focus. I know of a stone arch in a cemetery in Saratoga, but that is going to be hours away. I press my fingers to Teari's neck and feel a faint pulse. I bend and dip my finger in the pooling blood on the floor and touch it to my tongue. Damn. I grab the empty vial from my pocket, untwist the lid and scrape it through the pooled blood. Angel blood has got to help me. I don't know Teari's life story, but from what I just tasted, this could help me one day. I twist on the cap and shove the vial in my pocket as footsteps echo nearby.

Shay appears next to us. She grips the pew. "I read about this in a survival first aid book. I think it's shock."

"Oh yea?" I ask, trying my best to look nonchalant and not like I was just licking blood off the floor. "Angels can go into shock?"

"Why not?" Shay shoots back. "They're just giant supernatural offshoots of humans."

"Ok." I move hair off Teari's face. "What do we do?"

"Get the heck out of here," Jed warns. "I'm sure there's a car here somewhere. The priest would have needed to get groceries and travel."

"But did this priest hit the road when the dead started walking?" I ask. I glance at Sparrow. "How do we get him in a car?"

"Trunk," Shay blurts out.

The Scarecrow drove around with me in a trunk for a bit once. It wasn't fun rolling around back there. It did keep me contained. That's what we need to do with Sparrow. Contain him until we can fix him. I can't be cutting off any more hands today. I nod and begin collecting my things. "Let's find it."

The three of us head behind the altar to the elaborate door which leads to the priest's chambers. We search the office, every cupboard, every drawer, until Shay holds up a set of keys. "Score," she shouts. "A Cadillac."

"I hope it's got a big trunk space," I say.

Jed starts heading to a door at the back of the office. We follow him through a few hallways and out another door that leads to a garage.

"There we go," Jed says. "Every church like this has a similar layout." He unlocks the doors.

Shay searches the garage. "Keep your eyes open for gas cans or anything we can use."

"How far to the portal?" Jed asks.

I pull out my cellphone and load up Google maps. "It's almost a seven-hour drive," I say. "I'm not sure Teari is going to make it that far."

I show the screen to Jed. He nods. "I know how to get there from here." He makes a face. "You know, that's going to stop working soon. Surprised it's still got service."

Shrugging, I say, "Maybe I'm just lucky. You know how to get there?" I ask.

"I've been doing this a long time. Running, that is," he assures me as he starts the Cadillac and checks the gas gauge. "Well," he shouts over the engine, "someone wanted us to win today. There's a full tank."

"Good," Shay claps, "because there are no full gas cans here to fill the tank."

I reach for the garage door and pull up. We are greeted by the sound of shuffling feet and groaning.

"Crap!" Shay shouts.

I grab my blade and start chopping. There's about a dozen zombies looking to make us their dinner.

Shay lets off some head shots and I hold in the urge to tell her lay off the noise. Noise brings the dead.

Jed presses down on the gas and runs over the pieces of the corpses in the road.

My stomach sinks. No! He's frickin taking off. Now, I never did much to help him but what the heck?

Suddenly the brakes squeal and the window rolls down. "Meet me at the front steps," he shouts out the window before speeding to the end of the street and taking a sharp turn around the block.

"Come on!" Shay slaps my arm and heads inside.

We run through the hallways and offices until we reach the main area of the church again. I run down the steps of the altar, headed straight for Teari. Sparrow is shuffling near the back door like he knows what's up. Could he know what's up? Could Sparrow be in there and just unable to control the bloodlust since he's been infected with whatever it is these dead have? Wait. *It's just death*, I remind myself. They didn't change planes when they died. They're stuck here. It's just death. Nothing to be afraid of. We've died before.

"Help me lift her," I shout to Shay.

I grab Teari's shoulders. Shay grabs her legs and we shuffle her out of the pew and down the aisle of the nave. I walk backward as best as I can, arms burning. When I get to the door, I pause before kicking it open, hoping to knock over anything that might be lingering close and waiting for us. Hope surges as I see Jed rush out of the Cadillac and open the back door.

"Come on," he waves, "hurry up." He moves to the trunk and pops it open.

"I hope you could fit groceries from a trip to Sam's Club in there," I shout. "Sparrow's a big guy."

"He'll fit," Jed says.

I climb in the backseat and drag Teari in with me, resting her head on my lap. Shay bends Teari's knees until she can get the door closed.

I watch through the window as Shay and Jed run up the front steps of the church, open the door, and guide Sparrow out. He's able to walk down the steps. Sparrow grunts and groans and the rear of the Cadillac dips as he's settled in the trunk. I think... he must still be in there.

Shay and Jed slam the trunk closed and run to the front doors, each getting in. Jed shifts the Cadillac into gear and hits the gas.

I glance down at Teari's head resting on my lap. She's so still. I touch her cheek. It feels cool and she looks so pale. I check the pulse in her neck. It's faint. I move her arms and tighten the knots, trying to stop the flow.

My stomach growls. Being this close to fresh blood is going to be rough. The back of my seat moves as Sparrow knocks into it from the trunk. Seems the fresh blood is going to be tough on us both.

———

JED DRIVES like a bat out of Hell. He turns onto route 219, headed north. The cellphone in my pocket alerts us to turn around. I dig it out.

"This thing says we're going the wrong direction," I say.

"Nah," Jed says, accelerating. "We're going to avoid the busted down cars and roadblocks. I've been through these parts before. On my way to California."

"You drove to California?" I ask.

"There weren't planes flying when the dead started walking everywhere," Jed says. "They shut everything down."

"Sure weren't," Shay chirps in. "Driving was safest and fastest."

"Where did you two meet?" I ask.

There is a beat of silence as they glance at each other. Shay nods. "Nebraska," she says.

"You don't have to tell me," I say. I've been there. In that place where you don't want to tell anyone your life story and the terrible things that have happened to you. The way Shay tenses tells me a lot. Her walls are up. I'm not about to blast through them right now.

I brace myself as Jed turns right onto interstate 80. He passes two cars that are moving slowly. There's more broken down on the sides of the road. There's even some of the dead schlepping it down the highway. Jed weaves around them.

"Why'd you choose California?" I ask, settling my hand on Teari's chest. Feeling her faint heartbeat gives me an ounce of relief.

Jed clears his throat. "You know I've been on the run my whole life." He glances at me in the rearview mirror and in his reflection, I can see the blue aura that surrounded him the first time we met. Only in the reflection. "Months ago, the news stations were tracking the horde of dead. There were groupings of them all over the U.S. but the biggest one was in California." He clears his throat. "It moved strangely, stopping for days at a time before moving up the coast. I've been around long enough to know those things don't move in a coordinated pack like that. They're usually scattered."

I think for a moment, and he's right. Never once have I seen them moving as one giant group. Maybe little clusters here and there, but never a giant gathering.

"So, I had the thought that they must be following something... or, someone." Jed accelerates past three dead making their way across the highway. "I reached out to some of my contacts and they told me about the rumors of a tall, dark man walking his way up the coast. No one could tell what he was." Jed snaps his fingers and points into the rearview mirror at me. "But I knew. I knew because I never forgot the day you two showed up with Sparrow in that Canadian tuxedo."

"What's a Canadian tuxedo?" Shay asks.

Jed chuckles.

"Think jeans *and* a jean jacket," I say.

"Wow," Shay makes a face, "impressive. Wish I'd seen it."

"Nothing like it," Jed says as he slows to pass a family waving us down from their broken-down minivan. "Sorry," he mutters. "No room here."

"Keep going with the California story," I urge, settling my hand on Teari's chest to feel her heartbeat.

Jed clears his throat. "Once I started putting the pieces together, I headed that way."

"Why seek out Sparrow when you're trying to hide yourself?" I ask.

"Who better to hide with than a Hellion?" Jed asks. "I knew no one was finding him and the walking dead were keeping their distance. As far as I was concerned, being close to Sparrow was the safest option on the Earthen plane."

"It was," Shay says. "Most of the dead kept their distance when we got close to him."

After all the messed up things that have happened, at least a spec of good came out of it. Jed helped us, and Sparrow helped him. And he's helped me. Wait... why would he help me?

"Why have you stuck with me?" I ask.

Jed presses his lips together as he glances at me in the rearview mirror again.

"Why?" I urge.

"Because you're different than you were last time I saw you, Meg. You're stronger, darker, quicker. You've lost your spark." He tips his head. "What happened to you?"

I don't say a word. Didn't realize I was that easy to read. But I guess when you spend most of your life making bad decisions and killing Archangels, and stabbing your boyfriend in the heart to preserve the sanctity of the realms, I guess that changes you a bit.

"Whatever happened to you," Jed says, "is going to keep me safe. You owe me."

Damn. Jed plays a good game. I do owe him, a lot. Even though he pissed me off with that bullshit of tattooing Sparrow with runes of my blood to hide him from everyone, even me. It worked out though. I found him with other methods. And Jed has helped us. I haven't been out of the Earthen plane for long. Jed knows a lot more than I do about Archangels and demons.

"Shit," Shay blurts out and points. "Army men."

Jed pulses the breaks to slow the Cadillac and moves into the right lane. A row of Humvees blocks the highway. Men in green fatigues loaded with ammo and weapons are stationed at the roadblock.

"What is this?" I ask.

"Some kind of checkpoint," Jed says, rolling down his window.

"Just speed through them," I urge, my stomach twisting. "We can't stop."

"Nah," Jed says. "They'll shoot us dead." He rolls down all the windows and stops the car. "A caddy won't win against a Humvee."

Men in fatigues, carrying lots of guns and ammo surround us. "Where are you headed?" The one at the driver's side window asks.

"Saratoga Springs," Jed replies.

I hear the static of a walkie-talkie and footsteps nearing my window. My heart pounds in my chest. This is worse than when Raguel had me imprisoned in Heaven. At least there I had help with my father and Teari; there's no help here and there's nothing worse than a human man with weapons and an ego.

"We've got injured," a man shouts from my window. "Unlock the door," he orders. "Medic, medic, medic we need you at the on-ramp now," he hollers into his walkie-talkie.

"We have to get her home and get her help," I shout. "Just let us go!"

The locks click. My door is opened.

"Weapons, they've got weapons!" a soldier shouts from the other side of the car.

"Everyone has weapons you imbeciles!" Shay shouts.

The soldier that opened my door grabs my arm and drags me out. I fight. I slap and kick because that's what I do when manhandled on the Earthen plane; throwing punches or pulling out my blade would be a bad idea. "Don't touch me!" I scream. "We have to get her home and get her help."

"Why would you wait that long?" the soldier asks as he releases me and reaches for Teari's shoulders. Thankfully they don't seem to care much about our weapons. Maybe we look innocent enough. Maybe they've seen worse.

A whole crew of people show up and the soldier slides Teari on to a stretcher.

"What happened to her?" someone asks. I notice a red cross on the person's sleeve.

"She was bit." I motion to my hands. "She cut off one hand and then it happened again and she made me cut the other one off."

A medic checks Teari's pulse. "She's going to code soon," he shouts to the others. And then they are running her stretcher toward an ambulance.

"Wait!" I shout. "Don't take her away." I try to run toward the ambulance, but the soldier stops me.

"Let them do their work," he says.

I notice another soldier standing at the trunk. "What's in here?" he asks.

Jed is outside the car. He looks at me before saying. "Weapons for killing the zombies."

"And a little bit of food," Shay adds.

"You want to search it?" the soldier standing near the trunk asks the one in charge.

Shit. Shit. Shit. Shit. If they pop that trunk and find Sparrow in there, things will not be good. They're already not good and I didn't expect them to get worse. The small of my back breaks out in panic-sweat. I try not to act nervous. Damn it. If we'd just gotten to the portal we'd be home safe now and I wouldn't worry about being found.

The one in charge shakes his head. I guess he's got bigger fish to fry right now.

The soldier pats the trunk and points in the direction of the ambulance. "You can go wait for your friend while they fix her up."

We scramble into the Cadillac. Jed drives away, pulls off the Scranton exit and follows the signs to the hospital.

"That was close," Shay says.

"What are they going to do to Teari?" I ask.

Neither of them answer me.

A long time ago, Teari told Sparrow to leave me behind when I was injured. She didn't think I was worth it. I can't leave her on the Earthen plane, alone. I'm sure she'd do fine and eventually escape, but I just can't do it.

Jed parks in the hospital parking lot as close to the door as he can get. The place looks like a ghost town. Panic fills my chest. I've seen too many horror movies with fake hospitals and fake doctors.

Jed follows the signs for the emergency room and parks near the sidewalk.

"Go check on her," Jed says.

"And what about Sparrow?" I ask.

"We'll watch him," Jed says. "We'll be freezing our asses off in this weather while doing it."

I nod and get out. I jog toward the door, push it open, and make my way to the registration desk. The place is pretty empty. An old man sits on the far side of the waiting room. I stand at the desk. I hear voices in the back. I see a nurse running down the hall.

"Hey!" I shout. "I'm looking for my friend."

She ignores me.

"Hello," I say as I walk to the back.

No one responds. I follow the signs to the trauma bay. There are three medical staff working over the bed. I recognize Teari's long legs and pants.

"Hey," I say. "That's my friend."

No one replies, they're all too busy. I find a chair and move it to the open door of the trauma room. The medical staff move fast and shout technical jargon to each other like "tube her" and "Kelly clamps" and "another bolus" and "what the fuck is taking blood bank so long?". There's beeping from the monitors. This is like something from a war movie. I am taken back to a long time ago when I was brought into the ER, no longer pregnant and beaten half to death. I was in a coma. Teetering on the edge. But this isn't like what I experienced. The podunk hospital in Gouverneur had more resources than this place. At least they kept me alive. I'm not sure if this place is going to save her.

I sit in my chair and think of a game plan. We have Sparrow. And I have help. I'll have more help if I can get home. I glance out the window at the fading light. We are sitting ducks here. Someone is going to find us. I came here to find Sparrow and restore the balance, I remind myself. I don't need Teari for that.

I stand. "I'm going to come back for her," I say out loud.

"Sure," one of the nurses says as she hangs a bag of clear fluid on a pole. "It's going to be a while."

The staff don't seem to care much about me. But they are working their damndest to save Teari. That's all I could ask for. I show myself out.

A thin layer of snow coats the sidewalk and my boots leave footprints. Jed starts the car as I get closer. I get inside.

"How is she?" Shay asks.

I shrug. "No one could tell me."

Thuds come from the trunk.

"They'll help her," Jed says.

"We need to go" I start to say.

"And leave her here?" Shay asks.

I rub my face. "It's getting dark. We need to get to the portal. I have to get Sparrow to Hell before we're found."

"So we are leaving her?" Jed asks.

I say, "I'll come back for her."

———

Jed drives as fast as he can toward Saratoga Springs. I watch the shadowed forests from the window. We take I-84E and turn onto I-87N. Dark cities surround the Newburg and Albany exits. In the distance, there's lights. It seems some towns still have electricity. I try not to worry about how the Earthen plane will return to normal. They'll have to rebuild, bury the bodies after their souls leave, and put their world back together.

It's the early hours of the morning when Jed pulls into the stone driveway of the cemetery. I recognize the arch from when the Scarecrow brought me here.

Jed parks the caddy against the wrought iron fence. We get out and move to the trunk.

"I hope no one is watching," Shay mutters.

Jed pops the trunk.

Sparrow stares at us. I'm not a mind reader, but if I know anything about expressions, I'd say he's pissed. Although, if I were locked in a trunk for nearly eight hours, I'd be pissed too. Spending nearly one hour in a trunk made me want to punch Reuben in the throat.

"Come on, big guy," I say as I reach for his legs.

Getting Sparrow out of the trunk is a bitch.

We get him to his feet and guide him to the stone arch.

"To Heaven or Hell?" Jed asks.

"Hell," I reply.

He points to the words etched into the stone. "This can go to either."

"You can read that?" I ask.

He nods. "You can't?"

I can't fly and now I can't read. This moment ranks pretty high amongst the times I've felt inept.

"Tell me what they say." I point to the arch.

"Gradus ad infernus," Jed says and the space between the arch wavers. "Step to hell. That's it. Easy peasy."

I only know a little spell that Sparrow taught me before I knew who I was: "Angele Dei, illumina, custodi, rege et guberna." I glance at Sparrow. He was my guardian. Now, not so much. But the spell helped me travel before I learned to do it at will. I wonder what else it could do if I utter those words from my lips? Maybe they'd bring my father, King Gabriel. But then he'd be looking for Teari, and I don't want to answer that question.

I grab Sparrow's jacket at the elbow and help Shay lead him.

We step into Hell.

A Dark Welcome

We step into an open field. I know this place. I've been here before. My plane is just a dark reflection of the Earthen plane. We are a ways from Centralia, where my castle is nestled into the burning underground caves. *My castle*; it feels strange accepting it after all this time. Hi, my name's Meg. I killed Lucifer by sucking him dry of blood and now I live in a castle. Sounds impressive. Sounds a lot more intimidating than revealing I grew up in a trailer in the woods, raised by a Demon whom I thought was my father... yeah, I think I'll stick with the first introduction.

"Where do we go now?" Shay asks.

I point south. "You know it as Centralia, PA."

Shay makes a sound of despair. "Are you kidding me? We just came from Pennsylvania." She runs her hands through the blowtorch blue hair and tugs at the ends.

"Seriously," Jed says, disgust in his voice. "Please tell me you have functioning vehicles down here."

"We do," I say. "But I didn't leave any nearby."

"You didn't plan very well," Shay says.

"Nope," I say. "Sure didn't. But no worries, someone will find us sooner or later."

Sparrow makes a noise but it's muffled from the cloth wrapped around the lower half of his face.

"Come on," I urge him. Sparrow walks better than I expected him to across the stone driveway and onto the paved street. We start walking down Green Ridge Road, our shoes echoing in the darkness. We turn left on Lincoln Ave and head for the intersection. Curtains move as the few souls who haven't found a Safe House hide out, waiting for their inevitable destiny of finding out they're dead. They'll wait for eternity, lost, if they don't find a Safe House soon. We turn left on Broadway, following the signs for the I-87 south.

"Weird," Jed says. "If I didn't know better, I'd say we already traveled these roads today."

"These are different," I say, then I change the subject. "Do you feel any safer, now that you're in Hell?" I ask Jed.

He shrugs. "All I can say, is I've never been here before. But those Angels have their ways."

"Not here," I say confidently. I have my crew of Hellions and demons and I can't forget my family of basilisks waiting in the castle for me. I shudder, remembering their slimy skin.

We pass a restaurant called The Sleepy Owl. "I miss diner food," Jed says.

"Same," I say. "What I wouldn't give for a large chocolate milkshake and some salty fries to dip in it." My mouth waters. I'll get it soon. As soon as Noah makes his appearance. Before I can call on him, the sound of footsteps break through the quiet.

"What's that?" Shay asks.

"Dead walking," I wave, dismissing it. "They'll keep their distance down here."

I take two more steps and the sound intensifies, moving faster. Wait. What's happening?

"Shit," Jed shouts. He grabs Shay's arm and tugs her away from the walking sack o' flesh that's currently running at us.

I grip my blade and glance at Sparrow.

There's a dead man headed straight for us at a pace I haven't seen since we were running from the drug infused party where I found Sparrow.

My blade glows, anticipating battle. I stand in the middle of the street, glancing toward the shadows to make sure there's only one. It gets closer, nearly running. I advance toward it, raise my blade, and chop off its head. The dead man drops to the ground. I kick its head away from the body. I've seen plenty of horror movies, don't want it reconnecting.

"Hm," I say as I secure my blade. "Haven't had that happen in a long time."

"What does that mean?" Jed asks.

"They usually keep their distance here." I search their faces. "Maybe it's because there's so many of us?" I suggest. "Come on, let's keep going."

We keep walking, quieter this time. And I have the urge to go back and drive the caddy through that portal. I don't think it's wide enough. I glance behind us. It's tempting. I want to poof back to the castle but I don't want to leave anyone behind for the second trip. Last time it didn't end well.

Twigs break and echo into the night as dead linger at the tree line like heifers in the shade.

It's not long before Noah appears in the road ahead of me. I missed his face.

"Noah, where have you been?" I ask.

He looks to Hellsky dreamily. "Birdwatching. You know how we used to do. Watching those songbirds all day long. What happened to it all?"

"We'll get back to it," I say.

Noah focuses on the group. "Oh! You brought back friends and…" he leans around me and notices Sparrow in the back. "What the fuck did you do to Sparrow?"

I grab Noah and something in me stills his ethereal form. "Do not tell Nightingale." I glance back at zombie-boy. "Actually, you are not to leave my presence until we figure this out."

Noah chuckles. "No soup for you."

My stomach growls on cue. "I'll have to eat something else."

"But, seriously, Night is going to be pissed. Beyond pissed, actually. You went back to fix things." Noah shakes his head. "This ain't fixing things."

"No shit, Sherlock." I point at the other two. "This is Jed. He's going to help us. And this is Shay."

"What's Shay going to do?" Noah asks.

"Something," I reply.

"Kick some ass," Shay says.

"I like her," Noah whispers in my direction. "Why aren't we going *poof* back to the castle?" Noah asks. "It would be faster than this method of travel."

"I can't take everyone at once. And I don't want to leave any of them waiting," I say. "Actually. Go get the Hellions. Tell them where we are."

"And leave your side?" Noah's lips tip up.

"Don't screw me over," I warn. "You've done enough of that."

Noah's eyebrows rise.

"Shut up," I warn. "Go get the Hellions. They can fly us back."

"Why don't you fly us back, Meg?" Noah asks, holding back laughter.

"You little...shit." I reach for his throat but Noah disappears into the darkness.

Jed and Shay are staring at me. I'm not revealing anything.

"Let's keep walking," I say. I lead the crew. Sparrow scrapes his feet behind me. I miss his singing and his feather obsession. His quirks made all our travels less boring.

"What are Hellions?" Shay asks.

"Giant, scary demon men," Jed replies.

"But you said Sparrow was a Hellion."

"He was. Or is. I'm not sure. Hey, Meg, what the heck is Sparrow these days?" Jed asks.

"Damned if I know," I mutter.

We walk further, passing the signs for the highway. I notice the asphalt is really crumbling along this road and I wonder if Hell has a department of public works.

"Oh my god," Shay shouts. "What the heck!" She grabs on to Jed, shielding herself with his body. "What are those?"

Skeele lands first. A wide smile that downturns almost instantly. "You took too long. We were worried."

I throw my hands in the air. "How about, great job, Meg? Or, way to go Meg? Or, look you found Sparrow, just what you needed to do," I scoff.

Heavy footfalls hit the pavement as the other Hellions land. Tukka, Chel, and Klaus look ready to fight and it takes a few moments for their tense poses to relax.

"Jed and Shay," I tell Skeele. "They're important to Sparrow." I glance behind Skeele. "Where is Noah?"

"He's at the castle," Skeele says.

A giant shadow covers us. Clea is here, in argentavis form.

Skeele gives orders. Chel carries Shay.

It takes two Hellions to carry Sparrow. Tukka grabs him from one side, Klaus from the opposite. They lift him into the sky, their bat-like wings strong and quick.

Skeele holds his arms out to me. "Wanna ride?" he asks.

I hesitate. Last time he had me in the sky he dropped me a few dozen times trying to get my wings out. I prefer not to subject myself to that again.

"Child," Clea calls, beckons.

"I'm going back with her," I say, thumbing towards the argentavis.

"Guess I'm taking the other guy," Skeele says as he moves toward Jed.

Clea lands. I run toward her and climb on her back. Clea spreads her giant wings, hops a few times and launches herself into the air.

In the distance I can see the Hellions flying and Sparrow dangling.

"Child?" she asks.

A mother knows.

"Everything is really fucked up," I say.

"There will be darkness and there will be light," her voice is soothing. "It never stays the same. Like the ouroboros, we are forever moving."

"I'm not sure I can fix this. Sparrow was bitten. He's something different now."

"He's always been something different," she says calmly. "Time will show you the answer."

I rub my fingers through her soft feathers and close my eyes as chilled air brushes across my cheeks. After all the running and fighting, the cool air feels good.

———

When we land at the castle only a few minutes behind the others, Noah is waiting, kicking pebbles around the dirt lot. He better not have told Nightingale already. He looks guilty.

"What happened?" Skeele asks, motioning to Sparrow.

"It was really bad," I say as I slide down Clea's side, my boots hitting the hard-packed red dirt. "Really bad."

"What happened to Sparrow?" Skeele asks.

"He was bit by one of the dead on the Earthen plane." I walk closer to Sparrow and motion to his boot. I don't tell them about Teari and thankfully neither Jed nor Shay mention her.

Sparrow groans, twists his neck like it's stiff, and flexes his jaws from under the mask Jed put on him.

"He needs to go somewhere safe until we can figure this out." I rub my face, exhausted and fed up. I want him to be in my room, but after what we just went through, I don't think that's a good idea. The only place I can think of that will keep him safe from harming others is locked up. "Put him in the dungeon," I say. "With eyes on him at all times."

"Meg..." Noah whispers, concerned.

"We'll figure it out," I say. "We have to." I head toward the door, Skeele close behind. "Give Jed and Shay rooms close to mine."

"Where are you going?" Skeele asks.

"To shower and change my clothes and think." I wave my hand. "Noah, come with me." I can't let him out of my sight again. I can't risk him going back to Nightingale and spilling the beans.

I open the giant wooden door that's built into the cave opening; woodsmoke and pine, it smells like home. Strange, I fought so long to find home. A place where I could be comfortable. A place where I felt I belonged. It took a while to sink in. I had to marinate here for a while. When the Deacons were drilling me for answers, they knew. They could tell I was searching for home, a home that filled my darkness, that cared for me, that sheltered me. I just didn't realize it back then. But, finally, this is home.

———

"Did you feed the basilisk babies and momma?" I ask Noah as I search the closet for something to wear, feeling squeaky clean not that I'm not covered in grime.

"Unfortunately," Noah replies, distracted. He's throwing birdseed over the balcony railing and songbirds are diving to catch the seeds. "Those things are nasty."

"I've been told they'll help us." I find a pair of dark jeans and pull them on.

"Help us, what?" Noah asks. "Help us despise walking into that office?" He makes gagging noises. "I want to puke every time I go in there to feed them."

I grab a black T-shirt and pull it over my head before leaving the closet and finding my bag. I find the small vial of Teari's blood and hide it in my nightstand drawer.

"You don't want anything to eat?" Noah asks. "It's been a while since I went to find pancakes or fried chicken or green eggs and ham."

"No thank you, Sam," I mock.

"Filled up on a little Sparrow while you were over there?" he asks.

"Nope. There wasn't time." I zip my bag and take it back to the closet for storage. "I would have liked too though."

I do wonder what it would do to me. If Teari chopped off her limbs, the result couldn't be pleasant. Maybe I'd turn into whatever Sparrow is now. Maybe it would put an end to all of these years of fighting to live.

I close the closet doors and glance out the window.

"You should eat," Noah urges.

"I can't risk you telling Nightingale," I reply.

"You're just going to starve?"

"Wouldn't be the first time."

Who Roams Here?

The conversation in the Hellion lair is interrupted by a bright flash of light. We shield our eyes. Skeele steps in front of me, a large hand pressing on my hip until I'm behind him, his other hand grips a wicked blade.

"Meg!" It's my father. He's covered in sweat and blood, his draped robes stained. He grips his blade, glistening with ichor. His knuckles are white.

The brightness of his arrival is swallowed by the darkness of the Hellion's lair.

"What are you doing here?" Skeele asks in a low grumble.

I push Skeele away to get a good look at my father. "What have you been doing?" I ask.

"Goddamn dead are roaming the Seven Kingdoms of Heaven." He secures his blade and the Hellions calm. "What did you do, Meg? You went to collect Sparrow to set it straight. Everything was supposed to go back to normal. Now we've got Angels dying and that jackoff Raguel think's you've sent the dead as an act of war. They're planning to punish you." Gabriel searches my face, waiting for a response. "And I can't find Teari."

I swallow hard. Those Angels love a good punishment. "I didn't do anything besides collect Sparrow and then we came back here as soon as we could."

"Where is he?" my father asks.

I wave as I head for the door. "Come with me."

Skeele's heavy footfalls follow as I open the door to the Hellion's lair and step into the hallway. My father barely looks out of place right now. He's usually bright, jovial even. Now, not so much.

Skeele leads us down long hallways, down cascading staircases chiseled from stone, past hallways and doors I have yet to explore. The smell of woodsmoke and pine and the heat intensifies.

"Don't look too closely," Skeele warns. "There are creatures down here that have been locked away for ages."

Gabriel grumbles something about "goddamned monsters."

We come to a large wooden door with a Hellion standing guard. There's a large square cut with metal bars. Skeele motions for my father to look.

Gabriel walks forward and peers in the window. "Jesus Christ." He turns to look at me. "What in the name of God happened?"

"He was bit by one of the dead," I say.

Gabriel rubs his face.

I don't elaborate.

"And where the Hell is Teari?" he booms. "We are being ambushed by those things. Have you seen them?" His eyes widen. "They run. They aren't like the ones down here, Meg. They're fast, they're different." He rubs his face. "We must figure this out. I need my healer. Where is she?"

"I don't know," I lie. "We lost her while we were running. It was a complete mess on the Earthen plane. The dead were everywhere."

"I told you to bring one of us," Skeele says.

I shake my head. "It wouldn't have helped."

"So you didn't send the dead to the Seven Kingdoms of Heaven?" Gabriel asks.

"No," I reply firmly. "I didn't send them. I would never. As much as I would like to show some of those jerks a taste of their own medicine..."

"I heard you've been having a problem with the Deacons," Gabriel says.

I turn to Skeele.

"They're under control," he promises. "We have them under control. Whatever this is, it is not the fault of this realm."

"If it's not you, and it's not the Deacons, then they are crossing the thresholds unassisted." Gabriel rubs his face. "What a goddamned mess."

A hissing sound interrupts our conversation. Sparrow is at the door opening, his face gray, his eyes sunken.

"Christ," Gabriel mutters. "How are you going to fix that?" he tips his head toward Sparrow.

"I don't know yet." I glance at Sparrow, longing for a version of him that's a little more alive, a little less flesh craving. "Somehow, we'll fix him. We always do."

Gabriel reaches for his blade.

Skeele pulls his own.

"Calm down, chuckles," Gabriel says. "I'm going back, and I have to go back ready to fight." Gabriel looks at me. "There are only two kingdoms who will believe you. Mine and Nightingale's. The odds are not good. The others will come for answers. They will want retribution."

"What are you telling me?" I ask.

"This is war." Gabriel's eyes widen as he focuses on me. And then he's gone, in a flash and speck of light.

"Have you been feeding Sparrow?" I ask Skeele and the other Hellion.

"We gave him food," Skeele says, crossing his arms over his chest.

"Did you give him blood?" I ask.

Skeele shakes his head. "What if it makes him too strong and he escapes?"

I lean against the door and take in Sparrow's side profile as he looks at the moon out the tiny window of his cell. Once he drank from me and inherited my ability to travel. Hunting him down again would be a nightmare. Maybe Skeele is right. Maybe we keep him starved of blood. But what if the bloodlust makes him crazy?

"No spoons," I say to Skeele and the other Hellion. It's not too hard to dig yourself out with a spoon; I've done it before. "No posters either." Only one of us can be channeling Andy Dufresne.

We walk back to the Hellion lair theorizing how to fix Sparrow and how the dead are getting into Heaven.

"We are going to help," I say, opening the door. "Gather whatever we need."

"We've never been freely allowed within the Seven Kingdoms of Heaven," Tukka says. "This will be something new."

"It's better for us to go than wait for the Archangels to come to us," I say. I will never wait for an invitation to justify myself again.

———

I always thought I'd battle everything with Sparrow at my side. That's how it's always been. Now I head off to a realm that despises me to finish a battle I didn't start, without him. It seems wrong. It seems off.

"Ready?" Chel asks.

"No." I tighten the leather that holds my blade. "Noah," I call.

He appears, looking solemn.

"I'm going to need you to stick by Skeele's side."

"Sure," he replies.

"And don't forget to feed the basilisk."

Noah makes a gagging sound.

"How are you going to travel between realms?" Skeele asks.

"Like I always have." I flick my fingers out. "With a poof. The Earthen plane is the only place that stops me."

I grip Chel and Tukka at their wrists. *Poof.* We go to the Seven Kingdoms of Heaven.

THE FAST ZOMBIE WAR

CHEL AND TUKKA FLINCH AT THE BRIGHTNESS.

We all spin at the sound of a deep moan and motion behind us. Yup, the dead are walking here. They're walking fast. Two advance on us.

"Crap," I mutter, reaching for my blade.

Chel and Tukka move faster. They advance on the dead, chop off their heads, and kick the body parts away from each other.

I brought them to Babylon–neutral ground where the council meets. If we're lucky we can address all the Kings of the Seven Kingdoms.

"What happened to this place?" Chel asks.

Last time I was here the sidewalks glistened, the wicked were on display, and Babylon center was filled with angels going about their daily business.

Now there are streaks of blood staining the walkways. Bodies rotting. Little sparkle.

I try not to focus on the fact that they watched me kill and drain dry one of their own.

"Let's see if anyone's here." I head toward the large marble building nearby, remembering that the last time I approached this building there was a shackle around my neck and fresh wounds from a whipping across my back. I guess I haven't moved on. I'm really struggling with forgiveness.

Tukka grips the door, Chel stands ready for action. I take up the back, blade in hand. Tukka pulls the door open and we pause, listening for voices or footsteps. Chel nods for me to move inside. I take a few quick steps and take cover against a wall inside. The building is a mess, and it smells. Tukka makes sure the door is closed. The Hellions look very out of place here. I bet Remiel would roll over in his grave if he could see this: me roaming freely with Hellions in Babylon.

"Where are we going?" Chel asks.

"The courtroom." I point to a large door not far from us. "That's where they meet."

Tukka and Chel move forward, blades ready for action. I follow, alert and ready. Not only do we have to worry about the dead here, we have to worry about the angels.

"Ready?" Tukka grips the handle to the courtroom.

We nod.

Tukka pulls. The door creaks and he stops moving it as soon as the space is big enough for us to squeeze through without making more noise. I enter first.

The giant last supper-like table is still here. Seven chairs. No Archangels. Last time I was here I made a deal for Jack Cooper's soul and my freedom. I've spent far too much of my life fighting for my freedom. I shudder, remembering the Scarecrow's void of a face in this realm.

"Where are they?" Tukka asks.

"Not here." Losers. I guess they could be defending their kingdoms. I shouldn't judge them too harshly. I was hoping to appeal my innocence once and assure them that the dead being here was not because of me. I guess that will have to wait.

"Well, boys, I guess we should move on." I tug Tukka and Chel closer. *Poof.* We go to Gabriel's Kingdom.

———

"OF ALL THE BULLSHIT," Gabriel shouts as something large falls and breaks glass.

We appear at the front door. Tukka shoves it open and we run in together. He's under attack. There have got to be twenty corpses walking around. Tukka and Chel start chopping. I turn, taking up the back and chop off the heads of the ones trying to sneak attack us.

"Meg?" Gabriel shouts. "Is that you?"

"Yes! We're here," I reply. "Head toward his voice," I tell Tukka.

My father's house is trashed. Glass is broken, paintings ripped, furniture busted to woodchips.

Gabriel is standing on the dining room table, taking on ten of the dead alone.

We work fast, making our way around the room. Blood sprays the walls. Heads fall with heavy *thwacks.* Jaws snap.

"Meg," Gabriel says as he jumps down from the table. "Thank God. You made it just in time to save dear old dad."

I smile. "Brought a few friends. We stopped in Babylon, but it was empty. I couldn't tell other Archangels that this is not my fault."

Gabriel shakes his head. "They're all fighting. The dead keep coming and they keep killing angels."

"Not turning them?" I ask.

"I haven't seen them change," Gabriel says. "Only die. I've lost many from my Kingdom. Nightingale has as well."

I look out the windows and listen for movement. "Where are the rest of your kingdom?" Last time I was here there were servants and staff keeping up the house.

"Hiding. I hid them. Came back here for weapons." Gabriel heads toward the kitchen. "I needed to get food for them." He opens the cabinets, grabs a bag off the counter that looks partially filled, and begins loading more inside. "Those walking corpses ambushed me."

"The fast ones seem to do that," I say.

Gabriel finishes filling the bag and turns to us. "I'm taking this back to them. They'll be fine in hiding here, but Nightingale needs help. Her kingdom is small. No Legion of their own." Gabriel glances at Chel and Tukka. "We are going to need more help than just the three of you."

"Okay," I'll get more help.

"I'm taking this back to my people." He secures the bag across his shoulder. "Get to Nightingale's Kingdom. The sooner the better."

"Okay," I nod. "See you soon."

Poof.

A Tisket, A tasket, A Basilisk in a Basket

We return to the Hellion's lair. It's empty. Chel and Tukka go behind the bar to get blood and power up. The door slams open and Skeele enters the room, securing the door closed behind him.

"Good, you're back," Skeele says.

"Not for long." I head for the wall of weapons to get another blade and guns. "We have to go back."

"I'm not sure if now is a good time," Skeele says. It's the tone of his voice that causes me to pause and focus on the noises in the hallway behind the closed door.

"Skeele?" I ask.

"They're here," he says.

Shit.

"How is this happening?" I ask, shoving a handgun into my belt.

"They're coming through the portals. They've never been able to cross before," Skeele says.

"How do we stop them?" I ask. "Close up the portals? What?"

"We could," Skeele says, running toward the weapons and grabbing ammo and securing small blades on his belt. "If we close the portals, no one can travel between realms but those with your ability to *poof*. Then we'd still have to deal with the ones that are here."

"Blast the portals. Kill the dead that don't belong," I say. My stomach growls. "Noah," I call.

He appears.

"I need something to eat. Something sweet. Like Cinnabons or donuts or something."

"I was just feeding the basilisk." Noah wipes his hands on his pants. "One of those dead things came running in the office and I spilled their food. Hold your nose if you enter."

"Did you kill it?" I ask.

Noah shakes his head. "Didn't have to. Momma ate it."

"Wait, the basilisk eat the walking dead?" I'm suddenly no longer hungry.

"Just the fast ones, it seems," Noah says.

An idea is forming. It seems nuts but being nuts has gotten us this far.

"Leave one portal open," I tell Skeele. "The closest one to us."

"Meg?" he asks.

"We are taking them on a field trip." This is going to suck.

Poof. I check on Sparrow. He's still locked up. Still looking dead. The Hellion assigned to him appears eager to be elsewhere. I check on Jed and Shay. They've got the bedroom door secured and coated the room in spells.

"Watch where you're walking," Jed scolds as my boot scuffs the black hieroglyphs on the floor. He bends to fix the marking. "I prefer not to die in the middle of this."

"Sorry. I was just checking in," I say.

"You're all going?" Shay asks.

"We should be back soon." *Poof.* I go to my grandfather's office. The basket we moved the babies in is on the floor next to the tank. Klaus is there and he doesn't look thrilled.

I pick up the basket. "Remember what we did last time?" I ask. "We are going to do it again."

A slithering sound echoes from the ceiling. We're making momma anxious.

I dip the basket in the tank of water and move the baby basilisk. Hissing warns us but doesn't stop me.

"You ready to run?" I ask Klaus.

He makes a grim face.

"Noah," I call. "You're coming with us!"

Klaus grips the other side of the basket and we take off running for the front door. The momma basilisk follows. Part of me feels shitty baiting her with her babies. It's kinda cruel to do to a mother.

We run out of the office, down the hallway, down the stairs, and toward the front door that's carved out of the caves. Skeele is waiting with a running Jeep.

Noah flashes to the passenger seat. "I call shotgun."

Klaus helps me secure the basket in the cargo area and we scramble into the backseat. "Go, go, go!" we both shout at Skeele.

Skeele burns rubber, speeding away, turning right onto the nearest crumbling road.

"How far?" I ask.

"I can make it in ten minutes," Skeele says, determined. The Jeep lurches as he presses harder on the gas pedal.

The mother basilisk rounds the corner and flies toward us. She's a little faster this time, not letting us get too far ahead.

———

Skeele turns into an old graveyard. There's an arch in the distance, similar to the portals we've used elsewhere. He parks the Jeep with a skid and a jerk. We scramble out. Skeele and Klaus grab the basket o' babies. Tukka and Chel are waiting for us.

The mother basilisk moves closer.

"Wait until the last minute," Klaus suggests. "We don't want her to turn away."

For a split second I remember I've been banished from Heaven. I wonder what will happen when I show up there again. I don't have much time to think about it. The basilisk's sharp teeth are close enough to bite off our faces. We run through.

The portal drops us in a field. There's a castle in the distance, but not my father's or Nightingale's. Wonderful. There's nothing worse than not knowing whose backyard you've fallen into. Knowing these Archangels, I don't trust that they'll let us help them.

An arrow whizzes by and lands in Chel's thigh. "What the hell?" he shouts.

"Run," I suggest.

We head for a line of trees, the basket sloshing and basilisk babies squealing.

A dead man exits the tree line in front of us. He's walking quick, nearly running.

Something drips out of the sky. We look up to see the momma basilisk fly over us, swoop in, and grab the walking corpse in her mouth. She swallows it down.

"I have an idea," I tell the Hellions. "Get to Nightingale's Kingdom. Noah will show you where it is. I'll be right back." I wretch the basket of babies out of their hands and, *poof*, I go back to Hell.

I empty the baby basilisk into the tank and set the basket on the floor for later.

Poof. I return to where I left the Hellions. I was only gone a few minutes but they're not here. I hear crashing from the forest. It's either the dead or the Hellions, or the momma Basilisk tearing this place apart.

Nightingale's Kingdom isn't far. I poof from place to place, looking for the Hellions and the basilisk. Finally, I *poof* to Nightingale's castle.

The front door is broken. Thick wood is cracked and hinges bent. Nightingale's castle is under attack. I get a glimpse of the basilisk's tail through the front windows. I grip my blade and run up the steps to the front door. It's open. There's screaming, moaning, and crashing inside.

"Nightingale?" I shout as I enter the castle.

I hear a baby cry. Skeele's deep voice shouts something unintelligible. I follow the noise. There's blood everywhere. More noise coming from upstairs. I head that way, taking the stairs two at a time.

"Jack?" I shout, hoping someone can give me some guidance.

Sounds of battle come from each end of the hallway once I reach the top of the stairs. I go toward Nightingale's room.

Which way do I go? I'm not sure if I should turn left, but I do. This looks as bad as the damage on the Earthen plane. At least there was a little warning and time to prepare on that plane. People have been prepping for apocalypse conditions for decades there. Not the Seven Kingdoms of Heaven. No, Heaven has been basking in their righteousness and glory. The dead coming was like a hotel bathtub kidney removal after a night of heavy drinking with a pretty girl met on the internet. Unexpected.

Walls are busted in, expensive furniture broken, thick carpets torn to shreds.

I run to the room with the most noise.

Things happen fast after I step into the room. Skeele throws a dagger at the back of a dead man's head. The dead man trips. The dagger hits the wall. The dead man falls into Nightingale. Jack shouts. Nightingale tosses baby Thrush like a basketball toward Jack. He moves to catch the baby but notices Night about to be bit. Jack reaches for both. *Poof.* I catch Thrush. Jack goes for Night. The ceiling caves in. Four of the dead fall on Jack. Two bite his neck. Then one bites Nightingale on her cheek. The basilisk slides in the hole of the ceiling, eating as she goes. Noah screams, a noise like I've never heard. He roars like a pained lion, white light illuminates around him. My heart sinks.

Poof. I take Thrush to Hell.

Tiny Visitor

I appear in Jed and Shay's room with a crying baby.

"What the heck?" Shay asks as she stands.

I run across the room and thrust the baby into Jed's arms. "No time to talk. Protect this kid with everything you've got."

Poof. I go back to Nightingale's.

———

Skeele is checking pulses. Noah is bent over Nightingale's pale, crumpled form, gripping her tightly. They don't have to tell me; they're both gone. There was a time in my life that I didn't give a shit about anyone or anything. My heart aches like never before.

"Where did the basilisk go?" I ask.

"Out the window," Tukka waves. "To eat more."

I nod, feeling sick. I want to puke and cry at the same time. I can do neither.

———

Poof. I go to my father.

Gabriel is picking up furniture and making a pile of the broken stuff in the grass outside his door. He takes one look at me and stops what he's doing. "What happened?"

I tell him. The portals tend to just drop you somewhere if you don't give it directions, not always the same place. Fields, churches, bathrooms. You never know. I'm sure that hasn't helped here either. Kinda hard to prepare when a handful of zombies fall out of the sky. At least, that's what I think happened.

"Mother of pearl." He rubs his face and sits on the stairs of the wraparound porch.

I walk toward him and he pulls me down to sit next to him, one arm wrapped tight around my shoulders.

"What happens to them?" I ask.

"When the soul is extinguished, you simply cease to exist," he replies, solemn.

I wipe my eyes. "They won't come back?"

Gabriel shakes his head. "Not even Teari could have healed those wounds. I'm sure she's with them, up in the stars somewhere. Never thought I'd see a mess like this in my time."

I shake my head. "I didn't do this. Do the other Archangels know?"

He shakes his head. I should've known when Chel got arrowed in the leg.

"I'll leave the basilisk until it cleans everything up." I stand. "I have to go back to Hell now. The fast dead are growing in numbers there."

"We'll come help, just... give us a moment to collect the Legion or what's left of them," he offers. "But, you know what this means now?" he asks.

"What?"

"With Nightingale and Jack gone, Sparrow's now the king, until Thrush becomes of age."

Something sinks deep in my gut like a stone in mud.

"Their Kingdom cannot sit empty for long," he warns, squeezing my shoulder one last time before releasing me. "Go back to your realm. We'll be there soon."

The Liar

Shit got real fucked up. I thought it was before, but nope, this is next level.

The Hellions secure the main doors and clear the castle. We are safe in here, for now. We have patrols, security, and spells–thanks to Jed. The lesser demons are scouting Hell for more, but the portals are demolished. Only one remains.

I sit at the end of the Hellions bar, staring at a glass of blood. I swallow a gulp and do better at controlling the reaction of lust. I don't have to leave the room this time, but I cross my legs tight and think of the basilisk babies roiling in their basket. That's enough to change the mood trying to bloom in my lower abdomen.

"How do you think it happened?" Skeele asks.

"On the Earthen plane, me and Teari had found Sparrow. They were bit. Blood was dripping down the stone wall we were perched on. And the dead licked it like a lollipop." I push the glass away, disgusted with myself. "They drank Sparrow's blood. They drank Teari's blood. And it turned those dead souls into something we've never seen before."

Skeele nods as he takes it all in. "So Sparrow's blood is next level, huh?" He smirks. "No wonder you rarely come for the cheap stuff."

I make a face. He doesn't really have a clue what Sparrow's blood does to me. Better than a moon's over my hammy with bacon from Denny's. Better than the finest liquor served oceanside at a little bar in Key West. Better than Thanksgiving dinner at a real home where the grandma makes everything from scratch. These past few months, I've pined over him. I've remembered how wonderful it would feel to have him in my bed again. To share the bloodlust. To finally be together again. Now I'm not sure if we'll ever return to that. The tables have turned and suddenly I fully understand the phrase *you can't go back home.*

I was once a child and Sparrow was supposed to watch over me. He messed up and fled. And here we are now. Sparrow is mine and I am his. And he will be my walking dead man until I can figure out how to fix him.

———

Skeele walks to the fridge and gets more blood. He pours glasses for the others. There are new recruits in the Hellion barracks. We had to strengthen the numbers. The new ones make me uneasy. They're scarred and horned and colored various shades of reds and browns. They're unpredictable and wild like Hellions of old. They need more training, but there isn't time.

"Keep your chin up," Skeele reminds me.

I tip my head and try to not get lost in the memories of the old Meg. It's so easy to get sucked down into that spiral and put up the walls around me.

"I'm going to need a rum and coke," I say.

"Liquid courage?" Skeele doesn't change his expression. He knows the new ones are watching. He makes the drink and slides it across the bar to me.

I down the rum and coke, then stand. I grip my blade as I move to the center of the room.

"Listen up!" I start. "There's a swarm outside the north entry. We're going to clear it. Bring only blades. No guns. They're fast. They don't belong here. These are not our dead." I reach for the door. "Remember, nothing gets to the third floor."

The Hellions follow me, Skeele at my side as my first in command. It should be Sparrow.

Chel and a new recruit shove open the heavy wooden door. We have about twenty feet to the barricade fence the Hellions built. Ten feet tall and topped with barbed wire and cement barricades, it looks like something from the Cold War. Some of the Hellions take to the sky, their bat-like wings blocking out the dull sun as they slay the dead. I circle a path near the door, jabbing my blade through the fence into skulls as needed. I won't say that I don't trust them to keep the inside of the castle secure. They don't know what the third floor holds. They don't know that I have a baby from the Seven Kingdoms of Heaven in hiding. I was once hidden on a different realm. I didn't think I would ever do it to another child. Seems I am no better than my history.

———

I CHECK ON BABY THRUSH, Jed, and Shay. I knock three times on the door and give Jed time to clear the runes off the doorway so I can enter. Thrush has Nightingale's dark hair and Noah's blue eyes. He's sleeping in an old crib Noah found at an empty house in Buffalo. Noah sits near the window, his handsome face drawn. I don't know if he'll ever get over losing Nightingale. At least before he could see her in the Astral. Now none of us will again.

"Do you need anything for him?" I whisper, afraid to wake Thrush.

"Diapers," Shay whispers back. "Unexpired formula would be good. Or if you have goat milk."

"Hell isn't known for goats," I reply.

"Have the fast ones stopped?" Jed asks.

I shake my head. "Not yet." Being in this room makes me uneasy. "I've got to go." I motion to the marks on the floor. "Fix this."

"I always do," Jed says.

I leave, rubbing my face as I take the short walk down the hall to my room. I push open the door, close it, lean against the carved wood, and slide to the floor. What a mess.

Gabriel arrives in a flash of light.

I hear Skeele's footsteps outside my door. He's the only one allowed up here now.

"Hey, Meg," my father says. "I've got the Legion ready." He looks tired. We are all tired.

I stand. "That's good. The realm of Hell thanks you."

"It's the least we could do after you lent us that snake thing." He motions to the sky and rotates his finger.

"It's a basilisk," I say.

Gabriel shivers. "It's disgusting."

"Does the job though. Is it done up there?" I ask. "I'll have to get the Hellions together to go back and get it."

Gabriel paces near the window. "It should be done soon. There haven't been reports of the fast dead in a few days."

"Did you destroy your portals?" I ask. "A single point of entry has helped."

Gabriel nods.

A yellow flicker lands on the railing of the balcony. The songbirds are wondering what happened to their daily feedings. I walk to the bag of seed, scoop out a handful and scatter it on the balcony railing. I pause for a moment, watching smoke rise from the portal in the distance. The Hellions are burning the bodies. We used to welcome the souls. We used to count our strength on their numbers. Now we just want them to stop.

Gabriel clears his throat.

I sigh, knowing some bullshit is coming. "What?" I ask.

"The other kingdoms will not be sending help." Gabriel runs his fingers through his long white beard.

"No? After all I've done for them?" I say.

"They want to blame someone. They aren't fully convinced it wasn't you."

"I told you what happened. This was an accident. Who knew? And I'd like to go back in time and bring up the fact that the Seven Kingdoms of Heaven hired the Scarecrow to find me on the Earthen plane. If they hadn't started meddling in my life, this would have never happened."

Gabriel raises his brows and smirks. "That's my girl. Don't let this burn out your fire."

"Sure," I reply. I just wanted to take a shower and get some clean clothes on. I'm not sure why I always do that. I guess maybe it's because I went so long without hot showers and clean clothes. "I guess if the Kingdoms of Michael, Raphael, Raguel, Uriel, and Phanuel don't want to help me, I'll just go get the basilisk and let them clean up their kingdoms alone," I say.

"If you must." He watches songbirds collect on the railing and whistles a short trill.

I pause. Waiting. That was something Nightingale and Sparrow would do. Not my father. My heart is still heavy with sorrow for losing Nightingale. Funny how a little whistle could mean so much.

"Hm," Gabriel finally says. "I was hoping something would whistle back."

"They haven't gotten much interaction here lately," I remind him. "The birds are skittish."

Gabriel nods. "I'm going to get the Legion. Make sure your Hellions don't try to kill us as soon as we arrive."

"I'll do my best," I say.

"Oh, and one thing..."

"Yeah?" I ask.

"They're looking for Nightingale's baby. Do you know where he went?"

I keep my face placid. "No clue." I lie.

Gabriel nods slowly. "We've lost many these few weeks." He pauses, waiting for me to speak. I say nothing. "I'll be back soon," he finally says.

Poof. He's gone.

I sit at the balcony, stare off into the Hellsky, and think.

———

THERE'S a knock on my door.

"What?" I shout.

The door cracks open and I recognize Skeele's shadow. "Are you alone now?"

"Yes." I take off my jacket and toss it across the room on the chair before working on unlacing my boots.

He enters the room.

"What?" I ask again, annoyed.

"You shouldn't just let him come and go as he pleases." Skeele's brow is furrowed in concern.

"He's my father. He's of no worry to us." I get my left boot off and toss it aside before starting on the next.

"He is a king from the Seven Kingdoms of Heaven." Skeele steps closer. "You shouldn't be alone with him."

"Just stop." I shake my head in annoyance. "I don't need a babysitter. I can handle my father."

"But can you? Have you seen him at his worst? Have you seen the power of an Archangel who has been around for eons?"

I toss my right boot and stand. I'm taller than most but Skeele still towers over me. "I'm not afraid of him." I start unbuttoning my overshirt.

"You shouldn't be alone," Skeele lowers his voice.

I pause.

"I already have a boyfriend. I don't need another," I say.

Guilt floods me. Skeele has helped even when I hated him and let him know it. He's never left my side. He's always been there. He offered to feed me and cared for me while I healed from falling out of the sky. He's probably seen too much of me. I stop unbuttoning the shirt and drop my hands.

"You shouldn't be alone when he can drop by, unannounced, at any time." Skeele steps closer and grips the blade at his hip. "Someone should always be with you."

"I've been alone for plenty of my life."

"You need to be fed. You need–" Skeele pauses abruptly.

"What do you think I need?" I ask.

Oh, this is not good. I know Sparrow was feeding off random women and god knows what else he was doing. I'm not a fan of what he did to survive. But, I should be able to do what I want; the draw is there. I'd like to have a warm body in my bed at night. Someone to worship me in the midnight hours. I've had plenty of boyfriends before. Some who have hung around longer than others. Look at Noah. Although, he can't help it.

Skeele's eyes are fire as they take me in from head to toe. "There has never been a female ruler here. There has never been a female who will fight on the battlefield with us. Hellions are better than they used to be, but still..."

I let out a laugh but stop abruptly as he tips his head to the side. It's a very Sparrow-like move and makes me wonder if maybe Sparrow was never bird-like in his mannerisms. Maybe he was always Hellion-like in his movements. Maybe a Hellion and an Angel aren't that different.

"I still haven't forgiven you for dropping me out of the sky." I brush a hand over my shoulder. Memories and anger bubble in my chest. "No wings. Still. If you'd like to bring it down a few notches, remember that. There's not much great about me. So stop trying to pressure me into believing the Hellions give a fuck about what I am. I know what they are. I know what you are." I jab a finger in his direction. "I know what I came from. I know what I am. I am a liar, and a sinner, and a fuck up. Look at this mess I've created and you want me to hold my chin up like some pathological asshole. I am not like my grandfather." My fingertips tingle with anger. He's lucky I don't have my blade near or I just might stab him.

"They'd come out if you'd let them." His wings unfold a tiny bit to tease me.

"Get lost, jackass," I dismiss him then turn and walk toward the bathroom.

Heavy footsteps come after me. A giant hand wraps around my upper arm and tugs me to face him. Skeele is right there. His face inches from mine.

Something throbs in my core. I know what it is. Desire. I had it for Sparrow. Still have it for him. After that night of dancing before he got turned into zombie-boy, there was never any relief. And here I've been, walking around for weeks ready to pop.

Skeele isn't that bad. I've seen worse. The horns don't scare me anymore. And to tell the truth, when I woke to find him reading a newspaper at the end of the bed all those months ago, it was an image I couldn't get out of my head. Skeele's not like the others. He's not like the old pack of Hellions that did terrible things to me before I knew what I was. I shouldn't have said those words a moment ago.

He reaches forward with his free hand and tugs at the buttons to my shirt. They pop off and scatter across the floor, revealing the tank top underneath.

"I watched you heal from a sack of broken bones to this," Skeele says, his voice low, eyes half-lidded. "I sat at your bedside for months. Watching your every breath." He drops to one knee. "Please, Meg, let me be of use to you."

Now, I've done plenty bad in my life. I cheated and took what wasn't mine. I didn't start changing until Sparrow came into my life and I never tried to be better. He's been gone all this time. He fed off other women. We never promised anything to each other. And now I don't know if I'll ever have Sparrow again.

"Please, Meg," Skeele whispers again.

What would Andy Dufresne do? What would Sparrow do?

What would Bon Jovi do? I close my eyes. What would Meg do? Why do I always rely on the morals of men? Men do what they want. They take what they want. Why can't I? There was that one Bon Jovi song about a cheating dude. Sparrow sang it to me before...

Skeele holds out his wrist.

I see the throb of his veins and arteries. I suck in a breath. I've never had Hellion before. Skeele rises to his feet and holds his wrist closer to my mouth.

"You need your strength for what we are about to embark on," he urges. "Use me." His voice is dark, promising.

Damn. What do you do when a monster begs you to use them like a piece of raw meat?

I grab his arm and sink my teeth into his wrist.

BURNT

The shower is boiling hot as I wet my face and scrub the blood off. Red stains the water as it slides down the drain. My gut is full. My brain buzzing. I feel like I did a line of cocaine. I scrub my body, my hand lingering in the vee between my legs. Christ. That could have gone in a very different direction. It's hard to control the lust. I'm getting better at it. At least, I think I am.

I wash my hair and turn off the shower. Wrapping myself in towels, I dry myself in record time. No lingering. We've got shit to do. I leave my short hair damp to air dry and head to the closet. Knowing we'll be fighting, I grab leather pants, knee high boots, a thin undershirt, and leather jacket. The fit is good for movement and the extra leather should protect my skin if one of the dead tries to bite me. I glance at my bag. I grab it and throw a change of clothes in there. Since Noah is busy with other things, I'll have to get my own snacks. Heck, I'm lazy. Maybe I'll just skip the snacks. I feel like I could last a few days after fresh blood.

"Child?" Clea arrives near the window.

"Yea?" I ask, leaving the closet.

"Your father is coming?" she asks.

"He is," I nod. "He's going to help us."

"The Legion has never helped Hell in all of history. This will be new." Her ruby red lips press together in concern. "You look strong. Even without Sparrow by your side. You can help set this right."

"I sent the basilisk to Heaven to help them," I remind her.

Clea nods.

"Why are you really here?" I ask.

"Sparrow doesn't look good. I think he's getting worse." She fidgets with her gown. Pale fingers tracing the white embroidery.

"I know." My shoulders drop. "We must clear the realm before I can figure out how to fix him. Unless you have any ideas," I say.

She folds her hands. "I've none. Only concern for him and that room I cannot enter." She points to the wall.

Jed's spells are good. Noah is sworn to secrecy, he wouldn't do anything to hurt his own child. And since Thrush is all that he has left of Nightingale, Noah is on his best behavior.

I secure my bag across my shoulder. "Are you coming to fight with us?" I ask. "We could use the extra numbers. Gabriel doesn't have many Legion left and I'm going to feel really bad if he loses more down here."

Clea watches out the window. "I'll go. Since I've got nothing else to do." She disappears in a puff of smoke.

I secure my blade with the holster on my thigh and settle the bag over my shoulder. I circle the room, taking it in. It's hard to escape the feeling that I might never see this room again. I'm headed to war, well, back into war. A war with the fast-dead.

I leave the bedroom and make my way down the long hall and the winding stone stairwell. The familiar smell of woodsmoke and pine is thick in the air now that the castle is locked up and secured.

I roll my shoulders and try to set my mind straight. I said some shit to Skeele and then used him like a Slurpee machine. I reminded him that I hate Hellions. Old wounds are hard to bury. Now I have to step into war with them. I cinch the strap holding my blade a little tighter. These new Hellions are wild and I doubt Skeele, Chel, Tukka, or Klaus could stop them from turning on us. I've been on the receiving end of Hellions doing their worst. I can't let it happen again.

WAR AND REGRET

There is a vibrating energy to the Hellions' lair. They're fed, briefed, and ready to fight.

"Only kill the fast ones. The slow ones belong here. They are not the same. There will be Legion present from Gabriel's kingdom. Don't kill them. Don't eat them. They are here to help." I glance at Skeele. He doesn't look like he lost any blood, like I nearly drained him dry upstairs a few hours ago.

"We don't need their help," one of the new recruits mutters from the back.

"Hey," Chel says from the shadows, his voice low and threatening. "You'll take their help and thank them."

"We clear the realm. Then they go back," I say. "Klaus and Chel will stay to protect the castle. You all are coming with Skeele and Tukka." I pause for dramatic effect. "And me."

You could hear a pin drop.

We head for the door, Skeele walking by my side. He pushes open the giant, carved door at the base of the burning caves. The Hellions take to the air to get over the barricade.

Chel and Klaus wait at the mouth of the cave.

"Nothing gets to the third floor," I remind them.

Klaus tips his head. "What's so special about the third floor all of a sudden?"

"None of your business." I *poof* to the other side of the fence. It's been a long time since I've felt this powerful. Maybe Skeele was right. Maybe all I needed was a little fresh blood from a dark creature.

There are about ten bodies that the Hellions have already taken care of. They pull the corpses to a pile and set them on fire.

Hearing footsteps, I turn quickly to find Skeele walking toward me. It's intimidating; tall, muscled, leaning forward like a cat ready to pounce as he walks. He's decked out in Hellion gear, leathers and straps securing various weapons. His wings twitch in anticipation of flying.

The others take to the sky and survey from above.

"Why aren't you flying?" I ask Skeele.

"I could ask you the same," he replies with a dark grin.

"Don't," I warn.

"Would you like me to carry you," he points to Hellsky, "up there?"

"Nope." I grip my blade, ready to use it on any fast ones that come out of the surrounding forests. Or Skeele. "Is Gabriel here with the Legion?"

"Yes." He points in the direction of the last portal. "They are not far. We should be meeting them soon."

We walk in silence for miles.

"We could have driven," Skeele finally says.

"Nah, then we'd miss them." I point at myself. "Bait."

On cue a zombie runs out of the tree line. Before I can do anything, one of the Hellions drops from the sky and slices it down the middle. Two more drop down to grab the parts, toss them in a pile, and light them on fire.

Skeele makes a hand signal to the ones above and we keep walking. "Portal's up here," he says.

"I know," I say. "I remember. Been down here long enough."

"I was just–"

A blast rocks the ground and smoke rises from the direction where Skeele had just pointed.

"Gabriel!" I take off running as fast as I can.

This can't be good. A million things run through my mind. I've already lost Nightingale and Jack. And there's a strong chance I might lose Sparrow and Teari. I can't lose Gabriel too. They can't leave me to navigate this alone.

With Skeele's blood pumping through my veins, I run faster.

Bird in a Cage

THE PORTAL IS GONE. THE ONLY THING LEFT IS A GIANT dirt hole in the ground. Dark dirt like a giant bowl pressed in the soil, littered with a few rocks from what was the portal.

"Gabriel!" I shout.

A dozen or so of the fast dead come running out of the surrounding forest. The Hellions get to work. Heads fall, limbs drop. The Hellions split most down the middle so they can't reanimate while they burn.

"Did he come through?" I ask one of the new Hellions. "Did Gabriel or any of the Legion come through?"

"There was no one," the Hellion says. "We were in the air when we saw the explosion."

Poof. I go to my father's kingdom.

Something's not right. Dad's acting sketchy. I knock on the giant embossed door only to find it's open. The house is put back together. In such a short time? It smells like fresh paint and lacquer and baked bread. "Gabriel?" I call. No one answers. This house is empty. I walk through the middle hall and check all the rooms, through the kitchen and out the back door, down through the vast yard to the Legion barracks. The Legion training grounds. It's all empty.

Poof. I go to Sparrow's old house in the woods. It's empty too, but I'd expect it to be.

Poof. I go to Nightingale's house. It's burned to the ground. The giant skeleton of the basilisk is set within the ashes, bones charred to ochre. The ash smells familiar. But I am used to the smells of Hell now.

Poof. I go to Babylon.

"No!" a familiar voice shouts. "Get out of here, Meg!"

In the distance, I see Gabriel in a cage, much like I was once, a gleaming tall cage in the bright sunlight. There's no missing it. Sweat beads his brow and his hair glistens wet. His robes are gone.

"Get out of here!" he shouts, his eyes wide.

He doesn't have to tell me three times.

Poof. I go back to Hell.

Everything Falls Apart

"Where did you go?" Skeele asks.

"To find Gabriel." I try to dry my sweaty palms on my pants but they slide across the leather. "He's imprisoned. He won't be helping us."

I scan the perimeter of the field. The slow dead halt at my presence and waver behind the shadows. Others come through fast, jaws snapping. Angry, I ready my blade and go to work, helping the other Hellions. Dozens more than I saw in Nightingale's kingdom. When they finally stop, I help the Hellions drag the body parts to a burn pile. I am covered in gore and ichor. Rotting blood coats my pants from the splatter. The smell of the burning bodies fills the air. I hold back a gag.

Poof. I go back to my room. The castle is quiet. Jed's spells keep the sounds of baby Thrush inside the room next door. What a mess. I strip off my clothes and rinse myself off in the shower. I need to think. I need to figure out what to do. I wrap myself in a towel then head to the closet to find more clothes. I dress in record time.

Poof. I go back to the field. Tukka and Skeele are circling the field in the sky. Their giant bat-like wings block out the fading sunlight. I approach the nearest Hellion.

"Hey," I call to one with curled horns like a mountain ram. "Have any more of the fast ones come this way?"

"No," the Hellion replies.

"And all of the other portals were destroyed?" I ask.

"As far as we know. The Deacons were pissed that they no longer had the ability to move between realms and consult the Seven King-doms of Heaven," the Hellion says.

Goddamned Deacons. Those bastards have been nothing but a thorn in my side.

Skeele lands near me and walks closer.

"I'm going to check the other portals. And make sure the Deacons haven't rebuilt one," I head for the road.

Skeele nods. "We'll finish up here."

———

I walk down the center of route 54, headed for Interstate 81. The moon is my only light. My stomach growls and for a moment I wish Noah was still at my beck and call to feed me like a nice handsome butler. I don't see us returning to those days any time soon. I shouldn't have used my power to travel so much. It makes me hungry and there is no Hellion lair fridge with blood here. I'll have to suffer. It's fine. I can do it.

The sound of a car on the road interrupts the silence around me. I move to the shoulder and keep walking. It could be a lost soul who found a car, searching for answers like I once did. It seems like forever ago I was searching this plane with Sparrow. Forever ago I thought I knew everything but knew nothing at all. I didn't know who I was, I didn't know what I was. But Sparrow searching for that Snowy Owl was the distraction I needed. I can't remember the last time I picked up a feather. It's probably a good thing. Most brought visions of something terrible. I don't think I'll ever trust a feather again.

The car slows. "Want a ride?"

I turn to see Skeele in the Jeep. He stops, reaches across the passenger seat, and opens the door. "Get in."

Tired and hungry, he doesn't have to ask twice.

"You're going to check them all?" Skeele asks as I close the door.

"Yup." I glance at him. "You didn't want to fly or walk?"

"I knew you wouldn't fly. And I'm not about to walk the entire way." He shifts the Jeep into drive and accelerates.

It's a few hours to check the portal in Saratoga. It's dismantled. Not as badly as the one that was bombed near the burning caves, but close. The rocks from the archway are strewn about and broken down to dust in some places.

"The last one is across the Vermont border," Skeele reminds me.

My stomach growls. "What I wouldn't give for a platter of gas station nachos and a blue Slurpee."

"There's a place to stay up here," Skeele motions ahead of us to the mountain across the valley.

"What kind of place?"

"Where Hellions can stay when they're out on patrol. It's not much, but we can rest and there's food."

"Okay," I agree.

It's not long before he pulls into the driveway of an old cabin. It looks like it was once a bed a breakfast tucked into the mountainside. Cobwebs string from porch railings and a pale bulb flickers near the door.

We get out of the Jeep and Skeele walks up to the front door and opens it.

"No locks?" I ask.

He laughs. "Hellions don't need locks."

That thinking is what got my door broken down. I'll have to remember it.

It's spacious. Dusty. Reminds me of the Hellion lair back at the burning caves. I kick the door closed and head for the giant bed tucked into the corner. I take off my bag and drop it on the night-stand before flopping onto the bed and falling asleep.

———

I DREAM OF SPARROW. It's filthy. We're naked and sweating and feeding off each other. His blood is warm in my mouth. Delicious. It coats my throat and fills my stomach. It fills one need. There's another that comes with the bloodlust. A throb deep in my lower abdomen takes over. I throw a leg over Sparrow and take the lead. I've waited so long to have him like this. To be filled with him. It feels so good and I'm impatient. His hands are on my body, my hips, grip-ping and pinching my skin in all the right places. I rotate my hips and–

"Wake up," Sparrow says. "Wake up. Wake up. Wake up."

My eyes flash open.

It's not Sparrow.

It's Skeele. His eyes are half-lidded and his hands are around my waist.

"The hunger will never go away. If you don't do something about it, you're going to do something you regret."

Seems Skeele was right. Fuck.

———

THE VERMONT PORTAL is a two-hour drive. We encounter five of the fast dead on our way there. Skeele pulls over and tells me he'll take care of them. There is no chivalry in Hell. I get out and take one of them out.

"I said I'd get it," Skeele says as we drag them to a pile on the side of the road and light their carcasses on fire.

"I am not some maiden who waits in a car while you pump gas," I say. "This is my realm."

"It is your realm. And a Hellion protects their leader. It is my duty." He sounds pissed as he marches back to the Jeep and gets behind the wheel.

More silence.

I never knew the Hellions to be so moody. I've only known them to act on impulse and fuck shit up. Hm. Kinda sounds like me... Skeele hasn't been like that though. Neither have the others. I'm going to have to change my method of thinking. I wonder if there's therapists in Hell.

Skeele turns onto a dirt road after passing a sign for Green Mountain National Forest.

He stops the Jeep and we get out to inspect the ruins in the clearing.

This portal is demolished as well.

Annoyed at the mood and the lack of a portal for the fast-dead to come through, I decide to go elsewhere, alone.

Poof. I go back to the burning caves and leave Skeele to find his own way back.

I run down the winding stone stairs to the dungeon below. I turn right. Go straight, don't look at the creatures caged there. I run to Sparrow's door at the end. I peer at him through the barred window.

"Has he eaten?" I ask the Hellion stationed at his door.

"Nothing," is the reply.

"No blood?" I ask.

"No," the Hellion says.

Sparrow's skin is gray, his green eyes dull and milky. His dark hair is matted and oily. He turns at the sound of my voice. His jaw bites. He scuffs toward the door.

"Sparrow?" I ask. "How do I fix this?"

"He won't answer you," the Hellion says. "Can't speak a word, just grunts and moans and snaps."

I ignore the Hellion. "Tell me how to fix this," I say through the bars. Sparrow's teeth snap loudly and echo against the stone walls of his cell.

Out of all the movies I've watched, none can help me with this mess. Shawshank never turned into this clusterfuck. Andy Dufresne would roll over in his grave.

Sparrow always said we would be invincible together, but not like this. We cannot be invincible as he rots in a cell. I must figure out how to release him from this curse. The laws of the ethereal realms kept tearing us apart. Or maybe I keep tearing us apart. Maybe we were never meant to stay together, like Gabriel and Clea. Me and Sparrow could be nothing but a tragedy. Could I forgive him? Even if I fix him, could he forgive me? I did lose his book, after all. *Birds of Paradise* is nothing but a needle in a haystack here. I've known some people who would never speak to you again if you lost their book.

Skeele's blood has given me power. *Poof* – I ignore the warnings of weeks ago and blast through to the Earthen realm.

THINGS WE LEFT BEHIND

THE HOSPITAL IS STILL OPEN, THE BARRICADES AND military thinned to a single crew. The parking lot has a few more cars in it than last time. I walk to the emergency room doors and go inside.

"There is only one inpatient," the lady at the desk says and gives me directions to the room.

The elevator works. I take it to the second floor and pass empty rooms until I get to the big corner one.

I knock on the door before pushing it open.

Teari is sitting in a chair eating hospital food.

"You left me in Scranton, Pennsylvania," Teari scowls. "Of all places."

"What's wrong with Scranton?" I ask, looking out the window.

"It's cold." Teari throws her blankets off her legs and walks toward a cupboard on the wall. Using the nubs of her arms, she opens the cupboard with a rope that's tied around the handle and pulls out her clothes. "Help me get out of this disgusting gown."

I pat my pack. "I brought you clean clothes."

"I hope they're not hand me downs from you. You're much shorter than I am. I like my pants to cover my ankles."

"Beggars can't be choosers." I unzip my bag and pull out the clothes. "I actually stopped at Wal-Mart before coming here. They didn't have a women's big and tall section, but the men's had some good choices."

"Ugh," Teari scoffs.

I'm sure she's not thrilled to slum it in cheap clothes. She's always been dressed to the nines or in expensive combat gear. T-shirts and sweats don't quite compare.

Teari tries to take the bag from my hand. Since she's got no fingers, I drop the bag on the bed and sort through it, laying out all the items I bought for her. She motions to a few pieces. "I'm going to need some help," she says holding up her arms.

I untie the hospital gown and leave it loose.

"I thought you'd love these grannie panties," I joke as I hold out the underwear for her to step into. "And these big white socks are straight out of 1986. It's all they had. I promise." I kneel and hold the socks open for her to put her feet into. She picked out a pair of loose sweatpants. I hold them open for her to step into.

"Don't tie them," Teari warns. "I can't do the ties."

I nod and gather the T-shirt, putting it over her head before pulling the hospital gown away. The nurses in Gouverneur taught me how to get dressed like that. After, I help her into a zip-up hoodie.

"You want me to roll the sleeves?" I ask. The sleeve fabric just sways loose, unfilled because of her missing hands.

She shakes her head. "I'm just going to the bathroom before we go," Teari says.

I sit in a chair by the window and wait for her. I can't imagine going to the bathroom without hands. I wonder if she's drip-drying. My questions are answered when I hear her sniff and hiccup, doing her best to cry softly.

I shift in my chair, uncomfortable with the crying Angel.

Comforting someone is not my strong suit. Heck, I don't think I've ever comforted a person in my life. At least nothing more than a few pats on the back from an arm's length away.

Teari finally leaves the bathroom. I avoid looking at her face. I don't want her to feel like she has to explain the puffy eyes or redness.

"Get me the heck out of here," Teari says.

I hold up a finger. "Shoes. We almost forgot shoes."

"The hospital slippers are tempting," Teari says. "I can't really tie any laces."

"But I've got these." I open another bag and hold up a pair of slides. "Easy." I drop them on the floor in front of her.

I show her the way out and find a car in the parking lot with the keys still in it. It was too easy, but I guess someone on the Earthen plane wants me to win today. I'll take a win after all that's happened.

I open the door for Teari, close it, then go to the driver's side. It's an old Camry with plenty of legroom. Never thought I'd see myself driving an import. I close her door and survey the parking lot. I'm not sure what God looks like. Not sure this was left by him. I was told he's been gone for a long time... seems someone is offering guidance here. Probably eager to get me to leave.

After turning the ignition, I pull away from the hospital and head for the highway.

"What happened to your magical healing powers?" I ask.

"Too many blood transfusions. It will come back after a while." She holds up her hands. "I hope. The bones aren't done healing. Can't do much until I'm in tip top shape."

I guess that's what seems so different about her. She's lost some of her grace in the blood loss.

I fill her in on the shit show she missed while I abandoned her on the Earthen plane. I leave out a few details: Thrush, Nightingale's death, and my father being imprisoned. There will be time for that later.

"Sparrow's still a zombie," I say.

"Did he drink my blood?" Teari asks.

"He bit you. I'm not sure about the blood drinking part."

"My blood could heal him."

"Or not..." I warn.

"I can't give any now," she says. "What I have now is mostly donor. Billy-Bob Jenkins and Laura Doone don't have much in the way of angelic healing powers."

I nod. There's a tiny vial in my nightstand. I was saving it for something. Maybe this is it.

I drive to the Saratoga portal. The cemetery quite familiar now. The archway of the portal is demolished.

"Great," Teari says. "How will we get back now?"

"I'll take you," I say. "I just wanted to make sure it wasn't useable."

I take Teari's hand and *poof* we go to Hell together.

This is how a Heart Breaks

Teari's room is on the third floor. Just across the way from Jed and Shay and baby Thrush. Jed helped me with the runes on her door to keep her hidden. Later I'll talk to her about some tattoos, after she's had some time to heal.

After settling Teari into her new living space, I head to my room and grab the vial of her blood from the nightstand.

I make my way to the stairwell and jog down. Someone's coming up before I get very far.

I recognize the horns.

"What are you doing?" Skeele asks.

"Fixing him." I squeeze the vial in my palm before holding it up for him to see.

"Are you sure it's going to fix him?" Skeele rubs his chin. "It could do something... unexpected."

"Everything about this shit show is unexpected," I remind him, my eyes lingering on his mouth. I want to take him back to my room and finish what we started. "You're just pissed I left you in Vermont."

"I didn't need you to find my way back," he chuckles.

"Make the Hellion in the dungeon go away," I command.

Skeele nods. "As you wish."

I pause for a moment and let him get ahead of me. As I make my way to Sparrow's cell, the leaving Hellion passes me with a nod. I walk faster, eager to fix one of my problems.

"Open the door," I tell Skeele.

He walks in first and immobilizes Sparrow. I twist the cap off the vial of blood. Gripping Sparrow's upper arm to steady myself, I try not to focus on the fact that he's skin and bone now. Hallowed and sunken skin, he barely fights. His teeth snap together. I reach up on my tip toes and pour Teari's blood into his mouth.

Sparrow stops. He licks his lips. I shake the vial to get as much of the blood into his mouth as I can. When I'm done, a very small coating remains in the vial. I cap it and save it for later. I'm not below breaking the glass and licking the shards in an emergency.

Sparrow's head ticks to the side. A hand moves to his pocket and he pulls out a black feather.

"Sparrow?" I ask, desperation in my voice.

The milky coating clears, but something changes. Those aren't the Ireland-grass green eyes I remember. Were they ever green to begin with? He scans the surroundings, taking in the room, me, Skeele, the door. There's a sound forming deep in his throat.

Skeele lets go, grabs me, and drags me to the door. He slams it closed and locks it. Skeele holds my shoulder protectively.

"Where did he go?" Skeele asks.

"The only place he could go," I say. "He's been called back to his kingdom within the Seven Kingdoms of Heaven. With Nightingale dead, he takes the throne."

I didn't think it would happen so fast.

"What now?" Skeele asks, solemn and unimpressed.

Poof. I go to Nightingale's kingdom.

"Sparrow!" I call.

He's in the distance, inspecting the burned ruins of his home. His curse finally cleared, he returns to nothing. Just ash and bone and sorrow.

One of the Archangels are there. It's not Gabriel. It's not his own father; I killed him a long time ago. One of the other Archangels who thinks this is my fault is standing close to Sparrow and telling him something.

"Sparrow?" I call. "Will you talk to me?"

He turns, focuses. There's my Sparrow. Finally. He runs toward me. I open my arms, running forward to leap in his arms like some cheesy romance movie. I don't care. He's back. My Sparrow is back. We get closer and closer. My heart fills with a joy I've never felt before. I've waited forever to feel like this, to have him free. To finally have set everything right.

"Sparrow," I say. "You're back. You're you."

"Is that so?" Sparrow asks. His voice is strange, not like I remember. There is no lilt of wonder and hope on his tongue. No Snowy Owl words. No moonlight whispers in the slick heat of lust. I do not recognize his voice at all.

He moves his arm and in the bright Heaven sun something glints in his hand. Sparrow is a trained Legion Commander and a Hellion leader. He knows how to fight the greatest of enemies. Teari's blood brought his strength back. He moves quicker than I've ever seen anything move. A quick jab. Three to my stomach. One to my thigh. Another to my arm. He holds the small blade against my breastbone and as I catch my breath, air thick with betrayal settles in my chest.

"An eye for an eye. Grace for grace," Sparrow's voice is malevolent, filled with hatred, like nothing I've ever heard. "Except you never had a speck of grace. I'll have to take something else."

He pushes the blade deeper until I feel the tip enter my heart.

Poof. I go back to Hell.

I collapse on the ground of the Hellions' lair. I didn't plan to drop at Skeele's feet, but I do.

"What in the hell happened?" is the last thing I hear.

PART TWO

NIGHTJAR

Not Again

Skeele

"Christ," Skeele spit, followed by more swearing in Hellspeak as he bent to lift Meg from the ground. *Not again*, he thought. This can't be happening again. Skeele lifted Meg, one arm under her knees, another across her back.

The energy in the room went berserk. The new recruits were wild, shouting and shoving ensued. Duke and Chel did their best to calm them, but this was the kind of chaos that ensued when the throne was threatened. The throne of Hell was a coveted thing here. A shadowed realm where darkness reigned, the malevolence of the throne loomed, it had *presence*. Lucifer's throne steeped in sinister intentions, cunningly concealed beneath a shroud of deception woven by the very souls in subjugation. If Lucifer's rule was night, Meg's rule was day. She was a flicker of hope for the souls of Hell. Meg started to tame the veil; started to loosen the chains. The creatures of Hell would always require reining in, but for the first time in eons, the Hellions were doing it with minimal violence and death. It was paying off; the more souls a realm held, the greater the power.

Skeele lifted Meg, exhaling a breath of relief when he felt solid bones under her skin. It wasn't like last time. Last time he lifted her like this off the dusky grass of the backyard, it sounded like Rice Krispies crackling under her skin. He'd never heard nor felt the weight of someone with every bone in their body broken. She was nothing more than a sack of flesh that day and simply thinking about how she felt in his arms made his stomach twist.

Meg didn't remember, therefore ever since that day she never understood his need to protect her. She was hazardous to her own health ninety-nine percent of the time. Hellions didn't give a shit about much, but protecting their leader–they cared about that. They wanted to protect Meg because she was different. She gave them hope. Skeele never wanted to experience lifting her as a bag of bones again. Yet, here he was.

"Get them out," Skeele shouted to Tukka and Chel as he walked toward the bar. The energy of the room cooled as the other Hellions left.

Skeele dropped Meg's lifeless body on the bar and slapped her pale cheeks, trying to wake her. Blood leaked from wounds in her leg, arm, and stomach. The most concerning was the one over her heart. Gaping wide, he could see the slow pulse of her heart where her breastbone was pierced, and the skin torn back.

"I'll get the blood," Klaus shouted as he ran behind the bar, ripped open the fridge and tore out every bag of blood that was stocked there.

This wasn't medicine like on the Earthen plane. Heaven and Hell each had their own methods of saving a life. Too bad Skeele wasn't skilled at any of them–none of the Hellions were. They needed something more, but battlefield survival would have to do. Blood cured much. Skeele scanned Meg's injuries... he wasn't sure blood would cure this.

Skeele and Tukka tore open the bags of blood and dripped them into Meg's mouth. The wounds seeped, their flow never seeming to stop. Rivulets of viscous blood ran over pale skin and torn clothing.

"Wake up," Skeele spit from clenched teeth.

Nothing happened. Meg didn't swallow. The blood simply pooled in her mouth. She was barely breathing and Skeele was so worked up he didn't trust his eyes. Her breaths were shallow. He blinked. Was she even breathing?

"Pour it in the wounds," Tukka suggested.

"Can't hurt," Skeele said as he opened a fresh bag of blood and poured it over the stab wounds on Meg's chest and stomach.

Tukka ripped open another bag using his teeth and poured blood into the wounds on her arm and leg.

They waited.

Nothing happened.

Meg's breathing slowed. Each breath was further apart. Her head tipped to the side with the pressure of Tukka's fingers as he felt for a pulse, worry creasing his dark skin. Tukka shook his head. "It's barely, anything. This is not good."

The blood that pooled in her mouth slowly dripped down a pale cheek and pooled along the valleys of delicate ear. Meg looked worse than before. Worse than ever. She looked dead.

"I'm going to get help," Skeele said, running for the door. "Don't let anyone in here!"

A SPEC OF GRACE

Jed and Shay

Someone was pounding on the door. Jed and Shay made eye contact from across the room, then both looked at the sleeping baby.

"Make it stop," Shay said. "It's going to wake him."

Jed and Shay weren't parents, but they were playing the part, and sleep deprivation was straining their relationship. He had spent his whole life in the run, now he was a sitting duck and responsible for two lives.

Jed clutched a knife. Not just any knife, a small switchblade that he'd carved with runes and coated in magic. It wouldn't save them, but it would gain them some time if he had to use it. It would delay whatever onslaught came for them until help arrived.

Jed opened the door just a crack.

There was a Hellion there, the one Meg called Skeele. He was anxious, pacing, and–more concerning–covered in blood.

"Meg needs help," Skeele growled.

"What kind of help?" Jed asked, gripping the knife tighter in his hand.

"The life or death kind."

Jed stilled. "Sounds like Meg." He didn't trust the hulking demon, afraid that the Hellion might try to blast through the door and get the baby that Meg made Jed and Shay swear on their lives to protect and hide.

Skeele's arms went wide, "Are you coming?" he shouted.

Jed slammed the door closed and turned to face Shay.

"What?" Shay asked.

"I think something bad has happened," Jed said as he crossed the room to get his bag. "I have to go." Jed knew whatever happened, wasn't good.

"You can't," Shay's eyes were wide as she stood, reaching for him. "Don't leave us."

Shay knew how to survive the apocalypse of the Earthen plane, but Hell? Hell was a different matter. For both of them. She'd never been here before. He'd never been here before. He'd taught her as much as he could about the spells and runes over the days I had locked them in this room. But he had to go now. Because if something happened to Meg, they were shit out of luck.

"Tell Noah as soon as he gets back," Jed said, concern overtaking his voice. "Noah will know what to do."

Shay nodded, blue hair falling over her eyes.

"I'll come back as soon as I can," he promised, stepping closer and gripping her arm. "I'll be back."

Shay nodded but worry glazed her eyes.

Jed backed out the door, checking the runes along the floor and around the door lock to make sure they were intact. He locked the door and turned to find the Hellion.

Skeele was pacing, cracking his knuckles, and looking thoroughly on edge.

"What happened?" Jed asked.

Skeele didn't answer, instead he grabbed Jed by the collar of his jacket and ran for the stairwell. Skeele ran down four steps at a time dragging Jed along. Jed tripped and stumbled, slamming his knee against the wall as he caught his footing.

"Let go of me you asshat," Jed shouted, arms flailing as I dragged him through the air on the descent. "You're going to break my fucking neck."

Skeele let go. "We need to move fast." He kept running down the stairs, the sound of heavy boots echoing off stone.

Jed followed, shaking off nerves. He didn't know what he was about to walk into. But if Meg was in the room, that usually meant he'd be walking into a shit show.

Skeele led Jed to a Hellion-marked door on the first floor. He pushed the door open and dragged Jed by the arm of his jacket. Slower this time.

The metallic scent of blood was thick in the air. It only took seconds for Jed to see where it was coming from. There was a body on the bar, and it looked pretty lifeless.

"Come on," Skeele urged as he crossed the room.

As Jed approached the bar, a hand flew to his mouth. Shit. This was not good. Meg was dead. That meant he'd probably be dead soon. And so would Shay. And so would that baby.

"We need your help," Skeele said, rounding the bar.

Jed threw his hands in the air. "How can I help you with this?" Hands went to his hair and tugged. His life was over. Shay's life was over. And God only knows what would happen to the baby upstairs. The portals were gone, and Jed couldn't transverse the realms like Meg.

"Do something," the dark Hellion in the room begged. His eyes wide and black. "She's going to die soon."

Skeele was pacing and growling and muttering in Hellspeak.

"I can't bring dead people back to life," Jed said, he didn't deal in death magic. "That's a different type of–"

Skeele crossed the room and ripped Jed's backpack off. "You

know magic." He pointed at the tattooed runes on Jed's arms. "You know spells. You must know something that can help."

"Are you sure she's dead?" Jed asked.

Tukka checked her pulse again. "It's faint. Very faint." The large Hellion touched Meg's hair, leaving bloody fingerprints on her forehead.

The Hellions were savage creatures and as far as Jed knew, they didn't care about much. But it appeared they cared very much for this lifeless person. If only Meg knew.

Jed took his bag from Skeele's hands and poured it out on the portion of the bar that wasn't covered in blood. There were vials, papers, bags of sand, bags of bones, and other strange little trinkets. Jed was looking for the book. He sorted everything until he found it. The book was really nothing more than a palm sized sketchpad, but it was ages old and fell into his possession after meeting another Nephilim years ago. He flipped through the pages, searching. Searching for something. Anything that could help.

"Come on!" Skeele pounded his fists on the bar. Empty glasses clanged together; the pings of glass threatening to shatter added to the angst in the room.

"I'm looking." Jed's fingers danced over the stained pages, his eyes scanned in rapid movements. "Ok. Ok. I think I found something that might help."

Jed went to work. He marked the wooden bar around Meg's body with charcoal, sprinkled sand, and arranged small bones near her head and feet. Last, he chose a small jar of white liquid that luminated faintly.

"What's that?" Skeele asked with a growl.

"Do you know?" Jed asked, one brow raised. "Some call it grace. Or at least, that's what I was told." He tilted the vial and the liquid inside luminated brighter.

"How'd you get that?" Skeele asked, eyes narrowed on the vial.

"I inherited it." Jed flipped the cap and stared at the two Hellions. "Now I need you both to shut up or join in."

Jed chanted ancient words from the book. The runes of sand glowed, the bones rattled like a rattlesnake tail. He tipped the vial onto his finger and pressed it to Meg's forehead. Chanting more, the words that originally sounded off and hard to wrap his tongue around became fluid and easier to annunciate the more he repeated them. The spec of grace on Meg's forehead pulsed. Jed was backlit in blue light as he motioned for Skeele and Tukka to join in.

The two Hellions made eye contact in apprehension but finally joined and repeated Jed's words.

Meg took a single breath. Her wounds oozed. Congealed blood dipped and formed circular crests. The spec of grace on her forehead glowed brighter.

Hope rose in Jed's chest. It was working. It was working!

Suddenly, Meg's wounds began gushing blood. Rivers flowed out of her. More blood than the Hellions had given her. Blood spilled onto the floor and the speck of grace turned from white to black. Meg's forehead smoked. Her body shuddered. The smell was putrid as the smoke billowed toward the ceiling.

"No," Skeele stopped chanting. "What did you do?" He grabbed a rag from the counter behind him and wiped the dot of grace off her forehead.

"What the hell," Jed shouted. "You broke the spell."

"You were killing her," Skeele growled. "And now I'm going to kill you!"

IDLED WITH DESPAIR

TEARI

TEARI SAT ON THE EDGE OF HER BED. THERE WAS NO balcony in her room. No extra furnishings. There were plenty of clothes and a variety of prosthetic limbs Noah had brought her to try. She stared at her arms; the nub at the wrist, the nub at the elbow. Nothing had prepared her for this. Not the decades of training with the Legion or the decades of being King Gabriel's personal healer. It was rare for an Angel to lose a limb for good. They always grew back. Teari had some practice with that magic. But now, human blood pumped through her veins. It had altered her, stopped her powers. She'd told Meg they would come back but to be completely honest, Teari wasn't sure. And the thought of being limbless for the rest of her time was too much to handle.

Teari was trapped within a desolate chamber of despair. Surrounding her were frigid walls that echoed with the silence of abandonment. The air hung heavy with oppressive darkness, suffocating any flicker of hope that dared to linger. Teari had once soared among the Seven Kingdoms of Heaven, a radiant beacon of grace, her purpose to heal and protect. Now, her wings weighed heavy with the burden of her own suffering, rendered powerless by the loss of her hands. Tears streaked down her ashen cheeks, the remnants of a shattered spirit. Every breath was a struggle as if the very air had turned against her. Her wounds throbbed, a constant reminder of the Fast-Zombie War. Although, from her hospital bed on the Earthen plane, she hadn't seen the worst of it.

Teari glanced at the four walls of her room. There was no window. And she was sure she knew why Meg hadn't given her a window. The urge to jump out it and plunge to the rocks below was strong. Or... maybe it was glamour. Teari stood and walked toward the exterior wall. She rubbed her arms across the green plaster searching for something, anything. Perhaps something hidden that she couldn't see with the naked eye. She'd take any way out she could find. Teari stood on her toes, crouched on the ground, pressed her cheek to the walls, and inspected every inch of the room. She shoved the bed away from the wall with her shoulder and kept going.

"Let me out," Teari whispered. Something was surging in her chest, a feeling of panic she'd never felt before. She tore through the room, looking for an escape. She shoved and kicked, she tipped over the nightstand, shoved the small bed aside. The scabbed scars on her arms opened and oozed blood and serous fluid.

Is this how Meg and Nightingale felt all those times they'd been locked up? Empty and cold? Sad and lonely? Pissed off and hating the world?

Maybe Nightingale could help her. Night frequented the Astral plane but the only way for Teari to get there was to sleep. She lay on the floor, in the far corner, hidden by the disheveled room, and closed her eyes.

SOUL SEARCHING

NOAH

"SHE WAS ALREADY DEAD," JED SHOUTED. "I DIDN'T KILL her, you all did!" He pointed at Skeele and Tukka.

Skeele ran around the bar, headed for Jed. "I didn't kill her," he growled. "I'd never kill her."

"Who killed what?" Noah's voice pierced the room. He appeared in front of Jed. Protectively. "You won't kill my man, Jeddio."

Skeele paused as best he could. It was hard to stop the killing motion of a Hellion, but he managed. Then he pointed to the bar. "Meg," was all Skeele said.

If a ghost could pale, Noah did. "No. No no no no no." He ran toward Meg. "What happened?"

"She just poofed into the room at my feet all stabbed up," Skeele said. "We tried blood. Jed used some bullshit spell that burned her face."

"She took a breath!" Jed thrust his hands toward Meg's body. "You saw it! We all saw it. The spell was working."

"It was not working," Skeele shouted back, muscles tense.

Noah held up his hands. "Just shut up. Both of you." He touched Meg's face, brushing off the burnt skin. If she's dead or in between, she might be in the Astral. Noah placed both palms on each side of Meg's head and closed his eyes. His image wavered as he searched the Astral plane for Meg. If she were there, it might mean they could get her back into her body.

Noah searched. He searched and searched and searched. He looked between every shadow of the void of the Astral but found nothing. The Astral was infinite, but there were places that he and Nightingale had created. Places that a wandering Meg might find familiar. He searched for them. A red tree by a stream. A kaleidoscope of stars above a hilltop. A hot tub at the top of a snowy mountain. Each place he visited tore at his gut. The memories of Nightingale were strong, and even stronger was the knowledge that he'd never get to spend time with her here again. Noah tried to push thoughts of Nightingale out of his mind. But memories are a spiral of emotion. It was a battle Noah barely won.

He felt a coldness surround him. A familiar coldness. Clea was nearby. Noah scanned the Astral shouting for Meg one last time. There was nothing. He had to go back. He had to go face Clea and tell her that Meg was nowhere to be found.

————

"Oh child," Clea's voice was full of sorrow. Her ruby red lips pinched together. Everyone stared at her. "It seems this curse is familial. We lose children too often here."

Clea knew about loss. Lucifer had lost Clea then Clea had lost Meg to the Earthen plane in an attempt to save her. Meg had lost her own child before it had ever been born. Clea and Megs reunion was bound to be ended soon enough. It was all a vicious circle in this bloodline. Clea could see some of the future, with visions and omens, nothing she'd seen ever ended well.

"We have to do something," Noah said, moving his hands away

from Meg's head. He didn't know what to say. At least Meg was here. At least they didn't have to search for her bones like Gabriel searched for twenty-five years for Clea's. Noah knew the story. At least they had a tiny bit of closure, seeing her here, like this.

"Have you tried everything to save her?" Clea asked, her image wavering, nearly transparent.

"We tried blood," Skeele said.

"I had a spell and some Angel grace," Jed began collecting his items and placing them in his backpack.

"Angel grace?" Noah asked.

Jed nodded. "It didn't work." He pinched the vial between his fingers and held it up to the light before placing it in his bag.

Angel grace might not have worked, but they had an actual Angel in the castle.

"I'll be right back," Noah said, just before he disappeared. "Don't touch her," his voice echoed throughout the Hellion lair.

Love, Death, and Antidepressants

Forcing oneself to dream is never easy. Teari wasn't sure how long she lay on the floor; there wasn't sunlight drifting across a window to give her an estimate of the passing time, there were no clocks, she heard no footsteps in the hallway outside her door. Her eyes felt gritty and her eyelids restless. Her body didn't want to sleep, and her mind was a flurry of coercive thoughts as she tried her best to convince herself that she was tired. When she finally drifted off to sleep, her dreams were nightmares–they had been since she lost her hands. The fast-zombies forever chased her. Their snapping jaws and gnarled teeth threatened to bite the few limbs she had left. Sparrow was there and he was nothing she remembered. He bit her over and over again. He didn't hold back; he didn't recognize her as the healer and Legion guard who had fought by his side, who had once desired him. Nightingale didn't save her. She didn't show up and interrupt the nightmares like she used to. There was only radio silence from the Astral.

Teari woke a few hours later. Her shoulders ached, her wings ached, and her wounds had scabbed over again leaving a crust over the incision scars where the doctors on the Earthen plane had done their best to stitch her back together. It wasn't their fault that her arms looked like Frankenstein. They were doing the best they could. She didn't forget that if the group of them hadn't encountered the National Guard in Pennsylvania, she'd surely be dead, and her soul lost. Teari forced herself to thank her lucky stars every day, but it felt like a lie. She didn't feel lucky and most days, she'd wished she'd just died on the Earthen plane instead of living like this.

A single tear slid down her cheek. If Nightingale wasn't in the Astral, where was she? Teari knew she'd been gone from the Seven Kingdoms of Heaven for weeks. Without a word and unable to reach Gabriel or anyone else, she was certain Nightingale would come looking for answers in her dreams. But she didn't. And Teari wasn't sure what that meant.

Meg was keeping something from her. They all were.

"Teari?" a familiar voice asked.

She didn't hear a door open so it could only be Noah. He was a thing of the Astral but tethered to Meg's soul by lifelong friendship and sacrifice. It was hard to remember with his boyish good looks and habit for pranks and dirty jokes.

"What?" Teari asked from the cover she currently occupied, unmoving; not giving Noah an idea of where she was.

"I need your help." Furniture scraped across the tile floor as he followed her voice. "What the heck happened in here? It's a mess."

"Nothing." Teari rolled onto her back and stared at the ceiling. She blew a small white feather off her face. "Can you just go away?"

"Nope." Noah appeared over Teari. "We got a problem downstairs. The biggest of problems."

"Meg ordered me not to leave this room," Teari reminded him. "So I'm going to stay here." Teari rested her forearms on her head but moved them immediately. It was hard to get comfortable in any position.

"Yeah, about that," he reached down and grabbed Teari's upper arms, tugging her to stand. "You want one of the prosthetics?"

"I'm not going anywhere," Teari said as she stood. Her body was limp, lacking muscle tone like a doll.

Noah was already opening her door.

"I don't like the prosthetics." She waved her arms. "They're uncomfortable."

"Then leave them. Come on." Noah tugged at her shirt. "Meg's in trouble."

"Meg's always in trouble," Teari mumbled.

"You're not wrong." Noah swung the door open and dragged Teari into the hallway. "But right now she's dying, and we need help."

"How much dying?" Teari added air quotes when she said dying. Meg was always in some kind of trouble, her life always teetering on the edge of an early death. Not much surprised Teari anymore when it came to Meg.

It annoyed Noah when he shouted, "She's bleeding out in the Hellion lair! I could see her heart." He paused. "I mean, at least I know she has a heart now." His eyebrows rose in realization.

"Shit," Teari ran out the door, disoriented in the dark hallways of the castle and began running in the wrong direction. Noah righted her with a hard pull in the correct direction and led her down the stairwell and hallways to the lair.

Noah and Teari burst through the door of the lair. Teari ran to Meg's side. It didn't look good. It didn't look good at all. The air dripped with a metallic odor. There was so much blood. And the remnants of a spell. Teari brushed the sand away and destroyed the runes surrounding Meg's body.

Jed shouted in protest, but no one paid attention to what he was saying.

Skeele filled her in on what they'd tried. "Can you do something?" he asked.

Teari rested her arm on Meg's chest, searching for a sign of life. "I can't do what I used to." She bit her lip, wishing she had hands. After all her years of healing, she had never felt so useless. She couldn't do a thing without her healing magic.

"Have you tried giving her fresh blood?" Teari asked.

Skeele's back went straight. Teari would have to be blind to miss his reaction.

"Did she fix Sparrow?" Teari asked. "His blood would be the best option. They have a bond."

"Sparrow is gone," Skeele said. "He's out of the picture."

Teari frowned. "Gone?"

Skeele motioned to the sky. "I'm assuming he went home."

"Crap." Teari stepped away from the bar and paced for a moment. She looked at everyone, studying them. Jed wouldn't do. Even with his mixed heritage, Tukka was unhinged at the moment. Her eyes paused on Skeele, the only one in the room who was semi-calm, but Teari could tell under his skin he was ready to lose it. The worry on his face was different; deeper than the worry of a bystander.

"What are you?" she asked, looking at Skeele. She waved her nubbed arms in a flurry. "Who are you to her? There's a reason you're so upset that she's dying right now. There's something between you two?"

He cleared his throat and reset his demeanor. "Hellion First Command."

Teari knew the First Command was the closest to the leader of Hell. There was a bond. Duty and sacrifice demanded it. Even if Meg and Skeele never admitted it to each other. No matter how weak the bond might be, it would work the best. Without Sparrow, Meg was only tethered to Noah, and being a spirit of the Astral, he didn't have blood.

"Your blood will do." Teari pointed at him with the nub of her right arm. "Give her your blood. Right now. Before she's gone forever."

Blood Letting

Skeele

He knew what fresh blood would do to Meg. The lust, the lack of control. He'd seen it at the Vermont cabin. It wasn't safe to give her fresh blood with everyone watching. People talked and it was bad enough she didn't have wings; that fact brought enough rumors. He didn't trust those in this room not to spread the image of Meg high on fresh blood. The new recruits were probably already spreading rumors. Skeele knew they'd reach the Deacons soon, and they'd start meddling.

Skeele knew it was Sparrow who did this. Meg wouldn't get close enough to anyone else. She was dangerous to herself and others, but she kept her distance. She always kept her distance. There was a time when Skeele respected Sparrow, learned from him, grew into the Hellion he was today. But Skeele swore on the throne of Hell that he'd kill Sparrow if he ever saw him again. It was the only right thing to do. Sparrow deserved nothing more than death after what he'd done to Meg. She hated the Hellions, but she forgot Sparrow was one of them. That or she did her best to ignore it. He wasn't so special.

Skeele carried Meg out of the Hellion lair. She weighed nothing, a feather in his arms. The others didn't follow. They saw the time he spent with her during the months following her fall from the sky. It was Meg's room, but he had a space to sit and watch and protect. He had a chair that no one else sat in. But he never thought he'd be returning to it so quickly.

Skeele took Meg to her bedroom. He kicked open the door, entered, and set her gently on the bed. He turned and grabbed the chair Meg had used many times to lock him and the other Hellions out. He closed the door, locked it, and propped the chair against the handle. He couldn't risk anyone coming in to see this. And if she didn't make it, he wasn't sure he'd be leaving the room at all. It was his duty to protect and serve her throne. Yet, here she was, dead as a doornail under his watch. There was no going back if he couldn't fix this.

Skeele grabbed his blade from the holster at his thigh. As he walked, he held his right arm up and sliced across the soft, inner skin. Blood came quickly. He kneeled and held his bleeding wrist over Meg's mouth.

"Please work," he begged with a whisper. *She isn't supposed to die here*, he reminded himself.

Blood pooled in her mouth. Skeele felt stiff lips on his skin, but it wasn't like before; there was no firm tone to her lips, no draw from her mouth. No aggressive sucking, moans in her throat, or eyelids twitching in haste. None of that. She was simply there as he bled into her.

When the drops stopped, he pulled away. The blood slowly disappeared down her throat. Skeele felt a spec of hope since it didn't pour down her chin, wasted like the bagged blood in the lair. His gaze scanned her closely, waiting. Finally, he moved away from the bed, took the club chair from the far side of the room, and dragged it closer. He sat, elbows on his knees, fingers threaded together in worry. He waited.

———

Meg's chest rose. It was faint but visible in the fading light of Hellsky. Skeele moved closer. He pressed two fingers to her neck and felt a faint pulse. He grabbed his blade, sliced his wrist again, and rested it over her mouth. She didn't move. Didn't suck. But, her skin changed from pale deathly white to the slightest tinge of pink. When the blood stopped dripping, he licked the cut to close it.

Skeele examined her wounds. He'd been afraid to move her much when he carried her back to the room, but now that there were signs of life, he needed to care for her. He moved her limp arms out of her leather jacket, her head flopping to the side as he turned her. He ran his finger over the stab wound on her arm. It still looked fresh, but it wasn't dripping or oozing like before. It was healing. Next, he ripped the neck of Meg's shirt all the way to the bottom hem and pushed the fabric aside. He inspected the stab wounds to her stomach, his hand smoothing over the skin of her abdomen. They were gone. Just soft, delicate skin with a spattering of tattoos. Skeele's eyes moved to the wound over her heart. It was deep still. He could see the splintered bone; the red flesh of her heart was stitching itself together. The tattoo of the sparrow in flight was torn. *Good*, he thought. He wanted to cut off that tattoo. The torn skin through the center of it wasn't enough. He never wanted to see or hear the word Sparrow again. It didn't deserve to be on her skin in any form.

Skeele glanced down her legs. There was more blood. He unbuttoned Meg's leather pants and dragged them down. One large gash to her thigh was bright red and glistening, longer than his hand. If he knew anything, that must've hurt like a bitch.

Skeele collected the bloody clothes and threw them in the corner. He went to her bathroom to find towels and soap before setting them on the countertop and starting the tub. He couldn't let her sit in blood. It was bad enough that she'd sat in it for this long.

He did his best to move her gently off the bed. He slid one arm under her shoulders, another under her knees. Congealed blood spread across his arms. If Meg knew what was happening, she didn't let him know. Her eyes were still closed, her breaths were just as shallow as when he watched her take the last one in the Hellion lair. Skeele grabbed a washcloth and wiped the dirt and blood off Meg's face. He dampened her hair before grabbing shampoo from the shower and massaging it into the blood-soaked strands. He used the washcloth to rub the crusted blood off her shoulder. His thick fingers smoothed over her inked skin. When he was done cleaning her skin and her wounds, the bathwater was red. He drained it and refilled the tub with fresh water to rinse her.

Skeele changed the bloody sheets on the bed and searched for clothing from the closet. It was all jeans and leather and small. Skeele left the closet and went to the club chair he'd sat in for so many weeks waiting for her to heal the last time. He pulled the chair away from the wall and grabbed the leather bag that was shoved behind it. He'd needed clean clothes before when he refused to leave her side. Noah had brought him random clothing from his quarters. He chose a large button-down flannel. It wasn't what Meg typically wore but it was clean, and it would keep her warm and give him easy access to her wounds. He dried her and moved her to the bed, then dressed her in his giant shirt.

After, Skeele sat on the chair, his large hands gripping the armrests and he hated being here again. Watching, waiting, praying that she'd wake up. At least she wouldn't wake covered in death. If she woke at all.

———

THE DAYS and nights went on. Skeele bled for Meg. He poured himself into her until he was pale and weak and couldn't take it anymore. A Hellion only had so much blood. On the fifth night, he walked to the balcony, opened the doors, and stepped out into the moonlight. He didn't want to leave her alone, but he needed to feed himself. Skeele jumped off the balcony and spread his wings. His glide was uneven, his muscles weak and body drained.

Skeele knew he wasn't supposed to feed off the newly dead souls. They needed a chance to get to a Safe House, to repent. If he upset the balance, the Deacons would want justice. He couldn't wait. He couldn't hunt and he couldn't let the others know that he'd left Meg alone.

He found a house where newcomers were hiding. They didn't expect him. No one expects a Hellion. He crashed through the door and ate them just like the monster Meg had always accused him of being. It was hard to stop and not move on to another house. That's what a shit ton of fresh blood did to a Hellion, made them absolutely feral and uncontrollable. When Skeele's stomach was full, he walked out of the house, went to the sky, and returned to Meg's side. He didn't even leave bones behind.

———

SKEELE REMINDED himself that the last time Meg nearly died, she'd laid in that bed for months while her body healed and her bones mended. Patience was a virtue; it was just that his was wearing thin and he wasn't very virtuous to begin with. He had left Tukka, Chel, and Klaus to train the Hellion new recruits and take care of the last of the fast-dead.

There was a knock on the door. Skeele stood and walked to it. He moved the chair that held the knob, unlocked it, and opened the door.

Noah was there. "Is she still alive?" Noah asked.

"Yes." Skeele cracked the door open further so Noah could see the color that had returned to her cheeks and shallow breaths that had started days ago. Surprised that Noah didn't simply apparate into the room like he typically did. The ghost-man was in a bad way. Ever since witnessing Nightingale's death, Noah hadn't been the same. He never smiled. He stopped with the jokes. It was like he'd died that day as well.

"Has she opened her eyes?" Noah asked.

Skeele shook his head no.

———

Skeele had been sitting in the chair for days, waiting for her to wake. He was tired. Dead tired. After all his blood, she hadn't budged. No muscle tics, no noise from her throat, no twitches from under her closed eyelids. It wasn't looking good. Her breaths were shallow and far between and the wound over her heart was taking a long time to heal. Skeele reminded himself that she'd lost a lot of blood. He was sure the Hellions were cleaning it off the bar for days. And then there was that spell Jed had tried; who knows what that shit had done to her? Skeele cracked his knuckles as he thought about the next step.

The bed was enormous enough. And he was confident she would never know. He moved to the other side and lay down next to her. He sliced his left wrist the long way this time and deeper than ever before. He turned and laid it against her mouth and closed his eyes. If he never woke, at least he tried to save her.

Holding out for a Hero

I dream of Sparrow. My mind is fuzzy and foggy. My limbs feel like they're filled with cement. My eyes are so heavy I can't find the strength to open them. Everything I do is in slow motion. But Sparrow's here, finally. It took long enough. I can smell him, that darkness that led me to him on the Earthen plane. Wood smoke and cigars and burning embers. It seems my realm permeates from him.

Sparrow's wrist is against my mouth. His warm body is finally back in my bed. I've been waiting for this for a long time. I grip his arm, moving from the wrist to bite him along his bicep. He tastes good. Better than pancakes and Twinkies and orange soda.

I push him over onto his back and snuggle close, my lips moving to his neck. He tips his head away, one arm gripping me tight against him. I rub against his hard, muscled body. I want him to bite me. But he won't put his mouth on me, even when I try to move his face with heavy arms that feel like stone. Maybe it's been too long for him. Maybe he's holding back. I don't care. I'll take from him what I want. It's only fair. I lost myself in his memory for so long. It's my turn now. My turn to take what I am owed.

It takes a lot of effort, but I slide my leg over his, my inner thigh resting against his groin. I want to move the rest of my body. I can't find the strength. The blood tastes too good. I can't take my lips off his neck. I moan against his throat. His arm tightens on my waist. Fingertips brush the sensitive skin under my ass. I want to say things to him. I want to tell him I missed him. I want to whisper dirty words in his ear. I want to lick and taste the parts of his body I've been denied all this time. I force my arm to move, tugging, dragging his shirt up. Skin on skin never felt so good.

A deep growl rumbles in his chest.

A thunderstorm drowns out the noise in my room. The sharp crack of thunder. The pelting of rain. I can't make out his words. He's saying something.

"I can't hear you," I whisper in his ear. Biting, tugging, and sucking.

Sparrow's leg moves against mine and I feel the bulge in his pants. I move my hand against his face to turn him. He won't look at me. He must be holding back. Sparrow's always been like that. Chivalrous. Must be the last of his grace. Wait... did his grace come back? I try to open my heavy eyelids, but I can't. They feel so heavy, glued shut. I slide against him, over him. Pushing his clothing away.

––––––

SKEELE

During the night, Meg came alive. She writhed over him; her hips pressing against him, her hands rubbing, her hot mouth feeding greedily. Skeele looked away. She had the worst bloodlust he'd ever seen in his life. Skeele was barely holding on. He gripped the side of the bed frame and squeezed until the wood cracked. He was surprised he had any strength since Meg drained him like a leech.

Whispering in Hellspeak, a language Meg wasn't fluent in, the heavy downpour outside drowned out his words. She'd never know what he'd said. That was probably a good thing.

This was worse than anything he'd imagined. She was hellfire in his arms. Untamed. Wild. Insatiable. She held nothing back, like an animal in heat.

He had to slow her down. Skeele was demon bred, Hellion trained. He could tear her apart if he lost control. He wasn't totally certain she wouldn't do the same to him. She had taken Lucifer's place, but she still looked to be very much human. Small and delicate, even if her smart mouth led one to believe otherwise. She wasn't though, he'd seen her change. And he had entered this room fully aware that he may never exit.

Skeele gripped Meg's hips and rolled the both of them until she was under him. He held her wandering hands against the mattress and ran the tip of his nose along the column of her neck.

"Do it," Meg begged. "I like it. It feels so good." Her hips pushed up against his. "Fuck me while you do it."

Skeele knew she was bare, and he could feel the heat that radiated off her naked body through his clothing.

"Open your eyes," Skeele said, strain in his voice.

Meg shook her head slowly. "I can't. They're too heavy. I'm too tired. Do it, Sparrow. I've waited so long."

Skeele growled and ran his tongue along her neck. "Go back to sleep," he begged.

"I can't," Meg said, pushing her bare breasts against him. "I need you first."

Skeele nipped at her neck. He wouldn't risk taking her blood. He knew that she'd slay him the moment she woke fully and realized what she'd done. The look of shock on her face after the Vermont cabin was forever burned in his brain. Meg felt nothing for him. Wanted nothing from him. Was disgusted by him. That made it easier. At least he'd done his due diligence to protect the throne. That was his fate, his destiny. They bred him for it. He was alive to do nothing more. He fulfilled that promise.

Meg writhed underneath his body. The shirt he'd put on her became tangled and twisted behind her back. She was warm, her stab wounds nearly healed, her skin a bright pink. He moved and looked down between their chests. The stab wound over her heart was still open. At least the bone was healing but he was worried that it was still soft, that his weight could cause more damage. He didn't want to injure her further. Skeele released Meg's hands and moved down her body. It was hard to control himself. If this was going to be the last of his days alive, he wanted to be just as greedy as Meg.

But he couldn't. He knew better. She had to recover so she could set things straight in her realm. No one was going to know what to do with an Angel without hands, and whatever was hiding in that room next door with Jed and Shay. They couldn't be left with an empty throne and the threat of the Seven Kingdoms of Heaven looking for retribution from the Fast-Zombie War.

Skeele didn't flip Meg over and mount her like a wild beast. Instead, he grabbed her hands with one of his, preventing her from finding the horns on his head. He slid further down her body to the vee of her thighs. He would not satisfy his own need, but his mouth would hers.

JED & SHAY

Shay paced the room holding baby Thrush. Her arms rocked him quicker than she was comfortable with. Shay thought babies were fragile things that should be handled gently, but Thrush was only calm when he was rocked at a rapid pace. It worried Shay, that she might give him brain damage or that he might develop some strange fondness for being shaken when he got older. Shay tried not to think too deeply about it. The kid had barely survived being eaten during the Fast-Zombie war. Whatever methods she used to soothe him had to be better than what he experienced during that ordeal.

It had been weeks since they left the child in Shay and Jed's care. Every night they still checked his skin from head to toe for bite marks. They'd found none, of course. Only soft baby skin and the occasional diaper rash.

Shay paced near the door, waiting for Jed to return. She tiptoed around the markings on the floor, careful not to disturb the charcoal marks or piles of salt. Jed had protected them all for this long, she wasn't about to put them at risk. It wasn't that long ago that Shay had no idea that Heaven and Hell truly existed. Her prepper parents worshipped other books, like the Farmer's Almanac. Not so much the bible or churches.

Shay and Jed crossed paths in the Midwest. Jed was traveling to California to investigate the zombie horde that was moving like herded cattle. And Shay was simply surviving the apocalypse just like her dad prepared her to do.

Shay paused when she heard shouting from another area of the castle. She had a strong urge to leave the room and find Jed. She looked at the dark-haired baby boy in her arms and remembered her promise. She couldn't leave the room, she could only hope that Jed would come back in one piece.

Shay glanced at the bottles drying near the bathroom sink. Thrush didn't want anything to do with the formula Noah brought. They'd tried everything. Every milk. Cow, goat, sheep, almond and coconut. Thrush didn't want any of it and what he did take, he puked up not long afterward. Shay's clothes were perpetually stained. Jed entered the splash zone, but he usually had towels ready to soak up the baby vomit. Thrush's cheeks were slowly shrinking in size, dark blue circles had started under his eyes. The kid wasn't necessarily sick, but from everything Shay had read, Thrush was borderline malnourished. If this kept on, he'd be completely malnourished quickly.

Noah was anxious about Thrush not eating. He spent most of

his time finding something for his son to eat. They'd tried jars of baby food and infant cereals. Thrush would eat it, but it wasn't enough. He needed the milk for a few more months at least.

Shay saw shadows under the door. Someone was outside the bedroom. There was whispering, tapping, and then the door handle turned. Shay moved to the far side of the room, reaching for the spell cast shotgun with runes carved into the metal barrel.

The door opened.

Shay let out a sigh of relief as Jed stepped in and latched the door behind him. He leaned his back against the solid wood door and took a deep breath.

"Is she dead?" Shay asked.

Jed nodded.

"Shit." Thrush stirred in Shay's arms. She rocked the baby again. "What do we do?"

Jed made a face as he skirted the markings on the floor to get closer to Shay.

"She might come back to life. Skeele is going to try something."

"I don't think I want to know."

"It's probably better you don't. These people are freaks."

Shay tipped her head to her shoulder, a motion that told him they might not be so freaky. Shay had seen worse in humanity. Unfortunately.

Thrush started crying. Jed made a bottle of the most recent formula Noah had brought them. He passed it to Shay. Thrush pushed the nipple out of his mouth and gagged on the baby formula. Shay set the bottle down and shifted Thrush in her arms.

Tears started streaming down her face. "This kid is going to starve to death." Shay wiped at her face. "One day we are going to wake up and he's going to be lifeless in his crib."

Shay was crying, Thrush was crying.

Jed stood nearby feeling utterly useless. He couldn't save Meg and he was sucking at keeping this kid alive.

Thrush started nuzzling Shay's chest, leaving wet marks on her shirt.

"There's one thing we haven't tried," Jed said, reaching for his notebook of spells and magic. He flipped the pages.

Shay looked down at the baby and realized what he was talking about. "I don't think so."

"Why not?" Jed asked. "It's natural."

"I'm not his mother."

"You don't need to be his mother. Wet nurses rarely are."

"I've never done this before."

"It can't be that hard." Jed paused on a page and tapped his finger on the paper. "I think I found something that will work."

"Don't you need my consent or something."

"This isn't permanent." Jed paused. "You don't want to try?"

Thrush whimpered in frustration, his little arms and legs were limp.

Shay couldn't watch him fade before their eyes. They'd both promised to look after this baby. "Just do it."

Jed's fingers danced in rhythmic spell casting; he chanted ancient words from his book.

Shay's chest started to feel warm and full. She looked down to see wet marks where her bra was.

"Okay, I think it's done," Jed said as he closed his notebook and knelt near Shay. "Do you want help?"

"Have you done this before?" Shay asked, tears dripping down her cheeks. This felt strange and weird and she wasn't prepared to hand over so much of herself.

"No. But that doesn't mean I'm of no help." Jed brushed his shaggy blonde hair away from his eyes. He set a hand on her knee.

Shay lifted her shirt and pushed her bra aside. She'd never breastfed a baby before, but she'd learned about it in her parent's survival books. There were plenty of chapters on delivering babies and placentas and keeping children alive.

Thrush latched on and ate, and for the first time in weeks he didn't cry or vomit. He simply ate until the tears on his cheeks dried to salt and he fell asleep making faint snoring sounds.

"Was it bad?" Jed asked, moving pillows behind Shay's back so she could get comfortable.

"It wasn't terrible." Shay scooted down in the bed until Thrush was lying flat and she could release him. She looked at Jed. "This is way more than what I signed up for."

"But look at all the fun we're having. I told you there would never be a dull moment with Meg involved." Jed crossed his arms on the bed and leaned forward from his sitting position on the floor. He and Shay were almost nose to nose.

"You should have warned me in Montana that if I followed you, I'd be stepping into some mega shit." Shay pursed her lips.

Jed smiled. "What better have you got to do? Kill zombies and pick dumpsters for food?"

"I didn't get my food from dumpsters. I grew it and hunted for it."

"Okay. But had you stayed, you would have never experienced this shit show. You'd be so bored."

"I wouldn't be lactating to feed an angel ghost baby hybrid." She smoothed Thrush's hair away from his eyes and smiled, relieved that the baby had finally eaten something and kept it down.

"True."

Shay sighed, tired from the long day and the tears. She wanted nothing more than to sleep a few uninterrupted hours, but they needed to talk. "Tell me what happened downstairs."

Jed made a face, but he told her and then they planned, just in case Meg never woke up. What good was life on the run without a plan? Jed and Shay had been running their whole lives, just in different directions until that abandoned gas station in Montana. Jed ran from the Archangels and Demons who wanted to extinguish all Nephilim. Shay ran from a family who taught her to survive, who taught her to never forget, and taught her to never trust. Never trust a man, a woman, family. Because when the sun went down or the doors were closed, the truth would always come out when they thought nobody was watching.

––––––

MEG

We go on for days. Feeding. Fucking. Just like animals. Just like creatures of Hell. There's not much thinking, just primitive need. And if I had a rational thought during it all, I'd think I wound up exactly where I belonged.

Between the intimate moments, I have nightmares of dropping out of the sky, nightmares of Hellions coming for me, nightmares of zombies eating babies. But Sparrow wakes me from them. He holds me close and tucks my hair away from my face, whispering sweet nothings into the night. He protects me just like he's always wanted. I have never been more content. This is all I have ever wanted. Me and Sparrow. Sparrow and me. Being invincible together. Even if we never leave the bedroom. If we never have another adventure together, at least I have the memories of all those times we traipsed across each plane trying to figure out who we really were. I could stay forever locked in this bedroom with him. My eyelids are too heavy to lift. That's okay. I know what he looks like; the edges and planes of his body, the touch of his fingertips. I know. I'll never forget because when I'm with Sparrow it feels too good to be true.

––––––

I STRETCH, waking to the sound of gentle chirps and a soft whistle. I roll, satin sheets pulling away from my body. I open my eyes and blink a dozen times to focus. Skeele is sitting by the balcony, his back to me. He's feeding the birds like Noah used to do before everything went to shit. I smile at the familiar *tap, tap, tap* of heavy sunflower seeds bouncing on the railing.

It doesn't take me long to realize I'm naked except for an unbuttoned flannel that's falling off my shoulders. I look down and see a bright pink scar over my heart. I pull the sheets up and cover myself. Laying back, I stare at the ceiling and try to remember what happened.

Skeele stands and stretches, his shoulders slump. He looks pale and moves slowly as he closes and locks the balcony doors. He turns to me, face thin and gaunt, and startles. "You're awake," he says as he rubs a hand over his bare head and horns.

I nod, my mouth feeling like it's filled with cotton and sand. I'm so thirsty. My eyes feel dry and heavy like I spent the night in a smoke-filled bar. If I did, this is the worst hangover ever.

"I'll get Noah," he says, walking out of the room.

Noah comes bearing gifts. A Big Gulp sized orange soda, pizza, and BBQ wings. "Sleeping beauty awakens," he says.

I reach for the soda. Noah passes it to me, and I drink greedily.

"What happened?" I ask.

Noah sits. "You don't know?"

I close my eyes and the scenes flash through my mind. "I fed Sparrow a vial of Teari's blood. He changed. He went back to his kingdom." My face pinches. "He stabbed me." My fingers touch the scar on my chest, my stomach, my leg, and arm. I open my eyes. "He tried to kill me." I groan.

Every jab of his dagger flashes before my eyes. I want to scream. I pinch my eyes closed and press my fingertips over the corners of my eyes to stop the tears. I can't cry. I won't cry for him.

Every memory of me and Sparrow dies. Every wish to have him at my side dies. Every song, every feather, every Snowy Owl word... it's all dead to me. Forever. I thought Sparrow was different. We were connected. He was the only one who showed me love and caring and truth. He was my halleluiah, heroin, and reason to breathe. He turned out to be no better than Jim. He is no better than those Hellions from my grandfather's time. No better than the Archangels who locked me up in Babylon and whipped me.

It hurts. Worse than anything. Worse than Jim. Worse than John Lewis. Worse than that day the Hellions came for me on the Earthen plane. My eyes burn. My chest throbs. I want to puke.

Noah watches me, silent. I remind myself that I'm not the only one who has lost someone I love in all of this. It doesn't work. Sorrow is a slippery slope. I can't stop myself from sliding down. It's been so long since I felt like this. Empty. Dead inside. The last time I felt like this we were running from the dead and I didn't know who I was. I stopped in the middle of the road as a horde approached, ready to end it all. It would have been easy back then. There was so much less to think about. Fewer people involved. I rub my face, surprised that there are no tears. I can't do this anymore.

I button my shirt, throw the covers back, and stand; unsteady on weak legs. I move to the balcony, the walk feeling twice as long as I remember.

"What are you doing, Meg?" Noah asks.

I climb up on the railing, my knees wobbly and arms aching.

"Meg..." there's worry in his voice. But Noah hasn't ever stopped me from doing things. He's the best kind of friend. He lets me make my mistakes and then never lets me forget them.

"Skeele was right," I say. Bird seed crunches under my feet. A sunflower seed peeks out from under the curve of my pinky-toe. It's a long way down. "I need wings. Because I'm going to fly my ass to Heaven and put Sparrow in a fucking grave."

I jump.

Do The Thing
You Fear

I spread my arms, tip forward, and... drop like a sack of shit. The wings don't pop out of my back, there's not even an itch. The familiar scorched grassy lawn gets closer and closer to my face. My flannel shirt billows in the wind.

Noah appears on the lawn, waiting, arms crossed. He looks up at me, unimpressed. I get a sickening feeling deep in my gut. This is going to hurt. Shit. I should *poof* myself somewhere, but as much as I want to live, I want to punish myself for being so stupid. There is nothing better than punishment. Just ask John Lewis. There is nothing better than pain. Just ask everyone. Pain is a lesson in never forgetting. Pain will break every single bone in my body for the second time the moment I hit pay dirt below. If only my wings would break out of my back. If only I could soar like a Snowy Owl on a dark night, the frozen air ruffling my feathers, crystals of snow glistening in the moonlight.

I am not a Snowy Owl. I am not an Angel. I am merely an embodiment of Lucifer. I make eye contact with Noah. He's smirking. What a jerk. Nothing like a best friend to be smiling before you eat dirt.

Just before I'm about to hit the ground, strong arms wrap around my waist and tug up. Warmth wraps around my back. I'm finally flying but it's by no means of my own. From my periphery I see the bat-like wings of a Hellion.

A familiar voice in my ear. "You could have put some underwear on so the entire castle didn't have to see your bare ass."

He's flying fast. Air rushes into my mouth and I can't talk back. I can barely breathe. I ignore the tears in the corners of my eyes and let the wind blow them away.

Skeele flies away from the burning caves, over treetops and small towns. He finally lands on a single lane road next to a little river dotted with boulders. His heavy boots echo on the steel deck bridge. My bare feet land softly as Skeele sets me down as if I'm made of glass.

Skeele paces away from me. He's tense, his Hellion gear haphazardly hanging on his body. He looks like he's lost a lot of weight since before Sparrow tried to kill me.

"What is wrong with you?" I prod him.

"You were going to kill yourself? After everything you went through?" Skeele is shouting at me. He's lost his cool. It's completely gone. Not that I've ever known a Hellion to have a cool factor, but Skeele is approaching another level right now.

"How dare you assume," I take a step closer. "I was trying to get my wings!" I shout.

"I thought you gave up on that goal?" Skeele shouts back. "Or at least you should have waited until you'd fully healed."

"Don't tell me what to do," I step forward again and point at his chest. "Of all people, you threw me into the sky for the exact same reason. You tossed me so far up into Hellsky I almost puked."

"Yeah, but I gave you time to recover from nearly dying. There was a difference." He tips his head, focusing on a sound in the forest. One hand settles on his blade.

I grab for mine but there's nothing there. Just bare skin. My naked thighs aren't protection against much. Shit.

"Is it a fast one?" I ask, feeling unprepared.

Dark eyes settle on me. "We killed them all. Every one we could find. The portals are still down, and word is that the Earthen plane is rebuilding." He moves his hands to his hips and glares down at me. "It was just a deer or something."

"Fine. Take me home," I order.

"No," his eyes are dark fire.

I close my eyes ready to *poof*, but I go nowhere. Damn. My muscles feel weary, my throat dry. I'm too weak to travel at will. I hate when this happens.

"Take me home," I order, again.

"Not now," he backs away from me. "I'm not done," he says.

"I am the ruler of Hell. Do what I say." I rise up on my toes. It's the only way for me to get taller since I'm barefoot. I really should have thought about dressing for my adventure out the window.

Skeele laughs, sharp teeth gleaming white against his lips. "Don't threaten me," he warns. "Of all situations you're out here nearly naked and without a blade. What are you going to do, bite me?"

"I've done it before," I warn.

Skeele nods and smiles, it's an arrogant move. "I don't think you have it in you right now," he taunts.

I turn and walk away.

"Where ya going?" Skeele asks.

I rub my face and run my fingers through my hair. I look for a street sign or a mailbox to try to figure out where he brought me. I've been down here long enough that I recognize most roads that are close to the burning caves. But I'm not sure where we are right now. I'd remember a steel-deck bridge; there were a few near Gouverneur and they made your ears ring when you drove over them. I walk. I don't know what direction it is, north, south, east, or west but it's in the opposite direction of Skeele. Which is where I need to be headed right now before I do something stupid.

My throat is so dry. I lick my lips and try not to think about the food I left behind in my room. Poor Noah went through the effort to surprise me and I just left it there. I'd kill for a pizza right now. I step on a sharp rock and stumble. Rocks in the road never felt so sharp. But then, I've never gone traipsing around barefoot down here. Jim taught me better. Always be prepared. Always wear sturdy shoes, dry socks, and carry a few supplies in your pack because you never know. Jim's probably rolling over in his grave right now. Good for him. If anyone deserves to roll in their grave, it's him.

There are more skittering sounds in the tree line, leaves crushing and sticks snapping. It's hard to release the memories of the fast-dead running at me, ready to bite. I walk faster, my spine tingling in angst. I try to *poof* again. Nothing. Damn. I should've stayed in bed. I should've snuggled down into the soft mattress and piled blankets on top of me and ate pizza until my heart was content. I should've channeled a pig in mud and stayed put instead of throwing those blankets back and trying to force wings to appear out of my back. There are a lot of things I should've done, but regret is not my strong suit. I'm more of a carry on without compunction type of girl. How does one not regret leaving the house without shoes... or underwear.

I rub my neck; suddenly holding my head up feels challenging. My neck aches. My head fills with fog and I stumble. I step on another sharp rock in the road and go down. My hands hit first, grinding against the loose asphalt and tearing the skin of my palms. I throw my body to the side and land on a hip, trying to save the road-burn to my knees.

"Christ," Skeele's heavy footfalls come closer.

I close my eyes, my eyelids feeling heavy. Suddenly, I could care less about anything other than sleeping for a million years. I rest my head on the pavement and go.

———

THERE WAS a time when I would dream of ridiculous things. I'd dream of memories and fears and hopes and I always knew when

Nightingale was there, speaking to me through the dreams. You never realize how one person walking through dreams can mess with you, can help you remember that you're not alone, even in sleep. I miss it. She had a way of letting you know she was around, even when she was the farthest away. I've lost those moments though. Because Nightingale died. I watched her die. I watched one of the fast-dead bite a chunk out of her neck and then she bled out. I did nothing to save her. I've replayed it a million times in my head. I cut off Teari's arms, but I couldn't cut off Nightingale's head. Where would that leave us? An Angel without a head or an Angel without a body. Either way, it wouldn't have worked. How would she raise a baby being just a head? I guess her body could have grown back. But then, Teari's arms haven't grown back. So who knows what would have happened if I had chopped off her head. I have guilt from not experimenting with every possible way to save her. We could have sewn her head on another body and turned her into some Franken-stein-Angel-thing. I imagine she wouldn't have been too happy with that outcome. I'd be pissed if I woke up only to find my head sewn on twelve other men's body parts. Yuck.

Without Nightingale, I am left to my imagination as I sleep. I dream of fountains of blood. Chalices overflowing with thick red liquid. Orgies and naked Angels so attractive Michelangelo's David would blush. In my mind I know it's wicked, but it feels so good, it looks so good. There are no babies without mothers, no depressed Angels without hands, no Sparrow stabbing me to death, no Hellions with a mood. I could stay here forever and revel in the inde-cency of it all. It feels good here. I like it.

But... my legs are cold, and my ass is cold, and my throat is dry even though I've been drinking from the fountain like a horse.

I open my eyes and wait for my vision to clear. The blurriness takes a few moments to pass then I notice the roughhewn wooden walls and lack of furniture. I'm in a place that looks like the Hellion cabin in Vermont. It doesn't smell like Vermont though. It smells like an old town in winter. Like kerosene heaters and coffee and burning newspapers.

I roll to the side, find a blanket covering one knee, and throw it back over my legs and butt. I snuggle in and try to get comfortable again. But I get that feeling that I am not alone.

Someone is sitting in the room with me. I know that shadow. He's reading a book, using the window for light and the fireplace to warm his feet. I want to lash out at Skeele and tell him to get the fuck out of my space. I know better. Nightingale would have told me to chill the fuck out after terrorizing me in my dreams. And then she would have made me apologize to him. I do what she'd want, in her memory. It's the least I can do.

"I'm sorry," I say. "Okay. I'm sorry." I press my head into the shitty pillow I'm resting on.

"For what?" Skeele's voice is dull.

"I don't know. Whatever I did." I raise my hands then drop them onto the bed in frustration. "I've always done something."

"Usually." Skeele doesn't even put down his book. "There's a vial of blood on the nightstand. It might help."

"Okay." I should thank him. It's just, thanking someone when I don't want to is hard to do. I can't make the words come out of my mouth.

The sound of crisp paper flexing breaks the silence as he turns the page of his book. I can't look away from him, he looks like a freaking Ivy league scholar wearing black-ops gear. It gives me a feeling deep down in my stomach. I know, without a doubt, if something happens to me, Skeele will always be sitting in the room like that when I open my eyes again. No one has ever been there for me like that. No one.

"How long have I been here?" I ask.

Skeele shrugs. "A while."

"Hours?" I ask.

"Two days."

"Jesus Christ." I rub my face, turn, and reach for the vial of blood on the nightstand.

"You drinking that now?" Skeele asks, brows raised in exaggerated questioning.

I hesitate. "I think so."

He slaps his book closed and stands. "Drink it."

I twist the vial and down the thick liquid.

His heavy footsteps cross the room. "I'll be back," Skeele says as he leaves, slamming the door and locking it from the outside.

"Hey!" I shout. "Why did you lock me in here?"

"Because I can't take any more of your shit," he shouts through the door.

He has a point. I cap the vial and set it back on the nightstand before snuggling under the blankets. Warmth spreads from my throat to my gut to between my legs. Yeah, that's why Skeele left. We've been in a Hellion cabin before when the bloodlust was strong. I rub my legs, close my eyes, and imagine doing dirty deeds to someone, someone other than Sparrow, someone big and strong. Someone true and... real.

———

THE NEXT TIME I wake it's like the wicked thing that I am. My feet hit the floor before my vision clears. There were days when I slept fully clothed, boots and all already on, ready to wake and run. It's been a while. My bare feet stretch against the rough flooring of the cabin. I stand, taking the blanket with me and wrapping it around my waist to cover my legs. I feel disgusting, like I haven't showered in a week. My hair feels greasy, my skin coated in a film of... something.

"You ready to go now?" Skeele asks from the shadows near the fireplace. He waves his book. "I finished this a while ago. It's getting kind of boring listening to you snore."

"I don't snore," I snap.

Skeele chuckles as he stands. "I won't tell anyone you snore." He crosses the room and opens the door.

Poof.

I go back to my room at the castle. Skeele can find his own way back.

Nobody's Housewife

I've never been good at cleaning, but I clean my room like a good little housewife. Except, I'm nobody's housewife. So I guess I clean my room like a single lady. Except, I'm not a lady. I find a pile of ripped and bloody clothes in the corner of my room. There's a pile of bloody sheets as well. I make my bed and pick up a pair of shorts from the floor. Hm. I don't remember ever wearing these. I toss them in the laundry. I rearrange the bathroom. I take a shower and get dressed in dark jeans and a wide-neck, black T-shirt. I glance in the mirror and curse the bangs for a moment. My mind wanders back to the scene of the dead falling out of ceiling and killing Nightingale and Jack. My chest feels heavy, my eyes burn. I look away and swallow it down. Tears have never gotten me anything. They won't bring back my friends. They won't fix the fact that Sparrow is dead to me. They won't release Gabriel from his Heavenly cage or fix Teari. I rub my face until the sensation disappears.

After spending some time alone, I remember that I have a giant mess to deal with down the hall. Most important being the Angel-baby next door.

I leave my room, thankful that there are no moody Hellions waiting in the hallway for me. I knock on Jed's door and wait for him to open.

The door cracks slightly.

"Hey," I say.

"Wow," Jed opens the door further, relief washing over his face. "You're alive."

"Why wouldn't I be?" I ask.

He motions for me to come in. "Last time I saw you, it wasn't looking good." He nods to the bed. "Shay's asleep. It's been a rough night." Jed rubs his face. "The baby is teething."

I glance around the room and find Noah sitting by the crib. He waves one hand at me.

"This last week has been hell, Meg," Jed says, crossing the room to sit. "Thrush wants his mother. He cries a lot. It's heartbreaking."

I maneuver around the runes on the floor, being careful not to disturb the piles of sand and charcoal markings.

"Feeling better?" Noah asks.

I shrug. "I'm not really sure how I'm supposed to feel." I look at the baby in the crib. He looks just like Noah but has Nightingale's eyes. He looks smaller than I remember.

"Speaking of feelings," Jed says. "We can't stay locked up in this room forever. We haven't seen sunlight in weeks. We haven't had fresh air. When are you going to let us out of here?"

"It's not really safe to bring you all somewhere else." I tuck my hands in my pockets. "The Earthen plane is rebuilding. But Thrush can't go there." I shake my head, remembering my childhood. "I won't let him get lost and abused."

Noah's eyes flash to mine. He was there. He knows what I went through.

"Keep them here," Jed says. "Just keep us here, just not in this room forever."

At least Thrush could have his father nearby if he stayed in Hell.

The only problem would be making sure none of the Archangels from Heaven come looking for him.

"We need out of this room," Jed urges. It's the strain in his voice that makes me realize his clothes are rumpled and disheveled. Solitude isn't good for them.

"Okay." I pause for a moment to think. "There's plenty of abandoned homes here. We could find you all one."

"They'll need security," Noah warns.

"The runes work well." Jed points to the walls and door that he marked. "No one has come in. Not even a bug. They work well."

"You're going to do an entire house?" Noah asks.

Jed motions, nonchalant. "I've done it before. Do you know how hard it is to hide from Archangels and Demons on the Earthen plane? I've lived this long. I've been doing it since I was a kid. If anyone could rune a house, it's me." He crosses the room to his bag and opens it. "I'm going to need more charcoal, salt, and sand. Depending on the size of the house."

"Okay," I agree. "Okay. Me and Noah will go out later and look for something that's not too far away."

"I'll have to prep it before we all go there," Jed says, zipping his bag.

Noah glances at me and tips his head toward the door. We leave the room and I hear the soft scrapes of Jed fixing the charcoal runes on the threshold after the door closes.

"What about the Deacons?" Noah asks.

I smile. "I've always wanted to kill them. Maybe this is my time."

"Won't you upset some balance if you do that?" Noah asks.

"Nothing is balanced. The Seven Kingdoms of Heaven skew everything for their benefit. I'm not holding back because of the Deacons any longer."

———

Teari's room is dark. Really dark. It's calming. I've found the shadows are comforting these days. Or at least the shadows of my own home are. The shadows of a forest on the Earthen plane or a courthouse in Babylon will still make me want to shit my pants.

"Teari?" I whisper into the room.

"Go away," Teari says. Her voice is dismal, lifeless. Like she couldn't care less about much.

"Where are you?" I ask.

I hear furniture scrape across the floor. "Meg?" Teari asks.

"Yeah."

"There's a table lamp near the door. I can't switch it on since I don't have hands." Teari sounds depressed; there's no life in her voice.

I wave my arms in the darkness until I nearly knock over the lamp, then I steady it and click it on.

"Why are you sitting in the dark?" I ask.

"So I don't have to see what I lost," she replies, voice dull.

I open my mouth to say something, to compare, to let her know she's not alone. But it seems wrong. Instead, I say, "That sucks."

Her stumped arms crossed over bent knees. "Hi." She's leaning against the wall, her wings slumped and missing feathers. I am reminded of the time Nightingale molted and wonder if that's what Teari's is going through or if she's just depressed like a caged bird.

"What can I do?" I ask.

Teari shakes her head. "I don't know. I don't know anything anymore."

I sit on the edge of her bed. "You know lots."

Teari's quiet. She rocks back and forth as she asks, "Who stabbed you?"

My stomach pinches, my heart skips a beat. "Sparrow," I say.

"Why would he do that?"

I bite my bottom lip to make it stop quivering. There's something about a straight shot question that threatens to rip out your soul. But I'm not going to stew in that feeling. I'm going to embrace the hate for the man I once loved. "I'm sure there's a reason." I stand and make my way to the dresser where there are a few prosthetic limbs. I run my finger over the metallic claws. I never allowed Teari to touch my skin much, but when she did, it definitely didn't feel like this smooth metal.

I turn. She's watching me.

"I don't like them. They feel... unnatural," she says.

"Where'd you find them?"

"Noah brought them." She makes a face.

"He's always trying to fix things." I sigh. "Ever since he died."

"Maybe he's trying for redemption," Teari suggests.

"Isn't it too late for that?"

"Who knows?" She holds up the nubs of her arms and taps them together like Dorothy with her ruby slippers. "Seems I don't know much about how our realms work anymore."

"We'll figure it out," I promise.

"I need you to get me out of this room. I need to do something so I don't go crazy." She pauses and touches her face. "And I can't find Nightingale. She's no longer in my dreams. I think... I think something happened to her." She holds up her arms and I imagine her past mannerisms when she had hands. "She always comes in my dreams. Always. At least once a week to check in. I haven't seen her in so long. Since before I went to find you on the Earthen plane." Her eyes are wide and worried. "I think something has happened to her."

Shit. Something did happen to her.

"You're right," I say. "She's not just missing. She's gone. Forever."

Teari stares at me, her mouth slightly open, her skin pale in disbelief.

"She died when the fast-zombies infiltrated the Seven Kingdoms of Heaven. We went to help. Me and the Hellions. I brought the Basilisk. But... we couldn't save them. Nightingale and Jack died."

"Oh God," Teari's arms settle on the side of her head. "I knew it was bad. Where's Gabriel?"

I tell her about the cage.

"No no no. If Raguel and the others turned on Gabriel, it's not good." She looks at her arms. "If they have him, my home is gone too."

"I'm going to rescue him," I say. "Soon."

"Alone?" She stands and paces. "You can't go alone. They'll eat you for dinner. You need an army. You need to protect yourself." She turns. "Take me." She thumps her arms to her chest. "Take me with you."

"I don't think that's a good idea," I say.

"Perhaps. But it's a distraction." She holds up her nubs. "Maybe if I go back, I can get my powers again. Maybe I could heal. Maybe…"

All I can think is that I cannot lose another friend. It's been too many too fast. Teari is one of the few from the Seven Kingdoms of Heaven that I can tolerate. If I lose her and something happens to Gabriel, I'm alone in this mess. Completely alone. My stomach pinches. I can't do this alone. I can't go back to feeling like I did before I found Sparrow and found out who I was. Teari can't fight with me.

"You're not going to risk your life for me." I motion to her arms. "Wait until you're healed before jumping back into this mess feet first."

Teari moves toward the door. "Fine, but I'm going to need you to take me somewhere besides this room."

It seems to be a repeating theme. Everyone wants out of their room. No one gave a crap all the times I was locked up. Truthfully, though, Jed and Shay didn't have anything to do with those times. Teari was an accomplice once. I wonder if she regrets doing it to me. I don't like the idea of locking up my friends. They deserve freedom, but I'd also like them to stay alive.

———

"If you're going to go up against a healed Sparrow, you are going to need a little more training," Chel suggests from the shadows of the Hellion lair.

Between my hands, I slide my glass across polished wood and watch the reflection of thick blood sloshing. "I didn't train to go up against Lucifer," I say.

"Lucifer didn't know you," Chel says. "He didn't spend time with you and study your ways."

"You're going to need to surprise him," Tukka says. He crosses his arms and leans on the bar. "You're going head-to-head with a warrior who has trained his entire life."

Klaus moves to the wall of weapons, thick fingers tapping on swords and blades and guns. He chooses a small dagger and turns to me. "Sparrow nearly ended you with a blade smaller than his hand. Imagine the damage he would do from the sky."

"If he picked you up and dropped you," Skeele interrupts.

"I know." I stop him with a raised palm. "I know what happens in that scenario."

"So let us train you," Klaus suggests. He slides the small dagger across the lacquered bar.

I stop the small weapon with the slap of the palm and twirl it by the point before wrapping my fingers around the grip and lifting it. It's a very different feel than my blade and I wonder how it would feel to jab with this tiny thing. Must feel good since Sparrow used something similar on me. The thought of him makes my stomach twist. My scars ache in remembrance; it happened so fast, so quick. Like a dancer to a rapid beat of drums. *Stab, stab, stab. Poof.* My chest twinges. I look down at the scarred tattoo. I should've known better.

"Yeah," I agree suddenly. "You can train me."

———

Tukka waits in the center of the dirt patch outside the entrance to the burning caves. The sun has set and Hellsky turns chilled, the moon providing dim light. Tukka's boots crunch on the ochre dirt. I glance at the others, watching from near the front of the cave entrance before turning to face Tukka.

He's tall, muscular, his skin scarred from years of battle experience. Tukka's eyes meet mine. He's determined to teach me something tonight, I can see it. I've seen that glint in a man's eye before. The glint in the eye of a Hellion. I'll never forget it. We circle each other, sizing each other up. Without my blade, I'm feeling really inadequate as I grip the small dagger Klaus gave me. There's something about a blade that only cuts in the grip of its owner.

Without warning, Tukka lunges forward, his dagger flashing in the dim moonlight. I barely have time to move, holding my dagger up, it rings out as hilt clashes against hilt. Tukka moves back one step before lunging again, this time he jabs lower. I jump to the side, grind my elbow into his tipped shoulder, and shove him away. He sweeps his arm as he falls to the side, grabbing my ankle and trying to drag me down with him. I hop on my free foot as he rolls onto his back. He loses his grip on my ankle, and I step on his wrist before slamming my other foot down on his chest. Tukka is fast, but bulky. He's playing nice, keeping his wings out of the way. He could've used them by now.

I step away from him. "You're being too easy on me," I say, annoyed. "You're better than this."

Tukka smiles, showing sharp teeth. "I saw you the night you killed your grandfather, you're better than this too." He moves to his feet fast. He slaps the dagger out of my hand.

"Nice," I mock after he laughs.

He jabs. I dodge and weave around his jabbing arm, on the third one, I punch his wrist and kick his opposite thigh. He drops the dagger. I kick it away. Adrenaline is pumping, my heart races as I focus on showing Tukka I'm not as weak a fighter as they think I am. Danger has lurked around every corner of my life. I may not have wings, but I'm scrappy. I can punch a throat or kick some balls as good as the rest of the white trash girls I grew up with. Been doing it for a while now.

Tukka swings his big body around and his shoulder lands in my gut, sending me flying backward a few feet before I land on my ass. Dirt grinds into the palms of my hands as I try to catch myself.

"You fuck," I groan. One of the daggers is under me, the handle pressing into my spine. I grab for it then roll to free my hand. What luck.

Tukka comes at me again. I thrust my right hand out and cut him in the thigh with the dagger. It slices through his leather pants and thick skin like they are nothing more than soft butter.

"Ah," he kicks my hand.

But it's too late. Fresh blood does a good job at getting me off my ass. I scramble to my feet and show my own sharp teeth. Shit. The adrenaline from fighting and fresh dripping blood...

Tukka's eyes go wide before he launches himself into the sky with a powerful jump, his leathery wings beating hard, sending dust and sand airborne.

I jump and grab at his boot. Gripping on, I dig my nails into the thick leather and grab for the laces with my free hand.

He shakes me off like I'm nothing more than a snake in the leaves.

I drop to the ground like a cat and laugh. "Are you afraid now?" I ask.

Fresh blood drips down his boot to the ground in front of me. Tukka hovers a few feet over my head. "I've seen that look before. You don't fight fair."

"What look is that?" I ask.

"The same look on your face before you drained Lucifer dry for all of Hell to see." He beats his wings, rising higher, farther from me.

"No one in the Seven Kingdoms of Heaven is going to fight fair. Not even Sparrow." I tamper down the desire to drain him of every last drop of blood in his body. I don't need Tukka dead. I need him at my side.

"I think we're done here," he says as he flies toward the caves.

Noah moves closer. "That's my Meg, always making friends." He claps me hard on the back.

"What can I say?" I spread my arms. "It's a gift."

Noah laughs lightly. "Shitty gift."

"Better than nothing." I make my way to the entrance of the caves and tag this instructional moment as a win for Meg.

House Hunting

Teari and I trudge through the streets of Centralia. We walked from the burning caves, past the smoking vents in the hillsides, and headed west on Big Mine Run Road. Centralia in my realm looks very similar to the abandoned town in the Earthen plane. There's uneven, cracked roads and a few chipped white painted houses with moss covering rotting wood. I'd say, it's probably the only place that closely resembles itself on each plane. But that's what an abandoned town with fire burning underground will get you. It's a two mile walk to the crossroads of Centre Street and Locust Ave. There aren't many houses here; most are torn down, and the lots filled with forest trees. There are crumbling structures with rotting clapboard and thick mossy covered roofs further down the road. Those won't do for Thrush.

"Which way?" Teari asks, her wings making scraping sounds as they drag on the pavement, turning gray with dirt and leaving bits of white feathers behind.

I didn't intend to leave a trail of crumbs so we can find our way home. A small white feather rolls under my boot.

"There's Saint Ignatius Cemetery down Locust Ave." I point. "Or Centralia Fire company No. 1 in the opposite direction."

"Not optimal for a baby," Teari says. "There aren't any houses?"

We walk a little further.

"No houses that I'd want my family living in," I say. "I'm afraid the roof would cave in on most. At least the chapel in the cemetery is stone and solid, same with the fire company building."

I pull my jacket tighter around myself to ward off the chill of the evening air. We've been searching for a house for baby Thrush for days. We started farther away, in bigger towns with nicer houses but agreed that distance was not our friend. The Hellions and I need to be closer.

Teari rubs her face with the sides of her arms. "I can't believe we still haven't found a house for them."

Rain falls, and Teari wipes the drops from her cheeks. "Let's look at the cemetery."

I nod in agreement.

"He can't be here for long," Teari points at the ochre dust under her feet. "Maybe we shouldn't even be wasting our time looking for a house."

"He's safer here," I argue.

"No, you don't understand." Teari presses her lips together and sighs. "I didn't know how to tell you. He'll turn into a Nightjar if he stays here."

I don't enjoy looking stupid, but I've got no choice right now. I don't know what that is. "Explain," I say.

"Nightjars are manifestations of the souls of unbaptized children doomed to wander the night sky," Teari clarifies. "He is a child of the Seven Kingdoms of Heaven. Nightingale would not want that for her son. He must go back. We must baptize him in the fountains of Babylon."

"I'm not sure that's a good idea," I say. "There's no one to take care of him up there."

"He has an uncle," Teari presses, her voice low.

"Let him grow up with a murderer? No." I shake my head and wrap my jacket tighter.

Our footsteps echo on the deserted streets. Every so often, a dimly lit streetlight flickers when we walk under it.

"He'll protect Thrush," Teari says, trying to adjust her cloak.

I do my best not to look at her skeptically. "Protect him? Thrush needs protecting from him, not by him. I can't hand over a baby to the man who stabbed me to death."

Teari takes a deep breath, hesitating. "He could change. We all change throughout these immortal lives."

"No one changes," I snap back.

"No?" Teari challenges. "You haven't changed?"

I shake my head, my eyes downcast. "I haven't changed much. Taking the throne in Hell hasn't prevented me from doing wrong and making mistakes. It hasn't prevented me from being selfish."

Teari touches my shoulder; it's strange, not the light touch of fingers but heavier. For one of the few times in my life I don't pull away. "All right, Meg. You haven't changed. You're still the rash, foul-mouthed woman-child I met last year who couldn't tell the difference between Demons and Angels." She smirks.

"Still can't tell the difference," I mutter.

"Also, you've changed," she says. "For the record. You shouldn't downplay how far you've come."

I nod, wanting to change the subject. I don't enjoy talking about myself like this, it has always been easier with some self-deprecating humor instead.

The chapel in the cemetery comes into view.

"It's not that bad," Teari says as we walk toward the front door. Tall, brown grass sweeps at our shins as we make our way across the cracked sidewalk.

"The windows are high," I point. "The door solid."

Teari nods. "It's not a castle but it could do."

I push my shoulder against the heavy door and shove it open. Dust motes swirl in the evening sun rays shining through the window. My daddy always said I'd burn to a cinder if I stepped foot inside a church. It's never happened and he wasn't my daddy. But the fear always hits me as I step foot across the threshold of any religious building. Not here though. This feels like stepping into my castle.

Stone floors, arched windows, and an open space make up most of the chapel. The walls are lined with dusty shelves dripping with old wax and burnt-out candles. As we explore, I find there are living quarters off to the side with a small kitchen.

"It could be quiet," Teari says, knocking on the stone wall with her elbow. "No one outside would hear much through this."

"That's good." I kick at some sticks and leaves that made their way in. The place needs to be cleaned.

"Will the dead stay out?" Teari asks.

"It would be hard for them to get in here." We walk to the back of the chapel. "There's only two doors to reinforce."

"And the roof?" Teari looks up.

"It looked like slate when we were walking up. I'll have the Hellions check it out. We could make it strong so nothing can fall through."

Silence passes for a few moments. It would be a tragedy for Thrush to die the same way his parents did. I'll do anything to make sure it never happens.

Rain patters on the rooftop as it begins to downpour outside.

"I don't see any leaks," I say, inspecting the ceiling. "That's promising."

Teari shivers. "It's cold enough to freeze the balls off a pool table." She looks out a nearby window. "Does it always get this cold when the sun goes down?"

I shake my head. "Only in winter."

"Lucky us," Teari mutters. "What about a fence around the exterior so they could go outside in the day?"

I nod. "The Hellions could build it quickly. We can scavenge for panels."

Teari tucks her arms into jacket pockets. "This could work. It could be a home." She clears her throat. "It doesn't fix the Nightjar problem."

"Ask Noah," I say, trying to hide the frustration in my voice. "Thrush is his son. But, what I know is that Noah will not want that baby a realm away from him. Not after losing Nightingale. None of us wants him out of our sight. Sending him back to Heaven is going to be non-negotiable. I know Noah will agree."

Teari frowns and walks in a circle, thinking. "Just for the baptism at least?"

"I don't think that's a good idea."

"Save his soul."

"I already did!" I shout. "He almost died once." Memories of the moment the dead fell through Nightingale's roof flood me. I press my hands against the sides of my head. The biting, the blood... "If you had been there–"

"I wasn't," Teari shouts back. "Because I was in a hospital in bum-fuck Pennsylvania. Remember? You left me on the Earthen plane, alone, half-dead." She holds out her arms. "I would have loved to be there to fight, but I couldn't be."

"You're alive now." I say, trying not to take her words personal.

"Am I?" She steps closer to me. "Am I alive? Because every day I feel like shit. I feel like I shouldn't be here. Like I cheated death or something."

"You want me to get you a shrink?" I blink. "Life sucks ninety percent of the time for all of us. Just because I have my hands, doesn't mean I haven't lost *other* things." My fingers itch to pull the blade off my thigh holster, but I know she's not coming at me like this to threaten me, she's just working through the spaghetti in her mind. "You healed me before. I didn't hold it against you. I did what I had to do to keep you alive. You would have done the same for me."

Tears slide down her face and Teari comes at me with arms open. She hugs me, burying her face into my neck and crying, heaving as large sobs wrack her lithe body. I'm not a fan of hugs, I'm more of a tap them with a broom and tell them there, there type of gal.

I guess we all have to mature some time. I hug her back, careful not to touch her wings and knock off any more feathers.

"I just feel so useless," Teari says though the sobs.

"I have met a few useless Angels. That's not you." I pat her back, awkwardly.

"You don't have to say that."

"I wouldn't if I didn't mean it."

———

WE LEAVE the chapel when the rain stops.

"Everything looks different at night here," Teari says.

"Sure does," I agree.

Moaning from the forest makes my spine straighten. The memories of the fast-zombies are hard to bury. I grip the blade at my thigh.

"Shh," I say, holding a finger to my lips. "I hear something."

"Wing beats," Teari says.

I look up and see one of the Hellions pass overhead.

"They're protective of you," Teari says quietly.

"Yeah," I walk toward the caves. "Let us walk," I say into the night. "Just for once give me a moment of peace."

The wing-beats soften and grow more distant, their whispers replaced with the chirping of crickets and croaking of toads in the thicket.

"There was a time when you hated them," Teari reminds me. "When you couldn't be near them."

"That time still lingers. It's a process I've been going through." I try not to think about the gaunt, pale Skeele I woke up to just a few days ago and how I almost cared about the unhealthy way he looked for about five minutes. "I wouldn't dwell on my feelings for them."

Teari moves closer to me, hearing the rustling in the forest. "They'd do anything for you," she says. "That's a good thing."

Last time I gave a shit about someone doing anything for me, it got me in a lot of trouble. It doesn't mean much anymore.

Loyalty is a cage that's only as strong as those surrounding you.

Rescue Me

Gabriel has been trapped in the cage for weeks. His once magnificent wings looked torn and tattered, either from him trying to escape or something they did to him. We are quiet on our approach, so quiet Gabriel doesn't turn until just before we reach him.

Gabriel smiles wide, "Lord knows my Meg would come save me." He grips the bars of the cage. "Get me the hell out of here." His eyes are tired, his face pale.

"That's what we're here for," I say.

"I know why you're here," Gabriel said, nodding to the shadowed Hellions behind me. "Why are they here?"

"Because I need help," I say. "And they do what I tell them."

"Fair enough," he says with a sigh.

Skeele and Tukka pry at the bars, testing them. Next comes the big guns. Skeele starts the angle grinder. The noise is loud. We stand back, waiting. Sparks fly like fireflies.

Gabriel looks toward the building in the distance. "Get me out or they'll be coming soon. For the love of Pete, let's get this show on the road."

"Can you go faster?" I urge Skeele.

He glares at me. "Going as fast as I can."

I focus on Gabriel. "Who put you here?"

"That asswipe Raguel." Gabriel palms a fist and cracks his knuckles. "As if cleaning up the mess from those zombies wasn't enough to deal with. I'm going to end him."

Metal clangs as one bar falls away.

"There's something you should know, Meg," Gabriel grips the bars opposite the sparks. "Sparrow's back."

"I know," I interrupt.

"He's not what we remember." Gabriel's forehead wrinkles in concern. "He's very different. There's something wrong with him."

"Maybe this is his true self," I reply.

"There's more..." he trails off. "You know with his family curse his head has never been quite right."

Metal clangs again as more of the bars to the cage fall away. The racket will bring a Legion soon.

"I don't care." I say. "I'm going to kill him. It's a non-issue. His curse might as well be my revenge."

Gabriel nods, knowingly. I'm sure he's heard what Sparrow did to me. Being my father and all, I'm surprised Gabriel didn't end Sparrow himself. But then, why deny me the glory of revenge? My father knows me well. I'm out for blood and if anyone knows this version of Meg, I'll drain whoever does me wrong.

Skeele turns off the grinder, tucks it in his bag, and shoves the cut bars. Gabriel steps out. Free. That was too easy. I scan the empty sidewalks of Babylon. Not a soul in sight. Either they don't care I'm taking Gabriel or there's some shifty shit going on.

"We don't have any portals in Hell," I remind Gabriel. "There's only one way in."

We grab hands.

Poof.

Noah appears with inkpots and a handful of sterile needles. He drops them in front of Jed.

"Let's go," I say to Jed. "Get your tattoo gun."

Jed turns to Shay, "I'll be right back."

"It's going to be a few hours," Noah warns. "At least. I'll stay with him."

Jed looks uneasy. Shay looks uneasy. They haven't left this room in days, and they've been taking their new job of babysitting very seriously.

"It's fine," I say. "We just need some ink."

Jed crosses the room to grab his tools and breathes something quietly to Shay. Then he follows us out of the room.

I lead him to the second floor. There's an empty room near the stairwell with chairs and a table and good lighting. I open the door and wait for Jed to enter.

It only takes him a minute to see Gabriel waiting in the corner.

"Oh no," Jed backpedals. "Nope. Nope. Nope."

I grab his arm. Noah slams the door.

Gabriel squints at Jed. "Well, I'll be damned," he murmurs.

"I have spent my life avoiding Archangels and you brought me to one." Jed looks ready to lose it. His eyes are wide with fear and anger. "Is this some sick joke?" He glares at me. "I knew I could never trust you, Meg. Never. The things I've done for you and now this?"

"Calm down, boy," Gabriel bellows. "I'm not here for you." He frowns. "Damned surprised to see you upright and down in this realm," he raises his palms, "but the more days I live, the less this shit surprises me."

"He needs the runes," I say, holding out my arm. "He needs freedom from the other Archangels."

Jed tosses his equipment on the table. He glares at me. "This is not what I signed up for."

"We're in the same club," I move closer to Jed. "Gabriel is my father. The other Archangel's are rallying against him. Including Sparrow."

"Fucking Angels," Jed mutters, shaking his head. He points a finger at me. "You owe me big time for this." He sets his equipment on the table and starts prepping to tattoo Gabriel. "You owe me for the rest of your life."

"Done," I hold out my hand, pinky extended. "Pinky promise. I am forever in your debt."

Jed jerks his hand forward, curling his pinky around mine and staring into my eyes. "I am a forbidden creature. They will always hunt me."

I nod, understanding. Jed and I aren't all that different, he just doesn't realize it.

Jed picks up one inkpot that Noah brought. He sets it aside and motions for Gabriel to lay his left arm out on the table. "We'll do both," he says. "If you can handle it." Jed smirks.

Gabriel rests his arm on the table and Jed gets to work.

"Would this prevent Sparrow from finding Thrush?" Noah asks, tipping his head toward Jed, watching.

"The runes?" I ask.

Noah nods.

"I'd assume." I say. "But, wait. Are you suggesting tattooing a baby?"

Noah presses his lips together and tips his head in a maybe expression.

"I don't think that's a good idea," I say. Something just seems very wrong about tattooing a baby. I've done a lot of awful shit in my life, but I draw the line at that.

Happy Little Trees

Teari is helping me paint the chapel in the cemetery. Actually, she's spending most of her time pointing out what a shitty painter I am.

"There's a big spot by this window," she points with the nub of her left arm. On the right she's wearing the prosthesis with a claw for a hand.

"Why don't you paint it?" I ask, wiping a dot of paint off my face with my sleeve. The sage green color stains my black shirt.

"I can't," Teari replies, moving farther down the wall with her inspection. "There's another here."

The door blasts open and I drop the paintbrush. Skeele walks through with Gabriel, carrying a couch.

"Jesus Christ," I mutter, picking up the brush and searching for a rag.

"That's going to stain," Teari says flatly.

"Well maybe you should help clean it up," I snap.

"Where do you want this?" Skeele shouts. There's an edge to his voice, beyond simple annoyance.

"Wherever," I shout back. I find a rag on the nearby table and use it to mop up the paint splatter.

"I guess, you could always cover it with a rug," Teari suggests with a disappointed sigh.

"Is this good?" Skeele asks as he drops his side of the couch.

Gabriel follows suit and drops his side as well. A large thud echoes throughout the empty room.

"What the heck?" I startle with the loud noise. "Are you trying to wake the dead?"

"Thought they were already awake down here?" Gabriel chuckles.

The moment between me and Skeele is tense. "Just try not to damage the furniture. This isn't a pigsty Hellion lair. A baby has to live here," I remind him.

Skeele stomps out of the room.

"What the heck is going on with you two?" Teari asks.

Gabriel sticks around for the drama.

I wave, dismissing her concern. "Something crawled up his ass and died." I find the paint and go back to painting the wall.

Gabriel chuckles at my comment. "Never a dull moment in this realm. Absolute chaos. Better than when I did my time down here as a Hellion. That was eons ago though. I like what you've done with the place, Meg." Gabriel slaps me on the back as he walks through the room causing me to drop the paintbrush again. A large plop of sage green stains the floor.

"Fucking-a." I grab the brush. I didn't think about Gabriel remembering his time as a Hellion. Sparrow's mind was so screwed up I just assumed that my father wouldn't remember either.

Skeele kicks the door open again, this time he's carrying a coffee table. "Where do you want this?"

"Up your ass," I reply.

Teari laughs.

Gabriel's eyes widen.

Skeele drops the coffee table and leaves.

"Hey, try not to ruin every piece of furniture you bring in here," I shout.

The door slams. I slap more paint on the wall and swipe the brush furiously. My stomach growls. I try to ignore it.

"Maybe you should eat, Meg," Teari warns. "You're getting hangry."

"Who will paint?" I ask. It's nice to be needed for a menial task and not something life or death or end-of-the-world-esque. Painting is easy. Painting doesn't involve zombies or Hellions or murderous Angels or hunting for slimy Basilisk. I could paint all day with these low standards.

"I'll paint," Gabriel offers. He holds out a large hand and I notice the healing runes twisting up his forearms.

"Don't get your robes dirty," I motion to the paint splatter all over my clothes.

"Ditched those for good," Gabriel smiles. He's wearing jeans and a green flannel shirt with the sleeves rolled up. If it weren't for his giant size, he'd look absolutely normal. "Give me the brush. You go... get something to eat."

I hold the brush between two fingers and let Gabriel take it. "Are you staying here?" I ask Teari.

"I think that's safest right now," she says, inspecting my subpar paintjob.

"Fine." I wipe my hands on my pants and walk away. As I get close, the door flies open and I catch it with my hand before it hits me in the face.

Skeele's standing there, a nightstand in his hands, oozing bitterness. He doesn't apologize; instead he walks through the threshold and around me. His movement brings a breeze that smells like smoke and pine. It's a comforting smell, makes me feel like I am home, makes me hate him even more.

I slam the door closed as I leave. I jog down the steps and the walkway before veering off the path and walking between the headstones. Some are half-sunk into the ground, some are covered in moss and lichen.

Living in a graveyard is kinda odd but it's not a dangerous place to raise a child. There's nature and calm and hopefully we can keep Thrush hidden long enough that he'll have a peaceful childhood. Every child deserves that.

I sit on a broken headstone and stare off into the distance. Sooner or later, I'm going to have to have a conversation with Skeele about his crappy attitude lately. I can't have my first in command being a douche. He still listens. There's just, something else going on with him that needs to be cleared up.

My stomach growls again. Damn. I had pancakes and eggs and sausage for breakfast. It must be a different hunger. The one I try to ignore.

Noah shows up. Always when I need him most.

"I brought you this," he passes me a bowl. "It's cherry pie."

"Of all things," I say just before digging in.

"I was hoping the red color would help." He sits next to me. "You know, because you need to eat blood and you haven't had any in a very long time."

The pie is sweet, the crust flaky; it even has real whipped cream on top. I chew and swallow before replying to him. "I'm fine. I've survived plenty of dry spells."

"I worry about those around you."

I look at his face. Noah stares off into the distance, his expression placid, not letting on to what he really means.

"I won't harm anyone," I say as I take another bite.

"You say that, but I've seen you turn in the heat of the moment." He clasps his hands together. "I want you to stay away from Thrush until you've had blood." His voice is low, like he doesn't want anyone else to hear.

"I wouldn't hurt him," I say, trying not to let Noah's distrust ruin my day.

"There's plenty you'd promise me, Meg. But the truth is," he turns to look into my eyes. "I can only do so much to keep my son safe in this realm, and while I will be forever grateful that you brought him here, I will always worry that he'll be present during a moment that you can't control yourself."

Anger boils through my veins. Being hungry for blood makes it worse. "Everything I've done..." I take another bite of the pie to prevent myself from saying something truly terrible to him.

Noah wraps his arm around my shoulders. Usually, I'd pull away or push him away, but something's going on deep inside my soul. Something Noah can sense; he's always been good at that kind of stuff. He's always been there to get me into trouble, there to get me out of trouble, there to bring me back to reality.

"You've done a lot to help us, Meg. We'll never forget it." He squeezes me tighter. "This blood thing is new, and I've seen you at your worst. Thrush can't be around you when you're like this."

"You don't want me to see him?" I stab at the pie and shove more into my mouth. I try to focus on the deliciousness of the flaky crust.

"Not unless you're full. On the real stuff. Not the cold stuff the Hellions live on. Fresh blood, Meg. That's the only thing that keeps you reasonable."

Perfect. Here's Noah giving me an ultimatum that I'll never be able to fulfill. Damn him. I don't have Sparrow to feed from and the next time I see him it will be to kill him, so there goes that. And randomly feeding off a stranger will turn me into a hoe because I know how I get when the bloodlust is at full tilt.

"I know you'll figure out something," Noah says confidently.

I'll figure it out. Sure. This is one of those moments when I should cry silently as I stuff my face and let my best friend console me. I blink back the tears.

"Choke it down, Meg," Noah whispers, knowingly. "It's okay."

A bluejay lands on the gravestone next to us. I try to whistle a light trill, but pie crust gets stuck between my front teeth and it looks like I'm spitting my food out.

"I got you," Noah says just before whistling to the jay.

It talks back with a jabber of chirps and whistles and song and I am transported back in time, months ago when we were sitting in my room feeding the birds on the balcony. Me and Noah and Nightingale and Sparrow. I have to stop dwelling on the past, but the hard thing is, that past was the best months I've ever had in my pathetic life. It's hard to let go and move beyond that. Memories of joy aren't so easy to bury. I want to set them on a mantle in my mind and reminisce on Sundays and Christmas mornings. But two of those people are gone now. Dead and dead to me.

Jed and Shay are walking down the road. Jed's carrying Thrush. They bundled the baby in a hat and snowsuit. Shay is carrying a heavy backpack and if I know her it's packed with everything she needs to survive for a week, at least. They walk toward the chapel. Jed notices me in the cemetery.

I wave but stay put because Noah's grip on my shoulder tightens. A warning. The realization comes to me that this will forever be my view of Thrush's life. He's the closest thing I have to remember Nightingale. It seems everything must be kept at arm's reach, or further. It's probably better that way.

I finish eating the pie. I cram it into my mouth to fill the ever-growing void of darkness in the pit of my chest. It's hungry, starving, never fulfilled.

"You should go home, Meg. It's getting late," Noah suggests.

I stand to walk away, the tall grass swiping at my knees. Something hits hard under my boot. I bend to pick it up.

Seems I've found Sparrow's book. *Birds of Paradise* rests in my hand, caked in dirt and stained from the rain. "I've been looking for you for ages," I say.

"Haven't seen one of those in a while," Noah says.

"I lost this one when the Scarecrow came."

"Guess it's time to return it to the library." He holds out his hand, ready to do my dirty work as always.

"No," I say. "This isn't from the library. This is from someone's house. And I'm going to bring it back to them."

Noah's lips tip in a playful smile as I test the weight of the book in my hand.

———

"Has Thrush been baptized yet?" Gabriel asks as we sit down to dinner.

I'm grumpy because only half the people I want to see are here, and… I'd prefer sucking my dinner out of someone's jugular. Thoughts like that are beginning to feel normal, shameless. I nearly take the solid mahogany table draped with food for granted. Candlelight reflects off the polished wood, illuminating the wood smoke haze on the ceiling. Small bodies writhe up there. Basilisk babies have left their tank and taken to the ceilings. They follow me from room to room like puppies. It's creepy.

Teari drops her fork. I try not to stare as she fumbles with the prosthetic arms. At least she's trying to use them. That's an improvement.

"No baptizing that I know of," I say, scooping a giant spoonful of mashed potatoes onto my plate.

Gabriel grumbles something about the fountains of Babylon.

"What?" I ask as I pour gravy. A lot of gravy. I pour until I think it might fill the void in my gut.

"He must be baptized," Gabriel says as he cuts into a roast and serves himself a heaping slab.

"He's going to be a Nightjar, it doesn't matter," Teari says from her side of the table. She's holding a spoon between the claws of her right arm prosthesis.

"Why are you so certain he will turn into a Nightjar?" I ask. "Have you seen this happen before?"

Gabriel and Teari look at each other.

"What?" I urge.

"It's more than lore," Gabriel says. "You could ask the archangel Raphael. It happened to one of his children."

"How?" I ask.

"The story goes he had a child with a creature other than an angel," Teari says, concentrating on the spoon handle. "Her name was Demore. She was born of darkness. Which can only mean she was born in this realm. Which can only mean Raphael–"

"Was getting his freak on," I interrupt.

Gabriel chokes on his wine.

"You haven't heard Demore's call?" Teari asks. "All that time you spent wandering down here?"

I tip my shoulder up and make a face. "I heard a lot of shit."

"It's like plip-plop," Teari says. "It's like the sound of someone's eyes being pulled out."

"I don't think I've heard that," I say.

"Thrush should be baptized," Gabriel says. "If not, he'll be satanic. A creature of Hell."

"You'll never escape him because you'll hear him calling at night. Plip-plop. Plip-plop," Teari says, her tongue clucking the p's.

"He might even pull out our eyes," Gabriel says.

"You'll never forget that sound." Teari continues, "Plip-plop."

"I heard it once." Gabriel says. "Will never forget it."

I focus on Gabriel. "You heard it once?"

He nods, silently.

Must've been during his time as a Hellion.

"Plip-plop. Plip–" Teari says in a sing-song voice.

"Shut up," I warn her.

Teari stops, eyes wide as she grips the spoon with her claw and scoops a tomato into her mouth. She bites, red juice and seeds coating her lips.

"Is it a curse that can be broken?" I ask.

"By baptism," Teari says, around her mouthful of food. "I told you."

I shake my head.

"Who's getting a baptism?" Noah appears. He sits opposite me at the table and swipes at the blonde hair near his eyes.

"Meg," Teari says.

"Nope on a rope," I say, stabbing a giant piece of roast and cramming it into my mouth so I don't say something stupid.

Gabriel pushes his chair back and seems to be completely disinterested in the conversation suddenly.

"Have you ever heard of a thing called Demore?" I ask Noah.

Noah narrows his eyes and glances at everyone.

"Plip-plop," Teari whispers.

"Have you heard it?" I ask. "When you're out there searching for all the shit I ask for?"

"I hear a lot of things," Noah says.

"But have you heard the plip-plop of eyeballs being plucked out by a Nightjar?" I ask.

Noah leans back in his chair. "That's very specific." He shakes his head. "I can't say I have."

"It's a scam," I say, looking at Teari and Gabriel.

"Scam?" Noah asks, propping his feet up on the table and crossing his legs.

"Not a scam," Teari says.

I stare at Gabriel. He can't lie to me. "All lore has truth. He should be baptized. Just in case."

"Are you talking about Thrush?" Noah asks, dropping his feet and leaning forward in sudden interest.

"Thrush will be a Nightjar," Teari says. "Unless he's baptized in the fountains of Babylon."

Noah looks at me. "Nightjar?" he asks.

"These two are telling me that without being baptized, Thrush will turn in to a creature of Hell and his soul will be doomed to wander the night sky," I say.

"Plip-plop," Teari says.

"Meg's a creature of Hell, she's not so bad," Noah says, staring at Gabriel. His smile goes flat.

"Meg is half-darkness," Gabriel says. "She's where she belongs. Your boy on the other hand–"

"Is half Astral, half Angel," Noah says.

"From the wrong side of the Earthen realm," Gabriel says with a frown.

He would know. Gabriel and Noah both fell for a girl from the wrong side of the tracks. Nothing is easy after that. Especially with children involved. The jar of feathers on my nightstand tell a similar story.

"The Astral is darkness. It's nothingness." Noah runs his fingers through his hair and rubs his neck. "Thrush is half-darkness."

Gabriel circles a finger in the air. "Not this darkness. Hell is a different place."

"So I take him to the Astral," Noah says.

"There's nothing there," I say.

"I will be there," Noah argues.

"You can't raise him in nothingness," I say. "Don't subject him to a lifetime of loneliness. He's alive, he can't live in dreams and outer-space."

Noah taps a finger on the table, thinking. He knows it's not right. He can't deny Thrush a childhood of poor decisions and teenage high-speed chases. If he didn't live through all of the typical childhood mistakes and traditions, he'll be... nothing.

"Baptizing him is easy," Gabriel offers. "It can't hurt to just do it and prevent the Nightjar business."

I swallow the food in my mouth to say, "So we take him to Heaven and Gabriel will baptize him in the fountains of Babylon. Then we come back here. Good to go. No issues."

"It doesn't sound like a no issues kind of thing," Noah says. "You've never gone to Babylon without a complete shit-show ensuing."

I nod. "True. But maybe I go beforehand and kill Sparrow. Then there's not much to worry about." I talk around the food in my mouth. "When we rescued Gabriel no shit-show ensued."

Gabriel chuckles.

"What?" I ask.

"The other five Archangels will come for you," Teari warns. "Anyone with a brain knows that."

"Maybe I kill them too," I suggest.

"You can't go killing everyone in the Seven Kingdoms of Heaven," Gabriel says. "You have to maintain some balance."

Tukka breaks into the room, hurried, only pausing when his eyes meet mine. "There's a Deacon here," he says. "And it wants to talk to you."

"Fuck that." I cross my legs and get comfortable in my chair.

Noah, Teari, and Gabriel continue talking and planning.

"He says he's not leaving. He has a message from Sparrow," Tukka says.

The room goes silent.

My mouth wants to spew some vulgar shit. Rage fills my chest. I could slay the room with the rage. I stand, knocking my chair over and gripping my hands into fists. "I don't want to hear his name. Ever."

I leave the room and follow Tukka. He takes me to the cave entrance, and I am grateful that he didn't let the scum Deacon into our home.

"Sparrow sent a message," the Deacon says. One finger tugging at the collar of his black button-up shirt.

I stare.

"Sparrow's message is..." The Deacon looks like he saw a ghost.

I flash sharp teeth. "Spill it. My dinner's getting cold."

The Deacon clears his throat. "Sparrow says he wants his nephew back. Now."

"I don't know anything about his nephew," I lie. "As far as I'm concerned, his nephew died in the Fast-Zombie War alongside his mother and father."

"We know he didn't," the Deacon argues.

"How do you know?" I take a step forward.

The Deacon takes a step back. "He knows the boy is in this realm. We know he's here."

"Then go find him." I say, taking another step closer, ready to run him off my property like a hillbilly with a rifle and a copy of the Constitution in his back pocket.

The Deacon backs up.

"I have a question before you go," I stop the Deacon.

He pauses.

"Where is Demore?" I ask.

The Deacon's spine goes straight. "Don't say that name."

"Why?"

The Deacon turns and runs away.

————

"Are you going to take this stuff in to them?" I ask Teari, motioning to her one arm with the prosthesis.

"I guess I could. You don't want to go?" she asks.

I remember Noah's warning. I can't see Thrush unless I've been drinking fresh blood. And I haven't been drinking fresh blood. All I can see is Teari's jugular beating and hear the blood rushing through her veins. It's been distracting me the entire walk here. I'd be lying if I said I didn't think about draining her dry and leaving her body under a pile of brush near the firehouse. Hunger makes me think things I normally wouldn't.

"Take this stuff." I help get the bag over her shoulder. It's filled with salt, holy water, charcoal pencils, and weapons. Noah has been bringing over five-pound bags of rock salt but I've been collecting the finer stuff from the castle kitchen. "I can't go in there. He has it warded against me."

There are runes etched over the doorframe, more burned into the thick, wooden door. Salt lines the sidewalk. These past few weeks the Hellions built a ten-foot fence around the cemetery. There are more symbols burned into the fence and I'm pretty sure if I touched the latch holding the door it would burn my hand.

I hear the lighthearted giggles of a child on the other side. A few bubbles float into the sky and over the fence.

"He's happy," Teari says with a smile. "That's all we can ask for." She opens the gate and leaves me standing alone on the other side.

I walk the fence and check the runes and markings that Jed made to protect him and Shay and Thrush from being found or hurt. I inspect the Hellions' work and kick the fence in a few places, testing it.

"Stop it!" A shout comes from the other side. Jed's voice.

"I was just making sure it's stable," I shout back.

Hushed wingbeats hover nearby. The Hellions are watching. They're always watching. It's like they're uneasy. Like they know I could snap in a heartbeat. They're not wrong. I can feel it.

I keep walking, thinking about all the scary movies I watched as a kid. Dead cats coming back to life and corpses digging their way out. I recall the night Pet Sematary played on the TV when I was six to help me fall asleep. I never slept that night. I shiver at the memory.

Up ahead, there's an indentation in the tall grass. I walk closer, slowly, praying it's not a petrified cat. Green grass is a stark contrast to the black clothes the body on the ground is wearing. I'd recognize that getup anywhere. The crumpled form of a Deacon lies not ten feet from the fence.

Meddling bastards. I wave to the shadow in the sky to land. I shove the body with my booted foot and roll it. Stiff limbs fall back with a thud.

"Oh gross." I cover my mouth.

The Deacon is missing his eyeballs.

Plip-plop. Teari's sing song voice fills my head as Chel lands next to me.

"That's unfortunate," Chel says as he surveys the nearby forests. "Haven't found a dead Deacon in a long time. Actually, I've never found one."

"I wish I could exterminate every one of them," I say, looking up. More Hellions are on their way.

One of the new recruits lands opposite Chel. "Go back, get Gabriel," I instruct. He takes off as others land.

"What happened to its eyes?" Chel asks.

"A Nightjar or meddling Angel," I say.

"The portals are all destroyed. How would an Angel get here?" Skeele asks as he lands.

"I'm sure they'd find a way." I search the grass around the body, looking for clues.

The grass around the body twitches. "What was that?" I ask, moving closer. The Deacon's body convulses. Arms and legs jerking slowly then becoming violent. We all take a step back as the corpse moves, reanimating to something very un-Deacon-like.

Skeele readies his blade.

"Wait." I hold him back. "See what it does. I want to know what we are dealing with."

The Deacon twitches to its feet, its head jerking from side to side. Without eyes it can't see, but it can hear.

"What in the name of Christ...?" Gabriel asks as he lands next to me, his white Angel wings mostly healed from his prison stint in Babylon.

That's all the dead Deacon needs. A hint of noise draws movement. The Deacon runs toward sound; mouth open, jaws snapping, throat hissing. He doesn't move slow like the dead who typically walk my plane. No, he moves fast. Fast like the walking dead of the Fast-Zombie War.

Gabriel is quick with his blade. Skeele lets him go in for the kill. Gabriel slices the head off the Deacon and the corpse drops to the ground.

"That was interesting," I say, a million questions circling in my brain.

———

"I thought the fast ones were all dead?" I ask the group of Hellions.

"They were," one replies. "There are no portals to let any in."

"It must've died here," Gabriel says. "Died here and turned here."

"They were fast before because they drank Angel blood," I say. "That Deacon drank angel blood?"

"Perhaps not willingly," Skeele says.

"I don't think he drank the Angel blood willingly," Chel says, pointing to a scab on the Deacon's wrist. It could be from a needle.

The Hellions collect the body. Skeele takes the head, gripping it by its hair. Chel and a new recruit grab the body under the shoulders and drag it away. I don't want them flying with body parts. I don't want Jed or Shay to see what just happened outside the walls of their safe zone. They are risking their lives to watch over Thrush.

They drag the body away, down the street and across the way as we search the cemetery for clues but find none.

There's a thin line of smoke as they burn the body.

———

I meet with the Hellions to discuss the plan to keep Thrush and Jed and Shay safe. We settle on a team of Hellions, the best of the newbies doing around the clock patrols.

"Next on the agenda is Sparrow. I'll be going back to the Seven Kingdoms of Heaven to kill him," I say.

Skeele grunts from beside me. He mutters in Hellspeak after everything I say. Until I can't take it anymore.

"Why are you so goddamn moody? I ask.

Hellfire burns in his dark irises. The energy in the room shifts.

"I'm not moody," he makes a sound deep in his chest like a growl.

"Whatever," I mutter, annoyed.

"Everyone out," Skeele says loudly, pointing to the door.

The Hellions leave. I barely hear the door latch. I'm staring at the bagged blood in their fridge behind the bar, thinking of lowering my standards. I've drank it before. I'm not sure what's wrong with me now, why it's so hard to maintain control.

There's a sound behind me. I turn to a pissed-off Skeele. "All you care about is fucking Sparrow. You are obsessed. Let me tell you a little story, Meg. You want to know why you're upright and full of energy right now?" He stares.

"Noah gave me–"

"It has nothing to do with Noah. It has everything to do with the fact that we were locked in your bedroom for a week straight. You nearly drained all my blood coming back to life." His hands flex into fists at his sides.

"Okay. Well, thanks for that," I snap back.

He steps closer, invading my personal space. I can feel heat radiating off him. I tip my chin up.

"It wasn't even that." One hand falls on the wall behind my head as he leans closer, the tip of his nose touching my earlobe.

"It was all the fucking we did that you don't seem to remember. That's what's been pissing me off the most. You nearly killed me."

Just the Tip

The tip of my blade touches his chin. "That did not happen. I would never."

"Uh huh," he mocks. "That's a nice little birthmark you have on your upper thigh."

My breath catches. "That's not a secret," I say.

"Do it. I like it. It feels so good." His hips press against mine as he backs me against the wall. "Fuck me while you do it." He grips my chin. A hot tongue licks the side of my neck.

Now that sounds exactly like something I'd say. I dreamed I was with Sparrow. I guess all we did wasn't a dream. I look up at Skeele's face. Every memory, every recollection I have of that time; I erase Sparrow's face and paste Skeele's in there. Fuck.

It wasn't that bad. The things we did... It actually felt really good. So good. Too good. Seems the bloodlust screws with my reality. In my defense, I was nearly dead. I wasn't in my right mind. We all make mistakes. But, the more I think on it, was it a mistake? Seems Sparrow was the biggest mistake of my life. Skeele... maybe not so much. Sparrow tried to kill me, but Skeele never has.

His gaze doesn't break mine. His hand feels hot on my skin. I shiver as the mark from his tongue dries on my neck.

"I don't nearly kill anyone when I take their blood. I end them. I drain them dry," I say.

"Well, you left a few drops of life in me," Skeele says.

"Why would I do that?"

A sinful smile creases his lips. "You must enjoy having me around."

He could be right. I could enjoy having him around. He's decent enough and makes good decisions. He's scraped my battered body off the ground more than once and watched over me as I've healed. He could have been much worse. He could have been like the Hellions of the olden days. But he's not like Vine and the others. And I know deep down I do like having him around. He respects my lead, he offers help, he keeps the other Hellions in check. I couldn't ask for a better first command. He's also never tried to kill me. He feeds me when I'm hangry. What more could a girl ask for?

Skeele tips his chin up and presses his hard body against mine. Yes, I like it.

"Watch it," I warn.

"What are you going to do? Bite me? Jump off a balcony half naked? Obsess over the one man who tried to kill you?" His eyes are fire. "Make me move furniture?" he snarls.

"Well, you did a true shit job moving the furniture. Pretty sure you cracked most of those tables. I won't be asking you to do that again," I say.

"Good."

He tips his head to the side, ever so slightly. And I can hear the *whoosh-whoosh-whoosh* of blood rushing through his jugular.

"You haven't had fresh blood in weeks," Skeele says. "Everyone can tell. You're moody and bitchy and everyone is afraid of getting bit."

"You're a bastard." If I nearly killed him before, I might kill him now. "I'm not a rabid dog."

"Do it, Meg," he says. "Use me. You've been doing it for a long time. All the way back to the cabin in Vermont. Why stop? Now that you know the truth, you're free to decide. Eat." He leans closer, the tip of his nose rubbing against my ear. "If you want to fuck, I'm good with that too. It's been weeks since you writhed over my body. I won't hold back this time like I did all the others."

I close my eyes and try to tamper down the thirst. Now that the offer is on the table, my throat feels drier, the ache between my thighs harder to ignore. I could shove him away, or... I could use him, just like he wants me to. He is my Hellion Commander, the closest thing I have to a partner in this mess. It can be no strings attached. I learned my lesson with Sparrow. Just feed and fuck. That's all. Fill the need because I can't go head-to-head against Sparrow with that bottled blood the Hellions eat.

I smooth my hand over his chest, over his shoulder and rest my palm on his neck. "Don't get too attached," I say, leaning closer, licking his jugular.

One hand slams into the wall behind my head, the other curls around my waist pressing us closer together.

"Never," Skeele says. "Already forgot all those other times happened. If you didn't rule this place, I'd have already forgotten your name."

The bastard.

Poof.

I take him to my room.

Payback's a Bitch

Poof.

I return to Sparrow's Kingdom. Strong, filled to the brim with fresh blood. I stand in the shadows at the edge of the forest. His house has been demolished. The basilisk bones are gone. There is a new house built further back, this one less grand than Remiel's home. It looks more like the cabin Sparrow lived in while he was nothing more than a Legion Commander in Gabriel's Kingdom. As I observe, I wonder if he has rooms in the basement where he likes to lock up family members just like Remiel did.

I grip *Birds of Paradise* by the spine, the book is heavier than I remember. That's good because I have big plans for this book.

Poof.

I'm at his door.

Poof.

I check the back door.

Poof.

I look through the windows.

Poof.

I'm standing at the foot of his bed. He's sleeping. A tall, blonde

Angel-woman sleeps next to him. I can hear her blood pulsing through her veins. The *hush-hush-hush* of slumber. It's so soft. Relaxing. Slow. A lullaby.

How times have changed.

Sparrow once told me, *"I am your monster, your saving grace, your everything."* He asked, *"Will you love me forever?"* He promised, *"...we'll be invincible together."*

It was all lies. Lies darker than a cold winter night in Gouverneur. Darker than a Demon's son filling my head with deceits and my belly with child. Darker than what those Hellions did when they stormed my house. I thought I'd seen darkness before but seeing Sparrow like this and rubbing my fingers on the scar over my heart tells me otherwise. I've lived through his dark lies, but I am darkness now. I sit on a throne of bones. I rule a kingdom of the dead. I may not have wings, but I will have revenge.

Sparrow rolls. One eye peeks open. Ireland grass green. I will never forget. Before he can sit up straight, I throw *Birds of Paradise* at his head with all my might.

Sparrow blocks the book from hitting him in the face with the quick movement of his hand. The heavy book falls on the blonde, the corner of the spine hitting her ear. She wakes up and starts running her mouth.

"Who is that?" she shouts. "Sparrow?"

I could tear out her throat.

Poof.

I throw back the covers and grab her by the hair at the nape of her neck.

Poof.

I take her to the grassy knoll between the house and tree line. She's screaming. Whoever this chick is, she's not composed or strong like the other Angels I've met. She slaps at me; weak, untrained, pitiful.

"What are you doing?" she screams at me and cries like a child.

I shove her away and she falls.

Sparrow comes running out of his house. No shirt, black wings, low slung loose pants. Damn, if I didn't want to kill him...

The blonde scrambles to her feet, screaming.

Poof.

I lift her by the arm. Her blood is really pumping. I can't ignore it. Not with him watching. The desire to hurt him as much as he's hurt me is strong.

"Don't do it, Devil," Sparrow yells, pointing at me.

I do it.

I grip her neck and tilt her head to the side, then I sink my teeth in. Just a little taste to see what's so special about her. There's no tingle of ancient blood, nothing that lights my veins aflame like royalty or special powers. It's worse; the fact that Sparrow chose her, nothing extraordinary. He prefers soft weakness and someone so pathetic. I suppose she's pure, untouched, probably even stupid like a barbie doll. Maybe that's what turns him on now.

She faints and drops to the ground as I let her fall, her heartbeat slow and steady. She'll live to tell the story of the morning Meg came for Sparrow.

Sparrow disappears for a moment. He can still poof to travel it seems. He returns a second later, his blade ready and glowing. I reach for the blade at my hip and take a few steps to the side, readying myself. He could go after the girl or come for me. It's only a moment before he comes running toward me.

Poof.

I move behind him.

He turns, blade raised. I hold my blade up and they clang together at the hilt. He's strong, pushing against the hilt of my blade. I drop to the ground and roll away, swiping at his ankles.

Poof.

He's straddling above me. I punch him in the knee.

Poof.

I move away and get to my feet.

Poof.

Sparrow is behind me.

Poof.

I travel faster and faster, appearing behind him, at his sides, low to the ground. I kick him in the shin, the thigh, the balls. Then I move further away.

Sparrow pauses. It seems his ability to poof is weak. I remember those days, when the ability was new and I needed to be full health for it to work. But he could only travel because he drank my blood. The power will be gone soon and he'll have to travel by foot or motor.

Poof.

I slice his thigh.

Poof.

I slice his arm and slam my blade against the arch of his wing. Black feathers fall.

Poof.

I watch him from a few hundred yards away. Sparrow runs toward me, the wounds on his leg and arm dripping. I lick my lips, do my best to ignore it. Even after feeding from Skeele and the dumb girl, I want more.

Poof.

I move behind him.

Sparrow must've anticipated that. He's turned, his blade moving, he hits me in the upper arm, slicing deep.

Poof. I move away.

He points at me. "How'd you like that, demon bitch?"

His words are hurtful. Even though I hate him, each new example of how he's changed hurts. I recall the stab wounds, the pain. I use it. Nothing is stronger than pain.

Poof.

I grab him by the hair and climb his back like a hyena.

He grabs my injured arm, squeezes hard and pulls me off him, throwing me to the ground. I land on my back, the breath slammed out of me.

"No, you don't," Sparrow says through gritted teeth. His heavy boot lands on my neck, the tip of his blade pressing into the soft skin beneath my chin. "This is where I end your reign." He leans down, his wide shoulders casting a shadow over me. "Grace for grace."

"I never had any," I say with a smile.

"There are rules. One realm cannot obliterate another realm's policing force." Sparrow reminds me. "I'm the last one. You can't kill me."

"You're full of shit," I say, watching the blood drip down his arm.

"Those dead things killed them all," Sparrow says. "And you sent them."

"I didn't send anything. They licked your blood off that wall. Yours and Teari's."

His face doesn't flinch when he says, "You're lying."

"Nope."

"Raguel said–"

"He's wrong," I reply.

"But you..." Sparrow says. "I remember all those lies you confessed to me." His eyes narrow. "Lying lips are an abomination to God."

"I've been told he doesn't exist. What does it matter? The Angels lie more than anyone I have met. More than me. You're not supposed to be able to lie but it's all you asswipes do up here." I open my mouth as a drop of blood falls from his arm toward me. Yum.

Poof.

I move from under his foot to a good hundred feet away. I point my blade. His blood tastes good, strong. He's definitely leveled up. I guess that's what taking the crown does. He is the Raven King with his blackened wings.

"I want my nephew," Sparrow says.

I shake my head. "Died with his parents," I say.

Sparrow's eyes narrow. "There was no body." He grabs his blade, readying for another round. "He'll turn into something else. He won't stay a boy for long."

"I have no reason to care."

"Demore will come for him."

I embrace my inner liar and dig in deep. "I don't know what you're talking about."

Sparrow smiles. "Has she already come for him? We're missing a Deacon."

"Could care less about a Deacon. They should all die if you ask me."

"They maintain the balance of the realms."

"Bullshit," I say. "They meddle and toy and disrupt."

"So you know about the dead Deacon?" Sparrow asks with another smile, catching me.

I've told so many lies I can't keep them straight. Maybe the truth will set me free. Maybe I should just spit the truth like bullets at his head.

"You let these bastards lock up my father," I say. "You let him sit and rot in a Babylon cell." I tip my chin. "There was a time when you would die for him. For me. What about that?"

"Gabriel lied for you. He forbid the others from holding you accountable for the Fast-Zombie War."

"Unpossible," I use Sparrow's word against him. I guess it's not a lie if they're just spreading ignorance. They don't know the truth so they fabricated their own.

Sparrow makes a sound. "Your snake killed everyone."

"Believe whatever bullshit you want." I ready my blade and bend my knees, prepared to fight. "I came here to kill you."

Sparrow sprints, running for me, blade raised. Black wings spreading, he launches himself into the air.

Shit.

A second pair of white wings appear in the sky. Raguel. More flying angels appear behind him. Five to be exact. The surviving Archangels have come to help their brethren. Word must've gotten out. I turn and find the blonde is gone. She must've run for help and run her stupid mouth.

I don't want to leave, but I don't want to die here. I point at Sparrow with the tip of my blade. A threat if I ever gave one.

Poof.

I go home. Disappointed. My only satisfaction was throwing that book at Sparrow's head and watching it hit the blonde.

———

"Where were you?" Tukka asks as I appear in the hallway outside the Hellion lair. "You look out of breath." He sniffs the surrounding air. "Have you been fighting?"

"Mind your business," I warn.

The door to the Hellion lair opens quickly and Gabriel is standing there. "You're bleeding." His eyes zero in on the cut on my upper arm, concern wrinkling his brow.

"It's just a cut. I need–" I start to say.

Suddenly Skeele comes stomping down the hallway. "Come here," Skeele calls.

I stand my ground.

Gabriel tips his head, intrigued, taking in the dirt on my skin and sweat, the blade with drops of blood secured to my thigh.

"Don't be so nosey," I warn him.

"I only have concern for my daughter, who has clearly been up to something."

I raise my chin. "You forget, this is my realm. I do what I want."

Gabriel steps back and spreads his hands with a little bow. "I yield." He looks into my eyes. "Be careful."

Poof.

I go to my room. I clean my blade and set it aside. Then I go to the bathroom to get a good look at the slice in my arm. It aches. Blood is oozing out. I pinch the skin surrounding the cut and see white bone. Saliva fills my mouth. I might vomit. I can deal with a lot but looking at my skeleton is a little much.

I get my shirt off and search the cabinets for bandages. Teari's healing powers used to be really convenient. She could have fixed this cut in a few minutes. I find some gauze and antiseptic under the sink. I stand, my gaze falling on the tattoo of the sparrow. I want to scratch it off. I should've known better. I broke the first rule of getting tattoos: never put your boyfriend on your skin. It always ends badly.

There's a loud slamming sound as my bedroom door opens and thuds against the wall. I step out of the bathroom and find Skeele standing in the doorway.

"Can I help you?" I ask.

He enters my room and slams the door closed.

Shit. I'm in trouble.

"Did you go there alone?" Skeele asks, stepping toward me. His eyes roam over my body before focusing on the cut.

"I don't have to tell you where I go or what I do."

"Right." He sniffs the air. "But you smell like him. You smell like the putrid air of Heaven. You let him touch you?" Skeele's fuming.

"Calm down," I warn.

He stands one foot from me, the muscles in his shoulder and neck flexing. His hands make fists. "I am calm."

"I didn't let him touch me. I went to kill him," I say.

"Is he dead?"

"No."

"Why did you go alone?" Skeele asks.

"I wanted to kill him on my terms."

Skeele walks around me and turns on the shower. "And how did that work out?"

I look at myself in the mirror. Blood drips off my elbow onto the white countertop. I look pale, tired. "Not so good."

Skeele is behind me, inspecting the cut.

"It's to the bone," I say.

"I am nearly tired of seeing your bones," he grumbles. "Of everyone I've ever met, ever killed, ever come across, I've never seen their skeleton like I've seen yours."

"It's that bad, huh?" I joke, my laugh cut short by a quick intake of breath from the sharp pain in my arm.

His fingers touch the tattoo of a spattering of stars across my left shoulder and move to the anchor on my ribcage. "I like this one the best." He pushes the waist of my jeans down, revealing the heart on my right hip. He licks the cut on my arm and it seals the wound, staunching the bleeding.

"I warned you not to get too attached," I say.

He makes a face that's hard to read. "Telling you what I like doesn't mean I'm attached." He unbuttons my jeans and shucks them down my legs in swift, rough movement.

Jesus. That was hot.

He stands and leads me to the shower with his large, warm hand on the small of my back. "Wash, rinse, repeat." Skeele orders.

I want to tell him I give the orders around here and that I don't take orders from him. But I'm trying to be better to those who help me. I keep my mouth shut and step into the shower.

I wash, thankful that water isn't seeping into the cut on my arm. Soap would've burned like a bitch. Skeele waits near the door of the bathroom. He's leaning on the counter, one arm crossed over his chest and the other holding a book.

I wash my hair and wonder where this guy keeps getting books and newspapers. He's the only person I've ever seen read in this castle.

When I'm done, I wrap myself in a towel and open the shower door. "What are you reading?" I ask Skeele.

He flashes the cover at me. Different Seasons it says in red.

"Where did it come from?" I ask.

"The library." He makes a duh face.

"You just always seem to have a book when I'm injured." I point out.

"It's because I have to prepare for the long haul of sitting around and watching you come back to life. I stash a book. Or just keep one in my pocket. Because listening to you snore is boring." He pats the large cargo pocket of his Hellion gear.

I dry my short hair and brush my teeth. While I'm scrubbing away, the cut on my arm breaks open. "Ah," I say as it aches worse than before.

Skeele sets his book down and moves closer. He grabs a clean towel from the drawer and presses it to my arm. "Guess we better fix this."

My stomach clenches. He just fed me less than twenty-four hours ago.

"Don't be embarrassed, Meg," Skeele says. "I know it's nothing." He picks me up and takes me to the bed.

———

"You still want food?" Noah looks around me to the mound sleeping on the bed. "It smells like sex and blood in here."

"Don't be a hater," I warn. "I was injured." I point to the bandage on my arm.

"Looks like you're still injured," Noah says. "Ok. Fine. I take pity on you. What do you want to eat?"

"Two large coffees, with four creams and four sugars. Three Jelly donuts. And an enormous pile of crispy bacon." My stomach grumbles at the thought of a sweet and salty breakfast.

"You're a pig," Noah mocks with a smile hinting at the corner of his mouth. "But I will get this food for you. Because it is my duty to serve."

"Maybe, drop some donuts off with Jed and Shay and Thrush too," I suggest.

"Babies can't eat donuts." Noah frowns. He's so serious, so unlike my old Noah, but I guess we are all different these days.

"Live a little. Maybe the others would like surprise breakfast," I say.

Noah disappears.

I press at the gauze wrapped around my arm. There's a little blood seeping through which is strange. I would have expected it to heal after having fresh blood. It was a deep cut. Maybe it just needs more time.

Skeele moves, still asleep. The blankets are barely covering his ass. The deep vee of his spine and firm back are on display. Memories of last night fill my mind. There was lots of biting and positions I haven't tried before. My cheeks flush as I remember my favorite.

Noah appears. Coffees and plates of food. "Get that look off your trash face." He sets the food on the table. "I saw the way you were ogling at that poor Hellion boy."

I laugh. "He's not a boy."

"Hm." Noah looks at Skeele. "Definitely not. Does this mean you're broken heart is fixed?"

My spine stiffens.

"I guess it was too soon for that question," Noah says, looking out the window. "Poor sucker doesn't know what he signed up for."

"It's nothing serious. Just a living buffet of food. Remember. That's what you demanded I do. So that's what I'm doing."

"And having a little fun too." Noah's voice is dull. "I gotta go. Enjoy the coffees."

Skeele groans. He rolls to the side and shoves a hand out over the mattress. His face pinches. "No," he growls. His eyes are closed.

I stand and walk closer.

His body tenses and twists. Sweat beads his head. He groans and mumbles.

"Hey," I say.

He doesn't hear me. He's having a nightmare or something. I crawl across the bed and set my hand on his shoulder. He's hot, warmer than ever. I shake him. "Wake up."

Skeele's eyes open suddenly. He glances around the room before his eyes land on mine.

"I think you were having a bad dream," I say.

He reaches up, one hand sliding up the side of my neck and

around to the nape, gripping the hair at the base of my skull. He pulls me closer until our lips are almost touching. "You should eat," he says.

"I just ate last night and Noah brought coffee and donuts."

He sniffs. "I thought I smelled that. I thought it was you smelling like breakfast." His lips move across my jaw to my neck. "Just have a quick snack before that sugar-laden crap you eat," he asks. He moves my legs with his free hand and rolls me onto my back.

His tongue licks my neck, my collarbone. He slides the shoulder strap of my tank away and takes my breast into his mouth. It feels so good I close my eyes and let him explore. My hands rub his shoulders, his neck, the back of his head before gripping his horns.

He mutters in Hellspeak.

"What did you say?" I ask.

He pauses his sucking. "Touch the horns, prepare to ride." He chuckles as he tugs on my shorts, removing them in pieces. Next goes the tank. "No one touches my horns," he says.

I let go. "Oh. Sorry. I didn't realize." I bite my lip to stifle a moan as his tongue explores the vee between my thighs. He tugs me lower on the bed, until we are face to face again.

"I didn't say to let go," he says placing my hands on his horns again. "Don't go to Babylon alone ever again." He says. "Promise me." He moves my legs apart with his knee. He grabs a small knife from the nightstand and cuts his wrist, holding it over my lips.

"That's not fair." I want the blood more than anything. More than his warm body. More than his sinful tongue and erection.

"Promise me." He presses the drips of blood to my lips and then pulls away. "Promise."

"Ok. Fine." I lick my lips and close my eyes. My throat feels hot. My lower abdomen throbs with want and need. "I won't go alone."

He presses his wrist to my lips and lets me feed. "Don't go alone again. Take someone, anyone. Just don't go alone."

These Hellions have become far too concerned. I file it under things that annoy me, close my eyes, and focus on control.

The blood is good. His thickness and length that fills me, even better.

Skeele

Skeele watched her sleep. Propped up on his elbow, his other hand hovering over the bandaged wound on her upper arm. There was something wrong with it. She'd healed faster from worse and the blood soaking the bandage caused concern. He touched her dark hair, the line of contrast as it fell on her pale skin. Hell had never seen a woman on the throne like this. Never someone so small and soft and without wings. Skeele knew she could turn into a monster. He'd seen it the day she killed her grandfather, he'd seen the spark in her eyes when Tukka attempted to train her to sword fight, he'd seen it wavering on edge with her shifty moods. That didn't stop the others from talking. It didn't stop the Hellions from being extra cautious. They were afraid of her weakness, but he knew she could slay every one of them in a heartbeat. She'd barely stepped into her strength. That worried him. She teetered on the edge of true power.

He glanced at the bite marks on his arm. Demons are always hungry. Fresh blood made it harder to control. Skeele had to watch himself before *his* darkness was out of control, he didn't want to return to the old days. Meg deserved better. He'd vowed to be better.

Skeele wanted nothing more than a few more hours sleep; they'd been up most of the night and Meg had taken a little too much blood. But he couldn't close his eyes. The dreams had started the day Sparrow chose him to be Hellion First Command. They worsened the day he watched Meg drain Lucifer of life. It was always the same. Some type of fighting, her being injured, him praying that she'd wake up. Except, she never did in his dreams. She shriveled to a corpse and turned to dust. And it was always in Babylon. If Skeele did anything in his life it would be to keep her out of that city.

Skeele shook his head. He couldn't close his eyes. He had to watch her, just as he'd done all this time. It was his duty. He scanned her back, the swell of her hips. The rest–the blood, the sex–it was a benefit of the job. Or at least, that's what he told himself. He remembered her warning: don't get attached. He reminded himself that she felt nothing and was most certainly disgusted by him.

Skeele rolled out of the bed, found his clothes and his book. He grabbed a coffee and donut from the table near the balcony.

Poof. He went to his quarters and avoided the walk of shame. It was bad enough Meg didn't want him. He could handle the teasing from the Hellions, but the cold shoulder from her hurt. Even if he was simply doing his job. He had to be careful though, traveling on a whim was something new he'd never experienced, and he knew it was from drinking Meg's blood. It wouldn't last, so he enjoyed the power while he could.

———

MEG

Gabriel and Clea are standing on the lower landing of the winding stairwell. They don't hear my footsteps, and I slow, crouching near the banister to watch them. Suddenly I am transported back in time, the forbidden child who never had a home with her parents, watching them from the shadows. I close my eyes and imagine what it could have been like if my mother had lived and the two of them stayed together. We could have been a real family. I could have turned out much differently having not been raised by John Lewis. My throat feels thick as I imagine dinners at a large table with a boisterous Gabriel and serene Clea. Maybe they would have had more children, maybe the fractured bloodline wouldn't have ended with me.

Gabriel and Clea whisper in the shadows. Gabriel leans his shoulder on the wall, smiling, looking like a teenage boy. Clea looks up into his eyes. He says something and she laughs. Gabriel leans closer to her, touches her hair, pausing when his fingertips go right through the strands. Nothing will make you remember that your only love is a ghost like permeability.

I stand and keep walking down the stairs. My footsteps become louder and Gabriel finally notices me. He clears his throat and steps away from Clea, their intimate conversation changing into a formal hello and goodbye. Gabriel passes me on the stairs with a nod.

I stop next to Clea.

"Child," Clea says, concern marring her face. "What are you planning?"

"Things," I say. "I'm planning things." I don't tell her the truth for fear she'll talk me out of it.

"Whatever you do," Clea says, "This is not a lone wolf battle. You need the others. They need you."

"It's just easier to do it myself. Never could count on another soul before, why start now?"

"Times are different, child. You are different. You took the throne. Enjoy all the accoutrements." Her cool fingers touch my cheek. "I think I was wrong." Clea says with a frown.

"About what?"

"I handpicked Sparrow. I saw it in the stars that he would protect you. I told everyone." She looks out the window and over the tree-tops, her gaze lost in the clouds of Hellsky. "I was wrong. Whoever I saw, it wasn't him." Her image fades until she disappears completely.

I stand on the landing of the stairs alone. A pinching sensation intensifies in my gut. *It wasn't him.*

I run down the stairs, down the hall and into the kitchen. The kitchen staff clear the room. They must sense my need to fill the gaping void with food. It will do me no good, but it doesn't matter.

I go for the fridge first. I bite into blocks of cheese, pies, and puddings. I guzzle milk like a baby calf—straight out of the container. The smell of a fresh chicken roasting draws me next...

I leave the kitchen a disaster.

Poof.

Feeling like a fat-ass, I lay in the grass in the dull sun to digest and plan. My stomach feels like it might explode. I stretch my arms and legs out like a star and take deep breaths, trying not to puke.

I wonder if this is where I landed after my battle with Lucifer? I wonder if my body left an indent when it crash landed and broke every bone? I was filled with fresh blood back then. I glance to Hell-sky, nothing looks familiar from that night. I'm not sure if it would. I was high on adrenaline and blood and... love. Stupidly.

I am still for so long that a chickadee lands on my stomach and chirps. It pecks at my shirt, collecting the crumbs–probably from the pie–before flitting off.

I knew Sparrow wasn't the one the moment he stabbed me. How could you kill someone you love? We are not invincible together. At least he broke his family's curse. At least Thrush won't have to dedicate a portion of his life to being a Hellion like his uncle did.

I take a deep breath and unbutton my jeans.

"Jesus," Noah says, sitting cross-legged next to me. "Never thought I'd see the day that Meg nearly split her pants."

"It's bad. I know." I splay my arms and legs again.

"Are you waiting for the vultures to clean your bones?" Noah toys with a tall piece of grass, twisting it in his fingers.

"Maybe later." I close my eyes.

"Are we going to talk about the kitchen staff?"

"I said I was sorry."

"You scared them."

"I... I was... sad. Okay? Can they forgive me for being sad and trying to make myself happy by eating?"

"You ate *everything.*"

I sigh. "I'll go on a diet tomorrow."

Noah chuckles. "Please don't do that. None of us need to deal with Meg on a diet."

"Remember that time we skipped school and stole that car and drove to Seabreeze?"

Noah settles next to me, his hands behind his head. "Yeah, Meg. Those were fun times."

"We got in a lot of trouble."

"Sure did."

"Look at us now."

"Look at you. I never thought the little girl who sat next to me in Kindergarten would turn into this."

"The ruler of Hell?"

"A pig." Noah laughs loudly at his own joke.

I slap his shoulder. "You're supposed to be my friend. You can't say crap like that to girls."

Noah holds his stomach, laughing.

———

Poof. I'm standing in Jed and Shay's room. They're sleeping in the bed; Thrush is quiet in his crib. Noah is nowhere to be seen. That's good. I didn't want him to catch me in the act.

I do exactly what I told Noah I wouldn't do. I grab Thrush from his crib. Jed and Shay are shouting as I disappear with the baby. I find Gabriel next, his blue eyes wide as I interrupt him eating a ridiculously large plate of spaghetti and meatballs.

Poof.

We're standing beside the fountains of Babylon.

"This is the last place I expected you to take me." Gabriel looks severely disappointed as he wipes sauce off his face.

"Baptize him. Fast," I say.

Gabriel takes the baby from my arms. He whispers a prayer. Blesses his head and Thrush's. He dunks Thrush in the fountain, quick. Thrush waves his arms, startled and scratching at Gabriel. He lifts the boy, water dripping, his small mouth gasping for air. Gabriel chanting a prayer, a blessing, I'm not sure.

Thrush cries.

"Hurry," I urge.

Gabriel nods, praying faster.

He dips Thrush in the water again. It seems to be a long of a dunk. It's too long. The baby's arms stop moving.

Oh no. He's drowning Thrush.

"Stop!" I scream.

Gabriel's face twists, like he's fighting. "It's not me. I can't lift him."

"Get out!" I shout. "Get him out of the water."

"I'm trying," Gabriel says, but his whole-body jerks. Once. Twice. He goes under, water splashing and running over the side of the fountain.

I run toward the fountain only to see a dark shadow under the water. Like a giant mouth, it swallows Thrush and Gabriel whole.

No. No. No. Noah is going to kill me. I can't go back home without the baby. The water of the fountain ripples, clear and blue as the sky. Whatever happened, there's no blood. That can only mean they're alive.

The Scarecrow once told me that water was a universal conduit. It could take us places. Move us between realms like the portals. I see it now. The fountain in the center of Babylon is nothing but a giant portal. To where? I'm not sure. But I don't wait to find out. I jump in after them.

Under the water I can hear it. The clicks and croaks and monotonous hollow song. Nothing like the songbirds from my windowsill. It's mournful, like a whale song in the ocean. *Plip-plop.*

Two Minutes to Midnight

Cool water soaks my clothing as I follow the shadow, and I hold my breath until my lungs feel like they'll explode. Going through the portal makes me feel sick. I kick and swim until I break the surface, gasping and choking.

It's night, the water dark like ink. Raindrops fall from Hellsky. I hear water splashing, a child crying, my father grumbling. I follow the noise, scrambling out of the water toward the shore, the moon my only light. I slip on wet leaves and mud.

There is a cabin in the woods with a dim light on the porch. Moonlight illuminates the muddy footprints and I follow them before they fill with rain water.

Croaks and clicks echo in the forest. The hollow song of the Nightjar fills my ears.

"Mine," a cryptic voice booms.

I see the light of Gabriel's blade.

I want to shout that I'm coming. But I want to be surprise help, not anticipated help. I don't want the Nightjar to know I followed them. Wings would be good right now; I could fly over all these leaves and sticks littering the ground instead of sounding like a baby rhinoceros making its way through the woods.

Shouts from Gabriel make me abandon my attempts at being quiet. I run toward the cabin and shove my shoulder into the door. After three more shoves, it blasts open.

The scene in the cabin is something from a horror movie. I take a lot of life highlights from Shawshank Redemption, but this... this is something darker.

Thrush is floating in the air. His little face is panicked, silent tears rolling down his cheeks.

"Give him to me," Gabriel shouts, reaching.

"Mine," the cryptic voice hisses.

Demore looks like Dracula, changing forms from bird to giant winged shadow. A current of air circles the room, rustling the tendrils of her darkened form.

I grip my blade and stand next to Gabriel.

"Mine," it says.

"Are you Demore?" I ask.

"One should know their realm better," it replies. "You should know better than to steal my gift."

Thrush is quiet now as he watches, too afraid to cry or babble.

"He's not yours," I say.

"He's baptized," Gabriel says. "You're too late."

"Mine," it says. "My gift. They left it for me. My precious baby."

Gabriel signals with his eyes and the tip of his head.

We move together. Two steps for Gabriel to launch himself to Demore's height. It's four steps and a jump for me but I only make it a few feet in the air.

Demore screams, shrill and ear piercing. Thrush cries. The wind in the cabin whips stronger. Dust and dried leaves take to the air. Demore reaches for Thrush, her tendrils of shadow wrapping around his tiny body. She is nothing but darkness now, a flowing void engulfing him.

"Mine," she says as she disappears through a hole in the roof.

Gabriel punches at the wood of the roof. Splinters of broken wood fall around him. He punches it harder, and harder, until blood drips from his knuckles.

"Stop," I beg. "Don't..." I press my lips together and run out the door to escape the blood and search for Demore's shadow amongst the darkened hellscape.

I see nothing, but I hear her call and the cries of the baby.

"This way!" I shout to Gabriel. "The voices are this way."

I run through the forest around lone sacks of walking flesh that wander aimlessly in the night. When the moon rises above the trees, they will sleep like the dead. They avoid me, but Gabriel is a different matter; their jaws snap at him and they turn to follow. But we are too fast, running with everything we've got, trying to find Demore and the baby.

"I don't see them," Gabriel says.

I slow my pace and tip my head, listening for the mournful call of Demore and the cries of Thrush.

There's nothing. Just silence.

"Damn," I mutter. "I can't hear anything."

Gabriel taps my shoulder and points to a clearing in the forest. Moonlight peeks from between the rain clouds and reflects off water like a mirror. There's a dark cloud, independent of the murky weather and lower to the ground.

We make our way to the pond, blades ready.

Something slithers beneath the surface; ripples disrupt the pond of glass on the far edge.

Gabriel pats my arm and points.

"Do we go in the water?" I ask.

"I'm going over it," Gabriel says as he takes to the sky.

I watch from the shore. Like a loser. No wings. No partaking. Just shivering in my damp clothes and dripping hair as the rain turns into a light mist.

The closer Gabriel gets, the farther away the dark cloud moves until it disappears.

Gabriel searches Hellsky before returning to the shore.

"They're gone," he says.

"Have you ever seen anything like that?" I ask.

"I heard stories, but I've never seen anything like that with my own eyes." He wipes at his mouth. "We must find Thrush."

"I know." I say.

———

"Tell me why I shouldn't trap you in the Astral for eternity," Noah is seething.

"You don't understa–"

"I told you to stay away from Thrush and you took him to another realm," Noah says.

Now, Noah's always been understanding. The best friend a girl could have. We've been through plenty together but this... this is something else. I'm not sure he'll ever forgive me.

"Why did you take him?" Shay asks.

"Yeah," Jed adds. "Didn't you do enough damage already?"

"I had to get him baptized." I point to Teari and Gabriel. "He was going to turn into a Nightjar. I couldn't curse his entire life." I look to Noah. "You knew. You knew what fate held for him without the baptism. I couldn't let him turn into something else. Something like Elise. Don't you want more than a jar of feathers to mourn? Don't you want more for your son?"

There is silence. Most of the people in this room didn't know about Elise. They didn't know my unborn daughter died at the hands of the Hellions of before my rule. They didn't know she was a snowy owl who haunted the northern parts of Hellsky. She was two-thirds darkness and one-third light. She was the brightest light in the darkest places. She was the only child I'll ever have since that day I killed seven Hellions after they stormed my home and took more than just my spilled blood.

So I tell them.

I face Noah. "You're my best friend. You always have been. I couldn't let you go through what I did. That's why I took him to Babylon. I didn't know the fountain was a portal and Demore could get him. I didn't know." I reach for Noah, gripping his shoulders. "We are going to find him." I close my eyes and think of the jar of feathers on my nightstand. "If it's the last thing I ever do in this life, I will bring home your boy," I promise Noah.

The room is silent.

Guilt threatens to overtake me. They hate me. All of them. The flood of shame is overwhelming.

—

Skeele

Skeele stood with Tukka and Chel and Klaus. They glanced to him as the scene unfolded. Meg was being thoroughly chastised by her friends and family. He was waiting to see what she was going to do next. Tensions were high and he was glad the new recruit Hellions weren't present. They'd feed on the tension; it would make them wild. They were having a hard enough time tampering down their rage with the bagged blood and saving their wrath for only when it was needed.

Noah and Meg's relationship was deep. Skeele wasn't going to get between them. Noah had told him stories of their childhood. And he was glad that the demon who raised her was dead, or he'd kill John Lewis himself. Meg had faced more pain than most. More deceit, more heartbreak. Skeele kept worse from her. He had his own secret. And when she found out that Skeele's father was one of the Hellions who'd raided her home on the Earthen plane, he was sure she'd kill him in an instant. She'd kill him just like she'd killed his father that night. Skeele didn't have Angel grace or a mixed blood to help his cause. He was Demon, through and through. The gene pool was small; the bloodline, even smaller. There was no separation from his father. It was the worst secret he could ever keep from her. Deep down he knew he was different. But he doubted that was enough to sway Meg's thoughts. She already hated him. Only used him for food. It wouldn't hurt her much to end him. She'd find someone else. There was no fairy tale ending for Skeele and he knew it. Still, it was better to be born of hate and die of sacrifice. That was more than most had accomplished in his position.

––––––

MEG

I go back to my room to shower and change into clothes better suited for hunting Hell-bound creatures. Tonight, we search for Demore and Thrush. I have a good feeling about it. I'm not sure if I've ever been more confident about finding someone. I'm going to find that baby if it's the last thing I do.

Noah hasn't brought me any food since I got back. I'm guessing it's his way of rebelling and hating on me. It's fine. I can survive. I survived a long while without his help. I'll do it again. But truthfully, I could really go for a Moons over My Hammy from Denny's. My stomach growls. I do my best to ignore it as I take a shower and try not to think about how Noah's tether to me is thinner than ever. I swallow down the fear that it might snap and break and I lose the best friend a girl could ever have. I lather with soap that smells like bergamot and lemon and scrub the mark on my thigh harder and harder, wishing it would rub off. The ouroboros reminds me that I always fuck up good situations. I am continuously threatened with resetting the balance. The ethereal equilibrium means so much to Babylon and the missing God of the Earthen plane and Hell. It actually doesn't mean much to me. From what I've seen, fuck resetting the balance. I think it's about time I embrace the chaos. I might have already. Or at least maybe the kitchen staff have embraced my chaos.

I change the bandage on my arm and inspect the cut that won't seem to heal. It burns from the soap getting into it. I dab at the redness before wrapping my upper arm with gauze and securing it with tape.

Standing in the closet I chose leather pants, ankle-high boots with a steel toe, and a dark blue shirt with a wide neck. I can't stand the thought of hair or clothing touching my neck right now. I pack my bag with a jacket, a small blanket, and clean socks.

I move through my room, rearranging and cleaning up. I stop at the jar of feathers on the nightstand. Picking it up, I tip the feathers and watch them fall.

"Help me find him, Elise," I say. I open the jar and take out one of the white feathers with few brown markings at the tip, the quill sharp and firm. I tuck it into my pocket.

The room cools. My breath becomes fog.

"What do you want, Clea?" I ask.

My mother appears in the center of my room. She's translucent with ruby red lips; pale and beautiful as always.

"You'll be careful," she says.

"Of course."

"Did you eat something?" she tips her head looking hopeful. "You'll need your strength, child."

"I'm fine." I adjust my bag and secure my blade to the thigh holster. "Were you going to tell me?"

"Tell you?"

"About Gabriel. You and Gabriel. I've been seeing you sneaking off and finding you together in dark rooms," I say. "Were you going to tell me that you've been seeing each other again?"

Clea smiles sweetly. "It's not like before. You see, I am a speck of what I once was." She reaches for me, touching my dark hair. "We weren't ready to say goodbye all those years ago."

"So, you're just saying goodbye?"

Her smile disappears. "Perhaps. Goodbyes can be long." Dismayed but calm, she closes her eyes like she's remembering. "Our time is finite. Ethereal beings or not, it's still finite. There are curses, dark magic, mortal wounds, our souls can get locked in the Astral. What we had was finite."

I nod, understanding. Every joyful moment I had lasted a second compared to other moments.

"Keep Teari and Shay safe," I make her promise.

She nods in promise, her image wavering and fading like a light bulb flickering out.

"Are you ready?" a voice asks from behind me.

I throw the bag over my shoulder and leave the room, following the giant shadow of Skeele as he walks through the halls quietly. His wings are tucked tight to his back, and I wonder if he's going to act like there's a stick up his ass this entire mission. I might have to snap his neck–or bite it. One or the other will do.

I press my hand to my aching stomach. I should eat. I should quell the thirst. Licking my lips, I watch Skeele walk. There isn't time.

We meet the others at the entrance to the burning caves. Chel, Klaus, Gabriel, and Jed are there. Noah appears, wavering. Shay was moved to the castle with Teari. They'll keep each other company while Clea and Tukka watch over them. The new recruits continue their duties with orders to notify Skeele if they hear the sounds of Demore in the night. She could be anywhere, but I doubt she'd go to the castle in the caves.

We go back to the pond where Gabriel and I last saw Thrush.

The Hellions go to the sky, a flock of dark figures.

"I'll carry you," Skeele offers. "It will be faster."

"No." I walk away from him toward Gabriel.

Gabriel can take me. I don't look at Skeele because I'm already too ashamed of myself for what I've done. Gabriel rarely judges my decisions, and he was there when Demore stole Thrush. I can't deal with the feelings from Skeele right now.

———

WE LAND NOT FAR from where Gabriel and I left when Demore stole Thrush. The plan is to approach her cabin quietly and hope she doesn't disappear with the baby again. We will surprise her in our attack.

We walk in a scatter formation, taking up most of the road. Gabriel leads us to where we last saw Demore's cabin.

Skeele takes his place by my side. "I could hear your stomach growling from the Earthen plane."

I glare.

Skeele steps closer, very close. His upper arm rubs against my shoulder, and he tips his head to whisper in my ear so the others can't hear. "You know, it really hurts, Meg. You fuck me then kick me like a dog," Skeele says, his voice sounding rejected.

"Shut up."

"I know you're hungry." He shoves me a little with his shoulder, just harder than a nudge. "You don't have to ask. You can take."

"I said shut up."

The others have gotten a good distance away, following the cries of Demore. It wouldn't take long to catch up with them. They don't seem to care that I'm not with them. I look up at Skeele.

"Do you know how... humiliating it is to not be able to feed myself? To have to beg and hate myself afterward? The disgust. To have to force you to do it. And to feel..." I stop talking and start walking toward the group.

I've never been embarrassed about sex, but there's something about our relationship–what it was and what it's turned into–that makes my face hot. With others I've had no shame. But Skeele has always been so contained and strong and loyal to me, it feels wrong to use him like a happy meal. He sat by my bed twice now while I came back from the dead. No one has ever done that for me. All that time ago I woke alone in the hospital on the Earthen plane. I was alone when I came out of the coma. But here I wasn't alone. I always woke to Skeele watching over me. He deserves better.

With Sparrow it was different. We were wild and dumb. Young.

Heck, we didn't even know who we were for half the relationship. I was stupid for thinking it could last forever.

Heavy footsteps behind me and a strong hand gripping my shoulder stops me from walking any further. Skeele pulls me backward, my back tight against his chest. Leathery wings surround us, providing privacy. The moonlight overhead illuminates his arms as they wrap around me. He cuts his left wrist with his blade and brings it to my mouth.

"Don't…" I start to say.

"Eat," he demands in my ear. "When we find Demore, you're going to need your strength."

I know what's going to happen the moment his blood touches my tongue. I straighten my spine, close my eyes, and tell myself to keep it under control.

"Eat," Skeele says but before he finishes, my hands slap against his arm, pressing the cut skin to my mouth.

Mmm. There is no road under my boots. No hunt. No group searching for Demore and the baby. There is me, and Skeele, his thick blood, his heat at my back, the rumble of Hellspeak coming from his throat. I press my back against him as I drink, grinding my ass against his groin. I can't help it. It's what I do.

A thick arm wraps around my ribs and squeezes me tighter to him.

I drink.

The rumble of Hellspeak continues. Lips press to my shoulder.

I suck, the bloodlust burning me from the inside like a torch in the night.

Teeth press against my shoulder. I press my ass back harder. His arm grips me tighter. I want to go further. I want to shove his pants down, and mine, and fuck in the street unashamed.

But I don't do it.

I lick his arm until the sliced skin closes. I turn in his arms, hold up my own wrist and slice with the small blade from my waistband.

"No," Skeele says, a pained look on his face.

"You need your strength too," I say. "It's only fair. When we find Demore, I can't have you collapsing."

"I have the bagged blood."

"Not good enough," I say. "I don't know how you Hellions survive on that crap."

"It keeps the feral at bay," he says.

I press my wrist to his lips. "Then be feral tonight." I smile. "I give you permission to let loose."

He groans and looks away as I press my bleeding wrist to his lips. His mouth parts and I am thankful for his wings hiding us or the rest of the crew would be getting a good show right now. Skeele's lips press to the sensitive skin of my wrist and he draws. His gaze never breaks mine. Heat floods my lower stomach and I lean into him. One of his hands moves to my arm, holding it in place, while the other slides across my back and down, gripping my ass and pressing me harder against the bulge in his pants. I know that's not some obscure Hellion gear pressing into my belly. Of all the times I took what I wanted from him, I never thought it was because he wanted to or that something about me turned him on. Maybe I was wrong.

His eyes are dark as he stops, licks my wrist to seal the wound, grips me by the shoulders and pushes me back a few inches.

"Control," he growls. The blackness of his eyes shines.

"Are you telling me or yourself?" I ask.

He turns us before dropping his wings away and folding them behind his back. I straighten my clothes. I guess chivalry is not dead; in Hell at least.

Skeele motions for me to walk around him. As I pass, I glance down at his crotch. "You need some time alone with that thing?" I tease as I walk away and jog to catch up with the others. I don't miss his reply in Hellspeak that sounded like more cursing, and perhaps a threat.

———

A LIGHT RAIN mists the road. It smells like autumn, wet decaying leaves and a chill in the air.

"The pond is in that direction," Gabriel points at a heavily wooded area.

We see the lights of the cabin and make our way into the forest. The rain stops just as soon as it started and the lights of the cabin dim until they disappear.

We make it to the edge of the clearing where we all just saw the outline of the cabin, but it's gone.

"The cabin should be here," I say.

There's nothing but a break in the trees where the cabin should be. It looks like one of those paintings of a forest clearing with a backdrop of trees filtering the light.

The Hellions scope out the perimeter. Noah crosses the clearing, pausing to inspect the grass.

Plip-plop. The sound is faint.

"Demore is here," Jed says. "I can feel her."

I search the sky.

"This feeling has always saved me," Jed says before whispering a chant and crossing his arms to trace the runes on his skin.

I follow the sound. *Plip-plop.* It leads me to the pond we came through that night. Unfortunately, there is not a baby hovering over the center of it.

Noah disappears from the clearing and appears at my side. "Thrush is here. I think... we just can't see him."

Something moves in the water, disturbing the flat glass surface.

"When we saw the cabin, we had just come out of this water," I say. "We saw the cabin when it was raining a few moments ago."

"And?" Noah asks, moving to hover over the pond. "It doesn't seem special."

"A Scarecrow once told me that water was a conduit. We traveled through the water like a portal. I think we need to dunk ourselves to see it."

I walk into the pond as Jed tells Skeele. I go under the water until my hair is dripping and my clothing soaked, then I break the surface. Blinking a few times, I walk to the shore. The cabin is there, lights glowing from the windows. "Get in the water," I say. "I can see it. Water is a conduit to see it."

The Hellions and Gabriel move smoothly into the dark water.

"I'm not going in there," Jed says, standing his ground. "There's something wrong with that pond."

"Do what you gotta do, pal." I pat him on the shoulder and walk toward the cabin. The others follow, the cries of Demore becoming louder.

Through the windows we can see Thrush floating in the air, sleeping. Demore's viscous shadow circles the room. Her hollow notes and monotonous cries must've put him to sleep. I motion for someone to go to the roof, since that's how we lost her last time.

Skeele and Klaus fly to the roof, their boots landing gently. The shadow of Demore pauses its circling and changes shape into a ball around Thrush.

"Christ Almighty," Gabriel says. "She's getting ready to run again."

Plip-plop. Plip-plop. Plip-plop. Her hallowed call repeats faster and faster like a threat.

"I just hope we come out of this with our eyes." I step onto the porch, old wood creaking under my weight.

Demore weeps loudly. Thrush begins crying.

"Distract her," Gabriel says as he runs up the steps and blasts through the door.

I follow him, blade in hand. "Come here, Demore," I shout. "Come and get me."

Demore hisses. "Stupid." Tendrils of her shadow flow toward me. I chop at them with my blade.

Demore screeches. "He's my gift. My precious. My baby."

"He is not." I grab at her shadow-form but my fingers go right through her.

"I'll come for your eyes," Demore threatens. "All of yours."

The ceiling creaks before the Hellions break through. It must've collapsed under their weight.

Demore circles around Thrush and disappears through the giant hole in the roof.

"Mother of pearl," Gabriel runs out the door and takes to the sky. The Hellions follow.

Since I can't fly, I run.

Demore seems to be a creature of habit. She goes to the pond and suspends Thrush over it, just like before. Gabriel and the Hellions chase Demore across Hellsky. Noah hovers over the water, ready to catch Thrush when he falls.

Jed waits on the shoreline with me since neither of us can fly.

"This is ridiculous," Jed finally says. "Demore is playing with them." He watches Thrush hover over the water and Noah hover below him.

Jed crouches and empties his bag onto the sand at the water's edge.

"What are you doing?" I ask.

"I have an idea." He lays out a red square of cloth. "I've been reading up on this. I think it's going to work."

"I'm not sure this is the time for experiments," I say.

"They're not experiments," Jed sounds annoyed. "They've kept me alive this long."

He arranges bones and small black feathers on the square of cloth followed by vials of strange liquid and finally, a stick that he sets to smudge.

"What will this do?" I ask.

Jed points to the water. "You said that's a conduit?"

"Yeah." I nod.

"Then watch this." Jed chants strange words. His fingers dance in rhythmic and repetitive motions with the spell. The water in front of us bubbles softly. Steam rises. I look to Jed and when I look back to the water a white, wispy form is taking shape.

"What is that?" I ask.

Jed simply chants louder and his fingers dance faster.

The form coming from the bubbles solidifies.

It's Nightingale.

———

"NIGHT!" I start to move to her.

"Don't," Jed warns. "She's not here for you. I didn't call her for you."

I stop running toward her.

Nightingale looks just like the first day I met her: a black crop top and tiny red gym shorts with white piping-straight out of the eighties. She has headphones resting on her neck and she's wearing the big, clunky roller skates. She turns, her dark hair flowing down her back. She glides across the pond, skating. She twists and turns so fast her image is a blur. She whistles a melodic trill.

Noah turns away from Thrush.

It's hard to describe the moment Noah recognizes Nightingale. Everything changes. There's electricity in the air. The light from the moon dampers to a dreamlike haze.

Nightingale glides to Noah. She takes his hand and takes him into the air as though there is an invisible elevator. They circle as they rise until they are with Thrush.

Thrush floats between them and coos as he recognizes his mother. Nightingale whistles a gentle trill to Thrush before taking him into her arms and holding him close.

Plip-plop. Plip-plop. Plip-plop. Plip-plop. Demore comes from over the treetops, fast. Her mournful melody gets louder and louder.

"Mine," she cries out. "My precious. My baby. My gift." The dark shadow of the Nightjar soars faster to meet Nightingale.

Night holds out a hand. I'm not sure what she is but she has a power that stops Demore in her path. Nightingale's sweet, high-pitched chirping trills turn into guttural chatter that makes the hairs on my arms stand up straight.

"What are they doing?" I ask Jed.

He's standing at my shoulder, no longer chanting, and praying. "They're gonna fight."

Nightingale pushes Thrush into Noah's arms and then she illuminates, drawing all of the light from the moonlight until she's a giant, glowing orb. Demore's shadows grow and blacken, her tendrils draping the canopy of the forest.

I'm waving my hands at Noah, trying to get him to move back. Whatever they are doing, they are getting bigger and bigger and drawing energy from around them.

Gabriel sweeps down, white wings spread wide in all their glory, and grabs Noah and Thrush, bringing them to the opposite side of the pond.

Lightning crackles between the twisting balls of energy that Nightingale and Demore have become. They rise in the sky, swirling, crackling, screaming, and crying. Their forms shift and blur. They twist and jab. The wind picks up, blowing my hair out of my face until it's dry.

Without the water, I can't see Demore so good. I can't see her cabin. I step into the pond to soak myself again, submerging myself for a moment. My head breaks the surface. Nightingale sends a blast of light and electricity to Demore. The dark ball of energy shrinks and shudders in defeat.

The fight is over. Demore's cabin is dark. Her shadowed form roils behind the windows. Nightingale drops from Hellsky like a ballerina, landing elegantly on one foot. She glides across the water on her roller skates, twisting and turning like an ice skater. She stops in front of Noah and bends to talk to Thrush. She says something to Gabriel and he takes to the sky, moving away.

I face Jed. "That was the best idea you've ever had," I say as I walk toward the shore. "You saved Thrush." Nothing can wipe the smile off my face.

Jed smiles and shrugs a little. "Nothing can defeat a mother's need to protect her child."

"It was per–" Something grabs my boot and jerks me backward. Hard. I drop, catching my upper body and grabbing handfuls of sand. Water splashes in my face. It jerks me backward again, harder. I go under in the deeper water. I splash, waving my arms, trying to scream only for my mouth to fill with water as I'm pulled under. I try to kick but my legs are immobilized, held tight together by something strong. It pulls me deeper and deeper until I can no longer see the light of the moon past the surface of the pond. Water fills my mouth as bubbles of the last bit of air in my lungs rises to the surface.

Darkness Calls The Raven King

Skeele

"Where did she go?" Skeele shouted at the others. He flew closer, now that the battle was over, to find Gabriel. "She went under the water and never came out."

Gabriel frowned. "It's a portal. We went through it before."

"A portal to where?" Skeele asked.

"Babylon."

"No." Skeele shouted. He dove into the murky pond water, searching. He swam deeper and deeper until his lungs burned. He couldn't find anything. Nothing resembled a portal under the water. He broke the surface and chanted every portal opening phrase he'd come across. None worked. Nothing appeared under the surface.

Gabriel joined him.

Then Klaus.

"I can't find anything," Gabriel said as he broke the surface and caught his breath.

"Me either," Klaus said, spitting water.

Chel shook his head no.

Skeele's heart beat fast. He knew he didn't have much time. And goddamn him if his nightmares were going to come true today. He swam toward Gabriel, knowing he had enough of her blood to travel once. When he'd fed from her wrist at the start of the hunt, he hadn't taken much. He had one shot. Skeele grabbed Gabriel's shoulder and... *Poof*. Skeele and Gabriel went to Babylon.

———

MEG

I wake, coughing and spitting water from my lungs. It spreads across the cement floor I'm lying on, turning the gray dark. I cough hard, trying to get out all of the water. My chest aches, water drips from my clothes and hair.

There is a dark feather on the ground in front of me. A memory...

"...the last Argentavis feather ... "What did you show them, mother?" I whisper to the feather. There is an arc of static electricity, my fingertips tingle, my eyes widen and... I see... I see.

Wars. Blood and death. Good and evil. A dead Sparrow. A motherless child and a fatherless child. Light and dark. The Earthen plane and the ethereal realms. A burst of bright light. An explosion. Fear and pain. Emptiness. A dark, never-ending vat of emptiness that would suck every joyful moment right out of me."

Sparrow had a vision that day too. Clea had given us both feathers.

"What did you see?" I demand. "Remember when I told you we're invincible together?" he asks. "Yes, and Clea said the same thing." "I saw a dark future, one where we are separate." He closes the space between us and takes my hand again. "She showed me, Clea showed me."

I was afraid to lose the one person who had shown me love and caring and truth. Whatever he saw, it wasn't worth saving. Or maybe, it was exactly where we are today. Maybe he didn't care to try and change our destiny.

The Raven King is waiting on the other side of the bars. His dark wings are dripping with water. Those green eyes damn me.

"That was really inspiring what you all did back there," Sparrow says. "Best part was seeing Thrush alive. And that spell to bring Nightingale back." He slow claps. "Spectacular. The Archangels haven't seen magic like that in eons."

"Why didn't you just take what you wanted if you were there?" I cough up water and move to my knees.

"Nightingale forbade it." He crosses his arms and looks down at me. "I'm not going to mess with my sister. Especially in her Astral form. If I go after her baby, she'll put a roller skate through my skull."

I sigh, relieved. "Then why am I here?"

"You killed that Deacon. They want retribution." Sparrow makes a face. "There's something else they want you to do. But they won't tell me what it is."

"I wish I had been the one to kill the Deacon. It was Demore. His eyes were gone. He turned into a fast-zombie. Someone injected Angel blood into him." I pause for dramatic effect. "Who would have done that? We burned the body." I hold my throbbing arm. "I'll kill every one of them if you don't let me go."

Sparrow points to the opposite side of the cage. "It's open. Remember when you and your filthy Hellion's cut Gabriel out, the same passage is there for you."

I glance at the opening. It's a trick. It has to be.

The sounds of water splashing interrupts.

"Looks like we have a party," Sparrow says, focusing behind my cage.

I take the distraction as my moment to scramble out of the prison cell. I roll, pull myself up on aching legs, and climb through the hole in the bars. I hold on to the corner post, afraid of collapsing.

Turning, I see Skeele and Gabriel exit the fountain of Babylon. I've never thanked God before, but I consider it in this moment.

My chest hurts and ears ring from my near-drowning experience.

The other Archangels make themselves known from near Sparrow. Gabriel and the others exchange words. Wing beats resonate off the stone slab under our feet.

Skeele is at my side, soaking wet. Skeele's black eyes bore into mine. "Move," he says. "Be fast." He flattens his hand, lifts my leg, and puts my boot in his palm then throws me up into the sky.

My gut drops. I can't fly. What the hell is he thinking?

Sparrow drops like a hawk, blade drawn. I throw myself back and kick at his wrist. His blade goes flying. Michael comes next. No blade. He grabs my wrist and throws me higher into the air, laughing. I tumble, ass over teacup, in the air. My stomach threatens to empty itself. My arms and legs cycle. This fight has turned into a game of monkey in the middle; me being the monkey and not appreciating it one bit.

Sound like thunder and lightning erupts from the sky as Skeele, Gabriel, and the Archangels go at it with blades and swords.

Someone grabs me by the ankle. It's Michael. He throws me a hundred feet across the sky to Raguel.

Raguel grabs my wounded arm. I scream. I reach around with my good arm and grab onto his shirt. He tries to shake me off.

"You fuck," I seethe. I get a good grip and bite him on the hand.

He tries to shake me off, but I don't let go. I don't release my jaws until his blade comes out. I drop.

Poof. I climb Michael's back and bite him in the neck.

I nearly forgot the taste of Archangel blood and the power that comes with it. Maybe this is what Skeele meant when he said be fast. Eat fast.

Poof. I take it easy on Raphael out of respect for Teari. One bite on the neck. He collapses and falls to the ground. I wasn't expecting that. But it gives me an idea. *Poof.* I appear next to Raphael's body. I dig the snowy owl feather out of my pocket and collect the blood leaking from his neck into the hollow quill.

Gabriel lands near me, blade dripping with blood and out of breath.

Skeele lands next.

"She'll drain every one of you," Gabriel shouts at the Archangels.

Michael points. "She is filth. We are giving her to the Deacons."

Gabriel points his blade. I step in front of him and point my own blade. "You're not giving me to fucking anybody," I say. "I'll drain you dryer than the Sahara desert. Can your annoying ass live without blood? I don't think so."

Gabriel chuckles.

"You will leave me alone." I jab my blade at Michael. "You will destroy that portal." I point to the fountain. "And if I sense you've been working with the Deacons, I'll drain you all." *Poof.* I grab Raguel by his neck and show my teeth. "I'm that fast." *Poof.* I return to Gabriel's side. "You will truce with Gabriel and allow him to return to his Kingdom."

"You don't know–" Sparrow starts to say.

"Shut up." I warn. "He was here before you." I drop my blade and secure it. My bandaged arm throbs and it's all I can do not to hold it and weep. "Let's go."

I walk away. Gabriel and Skeele follow, keeping the pace on each side of me.

Live, Laugh, Toaster Bath

"Are you coming back?" I ask Gabriel as we walk down the road to his Kingdom.

The last time I left Babylon headed in this direction it was in a Cadillac. Now, Heaven doesn't look much different than the Earthen plane. There's busted cars, rotting bodies on the sides of the road, chaos and destruction still lingering from the Fast-Zombie War.

Gabriel takes note of the broken gate to his home. "I'll have to get this fixed first," he says, testing the gates motion. It sags and scrapes the road.

"You think they'll leave you alone?" I ask.

Gabriel nods. "If they know what's good for them." He smirks with a finger held in the air. "Ah, it's good to have the largest Kingdom in the Seven Kingdoms of Heaven. I'll have this rebuilt in no time."

"But Sparrow said everyone was dead. The Legions are gone." I walk past the gate, eager to sit on the shaded, rambling front porch of my father's home since the sun of Heaven is punishing me. I hold a hand over my eyes, wishing for sunglasses.

Gabriel laughs. "For Pete's sake, I'm a little smarter than your average Archangel. My Legion is fine and well. I hid them."

I scan his lands not noticing anything different or out of sorts. The house is there, giant and magnificent; the Legions barracks and training grounds down in the back, the walkways–although dingy– still in place.

I get closer to the house, remembering what he told me during the Fast-Zombie War when I came to find him. He did say he was bringing his people food and they'd be fine.

Skeele looks uneasy in this realm. I'm sure it feels about as far from home as he's ever been. He never gets more than ten steps away from me and keeps looking behind us and up to the sky. He flicks his wings every so often and I'm sure it's because he's sweating like a whore in church under this sun as well.

"I'm going to stay, Meg." He rests a giant, tattooed hand on the porch railing as I walk up the few steps and sit in the shade. "I'll be fine. Thanks for the hospitality in Hell." He reaches forward to shake my hand like a businessman.

"Any time you need to run from the law, Dad. I'm here for you." I press my palm to my throbbing upper arm.

Gabriel tips his chin at me. "You better get that looked at."

I rub my lower arm. "It's from Sparrow's blade," I explain. "He sliced me down to the bone."

"It hasn't healed?" Gabriel asks.

I shake my head.

"Hm." Gabriel rubs his scruffy beard, looking hard at the blood-stained bandage.

"Sparrow's you say?"

"Yea."

"You better have Teari look at that." Gabriel looks off in the distance. "You should probably go now. I'm eager to free my people from hiding."

"You don't want us to help you?" I tease.

"Not even a little bit." Gabriel doesn't attempt to move. He just stares me down like he really wants me to get the fuck off his land.

I guess I wouldn't want anyone to know where I hid my entire Kingdom of Angels either. Even though things are good between us today, I've seen families turn sour over something as minor as a curse. He can keep his secrets, I'll keep mine. Although Gabriel is my father, we might not always have such an amicable relationship. After all, he's been around for an epoch at least. And just like Teari said, people change. Just look at Sparrow. Look at me. I'd say look at Skeele but I sense he's always been halfway decent for a Hellion spawn.

"It was nice saving the realms with you," Gabriel slaps my back as I stand and move toward Skeele.

"I'd say 'anytime,' but nope."

I take Skeele's hand. From the shiver of his arm, I must've startled him. He spreads one leathery wing behind me like a shield.

Poof.

We return to a dark castle in the burning caves.

———

I PUSH open the giant wooden door to the cave, weary but triumphant. In the dim light I notice Skeele's Hellion gear is marred and dented. No one gathers to greet us, other than the creatures that scurry and slither in the shadows of the castle.

"I think I need a shower." I pull my damp shirt away from my skin. After being soaked in pond water and then battling the Archangels, I'm sure I smell ripe. I consider inviting Skeele along for the shower but as we get closer to the Hellion lair, he strays further and further from my side.

He's probably tired of me using him like a Golden Corral buffet.

"Make sure you see Teari about that arm," Skeele says as he points to my bandage.

"I'm going to see her next." I pause and reach out. "Do you want to have dinner... or a dinner. With everyone?" I ask. "To celebrate."

Skeele smiles. It's small and a bit shy, maybe because he'd never expect me to invite him to something like that. His wings hang, tired and dirty. He tips his head toward the Hellion door. "Everyone would like that. It will raise spirits."

I smile a little too much and try to ignore the awkward tension in the hallway. But I'm coming down off a shit ton of adrenaline and it makes me stupid. "Okay. I'll see you later."

I walk toward the stairwell that leads to my room and try not to look back at the Hellion lair door.

I run into Clea on the stairs. She appears to be waiting, wringing her hands in worry.

"Hey," I say. "What's wrong?"

She was deep in thought and her image fades as she notices me. "Where's your father?"

"He's in his Kingdom. He stayed in Heaven."

"Oh..." Clea looks out the window. She's upset. "He didn't tell me he wasn't coming back."

"Maybe he didn't plan on staying?" I say.

"He left without saying goodbye," she says. "It's fine." She wipes at her eyes. "It's not the first time."

"I'm sure he'll be back. Probably sooner than we think."

Clea nods quietly as she fades into nothingness.

Twenty-six years later and he's still breaking her heart.

I walk up the last flight of stairs and down the hall to the room where Shay and Teari are. I knock twice before opening the door. It's empty. Uh oh. Dread floods me. Just when things were going so well.

Poof.

I go to the cemetery, relieved when I hear the giggles of Thrush from behind the fence. I grab the handle of the gate but it burns my hand.

"Ah!" I shout as I wave my hand, trying to cool the burning skin. "What the heck?"

"Meg?" Jed asks from the other side. "Is that you?"

"Yes it's me."

The gate opens.

"Oh, thank God. We thought you were gone." Jed opens the gate wide and lets me enter.

They're all there. Noah, Thrush, Nightingale, Shay and a handful of Hellions.

"You were supposed to be at the castle." I remind them.

"They were safe with me," Nightingale says. She's holding a sleeping Thrush and cooing to him and rocking him.

"Where's Teari?" I ask.

Noah nods toward the front door.

I pass Shay who's talking closely to a Hellion about survival gear and easy to hide weapons. "Welcome back," she says with a smile as I pass her.

I open the door to the chapel and find Teari sitting in a chair and staring at the wall.

"How's it going?" I ask, closing the door and sitting next to her.

"What do you want, Meg?" Teari seems suspicious.

I lean back and pull the snowy owl feather out of my pocket. "I have something for you. Something that I think will help."

Teari holds up her nubbed arms. She clicks the hooks of the prostheses. "These puppies help me more and more every day."

"Then why are you sitting in here alone?"

She makes a face. "It's hard seeing Nightingale like she is."

"At least we get more time."

"True," Teari says. She notices the feather in my hand. "What's that?"

I grab her arm, pull it straight, and stab the quill into her soft skin.

"Meg!" Teari screams. "What are you doing?"

The quill empties of Raphael's blood and I set the feather on her lap. Teari's face turns red. She knocks off the prostheses, leans back on the couch, and holds up her nubs crossed on her chest. Slowly, her arms start growing. There's a commotion in the room as Jed and Shay and a few Hellions shove open the door.

"I knew we couldn't trust you in here. What did you do?" Jed asks me.

"Oh, just performing a miracle," I say. "But I'm hurt, really. Why must you always assume the worst of me?"

Jed walks over to Teari as her arms elongate into hands and fingers.

"I always assume you're up to some shit," Jed says. "But this is better than I was anticipating." He jabs me in the shoulder, playfully.

I fake a yawn and rub my arm, holding in a wince.

Teari's fingers have grown back. She waves her hands in front of her face, disbelieving.

"Oh my God," Teari exclaims as she stands. "This is the best." She runs toward me, throwing her arms around my neck and hugging me too tightly. "Thank you, Meg."

"It was nothing." I pat her back awkwardly.

She pushes me away, wrinkling her nose. "You stink."

———

SKEELE

Skeele stood at the wooden, lacquered bar and ripped open the bag of cold blood. He drank the entire bag without stopping to take a breath, then reached for another.

"Don't choke on that," Klaus said with his eyebrows raised in concern.

Skeele had been back for a few hours but had barely spoken. It was clear that he'd been fighting, but he had yet to tell them who he fought or who won. They could smell the air of Heaven that clung to his clothes, so they had a few clues.

"I can empty the fridge," Tukka offered, his dark red skin

reflecting off the glass door as he opened the fridge again. "We can restock."

Skeele simply shook his head in agreement.

Chel appeared from the shadows in the corner of the room. He grabbed a glass tumbler from under the bar and a bottle of whiskey. He poured the whiskey into the glass—more than a shot—and slid it across the bar to Skeele.

Skeele dropped the bag of blood, picked up the glass, and downed it in one swallow. He waved for Chel to keep them coming.

For a good thirty minutes Skeele alternated between drinking the blood and the whiskey. Tukka, Chel, and Klaus were starting to get concerned.

"Where are the new recruits?" Skeele finally asked.

"Some are in the barracks, sleeping," Klaus said.

"Half are on assigned rounds," Tukka said.

Skeele shook his head in satisfaction.

He finally sat in one of the barstools and slowed his rate of ingesting the whiskey and blood. The others stayed close, worried.

Skeele told them about the battle with the Archangels. He rubbed his face and horns. "I've been dreaming that she dies in Babylon," he said. "I thought this was the day."

"We won't let that happen, boss," Tukka said.

Skeele nodded in agreement. He'd do everything in his power to prevent it, but he couldn't get the image of Meg on the ground in that cage out of his head.

"Is there more?" Chel asked quietly.

Skeele nodded and cleared his throat.

Skeele's blade clashed against Michael's. He wasn't prepared to take on an Archangel alone. Michael shoved and kicked. Raguel fought dirty, ripping Skeele's wings from behind. Skeele roared in pain before kicking Raguel in the chest, sending him backward. Fighting in the air was unfamiliar to Skeele. Gabriel came to his rescue one too many times. He had started to feel like a burden in this battle. He had started to feel like they were going to lose. Worse, he watched the Angels toss Meg through the air like a doll. It took her too long to get her bearings and use her power.

The Angels had said things to him as they fought. Dirty pig, Disgusting Hellion, wretched dog. If Skeele was ever considered a skilled protector, the Archangels were more skilled at spewing sinful language from their tongues. It grated on his conscience. The words they used weren't that far from Meg's language when she said she hated the Hellions.

SKEELE WAS STARTING to wonder if maybe his father's kind of Hellion was better equipped. Hellions from Lucifer's rule weren't swayed by the foul talk, they'd give it right back and then some and follow up with violence. But the old Sparrow had taught Skeele to be different. Skeele had studied human and Angel ways. Humanity and angelology had become a part of him and as much as he hid it, he was struggling at the moment with the clash of emotions swelling inside him. His brain was running a thousand miles an hour processing everything that had just happened.

He was quite sure he could have handled it all just fine if Sparrow hadn't whispered to him when their blades clashed together. *"Don't you hear that heartbeat? That's mine. And I will take it."*

Now Skeele was on edge. He couldn't hear heartbeats from far away. It was just another threat.

Worse was the way he flew into the pond to find Meg. He couldn't get over it. He risked everything. His whole life. And the worst part was, she'd never know how much she meant to him. She'd only know him as a warm bag of blood and a disgusting Hellion.

Amidst the ruins of their battlefield in Babylon, Skeele stood alone. The echoes of the clash between the forces of Heaven and Hell still reverberated in his mind, but his thoughts were consumed by a different torment—one that cut deeper than any sword. Skeele's bloodline was known for being ruthless and cunning. Yet, his heart, blackened by darkness, burned for Meg.

He watched Meg and Gabriel, his eyes clouded with a mix of longing and bitterness. He had fought alongside Archangels and the leader of Hell. He'd hoped that his valor would change her view of him. But despite his efforts, Meg's heart remained distant, unyielding.

The weight of his unrequited love pressed upon Skeele like an invisible burden. He had watched Meg's attention and affection bestowed upon her friends and family, their mere existence eroding his spirit. Every smile she directed at another, every whisper of endearment he overheard, chipped away at the fragments of his shattering soul.

Skeele understood the futility of his desires. He knew Meg was not one to be possessed or tamed. Her heart was a tempest, feral and wild, resisting the constraints of any suitor, including him—the commander of her fearsome legion of Hellions.

His thoughts were interrupted by the sound of Tukka cleaning up the bartop. The war may be won today, but his internal struggle, his battle for Meg's heart, seemed an endless cycle of torment. She was obsessed with a man who tried to kill her and the fact that Sparrow's heart still beat was competition.

With a heavy heart, Skeele summoned his strength and resolved to set aside his personal anguish. There were battles yet to be fought, Hellions to command, and the leader of Hell to serve—without getting attached. He would carry on, his affection forever unreturned, but his loyalty to Meg unwavering.

Skeele stood from his seat and made his way to his room. As he took his first step forward, he promised a vow. He would be the fiercest warrior Hell had ever seen, not for the promise of love, but as an offering to the throne.

———

MEG

Teari inspects the cut on my arm. "It hasn't healed, even with fresh blood?"

"Nope," I say, wincing.

"This is easy. I've seen this before. Sparrow's blade must've been dipped in poison." She makes a face.

"You outdid yourself, Meg." Teari says. "I didn't need hands for this."

She calls for Noah. "Go get the baby basilisk."

Noah leaves, returning a few moments later with a covered wicker basket. He's making a face. "It's bad enough you make me feed these things," Noah says. "I don't like handling them."

"Be nicer, Noah," I say. "They lost their mom. She gave her life to the Seven Kingdoms of Heaven."

"Do they want the rest?" Noah deadpans.

"Stop arguing," Teari scolds as she pulls the basket closer, opens it and reaches inside. "These things are so slimy," Teari complains. The baby basilisk writhes in her hands, slime dripping on the floor. It stops moving when she places it near my arm.

The baby basilisk opens its mouth in anticipation, and she moves it closer until it latches onto the skin surrounding my wound. "It's like on the Earthen plane, with the leech therapy. The basilisk sucks the poison out."

I shiver. "Gross."

"They're good creatures to have around," Teari says. "We don't have them in the Seven Kingdoms of Heaven. Or the Earthen plane. The doctors at that hospital told me about the leeches, they've got to be the closest thing that resembles these there." Teari pets the basilisk. It breaks suction and twitches. Teari settles the creature in the basket before inspecting my arm again. "I think it got the poison out." She cleans my arm and wraps it in white gauze. "If this doesn't heal in a few days, you'll need to have the basilisk drain it again."

"Wonderful." I'd prefer a puppy or a kitten to the slimy basilisk.

MEG

Noah talked me into wearing a dress. It's low cut and tight and smooth against my skin. I've worn less so I'm not sure why I feel so uncomfortable.

Clea suggested opening the exterior doors so we can see Hellsky while we celebrate. It's a clear night with an infinite spattering of stars and a full moon.

I stare at Skeele who is standing in front of me, ready to open the door. He's wearing some kind of formal wear that's black and gray. He looks really good, even with the scruff on his face and the dark circles under his eyes.

"You ready?" he asks, one hand on the door.

"I think so," I say, smoothing my hands over the black satin dress. "Is this too much?" I ask.

Skeele focuses on the feather in my hair, then looks away and pushes the door open. "You look good," he says quietly. "The others will be pleased your ass isn't hanging out."

The formal ballroom is huge, with tiled floors and cavernous ceilings. Giant open archways let in the moonlight. The room seems too big for the dozen or so people who came. There are three tables in the center of the room. The pizza and drinks are off to the side. Another table has a record player set up and Nightingale glides over to change the song.

Noah appears at my side. "Meg," he smiles, "You're looking much better than the trailer park I pulled you out of."

I slap at his shoulder. "Just wait, a few drinks and you'll be wishing you left me back there. You can take the girl out of the trailer park but not the trailer park out of the girl."

I walk to the food table and get a plate with three slices of pizza and a mug of the spiked punch. I sit next to Teari as she's explaining the healing benefits of the basilisk to Tukka and Chel.

Everyone is lighthearted and chatting. There's no doom of impending Archangel fights. No threats from the Deacons. No chomping of fast-zombie jaws.

I eat the pizza and down the punch.

Nightingale dances with Thrush on her hip and Noah in front of her. The record player is blasting *Take On Me*. Thrush jabbers and moves his arms in what I can only imagine is baby dancing.

I Wanna Dance With Somebody comes on. The urge to dance is strong and Klaus must notice.

"Would you like to dance, my Queen?" Klaus asks with a bow and his palm out. He's wearing a purple button down and black slacks. His sleeves are rolled up, and it appears he's been cutting-a-rug for some time now.

I slap my hand in his and let him pull me to my feet. He drags me to the section of the ballroom where Noah and Night are dancing. Tukka dances alone until Clea shows up. I bust out every move I learned in Gouverneur elementary school and let the music take me back to a simpler time. I forget about basilisk and Nightjars and Scarecrows and Deacons. I let them evaporate from my mind and revel in the feeling of a full belly and warm night and clothes that fit and a day without a fight. I focus on that feeling of snow at Christmas and the hope of New Years Eve, Cadbury Eggs stolen from the local gas station because I wasn't getting an Easter basket from my fake dad. You know, simple feelings from simple times. Nostalgia stings realizing you can never go back, you can only remember that feeling. You can never go back home, you can only create a new home and better memories.

Klaus takes my hand and spins me, he pulls me close before dipping me and spinning me again.

"I didn't know Hellions could dance," I say, out of breath.

"We can do plenty of things," Klaus says. "Dancing is just the tip of the iceberg."

Time of My Life starts playing.

"Oh my god," I say. "I haven't heard this song in a million years."

"On day you'll say that, and it will be accurate," Klaus jokes.

"Do you know the dance from the movie?" I ask.

He makes a maybe motion with his hands but the smile on his face tells me he knows. Klaus takes both my hands and soon we are mimicking Dirty Dancing. I'm Jennifer Gray and he's Patrick Swayze and nothing matters but getting the final move just right. My dress isn't the right fit for all the twists and turns but I hitch it up so I can bend my knees better. Klaus doesn't get too close, but he does all the lifts and spins like this old movie from the eighties is his lifestyle.

"Are we doing the lift?" he asks.

"If you can lift me," I say backing up. I probably don't back up far enough, but I run at him and he swings me up into the air. My stomach flip-flops as the memory of being tossed by the Archangels hits. I push it away and plaster a smile on my face. My friends don't need to deal with my baggage tonight. I don't want to deal with my baggage tonight.

Klaus sets me on my feet and we laugh.

"You did it," he says, his expression so joyful he's almost handsome.

I curtsey like I grew up in a castle or went to a Miss Manners class as a kid. We all know better though. I learned how to curtsey from watching actors do it on TV. This is only the fourth time in my life I've ever curtsied.

The song fades and *Every Breath You Take* starts playing. Klaus gives me a questioning look. He knows I can't handle too much of the touching. I spin away from him with a promise to dance to something with a faster beat in a few minutes.

I make my way to the balcony and get a look at the stars. Skeele is there, hiding in the shadows. Lurking, and if I didn't know better, sulking.

"I thought you were Chel," I say, "He's usually the one lurking in the shadows."

Skeele tips his head but doesn't speak.

"Do you want to dance?" I ask, walking toward him.

"The song's almost over," he shakes his head but doesn't move away.

I pause, my confidence wavering. After all we've been through, the rejection throws me for a loop. I wanted us to have one night of fun, one night of relaxation. No rules, no wars, no realms, or rules.

Time After Time starts playing.

Something changes in Skeele's eyes.

Maybe he sees how his rejection hurt.

He reaches out with both arms, grips my elbows, and brings me to him. "What's wrong?" he asks. "Are you hungry?"

"No." I smooth my hands up his arms and consider telling him yes. "I asked if you wanted to dance." I search his face for an inkling of what he's thinking. He is stone. A statue. Unreadable. I sway to the slow song.

It takes a minute for Skeele to loosen up and move his hands to my hips. Maybe it's because all of our intimate moments have been in my room. Never in public.

"I never thanked you for coming to save me in Babylon," I say.

Skeele moves us back into the shadows so no one in the ballroom can see us.

"I will follow you to Babylon, to Hellsky, to the ends of the Earthen plane," he promises as he tips his head and touches his lips to my bare shoulder.

"Thank you–"

Poof.

Skeele is gone.

I step to the doorway and notice his figure in the shadows on the other side of the ballroom.

Damn, that stings.

Pour Some Sugar On Me starts playing and Nightingale whoops. She's dancing with Klaus and Noah is dancing around the room with Thrush as he giggles and drools all over his father's shirt.

Clea is laughing at Noah's dance moves and clapping her hands along to the beat of the song.

Poof.

I move to Clea's side. Her cold hand touches my elbow. "Thrush is adorable."

I nod in agreement, swiping at my hair to move it out of my face. My fingers touch the feather in my hair. The realization hits me that I will never have a moment like this of my own. I will never dance my own child across the ballroom floor because mine is lost, gone, nothing but a jar of feathers sitting on my nightstand.

Suddenly I feel ill. The three pieces of pizza and spiked punch crawl back up my throat. Maybe I should have eaten a little slower. I start walking for the door fast, not wanting to ruin everyone's evening with my vomit.

I move faster, then run.

"Meg?" Teari calls from behind me.

I open the first door I come to and thank the stars when I enter an empty room with a trash bin.

I puke up the pizza.

Teari is handing me a napkin. Tears sting my eyes as I hear baby Thrush giggling from the ballroom.

I pause. It still hurts, knowing that motherhood will never be for me. My womb is gone. Cut from–

"*When Teari healed you, she healed all of you. Even what you lost.*"

Oh shit.

"Teari," I ask quietly. "I have never had a period since I transformed."

She looks at me, questioning.

"When you healed me, a long time ago. You healed all of me." I blink hard at her, annoyed that she's not understanding. "Like my fucking womb. Teari, give me some details."

"Angels and Demons and what you are, we don't have periods." She clears her throat. "Do you miss that?"

"Absolutely not." I lean closer to her. "Why don't we have periods?"

"It's just the way it is." She closes the door and sits next to me. "Something to do with the immortality."

Okay. Okay. This could just be a stomach bug or bad cheese or anxiety. A year without a period... some women would kill for that. I should be thankful, exuberant. I should be rolling in my bed like Scrooge McDuck with all the money I've saved not buying feminine products.

"Why are you asking?" Teari touches my back. Her hand slides down my spine, pausing at my hips. Her eyes widen. "Oh..."

"Don't say it," I warn her.

"Meg." She stands and paces the room. "Meg, who's..."

I close my eyes and curse every decision I've ever made. "Get rid of it," I beg. "Please, Teari. Get rid of it."

Her hands raise in defense. "I can't."

"You can!" I stand. "You can and you have to." A bout of nausea forces me to sit again and take deep breaths. "Please take it away. I don't want it. Not like this. Not under these circumstances. Make it go away."

Teari touches the feather in my hair. "Maybe this is a good thing. Maybe it's what we all need."

"I don't need this." I shake my head and swallow down the giant lump of emotion in my throat.

She tries to calm me. "You've been through some rough shit, Meg. But it's going to be ok. This is... this is a miracle. Thrush was the first baby born in nearly a century."

I grab her arm. "It's not a miracle, Teari. This isn't Sparrow's." I stare into her eyes, ready to puke and scream and poof to the moon.

"Then who..." her hands fly to her mouth. "Oh Lord."

"You all did this to me." I point at her. "You made me use him for food. You and Noah." I hold back tears. This is the worst news in all of my life. "Why the fuck did you make me use a Hellion?"

"We didn't force you to fuck him, Meg." Teari says quietly. "We wanted you to eat. You were not well. We couldn't watch you go on like that."

I slap my palms together. "They go hand in hand. Do I need to write a book on it? The blood eating leads to the bloodlust. I drink the blood, I fuck anything with legs. I didn't make these rules. It's just the way it is."

Teari grabs my hands and holds them together. "This is a miracle Meg, whether you see it or not. It's a miracle." She blesses herself, like I'd expect an Angel to do. "I won't help you get rid of it. I can't. I'll do everything I can for you. But there's a heartbeat in your womb and I won't make it silent." She clears her throat. "You have time to figure this out. A Demon's gestation is much longer than an Angel's. There's time to make things right."

"How much time?" I ask, wondering how long I'll have to live like this.

"Usually about eighteen months or so."

Tears pour out of my eyes. I lean forward and heave onto the floor. After what happened to me and Elise, I can't do this again. I can't.

PROMISES, PROMISES.

I WAIT UNTIL EVERYONE GOES TO BED BEFORE GOING BACK to the ballroom. I change into jeans and a T-shirt and steal some bagged blood from the Hellion's lair.

My bare feet fall softly on the tile floor of the Ballroom. I veer away from the pizza and punch. There's empty plates and glasses at the tables. Confetti and napkins litter the dance floor. I tuck my hands in my pockets and pad to the record player.

It's on, the black ring in the center circling, static playing in an undulating hum. I flip through the records on the table and select *Time After Time*. It's been a long time since I listened to this on repeat and got lost in a mood. I set the record on the player and settle the needle. The record spins and the song starts. I bob my head to the beat, turn away from the table, and head for the balcony.

I grip the railing, take in a deep breath, and lean over the edge to look down. The railing presses into my stomach.

"You're not going to jump, are you?" Skeele's voice asks.

I turn to face him. "Not tonight. But, I can't promise about tomorrow."

He frowns. "Don't say that."

"Fine. I won't jump. Not until I get my wings." I cross my arms and turn again. My hand rubs the bandage on my arm.

"Does it hurt?" Skeele asks, focusing on the injury.

"A little."

Skeele grips my hips and turns me to face him. His eyes search my face. "Just a little?" he questions.

"It's fine."

He tugs me closer. "Are you hungry?" he tips his head, revealing the thick, pulsing veins in his neck.

I lick my lips. I'm hungry, but I'm not going to tell him. I'm trying to wean myself off him, I started the moment he refused to dance with me. My ego is too hurt.

"What's wrong?" he asks.

"I just wanted to dance."

His lips part. "You danced with everyone in the room."

"Except you."

"Is that all you want?"

"Yes."

The song repeats in the ballroom. The soft crescendo of the keyboard gets drowned out by the clock ticking percussion sounds. *Lub.... Lub-dub.* It's like a heartbeat.

"Okay," he says quietly as he holds me tighter. His dark wings spread, he steps up onto the balcony railing, carrying me, and jumps off. Skeele beats his wings, raising us higher into Hellsky.

He holds me tighter than anyone ever has, his face buried in my neck, the music playing in the background. I wrap my arms around his waist and tuck my hands into his back pockets. He spins and rocks us to the beat of the song.

For a moment I forget that his child is growing in my belly. I ignore the fact that he should know. He doesn't need this burden. He barely tolerates me most days. And no one should have to handle the baggage that I bring to this party.

Time after time I keep making the same mistakes. The same

stupid decisions. Living with my heart and not my head. Not this time. This time I'm going to do it differently.

What Skeele doesn't know won't hurt him. He'll finally be freed of me. He can have his life back. Heck, I never asked him if he had a girlfriend before I took him to my bed. I'm not going to be selfish this time. I'm going to be cognizant and compassionate and better than I used to be.

Part Three
Night Owl

TURNED TO GRAY

MEG

THE WARM BODY NEXT TO ME SHIFTS, DRAGGING THE sheet. I open my eyes. It's Skeele. Of course it's Skeele. It wouldn't be anyone else. He didn't leave after I fed. He was probably too tired. It's been weeks since dinner in the ballroom and things have been off between us. Not that they were ever really going well. He's still grumpy but does whatever I tell him. Every time I need him, he's there.

The aroma of coffee fills the room as a breeze blows through the open balcony doors. Noah left coffee and donuts. Not long ago I loved the smell. But today, it causes my stomach to lurch. I slide out of the bed and run to the bathroom.

"What?" Skeele asks, sitting up quickly, ready to fight.

I wave as I run, slam the bathroom door, lock it, and dry heave into the sink since there's no food in my stomach to puke up. I turn the water on high to hide the sounds. I don't want him to know. I don't want him to ask. From the corner of my eye, I watch the doorhandle to see if it moves, to see if he tries to follow me in here. I don't want to be caught purging my hopes and dreams into the sink.

It's nothing, I tell myself. *Just ate some bad burritos.* Burritos are never really bad though. I watch my distorted reflection in the sink plug. It could be worse. I could be broke and homeless and living on the Earthen plane. Yeah, that's it. I could be stuck never knowing that I was more than just a trailer-park girl in a small-town fighting like a rabid animal to live the American dream. I grab a towel and wipe my face. Look at me now.

I lean against the counter and press my face into the towel. *Look at me now.* I have fluffy towels, a proper bed, a kitchen with food, clothes that I didn't have to steal. Squeezing my cheeks, I swallow down the lump that's rising in my throat.

SKEELE

Skeele opened his eyes and lay still, listening to the sounds of Meg retching in the bathroom. Gnawing doubt and torment clawed at his heart. He gave himself to Meg, gave his body and his blood but he couldn't shake the persistent feeling that she despised him. She'd said it to his face enough times. His mind spun with uncertainty. The time they'd spent together in the darkest hours of the night seemed like a cruel illusion, tormenting him with false hope. He was sinking into a pit of self-doubt and despair. It had been hard to forget after his fight with the Archangels. He couldn't ignore their words.

Dirty pig, Disgusting Hellion, wretched dog.

Skeele stood and straightened the blankets. He collected his clothes, catching his reflection in the mirror. Shadows crossed his face. *I have pledged my life to her*, he thought, *why does she despise me? I make her physically ill. She can't even look at me.*

Skeele dressed quickly and left the room.

He walked through the halls of the castle within the burning caves. The pain of rejection would serve as fuel; he would remain loyal, a relentless warrior, a commander of unparalleled strength. He would ensure Meg's reign would be unchallenged, her enemies crushed. She could hate him, but he would forever remain loyal and serve. It was in his bloodline, his fate forever solidified in the stars of Hellsky. Meg could use him, that's what he was born and bred for. Serve the throne, nothing more.

Skeele was dizzy, his throat becoming drier with each step. He felt like he hadn't eaten in weeks. He tugged at the waist of his pants. They were looser than ever. He had fed Meg, but didn't take from her like before. Something internal warned him not to. He couldn't place the feeling, but he sensed she needed all the blood for herself. That wound on her arm wasn't healing and Skeele didn't want to risk her not being in full health.

He took one step down the winding stairs that led to the Hellion lair, and on the second step, something strange happened to his body. The fog in his brain intensified, he stumbled, then fell. Skeele rolled down the stairs like a tossed mannequin. He finally stopped at the first landing where the stairwell turned sharply. Dark red blood dripped into his eye, but he didn't care much because he passed out.

———

MEG

"I can't go on like this." I slap my hands on the table. "Last night I almost drained Skeele." I shake the memory and the fear away. "I could barely control myself. Klaus found him collapsed on the stairs this morning. I almost killed him. I can't do this." I run my hands through my hair and tug.

"He might understand," Teari suggests. "Maybe you should tell him. Then he can take proper precautions. He could carry extra bagged blood."

"No." I cut her off. "I want to know how to stop the puking. I want some control back–not that I ever had much, but this is worse. I feel like a dam ready to burst. Maybe it's the hormones. I don't know." I tug at my hair, ready to tear it out.

Teari holds up her finger. "I've been doing some research." She opens an old book. "I got this from the library in Babylon. There are actually a lot of historical books there."

"I don't really care." I lean back in my chair and set my feet on the table. I whistle a ho-hum trill. Just like the old days. I should stop that. "Just tell me how to get rid of this or survive it."

"Well, Meg," she shoves my feet off the table. "First you should remember that you are kind of like royalty now and you should have some manners." She flips through a few pages, and they crinkle like they've soaked in wine and dried in the sun. "You are not complete darkness." She reminds me. "You are half Angel. An Angel's gestation is about six months. You remember how quickly Nightingale had Thrush."

I nod.

"And Demons range from 18 to 20 months." She holds up a finger. "But you aren't full Demon."

"The father is."

"So there's that." She turns the crisp page of the book, and I make the mistake of looking at the pictures. Drawings in black and red of beastly looking creatures tearing apart vaginas and dead women laying on tables with their arms and legs askew and eyes deadened, wide open. So easily the pages could be illustrations from the movie The Shining with Demon babies hacking away at their mother's bodies just to make a grand entrance shouting "Here's Johnny!" amongst all the blood and gore.

"What the fuck, Teari?" I point to the picture. "Am I going to die giving birth to this monster?"

Teari slaps my hand away. "That's only what happens when they breed with humans." She clears her throat. "And we both know that you are not pure-blood human. You'll be fine. Remember Nightingale's delivery. You're a mixed blood, but the right kind of blood."

I cross my arms and stare at the ceiling. "So, if I don't get rid of this thing. I'm going to be a fat-ass for almost two years."

"You might grow in the belly, but you won't necessarily be a fat-ass, Meg. Maybe lay off the donuts." She closes the book. "You know you can't hide this from everyone. Some will tell you're pregnant immediately. They'll hear two heartbeats."

"Can the Hellions?" I ask, feeling like a jerk.

"Nope."

"Can the Angels?"

"Well, Archangels can. But regular Angels can't." She rubs her hands together.

"Does my father know?" I ask.

"I don't know," Teari says. "If he knows he has said nothing to me."

"I should probably get out of here before he sees me and finds out."

"Wait." Teari holds out her hands. "Let me just... check."

I grab her hands to stop her. "How about you just make it go away."

She elbows me and shoves my hands away. "I won't do that."

Her hands hover over my chest and slowly down to my belly. She frowns, a crease in her forehead. "Sit up straight."

I do, hoping for bad news.

One of her hands slides down my back. The other settles on my lower abdomen. She tips her head and closes her eyes. "You need more blood." She tips her head like she's trying to hear something. She moves her hands away and lifts the sleeve of my shirt to find the bandage still there. "This hasn't healed?"

"It's better than it used to be."

She pulls the gauze away revealing the deep cut. It's less deep than when it started but still oozes and aches every day. "Put the basilisk on it again. Every day for a week."

I sigh, grossed out.

"Do it, Meg." She hits my leg.

"Can you come do it?" I beg. "I like it better when you're there."

"I'm Gabriel's personal healer. I can't stay in Hell with you."

"I feel lost without you all," I confess to Teari. "Noah spends less and less time with me. He doesn't want me around Thrush. He just drops food and runs home to be with Nightingale and Thrush."

"You can't hate him for spending time with his family. Nightingale was dead, gone forever. Give him his time. He might not always have it." She wraps the gauze around my arm. "Go see Tukka. I told him how to use the basilisk."

"Fine." I sigh like a child. "So, you'll come for a weekend maybe?"

"Gabriel has me very busy here. We are rebuilding. Several Legion were injured in the Fast-Zombie War. I can't go."

"Fine. Be that way," I pout.

Poof. I return to Hell.

———

THERE'S a loud knock on my door. I throw the covers back and get out of bed to answer it wearing the old flannel I woke up in that one day when I jumped off the balcony. I open the door. Skeele's there.

"You haven't eaten in three days." His tone is annoyed.

"I'm not hungry."

I try to close the door, but Skeele's arm stops it. His big hand grips the edge of the door, holding the lock.

He says something in Hellspeak. I think he's calling me a liar but he never says it in plain English so I can understand.

He pushes the door open. I back up as he enters the room and closes the door behind his back.

"Nice shirt." His eyes linger.

"Thanks. I found it laying around." I sigh, knowing that I was too lazy to button the whole thing. "You can go back to your life, whatever you had planned tonight. You don't need to be here."

My stomach growls loud and it echoes. I cover my face with my hands, feeling stupid.

"Is that so?" His eyes lower.

"You have nothing to do tonight?" I ask. "You don't have to be here."

He walks closer. "I have something to do and that is feed my queen."

I let out an awkward, breathy laugh. My queen. "I'm not really a queen."

"You're not a king." He reaches for the shirt and peeks inside. "Definitely a queen."

It's hard to push him away when he's this close. Even harder to ignore the quick movement of his hands as he slices his wrist and holds it against my mouth.

"That's rude," I say, tipping my head back.

"Did you want to pray first?" The corners of his lips rise. He knows better, I'm not one to pray before meals. I'm not one to pray ever.

I scowl, grab his wrist, and press it against my mouth. "Mmm." The noise escapes my throat as I drink. It's been too long. His blood tastes like champagne on my tongue; tart and sweet and bubbly. It's warm, like he just came from a hot shower or working out. Since he smells like wood smoke and pine, it must be the hot shower. I savor the smell, close my eyes, and take a deep breath in as I lap at the blood dripping from his wrist like it's a melting ice-cream cone. I was supposed to let him go, not latch onto him like this. He probably had plans tonight and here I am holding the monopoly on his time. It doesn't take long for the heat between my thighs to become unbearable.

Skeele sniffs the air. He tries to hide it, but I can tell. I think he can smell the bloodlust. Or maybe he can just smell me. I'm not sure and right now, I don't really care. He pushes me with his free hand, pressing against my stomach until the backs of my knees hit the mattress.

It all goes downhill from there. I promised to be better. I promised not to be selfish, to be cognizant and compassionate. I guess I'll try another day. Tonight is a complete loss. I take from Skeele everything he gives; his blood, his thickness and length, his Demon tongue. And I love every second.

———

I WAKE ALONE and not ready to puke. I get my coffee and donut from the table near the balcony and think about how cultured I've become. I haven't had an orange soda for breakfast in at least a month.

The sun seems too bright today, the chirping of the birds too loud. I wander to the back of the room and curl up in the club chair that's against the wall. It smells like Skeele. I guess it should since he spent enough time sitting in it and watching me come back to life.

Four sips in and I realize what a failure I was last night. I did nothing I promised. I rub my face. What the hell is wrong with me? Bad habits are hard to break, especially when they feel so good in the heat of the moment.

As I finish the coffee, I realize Skeele never took blood from me last night. I guess he's holding back. Maybe he's so fed up with me he can't bear to do it. Maybe it really turns him off. I've never asked. I thought he used to enjoy it. He absorbed my ability to travel at will. Maybe that's why.

———

JED AND SHAY

The dead were wandering about quietly in the forest behind Jed and Shay. Sticks snapped, leaves rustled, moans interrupted Jed's teaching.

"Let's start with a warm-up exercise," Jed said, showing Shay how to stretch, twist, and tap her fingers into nimbleness.

Shay mimicked Jed's motions, her fingers moving faster and faster to keep up with him.

Jed watched her hands intensely. "That's good." His fingers moved in a rhythm only he seemed to know. He clucked his tongue lightly like a conductor so Shay could follow along to the beat. After three rounds he started with the first spell. Jed backed up in a circle, looking for the nearest walking corpse to practice on.

"That one," he jerked his chin to a dead man dragging his foot. "Like this." Jed's fingers danced as he cast a spell to freeze the zombie in place.

Shay's fingers followed along in the same dance, the same nimble spellcast. But no energy moved from her hands like it did Jed's.

Shay dropped her shoulders, defeated. "It didn't work." She flexed her fingers.

"Try again."

"I'm too human." Her voice was thick with disappointment.

Jed touched her shoulder. "I won't think less of you," he joked, the corner of his lips tipping up.

Shay swung at him. "You shit." Her fist landed on his bicep, and she moved to smack him again.

"I think you can do it," Jed said as he sprung away from Shay's fist. "You just need more time."

"It's been a long time. It's been forever."

Jed's eyes went wide and he held a finger to his lips. "Shhh. The dead will hear and come."

Shay paused and looked around. It wasn't long before the shuffling of feet started getting closer. "Shit."

"Let's go." Jed grabbed Shay's arm and tugged her in his direction.

The old Shay would have been pissed for not being asked which direction to run in, but she'd spent enough time with Jed to know that he had a knack for finding a way out. He'd never led her wrong.

They'd spent plenty of time on the run after meeting on the Earthen plane.

Jed and Shay ran through the forest in a roundabout path toward the burning caves.

"Should we go to the cemetery?" Shay asked. "To lose them?"

"We can't risk bringing a horde to Thrush." He ducked under a low branch then held it up for Shay. "If we go back to the burning caves, they'll just wander away. They won't get close. Meg's there. They won't go near her."

"Not like the fast ones did?" Shay asked.

"The fast ones didn't follow the rules of Hell." Jed slowed to check their surroundings. "These slow ones will just move on." He motioned for her to move faster.

Jed and Shay moved quickly through the forest. Once they found the road, they ran parallel to stay hidden. Soon the moans of the walking dead got further and further away. Jed and Shay slowed, only to hear voices not far away. They both came to a stop and listened.

Shay ducked near a fallen tree and focused in the distance. She pointed. Jed crouched near a thick tree trunk coated in lichen and followed her line of sight.

There were three men dressed in black with white collars. Deacons.

Shay tapped her ear. Jed shook his head. Neither could hear what the Deacons were discussing. The dragging footsteps of the dead were getting closer. Jed and Shay were stuck in the middle.

Shay's heart thumped in her chest as they waited. She didn't like the feeling of being trapped. She'd spend too much of her life stuck between safety and the bliss of freedom. She turned to see the decaying forms of the dead as they meandered toward them and estimated how much time they had. At the rate they crept and how easily they were distracted, Shay figured it was less than six minutes before they needed to move again. She focused on the meeting of the Deacons in the road. Hopefully the men in black would be done by then.

Skeele

Tukka grabbed Klaus by his beard, jerked until the giant Hellion dropped to one knee then rammed an elbow into his chest. Before Tukka could finish the move, Klaus twisted and kicked out his leg, tripping Tukka. The vigor that the two Hellions fought with might have worried a passerby, but the line of new recruits were watching with rapt attention.

Skeele clapped his hands together, ending the sparring match between the two. "Alright," he said with one hand raised, "double up and spar until one of you drops."

Skeele headed toward where Chel watched in the shadows of the trees as Tukka and Klaus rallied the new Hellions. They'd almost replaced every Hellion from Lucifer's time. They wouldn't tolerate defectors or any Demon who didn't support Meg's throne.

"Did you find something?" Skeele asked Chel.

"The portals are still down. I checked them all. Nothing but rubble."

"And Demore's pond?"

"It's still there and under guard. We could drain it, but the water would likely collect there again and refill."

Skeele was silent as he contemplated.

"We found something," Chel pulled a metal syringe from his pocket. "There was Angel blood in it."

"Used to inject the Deacon in the cemetery." Skeele touched the syringe.

"It was," Chel confirmed. "We found it in the depths of Demore's pond."

"Put it somewhere safe," Skeele said. "Out of sight." He met Chel's black eyes with the sound of running footsteps in the woods behind them. With a nod, both Hellions readied themselves. "The fast ones are all dead."

"They were," Chel gripped his blade and it glowed, ready for battle.

Skeele drew his blade and sidestepped until he was a few yards from Chel. The footsteps got closer as did the sound of heavy breathing. Whoever was advancing wasn't trying to stay quiet.

Blue shone through the dapple light of the canopy.

"Wait," Chel motioned to hold their position. "I recognize that hair."

Jed and Shay broke through, running and panting.

The Hellions secured their weapons and let their guests enter the training fields. The two stopped to catch their breath.

Jed bent over, hands on his knees. "Damn, I need to run more." He wiped perspiration off his brow. "Been a long time. Too long." He patted his stomach. "Getting comfortable is never a good thing."

Shay coughed. "I was kind of enjoying not running for my life on a daily basis."

"Why were you running?" Skeele asked as he sheathed his blade before crossing his arms and looking down at the human and Nephilim.

"We were training in the forest, past the cemetery and a horde came," Jed said.

"They don't move that fast," Chel said.

Jed held up his hand as he said, "As we were leaving, we found three Deacons in the road not far from here. We had to wait for them to leave. The dead caught up."

"Deacons?" Chel's brows rose in attention.

"Did you hear what the Deacons were saying?" Skeele asked, suddenly interested.

"No," Jed shook his head. "We can show you where they were."

Skeele nodded and motioned for Chel to follow. He had to see if the Deacons had left anything behind.

Of course, they hadn't left a single thing behind, not even a footprint. But the Hellions did a thorough job of surveying the area and tracking back to the crossroads.

"Did they have a vehicle?" Skeele asked Jed.

"Not that we saw." Jed did his best to help but he wasn't trained in tracking, only running and hiding.

"You have a spell or something that could help us gain some insight?" Tukka asked.

Jed thought for a moment before reaching into his pocket to pull out the ages old notebook he carried with him. "I might have something. Let me look."

Shay stood close, watching Skeele as he searched. Skeele caught her eye more than a handful of times before he finally walked over to her and asked, "What?"

"You seem different," Shay said. She was straightforward and honest.

"Nothing's changed." Skeele ran a hand over his head and horns as one runs their hands through their hair in frustration.

"Sure." Shay stepped closer to Jed.

"Why do you ask?" Skeele said.

"You seem tired or sick, and you've lost a lot of weight. You're the Commander of the Hellions." Shay lowered her voice. "Maybe you should see that healer, Teari."

"Not necessary." Skeele walked away from the human and continued on his searching until Jed cleared his throat.

"I found something." He motioned to Skeele and Tukka. "It's a spell that can rewind time but only for a few moments."

Jed's fingers tapped and twisted as he chanted the spell, motioning in the area of the road where they'd seen the Deacons.

Transparent leaves rolled across the road before the images of the three Deacons appeared. They were see-through and faded, like Clea's wavering image. Ghosts of the past. Skeele moved closer and watched their lips as they spoke.

"Dead Newcomers." He heard them say. "Her condition." He couldn't make out the full conversation just bits of it. "Unlawful." Shit.

"What did they say?" Tukka asked.

Skeele pressed his lips together. His stomach felt like a boulder had dropped into it. Skeele had been haunted by the day he ate the Newcomer family. The Deacons found out. They were after him.

———

MEG

The long table in the dining room is overflowing with food. Roasted chicken, piles of grapes, chalices of wine. I pile my plate high but find that I can only pick at it. The days of gluttony on actual food seem to be gone. Or maybe I'm just moody.

Everyone came for Saturday night dinner. We've been trying to make it a weekly event now that things have calmed down. With the truce from the Seven Kingdoms of Heaven, things have been a lot more relaxed.

Nightingale and Shay are mashing sweet potatoes for Thrush to try after he gets done chomping on the corn cob in his hand.

"He has two teeth coming through," Noah says with a proud smile. He tugs two wings off the roast chicken and wags them at Thrush. "Watch this." Noah tosses the wings toward the roiling shadows on the ceiling then holds his palms open with a surprised look when they don't fall back down. "Surprise!"

Thrush looks up then back at Noah before giggling uncontrollably. The sound of his little voice brings a smile to everyone's face.

"Teeth already?" I ask. "Are they sharp?" I point to my own teeth.

"They aren't too sharp," Nightingale says as she combs Thrush's hair to the side. "Did you invite Gabriel and Teari to dinner?"

I nod. "A few times. But they're busy rebuilding." I use air quotes when I say rebuilding because I'm tired of them using it as an excuse.

Nightingale frowns as Thrush whacks her with the corn cob. "I'll give them some nightmares. Maybe that will make them reconsider blowing us off."

"Perfect." I chew on a piece of the roasted chicken.

Two bones fall from the ceiling as the baby Basilisk drop them.

"You'll spoil them," I warn Noah. "They'll be like begging dogs soon."

"Are there dogs down here?" Shay asks.

"All creatures," Noah says.

"Can we get a dog?" Jed asks. "Are dogs allowed?"

"You can get whatever you want," I say.

The door to the dining room opens. Skeele, Tukka, Chel, and Klaus enter.

"Hey, where ya been?" Noah asks.

The Hellions make their way to the empty seats. Shay looks uncomfortable. She gets that way when a group of Hellions are around. I remember when I felt like that. I watch her until she focuses on me. I smile and nod, hoping the gesture offers her some comfort and hoping it doesn't make me look like some weirdo who stares at people.

"We were tracking something," Skeele says. He glances at the empty seat next to me but sits next to Tukka on the other side of the table. I try not to take it personally. My stomach growls loudly.

"You want more?" Noah asks, pointing to a second roasted chicken. "There's ribeye too." He raises a platter piled with steaks.

I shake my head, but Skeele raises his hand and reaches for the steaks. "Hope the kitchen didn't overcook these."

"They undercook everything these days just to get out of the kitchen quicker," Noah chuckles. "They're too afraid of Meg showing up and emptying the fridge."

Skeele's brows raise in question.

"Shut up," I threaten Noah.

Skeele motions to me and mouths, "Are you hungry?"

He's asking if I need blood. I don't want to answer. "I'll have a steak." I stand and reach forward with my fork, jabbing a large steak and dropping it on my plate. They're rare, red juice seeping across my plate. My mouth waters. I dig in and eat the entire thing in record time.

Everyone talks and plans and reminisces. It's like a family dinner from a Lifetime Christmas movie. It makes me feel good. Even better is no one brings up the fact that Skeele fell down the stairs nearly drained of life a few weeks ago.

I remind myself that Thrush isn't a Nightjar, and Nightingale is back, and Teari has her hands again. Things are looking up. My stomach churns. I think I ate too fast.

"I'll be right back," I say as I stand and walk out of the dining room. I hate missing any time from these get togethers. I've waited all my life to have something like this. Even though I feel like an outsider. I feel like I can't relax, I can't let loose like I used to. It's probably the giant secret I've been keeping. It's eating me away from the inside. I've kept worse secrets. There's plenty I've done in the past that I didn't tell a soul about.

Just as I'm reaching for the dining room door, it opens. One of the new recruit Hellions is letting himself in and he has a visitor.

It's a Deacon.

"What the hell are you doing here?" I ask. I look to the Hellion, Shule, "Why is that thing in here? Why did you bring a Deacon to dinner?" Anger is welling up inside me. I don't want to see a Deacon. I don't want a Deacon to see our Saturday night dinner. It feels like a violation, and I hate it. Anger swells, my fingertips tingle. "Get him out of here!" I shout. "Deacons are not welcome here. Ever!"

My stomach is growls loud.

"Meg?" Skeele's voice sounds like it's a million miles away.

My mouth waters. Someone touches my arm. I turn and find Skeele standing there, looking concerned.

"What?" I ask.

"It's okay," he says. "Shule didn't know."

"It's not okay." Damn him for talking down to me. Damn him for interrupting.

"Get the Deacon out of here," Klaus says, making his way toward us.

"That's what I said." I look between the two Hellions. Am I dreaming? Am I in the Twilight Zone?

"Listen to me when I speak." I glare at Shule, and his face is stone. "Get the fucking Deacon out of here."

"We need to discuss your situation." The Deacon has the nerve to speak to me.

"Close your meddling lips." I warn. "How dare you come into my home, uninvited?"

"We've been trying to reach you," the Deacon says, his voice flat and even. He's not scared, not even a little. "We need to talk." His eyes focus on my stomach. "We need to talk about your *situation.*"

"Don't," I warn. "Do not say one more word."

Suddenly, Klaus and Skeele are pushing me toward the hall and out the door.

"Get the fuck off me." I step away from them. "Get your hands off me and get this trash out of my home." I reach for my blade but remember I left it in my bedroom. I was trying to turn a new leaf, attending dinner without a weapon.

"Your situation needs–" the Deacon starts to say.

"No!" I turn my anger on Shule. "Why did you bring him in here?"

Shule lets out an awkward laugh, cocky. Arrogant. He opens his mouth to speak. But it's too late. The welled-up anger has to go somewhere, my body feels hot, thirst strikes. I can't listen to one more word. How dare they? Shule's jaw twitches. I move like a viper, teeth bared.

———

"Come with me," Skeele says quietly. I stand my ground and glare. "I don't want to force you." His voice is quiet so the others can't hear. How dare he?

I look down. There's blood on the floor. The Deacon is ghost pale. Shule is a mound of Hellion uniform.

Klaus looks uneasy.

Noah whispers to Nightingale and they disappear with baby Thrush.

Skeele says something but I can't hear him with the buzzing in my ears.

Jed grabs Shay and his fingers dance in spellcasting. They're gone before my next breath.

Shit. Our night is ruined. Goddamned Deacons and new recruits.

The Deacon backs up into the wide hallway. Skeele says something to Klaus in Hellspeak. Klaus moves around me and takes control of the Deacon situation.

"Let's go." Klaus motions to the Deacon. "Walk, Deacon. You know where the door is."

Saturday dinner devolves into me glaring at the black dress shirt of the Deacon as he walks away, watching his lips, making sure he mentions nothing about *my situation* to Klaus.

Skeele clears his throat.

I spin on my heel to face him. "What the hell was that?" I pace and find myself in the dining room with Skeele closing the door.

"What was what?" Skeele asks, crossing the room, giving me space.

I point, mad as a hornet. "You both interrupting me." I tug at my shirt, suddenly feeling claustrophobic. I can't breathe. "I had control of the situation. I don't need two Hellions butting in."

Skeele nods, his lips pressed into a straight line.

"What?" I shout.

Dark eyes land on me. "You didn't have control. You were very out of control."

"I was fine!"

Skeele spreads an arm toward the dining table loaded with uneaten food. "Then where did your guests go?"

A shudder of embarrassment rolls through me. "Home. I guess they were full."

Skeele chuckles. "That's not why."

"What do you even know? You know nothing." I point at the floor. "This is my realm. My castle. Mine."

"You live here alone?" He's very still.

I take one step forward, ready to pounce.

"You live here alone?" he repeats. "No one else lives under this roof? No one else eats at this table?" He rubs a finger across the polished dining table.

"How dare you?"

"How dare I question you?" he pushes.

The last spec of control leaves my body. I launch myself across the dining room. I toss an errant dining chair on its side.

"You want to fight." Skeele tips his head and cracks his neck with a smile. "Come on."

I reach for my blade, remembering I left it in my room. Pissed it's not on me, I grab a steak knife off the table.

Skeele's brows rise in jest. He reaches to the side and picks up two spoons.

"Don't be an idiot," I seethe, advancing toward him.

"Too late." He knocks the spoons together.

"It's your funeral." My stomach growls loudly. For a moment I revel in the hate of being controlled by blood. I pull a surge of energy from my toes and lurch forward, my knife slicing through the air in a swift arc.

Stainless steel clashes as Skeele crosses his spoons and catches the hilt of the steak knife. Serrated edge zips across spoon handles. In a powerful movement he thrusts the spoons forward and knocks my knife away. He dashes to the left, kicks a chair in my direction, and keeps going around the table.

I growl like an animal. "Running away?"

"Never." Skeele flashes a smile. "Just getting warmed up." He grabs a handful of grapes off the table and throws them at me.

I run toward him, step on the fallen chair, and leap onto the table. I kick a roasted chicken in his direction like a football. He leaps to the side, the carcass missing him and making a splat sound as it hits the wall. Grease leaves a giant mess on the wall as the chicken slides to its ultimate resting place.

"You know there are children starving in China?" Skeele picks up a fork and holds it out, threatening. "Probably some other places too."

"Then bring them these leftovers." I pick up a heavy candlestick and jump down, slipping on crushed grapes. "You gonna comb your hair with that?"

Skeele scrapes the tines across his bald head. "Feels good." He itches behind his ear and against his horns. "You want to touch them?"

"I'll rip them off your head," I promise. I drop the candlestick, pick up one of the fallen chairs, lift it over my head, and throw it at him.

Skeele moves to deflect the chair, but it barely makes it to him. The thing is heavy; it only goes a few feet in the air before falling on the ground with a loud thud and skidding across the floor.

"You're weak." Skeele kicks the chair against the wall. "Maybe you should eat something." He motions to a steak. "Or..." He grabs a knife off the table and holds it to his neck.

"Don't," I warn.

"Why not? It's what you want. It's what you need." He slices skin and a tiny drop of blood leaks from the cut.

"I'm fine." It takes every ounce of control to keep my body still and not jump on him. "Bastard."

"No. I'm not." He cuts his neck again. Two drops of blood trickle down his neck. He flicks his fingers. "Come on. We're fighting, remember?" His eyes crinkle. "Don't hold back."

I consider picking up the steak knife I dropped and throwing it at him, but I don't want any more blood. I'm not sure if I can control myself. My mouth waters, my stomach churns.

"It's been a long time since you invited me to your room." He flicks a wrist. "A long time since you had fresh blood. And we both know what happens when you do this."

"I'm fine."

"Really?" he chuckles, the sound of his voice deep and warm. "This is not fine." He motions to my whole being. "You lost your shit on a Deacon. At dinner. You yelled at that poor young Hellion and killed him."

The drops of blood trickle down his neck and pool in the valley of his collarbone. I lick my lips.

Pounding on the dining room door echoes throughout the room.

"Go away," Skeele shouts.

"Is everything okay in there?" Tukka's voice shouts.

Skeele shoots me a questioning glance. "Are you okay?"

The drops of blood flow to the base of his neck and collect in a tiny pool.

"Perfectly fine."

"It's wonderful in here," Skeele shouts. "Like a vacation on the beach."

"I heard noise," Tukka says, trying the latch.

"Go away!" Skeele shouts looking toward the door.

That's my moment, his eyes are finally off me. I pitch toward him, ready to slam him to the ground. But my foot slips on a greasy piece of chicken and I lose my footing.

Skeele hurdles forward to catch me.

Chivalry should have been dead in this room. It might've saved him from me. I grab Skeele's arm at the elbow and twist, knocking him to the ground with me.

Skeele grunts. "You've been training with Tukka again?"

I shift my weight and wrap a leg around his middle. "Nope. Been watching Escape from New York."

Skeele rolls, taking me with him. His hand slides on a pile of mashed potatoes that made it to the floor, probably when I kicked that chicken across the dining room table.

"Ugh," he groans. He reaches over and wipes his hand on my jeans.

"I'm not your personal napkin." I roll forward and shift my legs. I grab his sleeves and twist, locking his arms against his body.

"You got that move from old movies." Skeele lifts his legs, his thighs hitting me in the back and knocking me forward. I lose my balance and pitch forward, my nose inches from the pool of blood at his neck.

"Do it, Meg. You know you want to. Lick it off me."

"I'm full."

Skeele slams his feet on the floor and pushes up with his hips, tossing me off him as he rolls. Suddenly I am on my back, looking up at him.

"No." I thrash and slap. "No; this is not how it's going to end."

"Nothing has to end," he laughs, collecting my wrists and pressing my arms against my stomach. "We can keep going." He grips my wrists with his large hand, reaches for the knife that fell not far from us.

"Don't," I warn.

"What will you do, Meg?" He puts the hilt of the knife in his mouth, holding it as he slices his wrist. He spits the knife to the side. "Do it. I like it." His voice is low, promising, sinful. "Fuck me while you do it." He presses his bloody wrist against my lips.

"I hate you."

"I know." For a moment, the playfulness in his voice is gone, his expression turns pained. "Eat."

I drink his blood. He releases my wrists, and my hands move to his chest. His free hand roams my body, kneading and stroking. I grip his shirt and pull him closer, the heat between my thighs becoming unbearable. I lick the wound on his wrist and tug him closer. Firm lips dust mine for a moment before he bares his thick neck, pulsing veins, and small drops of blood from where he cut himself. I bite, I drink. Our hands are free to grab and touch. His blood is magic on my tongue, filling the void I've tried to ignore for so long. My brain buzzes with the *rush-rush-rush* of his heart pumping. Sweet and tingly like champagne, I drink like he's a never-ending fountain.

We roll until I'm on top. I tear at his shirt and feed from other places: the firm pectoral, the soft skin of his inner arm, the vee of his lower abdomen. He moans with each bite, his hips thrusting up in need. But I'm not ready for that yet. I'm too hungry. I waited too long. The bloodlust is strong, but my appetite is stronger. His hands are in my hair, gripping my scalp, tugging at my hair; the ache feels so good.

I climb his body like a siren slithering out of the ocean with one thing on my mind: fill this ache, fill this stomach, satisfy the need growing between my thighs.

Skeele rips my jeans apart and touches the warmth between my legs. "Christ," he whispers. "Why did you wait so long?"

I don't reply. I'm too busy licking his abdominal muscles before tasting. By the time I reach his neck, there isn't a spec of his body I haven't tasted, not a vessel I haven't fed from.

I'm ready to sate the bloodlust, brushing my lips against his, I settle his length at the softness of my center. We slide together. I moan.

Skeele is eerily silent. I stop my body. Stop taking what I want. Something more compels me to pause.

"Hey," I touch his face. "Hey."

Skeele's eyes are closed, his jaw slack, his head tipped to the side.

Oh no. I've done it again. Skeele is barely breathing. His pulse is faint. His breathing too slow. I shake his shoulder harder and harder, but he doesn't wake. I slap his cheek.

Panic rips through me. What if it was Thrush? What if it was Jed or Shay or Gabriel or Teari? A sickening feeling overtakes me. I am a danger to my friends. I am a danger to everyone. I can't be around them.

Poof. I go to my room. I don't bother to shower because I can do that where I'm going. I run to my closet and find my bag. I shove some clean clothes in there. I get dressed: jeans, a T-shirt and sturdy hiking sneakers. I take the time to brush my teeth and run my fingers through my hair.

I have one last thing before I go.

"I release you, Noah." I murmur into the darkness.

The thread that tethered us breaks. He is free. No more serving Meg. Noah can go be with his family. Something he never got to experience when he was alive on the Earthen plane because like the song goes, only the good die young.

Poof. I collect Skeele's body from the dining room. *Poof.* I tuck him into my bed because I actually do give a fuck. I can't leave him naked and drained on the dining room floor.

"I'm sorry," I whisper to Skeele. I steal a kiss and press my forehead against his. For a Hellion he's not so bad. Better than I ever expected. I shouldn't have been so harsh with him. I should have controlled my words when I was hungry and angry. But then, lust and hate are brethren, and I was speaking out of fear when I said some of those things. Still, he deserves better than what I have to offer. I told myself I was going to do better but I never did. Same old Meg. Same old mistakes. Not anymore.

———

SKEELE

Skeele woke alone in the dark. His mouth was dry, his body ached. His head throbbed like someone had hit him with a mallet. He sat up too fast and was so dizzy he had to lay back again. He rubbed his eyes and sniffed the air. He was in Meg's room. He groaned, remembering all they'd done, the feel of her naked body on his. Her mouth, her...

He sat up again. "Meg?"

There was no one else. Something was strange, off. He got up and searched the room, the closet, and the bathroom. She wasn't there.

Skeele adjusted his clothing before going downstairs to the

Hellion lair. He hadn't been taking her blood so he could no longer travel at will. He had to use his feet and he was starting to understand why Meg just chose to *poof* from place to place half the time.

The lair was empty except for Chel looming in the shadows like always.

"Hey," Skeele said as he went to the fridge and took out four bags of blood.

"Hungry?" Chel asked.

Skeele chuckled to himself. "Yeah."

"Where have you been?" Chel asked, sounding annoyed.

"I've been here."

"We haven't seen you for two days. And no one has seen Meg."

Skeele paused after swallowing a mouthful of blood. "Two days?"

He rubbed his face. "Did you look for me?"

Chel raised his hands, in defeat, annoyed. "Everywhere."

"Meg's room?" Skeele asked.

"No one answered the door."

"Why didn't you go in?"

Chel made a face. "And have her bite our heads off? No thanks. After the other night, everyone was too afraid of her. Even Noah."

Skeele drank from another bag and collected his thoughts.

"Goddamnit." He slammed his fist down on the bar top and ran out of the room.

Skeele ran up the stairs, four steps at a time, then he ran down the hall and burst through Meg's door. He turned on all the lights. He checked her closet. There was a bag missing and a pair of sneakers. He checked the shelf where she stored her blade. It was still there but covered with a leather sheet.

Her clothes were haphazardly spilled on the floor and dug through. Wherever she was going, she left in a hurry.

"No, Meg." Skeele gripped his horns and held in a roar of defeat. Meg was gone.

Warm nights, Dark beaches

Meg

Florida seems like a good choice. The panhandle this time. I'm ready for white, sandy beaches and turquoise water. Anything closer to Miami brings back memories of Reuben. I shiver. I don't want to remember Reuben and his dark void of a head as the Scarecrow.

The first thing I do is head to the bank. There's a branch down here. I walk inside and show the teller my license.

"You're going to want to get a new one of those." She taps the card as she slides it back to me. "You look different."

"I do?" I bend down to get a glimpse of my reflection in the glass separating us. I look at the picture on my license. "I guess I do," I agree. "I'll go to the DMV tomorrow."

"How can I help you today?" The teller is young, blonde, and cute like she just graduated from high school and wakes up every day with an ass-load of energy to count money and smile at the people of Perdido Key.

"I need to check my balance and I need some cash." I make a few calculations and then round up. "Five-thousand cash."

The girl taps on her computer keys. "No problem."

A man in a suit walks up behind her and they whisper to each other. My stomach sinks. Shit. I turn to look at the door and the video cameras in the corners of the lobby. I'm the only one here. My heart thumps.

The scratchy beeps of the printer pull me out of my panic.

"Okay, I just need you to sign here." The teller slides me a slip of paper. She rests the tip of her pen on the numbers in the corner. "This is your balance."

I lean forward and see a lot of zeroes. Thankfully the money I inherited has just been sitting in savings collecting interest.

"Just a heads-up," she says as I sign, "anything over ten thousand will require a forty-eight hour notice to pull."

"Gotcha." I set the pen down when I'm done signing. She slides me an envelope of money. I tuck it in my bag.

"Do you want to count that?" she asks. "Once you leave–"

"I trust you," I interrupt her, eager to get the heck out of the bank.

"Have a good day." She smiles and goes back to tapping on her computer keyboard.

I step into the hot Florida sun and start walking down the street. I smile to myself. The Deacons will never find me here. They're better off trekking me down to sell me an extended car warranty than knocking on my door to discuss my condition. Fuck my condition.

———

"I NEED A ROOM. FACING THE BEACH." I tap my fingers on the countertop and search the lobby for a gift shop. I need sunglasses in a bad way. My head is starting to throb from the sunlight. It's worse than Heaven. I don't remember the Earthen plane to have such a punishing sun.

"I'll need an ID and credit card." The man behind the desk stares at me.

"I have an ID." I slide it over to him then I search my wallet for an old credit card. It's my lucky day, this sucker doesn't expire for three months.

"You're going to need a new one of these soon." He waves the ID.

"I know. I look different."

"No," he says. "This expires at the end of the year."

"It does?" I take the ID back. "Well, I'll be damned."

"The DMV here is pretty quick. If you're moving here, you'll need residency." His brows rise. "Or are you just visiting? Nearly half the check-ins have been transplants from New York. Uh, the room is four hundred a night."

"Ew." I make a face and look at his name tag. It says Alex. "I used to live here so that makes me better than any typical transplant. I'll take the room for the week. Until I find a realtor."

"Oh yeah?" Alex asks as he scans keycards with his machine. "Where?"

"Near Miami."

Alex smiles and hands me the hotel room cards. "This is a lot quieter than Miami." He winks and I wonder if it's because he's friendly or a serial killer. I should probably work on my trust issues.

———

My next stop is getting a car. I can't be walking everywhere in this heat, and I need to find a house to hole up in. I'd rather be spending the day at the beach but instead I'm sitting in a chair at Crystal Automotive waiting for the sales attendant to confer with his manager about the drop-top Mustang I'd like to buy.

The two men walk toward me, and I stand. I force a smile, trying my best to remember my manners since I haven't been on the Earthen plane in a while.

"We have to disclose to you that the vehicle you want was manufactured before the Zombie War."

"Okay." Jeeze, I didn't realize... I need to read some newspapers and get a clue. The last time I was here the Earthen plane was a shit mess. But the little town of Perdido Key seems to have put itself back together pretty well. There's no blood splatter or brain chunks or rotting bodies, that I've seen.

"It just might... smell a little strange if you leave it in the sun with the windows closed for a long period of time. We've thoroughly cleaned it." One of the men looks at the papers he's holding.

It might smell. Great. The smell of coffee made me spew chunks one morning, I'm sure the smell of death might do the same.

"What else have you got?" I ask. "Money isn't an issue."

The two men look at each other and then walk me toward a sparkling new Jeep Grand Cherokee.

"Perfect. Let's sign papers," I say.

———

IT TAKES me four days to drive to all of the Catholic churches near Perdido Key. Holy Spirit Catholic Church on Gulf Beach Highway is the first to lose its holy water supply and any fountains on the premises. St. Thomas by the Sea is next. Then Saint John the Evangelist church. Then Little Flower Catholic Church. Finally, Our Lady Queen of Martyrs.

The fountains could be portals and destroying the holy water was just something extra because water is a conduit and I'm sure holy water could let lots through. I have to destroy it all, just to be safe. I smashed them.

When I return to the hotel from my last night of destruction, I extend my stay by another week.

"Having trouble finding a home?" Alex asks.

"Yes," I lie.

Alex opens a drawer and digs around for a moment. "Here." He hands me a card. "Check with Stacy. She's my aunt."

"Hey, thanks, Alex." I tuck the card in my pocket. "I'm going to call her in the morning."

What a great guy Alex is. So helpful. He has no idea what I am and what I've done. I like to keep the bar low. It's the best way to start a relationship.

As I walk to my room, my stomach grumbles loudly. Shit.

———

MEG

I dream of volcanoes in the ocean. Hot lava bubbling and splashing on rooftops setting everything near the coast on fire. There are coyotes running through my backyard. I'm watching it all and talking to a bird with brown wings and a white chest and telling it there's no volcanoes in Florida. Perdido Key is safe.

"Perdido Key?" the bird asks. "Are you at a roach hotel or something nicer?"

"I'm staying at Johnny's On the Beach."

The bird flutters off.

I wake up grumpy and hungry. The scar on my arm aches. There are a dozen donuts from yesterday on the dresser in a half open box. I rub my eyes and wish for fresh coffee. Noah isn't here so I have to be a big girl and drag my ass out of bed to go find some.

I put on the clothes I wore yesterday. They smell damp, like rain. I need to get more clothes and find a laundromat. My standards are pretty low but dirty, wet clothes is where I draw the line. I brush my teeth and wash my face then head out.

Alex isn't at the desk. It's an older man with a gray beard and waxed mustache twisted into points. I wave and try to act normal; not like the ruler of Hell in hiding. Not like a vampire looking for blood. I think it works since he waves back and wishes me a good morning.

I head to my car, drive to a McDonald's drive through, and order enough food for three people. I eat it all in the parking lot of a Marshall's department store. When I'm done pigging out, I'm going to one stop shop.

I buy shorts, tanks, clean underwear, a few bikinis, flip-flops, deodorant, and body spray so I don't smell like rainwater for the entire day. I wander by the book section and a book with birds on it catches my eye. *Birds of the World* it reads. The book draws me like an omen. I flip through the pages and land on a page with a little brown bird. A Nightingale. Something pings on my brain. I remember the dream I had last night. Shit. That wasn't just a random dream about apocalyptic volcanoes in Florida and cute little birds. Nightingale is back to invading my dreams.

I jog to the checkout and pay for everything. This has been the world's worst game of hide-and-seek. I gave up my location in record time. As I'm handing over my bank card, I tell myself that there are no portals in Hell. We destroyed them all. There's no way for anyone to get out and find me.

There are no portals in Hell. There are no portals in Hell. There are no portals in Hell.

"What's that, dear?" the cashier asks, her saggy upper arms waggling as she hands me back my credit card.

"Nothing," I reply as I grab my bags and run to my Jeep.

I'm going to have to find a new place to stay. I dig through my wallet until I find the realtor card Alex gave me. Stacie Realty on Gongora Drive. It's on the other side of the island.

I put the pedal to the metal and drive there as fast as I can. On the way, I open my windows and spray myself with the body spray I got from Marshalls, hoping I don't just wind up smelling like rainwater and cheap perfume.

I follow Perdido Key Drive until the turn for Gongora comes into view. The realtor office is a small house with giant elephant ear plants growing near the front porch. After parking, I walk to the door, feeling like I need a hot shower. I should've cleaned myself up before I came here. I shake my clothes, hoping to get rid of the smell of too much body spray.

The sign on the door says to let myself in, so I do. There's a lady with dangling flamingo earrings.

"Can I help you?" she asks, with a mild southern accent.

"I'm looking to buy a home," I say.

"Okie dokie." The sign on the desk says Stacy and I wonder if it's a typo. She rolls in her chair to pick up a stack of papers, then rolls back. "Have a seat. Have you been pre-approved for a loan, dear?"

"I have cash."

"Do you have proof of funds?"

I dig in my bag for the receipt from the bank the other day. "It's in here somewhere."

"While you're looking, tell me what kind of house you want. A condo, a single-family, new construction townhouse?" She talks with her hands moving.

"Something close to the beach and... not too fancy." I find the receipt and show it to her.

Stacy flattens the strip of paper on her desk and makes a surprised face. "Well, with this you can get whatever your little heart desires." She slides the paper back. "But let me pull up what we have for sale. Come around here." She pats on a free chair that's behind her desk.

I sit and smell myself. I tell myself I don't care. I used to smell worse. There were weeks I didn't bathe when I was a kid. "Sorry, I got stuck in the rain, my jeans are damp."

She flicks her wrist. "We get all types in here." She doesn't even wrinkle her nose as she points to the computer screen. "Okay these are what's on the market now. This one is near the beach. She points at a little bungalow with a rusty green roof and surrounded by palm trees.

"I like that one."

"You don't want to see more?" She turns to face me.

"I'm just looking for a home. Something simple."

"Well, eager beaver. Let me call over there and see if we can go look at it."

I lean back in my chair as she makes the phone call. *Woosh-woosh-woosh.* The pulsing in her neck draws my attention. Saliva pools in my mouth. It's been nearly a week since I almost killed Skeele. I get up and move near the door so I'm not tempted to do something illegal. Like suck every last drop of blood out of Stacy's body and leave her carcass for the next buyer to find.

Stacy hangs up the phone. "Let's go." She opens a drawer and gets out her purse before meeting me at the door. "Do you want me to drive you? Or do you want to follow me?"

"I'll drive myself."

I run to my Jeep and wait for her to pull out of the driveway. It's better if I drive myself, then I won't be tempted to lean over and bite her neck. I won't be tempted to grab the steering wheel and... I click the lock on my door. Focus, Meg. Focus.

———

THE STREET IS PARASOL PLACE. There's a crumbling sound as I drive over the white, crushed shell driveway. The house is small and painted peach, with green shutters and white picket fencing across the tiny front yard. Two red Adirondack chairs are on the front porch.

Stacy waves me to the front door. She's messing with a box hanging from the handle.

"I really like this," I say as I get closer.

She gets a key out of the box and enters the house. I follow. The interior is dated but everything that matters works. There's water, a shower, a kitchen, and appliances.

"I'll take it. But, can I get the furniture and curtains?" I ask.

"I can ask the sellers." Stacy texts on her cell phone.

"How fast can we close?" I ask.

"Money talks."

"Tonight?" I ask. "I'll pay fifty thousand over asking price. And I want the furniture."

Sleeping in a stranger's bed seems weird. But I slept on a mattress on the floor for fifteen years, and I'm pretty certain it was pulled from a dumpster. At least this place smells clean and I can wash the sheets or buy new linens another day.

———

STACY FROM STACIE REALTY makes the magic happen. I wire the money and have a key in my hand by seven p.m. She meets me at the hotel for the final paperwork.

As I'm leaving, bags in hand, I notice Alex is working the desk.

"Hey, Stacy!" He waves.

I say my goodbyes and thank-yous and amaze myself with my good manners. Gabriel would be proud. Teari too. The Hellions would be flabbergasted.

I drive to Marshall's, buying a new coffee maker and a few mugs, then head to the little house on Parasol Place.

I like the sound of the Jeep's tires crunching on the seashell drive. It doesn't feel like home, but I've spent most of my life with nothing feeling like home. I think of my little white house in Gouverneur. It was the first home I had to myself. But then Jim came along, and home became something I'd rather not remember.

I unlock the door to my little beach house, go inside, and take a breath of relief. If I never leave the house, no one from Hell will find me. They won't be searching every home in Perdido Key, and I didn't leave a forwarding address at the hotel.

I get my packages out of the Jeep and the first thing I unpack is a fancy coffee maker and two bags of coffee. I wash the mug and leave it to dry by the blue, ceramic sink.

If I do anything during this time on the Earthen plane, it will be to never sleep again. I'm not even going to blink, I can't risk giving up my hiding place to Nightingale.

———

SKEELE

Skeele stood in the living room of the chapel in the cemetery. Scowling, with arms crossed, he waited for Nightingale to exit the bedroom where she was putting down Thrush for a nap.

"Can't you go do it?" Skeele asked Noah.

"Baby wants his momma. And baby gets what baby wants." Noah sat down and crossed his legs. "Want something to eat while you wait?"

"No." There was one thing that Skeele wanted and that was to know exactly where Meg was. He'd come the instant Noah had news only to find out it wasn't Noah, but Nightingale who'd tracked her down.

The door to the bedroom finally opened and Nightingale skated through. She turned to close the door softly and held her finger to her lips when she faced the impatient Hellion.

She whistled a light trill and waggled her fingers at Noah. He smiled. The entire scene tore at Skeele's heart. He'd never have something like this, a family, a child. Or someone who loved him unconditionally and wasn't afraid to show it.

Skeele closed his eyes and took a deep breath. He reminded himself that he was eager to let her use him. He told Meg himself, *use me.* He'd said it too many times. And that's exactly what she did. He got what he asked for. She warned him not to get attached, so he didn't. At least that's what he let her believe.

"I know you've been waiting," Nightingale said as she skated closer to him. "Meg is safe. I could hear the ocean and cars."

"What ocean?" Skeele asked, wanting more details.

Nightingale held up a hand to slow him down. "She's on the Earthen plane. Last time she ran away there she was in Florida. She told me some things before she woke up. I'm sure she's realized it was me visiting her dreams by now. She's in Perdido Key. She's safe." Nightingale leans closer to Skeele. "But she's hungry. Very hungry. This will not end well." Nightingale gave him a knowing look. "There's lots of human blood there. Fresh blood. And they don't stand a chance against the ruler of Hell." Nightingale cleared her throat. "The Earthen plane doesn't have many people left after the Zombie War. If she loses control, she's at God's mercy. That is his plane."

Skeele moved to the door as though crossing realms was nothing more than a hop across a puddle. "I'll go get her."

"Slow down, homeboy." Noah closed the door. "You can't just ram it on in there and drag her back here by her hair."

"She won't do what others tell her," Nightingale said.

"You're going to have to trick her." Noah looked Skeele up and down. "You're going to have to glamour yourself. Change your name. Fit in with the humans."

"Fine," Skeele said. "I can do that."

"You need to do it really good," Noah said. "She'll run somewhere else." There was a knock on the door. Noah opened it and let Jed inside. He was carrying a small pouch.

"One last thing," Noah said. "You're going to need a few tattoos, so the Angels don't come looking for you and try to throw you out. A Hellion being on the Earthen plane is not a light event. Sparrow killed and destroyed. The grouping before found Meg and..." Noah pressed his fingers to the bridge of his nose and took a deep breath. "They can't find you. She can't know it's you. The Earthen plane is her safe place. She always runs there. She always runs home."

"This is her home," Skeele corrected.

Noah smiled, but it was a little bit sad. "It is and she's almost accepting of that."

Jed sat at the table near the window and opened his bag. He took out pots of black ink and his tattoo gun. "Maybe you can change that," Jed suggested.

Noah herded Skeele to sit across from Jed and motioned for him to pull up his sleeves.

"So, what's your style?" Jed asked. "Eagles, Celtic crosses, Chinese characters?" His brows rose in question. "Please don't tell me it's tribal art."

———

Skeele was at the chapel for hours and when he left, he'd gained a textbook worth of knowledge about the Earthen plane and how to pretend to be human. They'd even given him some dating advice. The night air felt strange against the forest images tattooed from his wrists to his elbows. It was Vermont. And underneath the coniferous trees were deep runes that would hide him from the Angels and other otherworldly creatures.

Skeele took to Hellsky and flew back to the burning caves as fast as he could. He had bags to pack and needed to have a conversation with the other Hellion Commanders. He wasn't sure how long he'd be gone.

———

MEG

I binge on movies to pass the time. I order takeout and drive to McDonald's on the other side of the bridge to get coffee twice a day. I tell myself that if someone from Heaven or Hell is here, they are less likely to notice me through the tinted windows of my Jeep so it's a safe option. But I smashed all those fountains at the surrounding churches. If someone were coming for me, it's going to take a while.

Today, the beach is loud. There's maybe twenty other people here but all I can hear are their heartbeats pumping through their bodies. The worst of it are the kids. Their little hearts pump super fast. With the *hush-hush-hush* of it all, I can't focus on anything. I pack up my chair and towel and walk back to the house.

I won't drain anyone's blood. I won't drain anyone's blood. I won't drain anyone's blood.

I get in my Jeep and go for more coffee. My first stop is the Publix grocery store across the Theo Baars Bridge. Thunderheads billow in the distance, lightning starts over the ocean. I challenge myself to get in and out of the store before it rains.

People are staring at me. I lick my lips. This is dangerous. I keep my sunglasses on, pull my hat low, and nearly run with my cart to the coffee aisle. I grab five bags of coffee then head to the refrigerator section for creamer. I pass the fresh meat in coolers and pause. I have an idea. I grab the bloodiest steaks and roasts I can find. If I can't have human blood, maybe some ultra-rare steaks will do.

As I'm leaving the grocery store. The storm thickens and starts rolling in from the Gulf. Right on time. Thunder booms. I run to my car and just as I close the door, the rain pours down. I drive back to the beach house, the bloody steaks calling my name. Just as I turn onto Parasol Place lightning strikes the lamp post.

"Ah!" I scream to myself and take my foot off the gas. My heart is beating a thousand times a minute and the hairs on my arms rise.

If I didn't know better, I'd say God was trying to scare me out of his realm. Maybe this isn't my safe haven. Even though Lucifer and the Archangels told me God was gone. There is some presence on the Earthen plane. God or not.

———

Skeele

Skeele carried a single leather bag and was dressed in jeans, a short sleeved button-down with palm trees printed on it, a baseball cap, and sneakers. He'd preferred his Hellion boots, but Jed and Shay told him they'd draw too much attention. The sneakers felt strange on his feet.

"Show me how to do the glamour again," Skeele asked Jed.

Jed told him what words to say. "It won't fade, not until you come back here," Jed said.

"Are you sure?" Skeele didn't want to be a sitting duck on the Earthen plane. The runes would hide him but if he was walking around the Earthen plane looking like a Hellion, everyone was bound to notice.

Jed stood on the edge of the pond near Demore's cabin. It was night and the other Hellions were keeping the dead of Hell at a distance. They couldn't risk any falling into the portal and making it to the Earthen plane.

"You're going to do fine," Nightingale said with a chirp that sounded like a hiccup.

They were all wary of Skeele going alone. He hadn't spent much time on the Earthen plane and the bags of blood in his pack weren't going to last long. Time was not on his side. He had to woo Meg and get her back where she belonged. Since her disgust was clear and she wanted nothing to do with him on a relationship level, Skeele would have to pretend to be someone else, someone Meg might cling to in her darkest hours.

Jed did his thing. He chanted strange words and his fingers danced in rhythmic spellcasting. A small area of the pond bubbled and then opened up into a dark void. Shay stood by, soaking up the lesson in opening portals to other realms, her fingers tapping in copycat motions. Now that Thrush had his parents, Shay had nothing better to do than learn everything Jed offered.

Jed paused his chanting and nodded at Skeele. It was time for him to go. Skeele jumped through the portal and was transported to the Earthen plane.

———

Skeele landed in a crouched position on the white sandy beach of Perdido Key. Sand slid under his feet. His back felt loose without his wings. The moonlight gave him some light to see by and he was thankful that no one else was on the beach to see him arrive. He stood and took in his surroundings. He had hours before sunrise, so he went straight to where Meg was supposed to be.

Skeele walked Perdido Key Drive until he saw the sign for Johnny's On the Beach. The hotel was small but the light out front flashed vacancy. Skeele tipped his hat lower and went inside.

The guy at the desk looked at the clock when Skeele walked through the door. "Just get into town?"

"Yeah," Skeele said. "I need a single room."

The guy at the desk tapped on his computer keys. "I need and I.D. and the room is two-fifty a night for a parking-lot view room."

Skeele pulled a roll of cash out of his pocket and a blank I.D. card Jed made with magic.

The guy took the cash and made a keycard. "Room two-twenty-five." He pointed toward a hall to the left.

Skeele walked the long hallway of the motel with slow footsteps. He'd never been to a place like this, and the smells were overwhelming to him. There was food, mold, liquor, dirt, body odor, sex. He wondered if this was how humans lived on the Earthen plane, like animals in the forest. The one thing he couldn't smell was Meg. Either she covered her scent here or she wasn't staying at this motel any longer.

Skeele stopped at room 225 and opened the door. The first thing he did was cover the large mirror over the dresser with a sheet. He wanted to break it because even with the glamour, his reflection was his true self. He stood in front of the sheet-covered mirror, tore the sheet down. He was a Hellion in the reflection, his horns tucked under the baseball hat and sharp teeth behind his lips. He punched the mirror and the glass shattered.

He stashed the blood from his bag in the mini fridge. He could survive on regular food for a while. But he might need the cold blood depending on how long he was on the Earthen plane.

In the morning, he left the room and searched the hotel for any sign of Meg. Skeele stood outside every room and took a deep breath. He grumbled when he concluded Meg was no longer at the hotel. He assumed she must've realized Nightingale had tracked her and got out of there. Skeele made his way to the lobby. He picked through the pamphlets for restaurants, beaches, state parks, and attractions. He took a few and tucked them in his pocket. Noah mentioned taking Meg on dates to new places. He'd have to start with the pamphlets because he didn't know jack about this place. If they were in Hell he'd take her to the black-sanded beaches and salt mines. But she'd told him not to get attached, so he planned nothing.

The sun pouring through the front doors of the motel lobby was bright and reminded him of the punishing sunlight of the Seven Kingdoms of Heaven. Skeele tipped his hat down to shade his eyes and exited the hotel intending to track Meg.

———

SKEELE WANDERED the walkway along the beach and stopped at one of the little tourist shops where he picked out a pair of sunglasses. Further down Perdido Key Drive there were medical buildings and a pharmacy. He went back to the hotel intending to search that section of town in the morning.

Skeele stopped at the library on his way home. He didn't have a library card, but he could browse. He nodded at the woman sitting behind a desk.

"We close in thirty minutes," she said as he passed, snapping her gum.

"I won't be long," he assured her.

Skeele stopped at the magazines and thumbed through them. He had to get a quick education about the Earthen plane if he was going to trick Meg into thinking he was something other than a Hellion. And he needed a new name. After reading most of the front covers of the magazines, he decided Kal would do. It was close enough to his real name he would answer to it. Less chance for confusion.

———

MEG

I leave my house and drive down River Road toward the clinic. I made an appointment to end this. It's a very hush hush, unlabeled office. They do things that some might consider unethical, things that a decent human being might never do. Unfortunately, I'm not a decent human being any longer.

Saliva fills my throat, threatening vomit all over my new car. I grab a bag from the door pocket and hold it in my lap. The nausea this morning is horrific. It's like the creature in my belly knows it's eviction day. I'd be pissed too. I'm a shitty host. I doubt growing on coffee and shame is a delightful diet.

Giant white clouds are rolling over the ocean. They look like a mountain and there's a layer of darker clouds below them. Just as I pull into the small parking lot, rain drops start hitting my windshield.

I check the clock. I've got five minutes. I'd like to run in and avoid the rain but the lady on the phone told me not to arrive early. She said arrive right on time due to the delicate matters they handle there. The cloudy day turns into a monsoon too quick.

I find a peppermint in the console and pop it in my mouth, hoping it will help with the nausea. I dig around for an umbrella but don't find one.

In typical Florida manner, the rainstorm comes with thunder

and lightning. Lightning strikes near the beach and across the bridge to the mainland.

9:55 am. It's my time. I open the door to the Jeep and get out. Without an umbrella, I ready myself to run. I slam the door closed and hold a hand over my eyes. I leap over a puddle to get to the sidewalk. There's tall shrubbery hiding the front door. Just as I step up onto the porch, lighting strikes the roof. The hairs on my arms and neck stand up. I smell smoke. I look up to see fire starting near the corner of the building. Dark smoke turns to orange flame. The door opens and a handful of people run out.

"Do you have an appointment?" a dark-haired lady with giant red glasses asks me.

"Yeah."

"The building is on fire. You'll have to reschedule."

She leaves me standing alone in the rain, next to the burning building. Sirens blare in the distance. I turn around and walk back to my Jeep, no longer caring that I'm being doused with rain. I get in my vehicle and don't bother putting on my seatbelt. I start the car and drive away. I make my way to Perdido Key Drive and turn onto the unnamed road with a local pizza joint. A medium cheese and two-liter of cola. All for myself. I cry when I take the first bite of pizza. I tell myself it's because the crust is so chewy and the cheese so stringy and the sauce light and sweet, just like I like it. I've never had more delicious pizza. I've never hated life more than this moment. I had a plan and now it's fucked.

THE NEXT DAY, I call the number to the office that went up in flames yesterday. No one answers. I take it as a sign to come up with a new life plan. Leaving my little house I walk to the beach, the seashell driveway coating my flip-flops in white dust. After finding a quiet spot on the sand I sit on a towel, kick off my sandals, and dig my feet into the sand.

Since my standards are low and I'm alone on the beach, I take a raw steak out of my bag. I unwrap the one pound of bloody meat, rolling the plastic down to cover my fingers. Then I eat the entire thing like a starved man biting into the best bacon cheeseburger of his life. It's messy and I wipe my mouth on my arm more than once until there's red streaks left behind.

"Are you okay?" an old man with a white beard is staring at me.

I smile, then stop because my teeth are probably coated in cow blood. "I'm wonderful."

My stomach has stopped growling and I can no longer hear the *hush-hush-hush* of every passing person's heart within a mile radius of my location.

"You have the zombie disease?" the bearded man asks. "I thought they were all killed."

"No." I chew and swallow and wipe at my face.

He moves away from me. "You should really see a doctor then."

That's probably the best recommendation I've received in a long time.

———

I sit in a cold, bright waiting room.

"Meg," the girl at the desk calls and waves for me to go to her.

"I'm Meg."

"I need photo ID and insurance."

I get out my walled. "I'm paying cash." I slide her my ID.

She scans it, pausing before handing it back to me. "You're going to need a new one."

"I know it expires."

She stares.

"I look a little different too."

She blinks twice. "It says you live in New York."

"I used to."

"Half of New York is uninhabitable. I'd change my address."

"Sure." I thank her for the guidance.

There's an old man in the corner watching the news. After fifteen minutes they call me back to an equally cold and bright exam room.

A tired-looking man enters the room. "Good morning, Ms. Clark." The doctor uses a touch screen iPad. "So, you're having trouble staying awake?"

"Yes." I press my hands together and try not to act sketchy.

The doctor looks at my face. "You look tired."

"That's the problem. I'm always tired. I can't stay awake."

"Hm."

"I've tried coffee and energy drinks."

"Do they work?"

"Sometimes."

"Have you ever been diagnosed with narcolepsy?"

"What's that?" I ask.

"I'll take that as a no." The doctor taps on his computer screen. "Let's try a stimulant. The other option is antidepressants."

"I don't think I need antidepressants."

"Uh-huh. After the zombie apocalypse half the country is on them." He sighs. "They're on backorder anyway. If you find any let me know. What pharmacy do you want to use?"

"The one down the street."

He focuses on the computer for a few moments. "You should have some testing. Stop by the lab for some bloodwork. You want an MRI?"

"For what?" I ask.

"To check out your brain. They're expensive and I see you are self-pay."

"I have money."

"It can cost up to three grand." His brows rise.

"Nah," I dismiss the idea with a wave. "I'd rather not." What if they find nothing in my skull, or worse, what if they find something?

"Okay. Do the lab work. Try the meds. Come back and see me in a week. Unless you have a primary doctor you usually see."

"I don't."

"Most don't." He stands and nods. "Thank you, have a nice day."

Wow. Times have changed. He didn't even listen to my heart or my lungs. What if I was a fucking robot sitting here? He'd never know. What if I had no heart, no pulse, no lungs? He just collected my two-hundred bucks and did a little clickety-clack on his computer and walked out the door.

I leave the urgent care and stop at the lab next door. Seems everything is electronic these days, no more slips of paper to carry around with doctor scribble. The nice young man at the lab takes five vials of blood. I think I should have skipped that, but I want this doc to help me out so I'm going to do what he orders. I probably shouldn't be giving up much of my blood since I have nothing to replace it with.

I drive to the pharmacy and pick up the pills. I twist the cap and pour out two into my palm. I swallow them down with a swig of cold coffee.

———

I sit on the beach and watch two college looking lads play volleyball. They're sweaty, their abs glistening and biceps flexing in the hot panhandle sun. I could bite every inch of them. I could lick them both from head to toe and leave them emptier than a cheerleader's head during final exams week. But that wouldn't be nice. Do better, Meg. Do better.

I press my lips together and focus on the magazine in my hands. I don't really care about the latest celebrity scandal but there's post-Zombie War info in this. It seems all the tabloids have taken to the post-War stories, interviews, and recollections. There are stories from famous actors who survived all locked up in their mansions with plenty of food and security. What a crock.

I stop flipping the pages to the magazine when a picture of a bunch of kids catches my eye. There's probably twenty of them, varying ages. The story is about all the children turned orphans after the Zombie War. I read the article. They're searching for families to adopt them. It must suck, losing everything in the Zombie War; your family, your parents, your home. I lost a lot in the Zombie War too. My boyfriend, my dignity, all the blood in my body–I glance down at my chest–a perfectly good tattoo. I should get that fixed.

The article gives me an idea. Since the clinic was destroyed and I haven't grown the balls to find another one further away, I consider the alternative. If I can't get rid of the creature growing in my belly, I can leave it behind for someone else to deal with. I don't feel as guilty. At least this decision won't end in death. The images from Teari's book flash through my mind. Mothers being torn apart by tiny monsters with little horns and sharp claws. Blood everywhere and torn open vaginas and stomachs. She assured me that wouldn't happen. But I trust no one. If I survive the delivery, God can keep his monstrosity on the Earthen plane. No one needs to know. I glance at the runes on my arms. Maybe I'll lower my standards even more and tattoo the baby like we considered doing to Thrush. Maybe if no one knows and no one can find it, then I'm absolved of guilt and wrongdoing. Skeele won't ever have to know. I'll just tell Teari I miscarried and bled it out one night. She'll never have to know either.

I pack up my beach chair and go home to call the adoption agency listed in the article.

———

"Ms. Clark." The doctor sits down and rolls his stool closer to me. "We tried to call you about your labs."

"I don't have a cell phone or answering machine." I'm probably the only person on the Earthen plane without one. It makes me feel special.

"I see that. You should get one. Or a secretary to sit at your house and take calls." His dry tone really hits.

"Nah. I lean back in my chair. I like the freedom."

He smirks. "You won't be enjoying it for much longer."

"Huh?"

"You have elevated hCG."

"No clue what that means." I tap my fingers on my legs.

"You're pregnant."

My mouth goes dry. I sit up and choke back the bile rising in my throat. I know this already; I just don't want any more evidence of the truth.

"You didn't know?"

I shake my head. Lies.

"You have to stop taking the stimulants." He clicks on his computer. "You can't take them pregnant. Do you have an obstetrician in mind? You'll need to find one."

"Can't you do it?" My throat is dry, feels like I've been chewing on cotton.

"I can't." He focuses on me. "This is unexpected?"

I nod.

"Do you want to be pregnant? These are dark times, but we are rebuilding; we lost a lot of good people in the zombie war."

"I don't want it." Tears burn in the corners of my eyes. Saying the words out loud sounds horrible. I was scared but I'd wanted Elise. This thing inside me, it's not the same.

He makes a face of disappointment. "I'll write for the morning after pill. We caught this early. This is why you are so tired." He sets his computer down and leans forward. I notice his badge. Dr. Jordan. "Give it a week. If you're still sure, then take the pill. Either way, stop the stimulants until you've decided."

"Sure." I stand, ready to run the hell out of there and bury my head in the sand from humiliation.

"I'll send over a prescription for prenatal vitamins as well. You decide which pills you take."

"Thanks." I reach for the door and run out of the urgent care.

———

I give the pharmacy a few hours to fill my new prescriptions. I take a walk on the beach and feel like shit the entire time I'm there.

Mark's Pharmacy is empty when I stop in to pick up my new prescriptions. I'm not sure if Mark is the guy in the white coat behind the counter, but he looks at me, judgingly. A medical professional with a name like Mark should be a little more approachable.

"I'm going to assume you'll take one or the other." He rings up the prescriptions. "One-hundred and thirty-five dollars and ninety cents."

I pay cash.

On my way out I run into a tall man looking at the gum selection. I drop my bag. "Sorry." I tuck the pharmacy bag in my pocket.

"No problem." The man smiles at me awkwardly.

My eyes fall to the beating pulse in his neck. I lick my lips and force my gaze to his face. He's handsome in a southern manly man kinda way. He was probably one of those guys that had a stash of guns, booby-trapped property, and a boatload of survival food. Maybe that's why he's so awkward. Too much time alone. Be nicer, Meg. I smile back at him because that's what normal people do.

He opens his mouth like he's going to say something but turns and walks away instead. Weird. The Zombie Apocalypse really ruined social interactions here.

———

SKEELE

Skeele knew the moment Meg entered the pharmacy. He moved behind the shelving and pretended to look at soaps. He recounted the lessons Noah had given him before leaving Hell. *Don't be too pushy. Don't growl. Buy her some gifts. Take her to dinner.* It was a lot of information and most of it fled him in the moment. His mind instantly went black because Meg looked tired and weak. Her skin was pale. Noah didn't tell him how to approach Meg if she was looking like absolute shit warmed over. Guilt tugged at Skeele. Meg needed blood; she'd clearly gone without since she'd escaped to the Earthen plane.

She got a bag from the back counter.

Skeele moved closer, ready to make his move. He didn't have any pickup lines and he wasn't sure he could charm her. She just didn't look in the mood to talk to anyone let alone a complete stranger.

Meg was walking toward the door. Skeele had to act fast. She looked distracted, her head down and focused on the floor as she walked. It was like she didn't want to be seen. He stepped into the aisle. Meg ran into him and dropped her bag. He bent to pick it up, but she was too quick. Skeele didn't know what to say so he smiled. He was happy to see her and a little stunned that he'd finally found her.

Skeele wanted to say something, but nothing would come out.

He walked away.

Meg left the pharmacy.

Skeele felt like an idiot. He watched her get into a Jeep and followed her. It would be a challenge following her on foot, but Perdido Key was small and now he knew what kind of car she drove.

Meg took a right onto Perdido Key Drive. Skeele followed her, trying his best not to run full speed and make a spectacle. The slow-moving traffic in Perdido Key was a blessing if Skeele had ever come across one in his life. He kept up with Meg's Jeep and hid behind a fence as she pulled into the driveway of a little beach house. It was cute, colorful, and bright; the complete opposite of the castle in the burning caves of Hell. When Meg got out of her SUV and went to the door, short shorts and tanned legs, Skeele thought she almost looked like she belonged here.

———

MEG

I need to stay awake. It's been three weeks now. Three weeks without fresh blood. And I can't remember the last time I slept. All I know is that no one has found me.

I stare at the pills Dr. Jordan gave me. I still haven't taken either of them. I rub my face. I need to do something else. The coffee isn't working anymore, and I can't think clearly.

This is Florida. Land of the free. Home of the crackheads. There are other ways to keep my eyelids open. I wait until dark and leave my house on foot. I don't want anyone to know what my car looks like. I walk down the main road to the gas station near Theo Baars Bridge. I've seen some sketchy people there. I wait near the entrance to a 7-Eleven for some shifty looking shit.

A man with greasy hair and limited tooth count lingers on the opposite side of the gas station. I stare at him. He stares at me. I rub my nose. He walks over.

"Hey," he says.

"Hey."

"You looking for some C?"

"Yeah. I brought cash."

"You want C or rocks?"

"Just the C." I reach into my pocket and pull out a bundle of cash.

"Whoa. Not here." He glances behind us and past the gas pumps, then motions for me to follow him. *Whoosh-whoosh-whoosh.* All I can hear is his jugular pumping. I lick my lips and follow. I follow him to the darkest shadows behind the building. It smells like rotting garbage next to the dumpster. I hold back the gagging feeling. Urgency prickled my spine to get this over and done with.

He digs in his pocket and pulls out a baggie with white powder. "It's five hundred."

I count the cash and we make the deal.

"Are you always here?" I ask. "When I need more."

"Usually." Rotten teeth peek out from behind dry lips. The combination is revolting. How could I ever think a Hellion was disgusting after looking at this specimen of humanity?

I leave the gas station and jog home.

I open the front door, slam it closed, and dig the baggie out of my pocket. I hold it up to the light. White crystals sparkle in the fluorescence. I've tried a lot of things and done a lot of awful shit, but this, this is me turning a new leaf. The coffee isn't working. I need to stay awake. I can't get found by Nightingale or the others.

I walk to the kitchen, dip my finger into the baggie and rub the white powder on my gums just like I've seen all those detectives do on TV.

Not only do I not sleep, but I also have so much energy that I clean the entire house by the time the sun rises. The toilets are scrubbed, every tile in the shower is sparkling. I can do it. I can do this and stop whenever I want. Whenever I get this thing out of my womb.

I stand in front of the bathroom mirror and turn sideways. I rub my hand over my stomach. It doesn't look any bigger. It's nice and flat and bikini ready. No one will ever know.

After looking at myself in the bathroom mirror for a few more minutes, I conclude I look like shit. The dark circles under my eyes look like they belong on a raccoon. My skin is pale, my hair dull. I slap my cheeks, but no redness appears. I need more bloody steaks, but I can't be going into the grocery store looking like the dead. I head to Mark's Pharmacy to get some makeup.

I LEAN down to look in the makeup aisle mirror with a handful of options. All the lipsticks look too bright and too pink against my pale skin. The foundations are too dark. I find a foundation that says

"Snow" and rub it on the back of my hand. Jeeze, if snow is my color, then I'm beyond pale. I've never known myself to be this pale. I'm in Florida for God-sakes. I've spent half the week on the beach. I should have a sun-kissed glow by now.

I throw Snow into my basket and then grab another foundation that's two shades darker. Maybe I'll fake my color. Same with the lip colors. I decide on Dusty Rose and Carnation Mauve. Hopefully one of them will bring life back to my lips. I search for bronzer next.

As I'm walking down the aisle, inspecting my options, I get the feeling I'm being watched. I glance out of the corner of my eye and notice a tall man in jeans and button up shirt lingering nearby. I recognize him from the other day.

"Can I help you?" I ask.

"Hi, my name's Kal." He holds out his hand to shake.

I want to be annoyed but there's something so innocent and happy about the guy. I'm not one for shaking strangers' hands but this guy seems like he needs the greeting. "Meg," I say as I shake his warm hand, noticing the tattoos of pine trees snaking up his forearms.

"That's a nice name. Hey, would you like to go to dinner tonight?" he asks.

"Whoa buddy. Straight to the point."

"Sorry," he lets out an awkward sigh. "I know you don't know me, but I've seen you here a few times and you're always alone."

"You assumed I was single?"

"Kinda."

His smile is friendly, and he has a good vibe. I've been here alone, no friends, no boyfriends for weeks. Some socializing might do me some good. Some socializing might do him some good. I'm not one for picking up charity cases but what else do I have to do? I've completely failed at staying hidden in my new home. I might as well embrace leaving the house now.

"Well, Kal," I check him out. "You are correct. I'm single and ready to mingle. Where do you want to meet?" I head for the self-checkout and start scanning my items.

"Lady's choice."

"Oyster Bar near the bridge?" The place looks like it would have good food and I nearly don't care what the food tastes like as long as they have orange soda.

"Great. Six?" He looks at his watch.

"Six is good." I head for the door.

"I can walk you to your car." He skips ahead of me and holds the door open.

Damn, chivalry is not dead with this guy. No one has held a door for me since I got here. The Earthen plane has a bit to learn from Kal.

"The sun is so bright today." Kal pulls a pair of sunglasses from his pocket and puts them on as he follows me to my car.

"Sometimes it gives me headaches. I just have to close all the blinds and hide indoors." I want to say that I miss the ochre dimness of Hell. But that's not a conversation I can have on the Earthen plane.

I unlock my doors and notice the clouds collecting over the Gulf of Mexico. "What if it rains at six?" I ask.

"Neither of us should melt."

Kal opens my door. I get in and roll down the window as he closes the door. "We can meet at the restaurant."

"Do you do this a lot?" I ask.

"What?"

"Pick up strangers at the store. What if I'm a serial killer or a vampire or batshit crazy?"

Kal shrugs like it's no big deal. "Met a few of those. You don't fit the bill."

"You met a serial killer, a vampire, or a batshit crazy chick?"

"All the above." He looks at the clouds over the ocean. "I'd still like to meet you for dinner even if it rains."

"Okay," I say. "But I've warned you."

I start the Jeep and drive away. I watch Kal watching me in the rearview mirror. He looks like he just won the goldfish in the ball toss game at the summer carnival. Poor sucker.

———

Skeele

His first lie was his name. Kal is innocent enough, but Skeele would rather shake some sense into Meg and drag her back to Hell where she belonged.

His second lie was telling Meg she didn't fit the bill of being a vampire or batshit crazy. She sure as shit fit the bill. But she had to be crazy to sit on that throne.

Skeele tugged his hat lower and started walking to the hotel. He was thinking about what he'd have to do if he scared Meg off. He listened to the ocean waves crash against the beach in the distance. For some this was very much a vacation, but Skeele found the sun too bright, the heat too hot, and the clothing too uncomfortable. And then there was the lack of free blood.

He passed a small house with a handwritten sign that said *For Rent*. Skeele stopped walking and considered. He couldn't stay at the hotel forever and if he wanted to invite Meg over, he needed a proper place to bring her too.

Skeele knocked on the door.

———

Meg

I walk the main road to the gas station near Theo Baars Bridge. I wait near the entrance to a 7-Eleven for my greasy-haired drug dealer. He shows up after ten minutes and motions for me to meet him around back.

Whoosh-whoosh-whoosh. I hear everyone's blood pumping. The drug dealer, the woman pumping gas, the teenager walking across the bridge. I try to focus on his mouth moving, I can barely hear him over the sound. *Whoosh-whoosh-whoosh.*

My dealer digs in his pocket. "Seven hundred."

"What?" I make a face. "That's more than last time."

He smiles, showing missing teeth. "This is how it works, sweetheart."

There's something about him, something slimy and fucked. *Whoosh-whoosh-whoosh.* I can't deal. Saliva fills my mouth. *Poof.* My teeth are on his neck, and I drain him of his blood in record time. It tastes better than anything I've had since arriving on the Earthen plane.

I drag his lifeless body down the ravine to the lagoon. I crouch so the cars passing can't see me. Wait. Wait. I check his pockets and pull out a handful of powder filled baggies from one pocket and a roll of cash from another pocket. Then I roll his body into the lagoon. The gators swim over immediately.

Standing, I back up into the shadows to calm down and take in my surroundings. No witnesses. Just the gators who seem more than happy with the free meal.

Poof.

I go back to my house and get ready for my date with Kal.

———

Skeele

Skeele checked his watch. Meg was seven minutes late. The hostess on the other side of the glass doors to the Oyster Bar was staring at him. It was making him uneasy. He glanced through the glass to find the hostess smiling at him. He bristled and tucked his hands in his pockets.

Meg's Jeep finally rolled into the parking lot of Oyster Bar and stopped in a parking space.

She was wearing jeans and a T-shirt. He would expect nothing less and was sure he'd never see her wear a dress again like the night of the celebration dinner.

The only difference in her outfit than what she typically wore in Hell was the flip-flops on her feet. Her toenails were painted black.

Skeele walked across the parking lot to meet her halfway. "I was afraid you weren't coming," he said.

Meg smiled and Skeele noticed the layers of makeup on her face.

"Are you feeling okay?" he asked. "You look tired."

"Gee, thanks," Meg had a sarcastic tone, but her eyes were hidden behind sunglasses.

"I didn't say it to be mean. We can reschedule."

"Nope," Meg said. "I'm hungry."

They crossed the stone parking lot. Skeele jogged ahead of Meg when they got to the door. He held it opened and ushered her inside with his hand on the small of her back. Her T-shirt was cropped short, and his fingers pressed against Meg's warm skin. He wanted to touch more, but he was trying to be a gentleman.

He wanted to ask her why she left him drained of blood and with blue balls in her bed. But he was trying to lie about his identity.

Meg was staring out the window at the shore birds as they pecked the grass.

"What are you thinking about?" Skeele asked. "You seem like you're a million miles away."

Meg pointed to the white bird with stick legs. "I'm trying to decide if that's a Snowy Egret or White Ibis." She leaned closer to the window. "The ibis has a pink face. The egret has a yellow patch around their eyes. I can't tell the colors from here."

"Can I get you some drinks to start with?" a perky waitress with red bangle bracelets asked.

"Rum and coke," Meg said. "And an orange soda."

"Beer. Whatever you have on tap," Skeele said.

"I'll be back for your orders in a minute." The waitress paused to stare at Skeele.

"Bye now," Meg broke the waitresses longing over her date.

"Why are you so interested in the birds?" Skeele asked Meg.

Meg signed and ran her fingers through her short hair. "They bring me back to a simpler time." She toyed with her fork. "Remind me of old friends."

Skeele knew. He'd been there for the birdwatching. And he wondered if he was included in the old friends comment or if he was simply just a sack of blood for her to use at will.

———

MEG

I try not to think about my friends in Hell. It's better not to think about them since they are better off without me. Noah has his family. Skeele can move on to whatever life he had before I showed up and ruined it.

I cross my legs and try to quell the ache there. It started the moment Kal put his hand on my back, the second he touched my skin. I'll be damned if it's not the bloodlust rearing its ugly head. I've been so good. So, so good. It's been weeks. I'm surprised I didn't fuck a log after I drained my drug dealer. Somehow locking myself in my house prevented that. But now I'm here with a hot-blooded man who doesn't really seem like my type, but could be. I'm starting over, turning a new leaf. Maybe my type is Kal now. He's nice to look at, even if his head is close shaven and he always wears a baseball cap and seems a bit too nice.

I can't deny feeling better since having fresh blood. It's not like Skeele's, but close, close enough for a starving girl who survives on blood but tries her darndest to ignore that fact.

Kal orders steak. Rare with a side salad and French fries. I order shrimp fettuccini Alfredo. I skip the salad and get mozzarella sticks.

Kal asks me about the rest of the day, and I lie to him and say I walked on the beach and read a book.

"What book did you read?" Kal's eyes light up.

What a dork. I guess it's not the worst thing to get excited about.

"A Marilyn Monroe memoir."

Our food shows up and we chit-chat about Florida and the weather and what we do for work. I find it odd that we are both independently wealthy and don't have jobs. But times are different now on the Earthen plane. I read in a magazine that insurance companies had a heck of a payout to plenty of survivors. Being eaten by a zombie didn't fall under any act of God so they had to pay up on all their policies. Most of the survivors had large payouts. Kal's situation is probably one of them.

"Do you ever think of working?" Kal asks. "There's a blood bank across the bridge that's hiring."

I pause, a large forkful of pasta near my mouth. "I don't think that's a good idea."

Kal shrugs. "I thought about doing it to pass the time." He tips his empty glass at the waitress, and she brings him a new beer. "You know what they say, idleness is the devil's home for temptation."

"Do you all want dessert?" the waitress asks as she sets Kal's fresh beer down.

"Chocolate cake," I say. "With ice cream."

"And you?" she looks longingly at my date. I want to kick her in the ankle and tell her to get her own man. This hunk of awkward bookish flesh is mine. At least until I scare him away or kill him. With my record both are an option.

––––––––

We watch the evening clouds thicken. Lightning illuminates the thunderheads over the Gulf.

"I like watching this." Kal points to the clouds. "The weather has never been like this anywhere I've lived."

"It's nice to watch until the lighting strikes too close." I push my chair back. "We should probably get going or we're going to get doused."

Kal stands and throws a few large bills on the table for the bill. He waves to the waitress and thumbs toward the stack of bills.

I didn't count what he left but I'm guessing he overpaid.

As we make our way to the front door, raindrops start falling.

"Where did you park?" I ask.

"I walked."

"You want a ride home?"

"Sure."

We run across the parking lot. Kal opens the driver side door and touches my back as I get in. It feels good. Skin against skin. Tingly. I know it's the blood lust talking but I can't ignore it. Kal slams the door and runs to the passenger side. The rain downpours, soaking him. Kal gets in.

"You barely made it," I say, starting the Jeep. "I think I have a towel back here." I turn and stretch to the back seat, reaching for the towel. Every good Floridian keeps a towel in the car for the summer rainy season. Usually, the wind will turn your umbrella inside out. It's better to run for cover and dry off after.

I feel warm fingers touch the skin on my side, his fingertips just skimming, making my spine tingle. Jesus. Why is he touching me like that?

"What?" I ask, dragging the towel and tossing it to Kal.

"You have a bruise on your hip." Kal dries his face with the towel. He pulls his wet shirt away from his body.

"You can take it off." I back out of the parking spot and head for Perdido Key Drive. "I hate sitting in wet clothes."

Kal tugs his shirt off and dries his neck and chest. His elbow knocks me in the shoulder. The guy is too big for the SUV.

"Sorry." He touches my shoulder, the one with the Scar from Sparrow's blade. I wince. "I didn't mean to do that."

I bite my lip and hold in a sound that wants to come from deep in my throat. This dude is too touchy and there was a time that I'd rather punch a man than let him touch me this much. But the blood-lust doesn't care about my feelings; it's soaking up every touch, every glance, every flirting tip of his lips. Oh my God what's wrong with me? I used to be so strong and edgy. Now I'm ready to melt like a long-haired blonde woman on the front of a romance novel.

I never ask Kal where he lives. Instead, I drive him to my house. I consider pulling off onto a dead-end road to bone him in the jeep. I still might. We've got a few more minutes before I have to turn onto Parasol Place. He doesn't say anything, he doesn't give me directions. The energy in the Jeep is tingly and hot and if I didn't know better, he doesn't want to go home. He's no better than me. Maybe that's the way it is here now. After nearly dying, all the survivors are horny and lonely.

The rain has turned into a deluge, ponding the streets and putting a hurt on my windshield wipers. It's the kind of white-knuckled driving no one talks during. I decide not to pull off onto a dead-end road because I can barely see the road.

I turn onto Parasol Place and park in my driveway.

"You want some coffee?" I glance at Kal's naked upper body. He must work out.

"Coffee sounds great." He reaches for the door handle, jumps out and rounds the Jeep to open my door. He holds the towel over our heads as we dash to the front porch.

Lightning strikes nearby, electrifying the air.

"Does that happen a lot here?" Kal asks as I search for my house key. He rubs his arms, no doubt the nearby lightning making his hair stand up.

"The lightning? Florida has the most lightning strikes out of anywhere." I shrug. "It happens."

"We better get inside." Kal rubs his arms with the towel then drapes it across my back and dries my neck.

That's it.

I shove the door open, grab him by the wrist to pull him inside, then slam the door closed.

"You are very flirty," I say, locking the door and invading his personal space.

He smiles, slowly, while looking down at me. His back is pressed against the door and my arm touches his side as I turn the lock.

Kal touches my chin, tips my face up to meet his, and puts his hands on me. He doesn't need to ask how far I want to go on the first date because I'm a grown ass woman and I'm already unbuttoning his jeans. The warmth of his lower abdomen seeps into my knuckles as I work the buttons.

"You want coffee first?" he asks, his hand moving into my hair and tugging my head back.

"Fuck the coffee." I kick off my flip-flops and reach for the hem of my crop top. If we were in Hell, I'd be able to use the bloodlust as an excuse for acting like a ho. But on the Earthen plane, there's no good excuse for taking Kal to my bed after one date.

Kal touches me everywhere. His big hands grip my breasts, his tongue licks my neck before his warm lips kiss down my chest. His hands slide into the waistband of my jeans, and he tugs them down. I kick them away.

"You're not wearing underwear," he whispers.

"I'm not apologizing for it." I tug at his jeans, trying to control the urge to *poof* him to the bedroom and have my way with him.

His teeth nip my skin, and he grabs me by the waist, lifting me up onto the nearby countertop.

"Are you sure–" he starts to ask, only to be interrupted by my legs wrapping around him and pressing him into me.

———

I WAKE to the soft breathing of a large body in my bed. I roll to the side, my eyelids heavy, my legs sore. My eyes focus on the nightstand clock. It's three a.m.

Shit. Shit. Shit. Shit. I fell asleep.

Nausea sneaks up my stomach. I slide out of bed and run to the bathroom.

I hurl up the fancy dinner Kal bought me and wish for blood. The drug dealer's blood should have lasted me longer. All it did was make me horny. There were days when I fed from Skeele more than once, but this feels extreme.

I start the shower. A cold shower will wake me up really good. Then I'll make some coffee and watch a movie and think of a good lie to tell Kal for why I left him in my bed alone.

I notice the bruise on my hip. There's a new bruise on my thigh, but that was from Kal carrying me across the house while I did unlady-like things. I'm not sure how he walked while I did that. I lather and rinse and wash my hair and think about how he didn't seem to notice the birthmark on my upper thigh. Maybe men on the Earthen plane are no longer impressed with tattoos and scars and strange birthmarks.

———

THE COFFEEMAKER DOESN'T WAKE Kal. Neither does my cursing as I search the TV for a movie. I want to watch Shawshank Redemption like the good old days, but the only things playing are horror and teen dance movies. I settle on horror and hope to scare myself awake. I wrap myself in a blanket from the back of the couch and sip at my sugar and cream laden coffee. My stomach grumbles and I consider finding a snack since my dinner is gone. There's one last bloody steak in the fridge. I could eat that, but I don't want to risk Kal walking in on me as I eat raw meat like that old man on the beach.

Kal is standing in the doorway, watching me. "Are you hungry?" he asks. It sounds familiar. I'd like to say yes. I'd like to tell him I'm hungry for his blood and that I want to screw and bite his neck. But I'm on the Earthen plane now, and Kal is a normal guy, a nice guy.

"Do you want me to make something?" Kal asks. "Or do you want me to go?"

I glance at his nearly naked form, the bulge in his boxer-briefs. No, I don't want him to go. I can still feel the urge from the blood-lust. He should stay so I don't wind up fucking a log in the backyard. My new neighbors wouldn't enjoy witnessing that.

I lift the blanket and ask him to sit with me. Kal stretches an arm across my back, and I lay my head on his shoulder.

I blink and take a mental snapshot. I file it under *the way things could have been*. We could have been a sweet young couple who survived the Zombie Apocalypse and help repopulate the world. We could have been something normal and nice. Like dinners on Sunday evenings and weddings and first birthday parties and proms. But that will never be because I am the ruler of Hell and Kal is a normal guy. Even though this charade just started, it's going to need to end. If he stays in the picture, it won't end well. I don't want to feed him to the gators. That would be tragic.

Kal taps my hip with his hand. "Are you okay?" he asks.

"I'm fine." I stretch my hand across his bare chest and to his shoulder, up the side of his neck and stretch my fingers across the back of his head.

Kal groans and he tips his head just so. *Whoosh-whoosh-whoosh*. If I didn't know better, I'd take it as an invitation. I take it as an invitation for other things. I move to my knees and straddle his lap and curse the bloodlust for ever existing.

———

Noah, Jed, Nightingale, and Shay

"He's found her," Nightingale told the others at the table. "I didn't approach her in the dream. She hasn't slept in a long time."

"Let her sleep," Noah said, shifting a sleeping Thrush in his arms. There was a wet drool mark on his shoulder, but Noah ignored it.

"How long will it take Skeele to bring her back?" Shay asked. Jed was in the middle of updating the runes on her arms. Shay's blowtorch blue hair contrasted against her pale skin and dark clothing in a newly shortened haircut to her chin. Shay sucked in a breath as Jed tattooed deep over bone.

"Sorry," he said as his thumb rubbed her skin to soothe.

Nightingale and Noah made eye contact. Jed and Shay had spent every moment together since Thrush had his parents back. Now they were on standby. Guardians for Thrush in case something happened to Nightingale or Noah again. Without Meg in Hell, there was bound to be some drama initiated by the Deacons. They didn't like that they had no control over Meg.

Rumors were starting. Someone had destroyed portals on the Earthen plane. The Deacons had already come knocking on the doors of the burning caves. Clea distracted them and sent them away. But it wasn't enough. The new Hellions had mouths that spoke freely at whatever post they were stationed. They were instructed to bring the rumors back to Klaus and Chel, but some had loose lips and spread their own rumors. The demons of Hell knew the throne was unseated. Meg wasn't as visible as she had been.

There was a knock on the door.

Nightingale moved to answer it. Chel, Klaus, and Tukka entered the room. Suddenly the chapel in the cemetery felt very small.

Klaus was carrying a bag. "This should be everything."

Nightingale took the bag as Jed stopped his tattooing, wiped Shay's skin, and rubbed a layer of healing balm over the fresh ink.

"Are you ready?" Jed asked Shay.

Shay nodded and stood.

Tukka grunted in disapproval. "They are nothing alike. This will not work."

Nightingale pulled clothing from the bag and held them up to Shay. "The clothes will fit."

"Her hair is blue," Tukka motioned to Shay's hair. "Meg's is black. Everyone will know it's not her." He was agitated. "She doesn't even have Meg's tattoos."

"Or her attitude," Klaus said with a smile, trying to lighten the mood.

"Hush, all of you." Noah patted Thrush's back, soothing him to sleep again. "She has a few of the tattoos. Jed still has time to add more."

"Here," Nightingale thrust the clothing into Shay's hands. "Go change."

"Come with me." Shay tugged at Jed's shirt as she headed to the bedroom.

Shay closed the door behind Jed and listened to the chatter in the living room.

"They don't want me to do this." Shay tossed the clothing onto the bed and kicked off her boots.

"It doesn't matter." Jed turned his back like a gentleman. "We have to do something until we can get Meg back where she belongs."

"What if she never comes back?" Shay asked. "I'm a human. I am not whatever magical creatures you all are. I don't have wings or magic or battle training."

"Meg doesn't have any of those either." Jed pressed his ear to the wooden door to hear the others speaking.

"She has something that keeps you all in check." Shay pulled on a pair of jeans that were a little too tight on the butt. She changed her shirt to the wide-necked blue T-shirt of Meg's. "Okay. Turn around. Tell me how bad this is."

Jed turned and walked a circle around Shay. "I think this could work." He stopped in front of Shay and frowned.

"It's the blue hair, isn't it?"

Jed shook his head in defeat. "Everyone knows you have the blue hair. We have to hide it."

"It took a really long time to get this shade just right." Shay was annoyed. "If you fuck it up..."

Jed's lip tipped to form a half smile. "Say it like Meg would."

Shay closed her eyes and took a deep breath, collecting every speck of attitude and edge in her person. "If you fuck it up, I will drain you dry." Shay opened her eyes.

Jed was nodding in approval. "That was pretty good." He held out his hands and his fingers danced in rhythmic spellcasting. "Let's just add a little glamour so as not to fuck up your blue."

When Shay left the bedroom, the visitors in the living room were silent, judging, and one of them eating crow, figuratively.

"Fine," Tukka said, his tone dull. "But don't let anyone get too close to her. Meg has blue eyes."

"We will make sure," Klaus said, reaching for the door handle so they could leave.

Chel motioned for Shay to follow them. "After you, Queen of Hell."

———

SKEELE

Skeele waited two days before inviting Meg out again. That's what Noah and the others had told him. *Don't seem desperate, give her distance, don't be overbearing.* All their dating advice ran through his head daily.

Skeele set his book down and walked to the small fridge to get a bag of blood. There were only two left. This was taking much longer than he'd planned. He thought about the blood bank on the other side of the Theo Baars bridge. If something didn't change soon, he'd be applying at that blood bank for a job. Soon.

Meg wanted to go to a dive bar on the water. The food was good, but she'd warn cutoff jean shorts and a tank top. Every man was looking at her and she didn't even realize it. And Skeele figured the damn woman would walk around naked daily if she could. Possessiveness thrummed in his chest as he glared down a college kid at the bar. It took the guy entirely too long to stop looking at Meg's legs. If only these dudes knew what she would do to them.

Skeele did all the things; a light touch to her back, plenty of smiles, touched her hand as they talked, asked about her day. It wasn't hard to notice that underneath Meg's smiles she was hiding something.

She was thinner than ever and started wearing makeup to cover the blue crescents of fatigue under her eyes. Skeele didn't like it. He was sure she was trying to wean herself off the blood and that was why she was at the doctor's and the pharmacy so often. He'd heard her vomiting enough times and he was starting to think it wasn't because of her disgust of his Hellion form.

This night wasn't much different from the last night they were together. Meg invited him back for coffee. As things were getting hot and heavy in the kitchen Meg paused, covered her mouth, and ran to the bathroom.

Skeele heard her retching and went to the sink to get her a glass of water. Demons knew better than to deny themselves blood. Meg's battle was impossible; she'd never wean herself off the blood. He couldn't shake the feeling that this didn't make complete sense. She'd been denying herself fresh blood for a while-the vomiting started back in Hell. He remembered her cut arm. Maybe it's the poison working its way out? Skeele wasn't a healer, and he could only guess what was really going on with her. He just hoped he could convince her to go home as soon as possible.

Skeele set his hand on the countertop and felt something granular pressing into his skin. Skeele wiped the counter, fine white dust collected near his palm. He noticed a bag hiding behind the toaster and pulled it out. Skeele tasted it. This wasn't sugar or salt.

Suddenly it was starting to make sense. Her thinness, her lack of sleeping. Skeele wanted to slam a fist into the cabinets, but he didn't want to scare her. He pocketed the bag of white powder and went to the bathroom to help.

Skeele knocked on the door until Meg opened. He handed her the glass of water as she was putting toothpaste on a toothbrush.

"Thanks," Meg said.

"You want me to make something to eat?"

"Since I flushed my dinner down the toilet?" she asked. "Sure."

"What do you want?"

Meg thought for a minute. "Spaghetti."

Skeele wasn't much of a cook, but he figured he could handle spaghetti. He read the instructions on the box to make the pasta. After draining it and mixing it with jarred sauce from the pantry, Skeele had an idea. He took two bowls out of the cabinet and filled them, then he grabbed a knife from the drawer. He stood with his back to the hall where Meg was cleaning up and sliced his arm, dripping fresh blood into Meg's bowl of spaghetti.

"Smells good in here," Meg's voice broke the silence.

Skeele turned on the sink and rinsed off the knife. He licked his arm to seal the wound.

"Hey, just in time," he said as he stirred Meg's dinner, mixing the blood into the sauce.

"I'm starved," she said, taking the bowl and sitting on the couch.

Meg

Kal can cook. I've never tasted a bowl of spaghetti so delicious.

"What did you do to this sauce?" I ask.

"Poured it out of the jar," Kal says. "You think it's good? I've never made it before."

I stare like a weirdo. "You've never cooked spaghetti before? Have you even lived?"

He laughs nervously and rubs a hand over his head. "I mean, I've had spaghetti before, I just don't cook it. It's one of those things. Have you made cheesecake?"

I shake my head.

"See. Some things we only buy."

I get up to clean and reach for Kal's empty bowl. "You want more?" I ask.

Kal gets up and follows me. "No. I'm full. Two dinners are enough for me."

"Apparently not for me." I set the bowls in the sink and turn on the water. I notice a splash of red on the side of the sink.

"I'll clean up later." Kal turns me and touches my neck.

"You sure?"

"There are better things to do right now." His eyes drop to my lips and heat spreads across my abdomen. Suddenly I feel like I'm in the tormented state of bloodlust. That spaghetti must've been magical. Maybe it was the act of a man taking care of me. Maybe that's what did it. He takes off his shirt and reaches for mine.

We make it to the couch again. Kal sucks in a breath as I lean into him and press my teeth to his neck. I want to break the skin. I want to bite hard and taste the blood. But I don't because Kal is human and I'm on the Earthen plane. And I'm trying to do better.

Kal's hands tighten on my hips then he jerks me down onto his hardness. "Yes, my night owl," his voice is low. The words sound more like a muttering, like a secret he wants to keep to himself instead of share with me, like a prayer to the darkness, a mantra to the night. I get the feeling those words weren't meant for me to hear. Perhaps they were meant for someone else, not a fling after a few nights. Kal's probably using me to forget someone else. I can't say I haven't done that before.

My night owl. I kiss his neck instead of draining him dry and I consider, as our bodies move together, languid and slow, maybe I should leave Kal so I don't hurt him like I've hurt the rest of my friends. He deserves better than what I'll do to him. I'll break him. I'll burn him. I just might lose control and kill him. The urges have been harder to contain, after all.

And, like he hears my thoughts, his arms pull me close, wrapping tightly and rolling us until I am below him, taking his weight and thrusts as he kisses me, whispers on my lips, "Stay."

I must be easy to read; in the short time we've been together Kal can sense I'm ready to run away.

————

Skeele

Skeele didn't know the glamour translated his Hellspeak. He didn't know Meg finally heard what he had been calling her all those nights she took him to her room. All those nights he promised on his honor to serve her without getting attached.

He couldn't ignore she had that look the veil of night could not hide. That same look she got when she was ready to run. He'd seen it before, felt the pulling away. He reminded himself that she was feral and wild. *Don't get attached.* He could be loyal and serve her throne as he'd promised.

The bloodlust was her addiction. He knew how to keep her focused and present, a little blood, a bit of his body, and she'd stay for a few moments longer. It was manipulative. He knew that but it was for her safety. Meg was running from herself, and Skeele was taking his time on the Earthen plane since the Deacons wanted his hide in retribution.

————

Meg

I decide to spend my day at the beach and take a break from Kal. I haven't had blood in a week, and being around him is getting dangerous. I wanted to sink my teeth into his neck the other night. If I know anything about myself, I'll lose control and do it. Then I'll have a mess to clean up. This is why I left Hell, being a danger to others is no fun at all. It's better to be alone.

The bag of C is missing from behind my toaster. Either Kal found it, or I can't remember moving it. Not that this would be the first time I can't remember what I've done. It's happened before. I'd like to think Kal didn't touch it. He's too good to do something like that.

I walk in the tide, my footprints sinking in the sand. I decide when I get home, I'm going to take the morning after pill that Dr. Jordan prescribed me. I think that's the best option for me.

I walk a good few miles before I notice the cooler breeze. Beach-goers are leaving in droves. Soon, I'm the only one left and my walk home is peaceful: nothing but the sound of the waves and the thunder rolling in.

There's a single man lying on his stomach facing the ocean, read-ing, and watching the storm clouds form. I'd recognize that ass anywhere. It's Kal. So much for avoiding him.

"Hey," Kal moves to his feet. It's a sight for sore eyes. He's ripped and slightly tanned and fills out his board shorts perfectly. He's too perfect. I could eat him whole but then I'd be sad that he would be dead.

"Hey," I wave and walk toward him.

"This water is amazing," he motions to the turquoise water of the Florida panhandle. "I've seen nothing like it." He pauses, his head tips. "What's that?"

Kal raises his arm; the hairs stand on edge. He reaches forward and touches my hair.

"It's sticking up all over the place," he says with a little laugh.

Oh no. I read about this in a safety pamphlet at the doctor's office. Static energy fills the air. BAM! A bright burst of light explodes around us.

Somebody That I Used To Know

The Deacons

The Deacons couldn't leave a Hellion lying unconscious on a beach in the Earthen plane. Especially with the glamour shocked out of him. He had runes to hide him, but a Hellion was a Hellion and the naked eye saw what it saw. There was no hiding now that the ruler of the Earthen plane had called them out with a bolt of electricity.

There is really one entity that keeps the world running. The cleanup crew. The scavengers, the vultures, the worms and dung beetles. The Deacons do the same for the realms. The cleaners, the scrapers. The Deacons make sure every soul has time to repent. Heaven or Hell is a choice, the Earthen plane a playground. But there were rules as old as the beginning of time that have waned and wavered. Rules for balance and rules for retribution. And, there was the simple fact that the Deacons favored the Seven Kingdoms of Heaven, although Meg had seen that firsthand. It wasn't a surprise to her. But times were changing, realms were shifting, the fast-Zombie War brought forth transformation; not just in the Seven Kingdoms of Heaven but the Earthen plane as well. The Deacons had seen the change in Hell with Meg at the throne. They kept close tabs as her kingdom grew by leaps and bounds. Plenty had died in the fast-Zombie War, plenty had woken in Hell, plenty had left the Safe Houses without ever ascending. Suddenly, Hell wasn't such a bad ending for many.

Skeele and Meg lay unconscious on the beach. The lightning strike left matching Lichtenberg figures in fernlike scars down their back and arms, mirroring each other. Whereas a human's scars from such an event would be red, theirs were blacker than any ink. Scorched to their bones, it was a message left to be interpreted in a variety of ways. But predominantly as, Stay Out!

Meg had been told there was no God and many times she'd formed her own conclusion that a true being was not there, but an energy was. That's the only explanation for how she found Sparrow so quickly. Now that energy wanted Meg and Skeele out of his realm. Or perhaps, it could no longer stand by and witness Meg's self-destruction.

The Deacons arrived in record time. They scooped the two bodies off the sand and walked them into the ocean. They moved calmly and with ease. The one carrying Skeele's giant body lifted him as if he were no more than a child's size. Each Deacon chanted the same phrase that turned the water into a portal and brought them to a Safe House.

———

MEG

I never thought I'd see this room again. The desk opposite me draws up feelings that I'd rather not experience. Last time I sat in this chair, I did not know what I was. I was nothing but a wandering soul on the wrong plane looking for trouble.

"Tell us what happened," the man from the center of the desk-of-questioning says to me.

"Nothing happened. I was walking on the beach and got struck by lightning." I rub my sweaty palms across my white scrubs.

"Something definitely happened," the one on the right says.

I press my lips together. I'm not answering to these fucks. I'd kill everyone in this room if I could.

"You should take better care of yourself in your condition," the one on the left says.

"My condition? What's wrong with my condition?" I ask, crossing my arms.

He presses his lips together before looking at his friends. "Let's start with the drugs."

"Lots of people do drugs." I shrug, annoyed. "No biggie."

"In your condition?" the one in the center says. "Do you realize what you could have done?"

"My condition is fine. Tip top shape." Nausea rolls up the back of my throat, but I swallow it down. I won't let my body show them I am a liar. I haven't had much control over myself these past few months, but this instant I will.

I should have taken that pill the day Dr. Jordan wrote for it. I should have ended this immediately. Never once did I think the thing in my belly would put a target on my back.

"You know," I cross my arms, "I'm still unhappy that you never gave me back my guns last time I was here."

The men don't say a thing.

"I'd like to give this place zero stars." I hold up my index finger and thumb in a circle.

"That doesn't matter here," the man in the middle says.

"It should." I rub away the ache from the mark down my arm left by the lightning strike.

The one on the left waves toward me. "Maybe you should come back later, when you can tell the truth."

"Whatever you think is the truth is most likely wrong," I say.

"Sparrow told us—"

I stand. "Don't." I point at them. "Don't you dare. This is my realm. I rule here. I am truth. Sparrow knows nothing!" I grip the back of the chair. "Let me the fuck out of here now!" I pick up the chair and throw it at the men. The chair hits their desk and falls to the ground. The men sit still, unscathed, unshocked, uncaring.

The one on the right waves to a Deacon near the door. If everything runs like the last time I was here, this is my Parole Officer. Poor schmuck. They assigned this Deacon to take me back and forth and hear me repent. I'm not sure if this is like regular Containment, because I'm not just any prisoner. I've noticed a few things: Newcomers wear maroon scrubs and they put me in white. I never got my Qualifiers checklist, an intake form where we write all the information we can remember and our greatest sins. Nope, they must've saved mine from last time I was here. The sins are the same. I'd probably need an additional sheet or two to include everything now.

The Deacon walks me back to my cell. "You'll be safe here. Safer than you've been out there."

"Shut up," I seethe.

The Deacon's mouth snaps closed, and he looks uneasy. The first time I was here, I thought they were helpful and kind, but then they sent a Scarecrow after me and colluded with the Seven Kingdoms of Heaven. I've realized that they are not helpful or kind, simply prying and meddlesome. Maybe they help the lost souls repent and guide them to where they need to go, but when it comes to me, they've brought nothing but trouble.

Prisons are all set up similar. They have me in a basement, no windows. I think it's solitary confinement. Probably for the better. They can't risk putting me in with the others. What an influence I would be on the newly dead.

There's a six-pack of Ginger Ale on my bed.

"The kitchen sent it," the Deacon says. "For your upset stomach."

"My stomach is fine."

"Uh hm." The Deacon opens the door to my cell.

I wander inside and he slams it closed like I am some dangerous criminal.

I've tried not wandering inside after Deacon opens my cell door. I've tried faking him out and running in another direction. I didn't get far. I can't walk through bars of iron, and I don't know the layout of this prison. Truth is, I'll run into a wall before I find a door. No, I can't run screaming down the halls. I have to be smart. I have to watch them and plan my escape. Just like last time.

The Deacon leaves with a jingle of his keys. I turn on the sink and splash water on my face, trying not to puke. I don't want him to hear me. My hands shake under the stream of water as I splash it and rub my face and neck. I'm not sure if it's the thing in my belly or the lack of C making me feel like absolute shit. Maybe it's the food here? I grab a ginger ale, crack it open, and sip.

I'm not sure how long I've been here. I was out for a while after the lightning strike on the beach. I would have thought living through that would have taken care of things. Seems it didn't. Hell, I wouldn't know. I need a meeting with Teari so she can answer all my questions. Poor Kal, though. I'm sure he's deader than a doornail.

I settle on the bed, put my hands behind my head, and cross my ankles. Since I have nothing better to do than wait for dinner, I take a nap. Maybe Nightingale will find me since she enjoys snooping so much.

My nap doesn't last long. Something roars like a wild animal from a few cells down. I sit up in bed. I thought I was alone. I stand and move to the bars, gripping them, pressing my face against the metal to see what's happening.

There's four Deacons in the hall. They're carrying electric batons; I can hear the static zapping. Scuffling ensues, slaps and punches echo. The Deacons are yelling at someone.

I wait, holding my breath to see who walks by. A giant form shuffles and shoves. I'd recognize those horns anywhere.

"Skeele!" I shout. He's cuffed and electrified batons threaten to zap him from all sides as he walks. He sneers, his eyes filled with hate like a wild animal trapped in a zoo.

I reach out from between the bars only for a Deacon to slap my arm away. The motion shoves my injury from Sparrow's blade into the bars.

"Ow," I shout, "You don't have to be such a dick. Just let me talk to him! Skeele!"

They don't let me talk to him, they take him away and he doesn't even seem to recognize me.

Maybe he's mad? I'd be mad at me for leaving like I did. I never said goodbye, I just disappeared. I never told him about… damn.

———

SHAY AND JED

Shay stood in the middle of Meg's room feeling uneasy. "This seems so wrong," she said.

Jed was brushing crushed bird seed off the balcony railing.

"What's this?" Shay picked up the jar of mottled feathers from Meg's bedside table.

"I'm not sure," Jed said as he walks into the room. "But judging from the scarce decorations in this room, if it's here then it's important to her."

Shay set the jar down and wandered around the room, then the closet, then the bathroom. "Do I have to stay in here?" she asked. "It really feels like a violation of her privacy."

Jed followed Shay. "Look, we are doing her a favor."

"No one will know." Shay made her way to the balcony for some fresh air.

Jed stood next to her, scanning the tree line. He saw movement and pointed it out to Shay. "That creature would know if this room were empty."

Shay leaned forward and squinted. "What is it?"

"Probably a demon."

"You don't think it's Demore?" Shay asked.

Jed shook his head. "It's too early in the night for Demore." He took a piece of sharp charcoal from his jacket pocket and began sketching runes of protection on the balcony railing. "It could be another Deacon."

"Meg drinks blood," Shay said. "Are they going to want me to drink blood?"

"You don't have to drink blood. You're human."

There was a cry off in the forest. It sounded like an animal or a bird. But Jed and Shay knew it could be something else.

Shay's breasts felt warm as milk letdown.

"Ugh." Shay touched her chest and felt wetness. "Is this ever going to stop?" She knew it could go on for weeks while her milk dried up. Now that Nightingale was back, Thrush didn't need a wet-nurse.

Jed touched her arm. "Come inside, I'll help you with that."

———

Nightingale

Nightingale sat in creaking rocking chair. Thrush tucked against her chest.

"How long will you be like this?" Noah asked.

Nightingale smiled. "Forever." She kissed her baby. "Forever and ever."

Noah flashed from one side of the room to the other. "We can stay like this?" He knelt beside her. "No more sneaking off to the Astral to be together?"

"No."

"And Thrush?"

"Will grow and find his place. Then it will just be us."

Noah dropped his head. "I never thought we'd be together again." He paused for a moment. "What about Jack?"

"He's gone." Nightingale looked away, remembering the ambush during the fast-Zombie War. "He went wherever I went. The only thing that brought me back was Thrush."

Noah nodded, solemn. He reached out and touched Nightingale's cheek, the scars that marred her skin.

Nightingale turned away. "Don't." She wasn't ready to deal with the scars and what had happened. She only wanted to revel in the joy of having her baby in her arms again.

"Will you search for Meg tonight?" Noah asked. "I feel like there's something very wrong."

Nightingale stopped rocking. "What's wrong?"

"I lost my connection to her when she left, but for some reason," Noah paced and ran his hands through his hair. "For some reason I feel like she's nearby."

Nightingale stood and took Thrush to his crib. She lay him down gently and patted his back until he was deep asleep. She left the nursery and closed the door.

"You think she's here in Hell?" Nightingale asked Noah. "Skeele didn't bring her back to us."

"I know. There's still a connection though, weak but there. She's back on this plane."

Nightingale made her way to the bedroom. "I guess we better find out where she is then."

———

MEG

I wish I could *poof* out of here. But the lightning strike did something to me. I trace the marks on my arm. I was a complete idiot for releasing Noah from our tether. If I'd never done that, I could summon him to this place. He'd be able to find me in an instant and help set me free. It's better this way. I've had to rely on myself my whole life before. There's no difference now. The more I think of it, the more I realize I've been around too many people. My inner circle is much too large. I need to shrink it down to one. Single. That's the best way to do things. Look what happened to poor Kal.

I fluff the flat pillow under my head by beating it with my fists. It doesn't do much. The pillow has the fluff of a piece of cardboard.

"Breakfast," a Deacon slides a tray into my cell.

I get up and see what they brought me.

More slop and plastic silverware. I sit on the floor and lean against the bed while I eat the cold oatmeal with strange milk and a brown banana. Either the food budget is tight or they're punishing me by way of my stomach. The food was strange last time I was here. Unpasteurized milk that stunk and odd meats.

My shirt catches on something sharp. Peeking from under the mattress, tucked between the spring and metal frame, is a tarnished metal spoon. Anything metal is a prize when you're locked in a cell like this. This thing looks old. I hold it in my hand and rub my thumb over the smooth handle.

Last time I dug my way out of jail, I had to steal the spoon myself from the galley. Those were the days.

"Hey," I whisper down the hall.

Skeele doesn't answer.

"Hey, are you there?" I ask again.

This is probably a bad time to shout between the bars that I've got a fetus in my belly and it's his. That seems insensitive and I've been enough of a jerk to Skeele. I've got to tell him sometime and we need to get out of here.

I pace in my cell and think of a plan. I rub my fingers on the spoon, fidgeting. I crawl across the bed and hang my bedsheet along the back wall and make it look like I'm just a slob who doesn't make their bed in the morning. If I dig under the bed, the sheet could hide it. I leave it like that to see if anyone notices throughout the day.

The doors squeal. Metal on metal. Plenty of footsteps follow.

Four Deacons walk by dragging Skeele. There's blood dripping down his back, a trail streaks across the floor. Thick and coagulated. My mouth waters.

I move to the bars like a starved lioness. "Skeele!" I shout. "What did you do to him?"

No one answers. The Deacons don't look at me.

After they leave, I reach out and touch the streaks of blood on the floor. I collect some on my fingertip and smell it. Damn. Saliva fills my mouth. I lick the blood off my fingers and reach out for more. I move across the front bars of my cell, scooping as much of the streaks as I can reach. It's disgusting. Dirty. It tastes so good. I miss his blood.

"What did they do to you?" I finally ask, hoping he'll answer.

He doesn't.

I lick the redness from between my fingernails, I close my eyes and try to poof; nothing happens. That lighting strike really fucked with my ability to travel at will.

———

Rolling over in the squeaking bed, a spring pokes me in the back. I open my eyes and hold my hand over my mouth. I take three deep breaths, hoping it will pass.

"You feeling okay?" My Deacon is here, prying eyes and imploring tone.

"Never better." I lie. "Tip-top."

"Be ready in thirty minutes. You're going to Questioning again today."

"Joy."

Another Deacon brings me a tray of food and slides it through the access near the door. I eat some of the toast while I get ready. There's not much to do. I don't want to wear my dirty clothes, so I keep wearing the white scrubs they bring me each day. I wash my face and scrub my neck. Then I wait until my Deacon returns.

I stand at the bars and press the side of my face against them, trying to see down the hall to the cell where Skeele is being kept.

"Hey," I whisper. "Hey, are you there?"

A grunt replies.

"What did they do to you?" I ask.

The Archangels tore up my back once before. I'm surprised the Deacons would employ similar methods of punishment. I've never seen them hurt a person before. While they've meddled and gotten people hurt, I've never seen them deliver a punishment.

The thirty minutes goes by fast. Deacon collects me from my cell for more questioning. It's always the same questions. I'm tired of it.

"Come on, Meg." Deacon motions for me to leave the cell.

"What did you do to Skeele?" I ask, crossing my arms and standing my ground.

"That's not open for discussion." He motions again. "Time to go."

"I don't want to go. I want to know what happened to him."

Deacon leans forward and lowers his voice. "We know you licked his blood off the floor."

I swallow down my shame. "So? It's what I am. You know that."

"It means something."

"Yeah. It means I'm hungry for more than the slop you've been bringing me every day. What do I have to do to get a rare steak or a bag of blood in this joint?"

Deacon smiles. "Let's go."

"Skeele?" I shout and run for the hall.

Deacon grabs me. He's strong, but after that little bit of fresh blood, I'm stronger. I tear myself away from him and run down the hall to Skeele's cell.

His large form is lying on the bed, his torn up back on display. His arms and wings hang over the bed and drape on the floor. He looks entirely too large for the cell and the furnishings. He's not moving.

"What did you do to him?" I snap.

"He'll be fine. He's a big boy."

"No one deserves that." I reach into the cell but he's too far away. I want to shake him awake to make sure he's okay.

"If you knew, you might change your mind," my Deacon replies with a sarcastic tone.

I glare at Deacon and consider injuring him. I might be able to do it. I can't *poof* from here to there, but I have a spec of extra energy from the blood. I'll probably have the blood lust soon too.

I grip the bars of Skeele's cell.

"You can't help him," Deacon says.

"Why not?" I argue.

"He's killed."

"He's a Hellion. It's his job," I say.

"All are forbidden from preventing Newcomers to Hell from reaching a Safe House to repent and find their place."

"He killed a Newcomer?" I ask. "He would never. Skeele is as straight as they come. All rules, no breaking them. It had to have been a mistake."

"It wasn't. Let's go. They're waiting for you."

———

IN THE NIGHT, I hear a strange noise; a cooing. I can't be too deep if there's an animal this close. I slide my arm behind the bed and chip away at the old cement. The old spoon works as well as can be expected. I barely hear the small pieces of cement falling to the floor. I work on digging for a few hours, until my fingers are numb and my arm is sore. When I'm satisfied with the hard night's work, I collect the small pile of cement chips and dust and put it in my pocket. The cooing noise stops not long before sunrise.

———

"SUNDAYS ARE FOR VISITORS," Deacon says.

"No one knows I'm here."

"I think you'll be surprised to see who knows." He motions for me to move. "Come on. Might raise your spirits."

He walks me up three flights of stairs. The layout starts to look familiar. There are windows and more cells that turn into real hallways with solid doors. He opens the one that says *Visitation*.

Clea is waiting, sitting with her back straight and hands folded on her lap, still as stone.

"Child," she says as I enter. "It's been too long."

"How did you find me?" I ask as the Deacon leaves.

"A mother's tether is forever strong." She motions for me to sit with her eyes. "Nightingale has been looking also. She said you haven't been sleeping very well. She hasn't been able to invade your dreams."

I've missed her paleness and red lips, the way her figure wavers like she's about to flitter away to the Astral realm.

"What happened to your neck and arm?" she asks.

I hold up the arm with the dark marks. "Struck by lightning."

She stares, intensity in her eyes. "It's best you're here then."

The door opens and Skeele walks into the room. I step to the side to make space for him. He doesn't look so hot.

I hold back the feeling of excitement at finally seeing him in his semi-normal state.

Clea's expression turns concerned as she examines him from her seat. "You as well?" she asks him.

"What?" he asks.

"Your hand." Clea points.

Skeele is wearing the same white scrubs as me and since we've been here, I've only seen him in passing. Now, I see the marks on his hand and the side of his neck. Lightning scars, just like mine.

"What the fuck?" I say as I grab his wrist and pull his arm out straight. "How did you get those?"

Skeele doesn't answer. He makes a face like a kicked puppy.

"When I was on the Earthen plane, I was on a date at the beach with a nice guy named Kal. We both got struck by lightning," I say.

Skeele is silent.

"How the fuck did you get struck by lightning?" I hold up my arm against his. "Why do these scars match?" I tug at my shirt, showing him the blackened fern-like patterns that extend from my neck, down my chest, covering the disfigured Sparrow tattoo. "You're fucking Kal, aren't you?"

"You ran away," Skeele finally speaks.

I look at Clea for support but she's too busy watching us intently.

"You lied to me," I say.

"Yes."

"You hunted me."

"It wasn't hard." Skeele touches the marks on his hand, the forest tattoos on his forearms. "Jed taught me the glamour. If you are going to be mad, be mad at everyone. We were trying to bring you home."

"Don't tell me who to be mad at." I control the urge to attack like a rabid animal. I want to. My emotions are teetering on the edge.

"Child," Clea interrupts. "I'm bringing the others to see you. We have to figure out a way to get you out of here."

"I already have one." I whisper. "I've done this before."

Clea blinks.

"It was a bit of a different situation, but I figured it all out." I make a shoveling motion with my hand.

Clea makes a face. She doesn't understand and I just turn out looking stupid, jerking my hand around.

I lean forward. "I'm digging a tunnel."

"Come on," Skeele exhales a breath of exasperation.

"I'm halfway. I've done this before." I reach into my pocket and pull out a handful of cement and dirt. "I'll be topside in a few weeks."

"We can't stay in here for weeks," Skeele rubs his horns.

"Regardless, I will bring the others back here to see you," Clea says.

"No." I slam my fist on the table. "I don't need them."

"We all need someone, child." Clea folds her hands and leans closer to me. "If anyone needs someone, it is you right now."

"I don't need anyone." I stand and move away from the table. "Don't bring them here. I don't want to see them."

Skeele twists in the bench to face me. "You're not thinking straight."

"What do you know?" I snap. "You just partook in the greatest mindfuck of my life. How could I think straight?"

I walk to the gate and tell the Deacon that I want to go back to my room. He takes me without question, leaving Skeele and Clea to continue their discussion.

I flop down on the bed and press my hands over my eyes. This is all turning to shit. I'm trying to keep them safe by not involving them, that's why I went to the Earthen plane. Now Clea is going to bring them here. This is exactly what I don't want. I don't want my friends to see me like this; weak, emotional, restrained against my will. It's been a long time since I was like this. Not since Jim. Not since that first group of Hellions that nearly killed me.

———

NOAH HAS a giant grin plastered on his face. I knew I shouldn't have come to see them. I should've stayed in my cell and ignored my Deacon when he came to collect me for visitation.

"Where's Thrush?" I ask, worried.

"Jed and Shay are watching him," Noah says. "Never thought I'd get to see you in lockup. Jailbait all your life and now is when you get put in the slammer."

I roll my eyes. "We could easily change places."

"I'm not so sure about that," Noah winks and scrubs his hair. "I'm too pretty for this place. You know what they say."

"This isn't like the Earthen plane prison," I say, crossing my arms and leaning on the table.

"Are you well?" Nightingale asks.

"I'm fine." I glance to the door, expecting a Deacon to bring Skeele out. My right hand moves to my pocket and slowly shakes the cement and dirt out.

"We are going to get you out," Noah says.

———

THE HELLIONS VISIT the next week.

Klaus, Chel, and Tukka look out of place in the visitation room. They take up so much space I pause at the door, afraid to enter. It seems like there isn't enough air in the room to breathe with them all there.

Klaus smiles. "There she is." He pats his pockets. "I brought you something." He pulls out four vials of blood.

"You can bring that in here?" I ask.

"They didn't search us," Chel says, leaning into the sliver of a shadow against the wall.

"Have you gotten in any fights yet?" Tukka asks, baring his own fangs. "I've got a bet going."

"Kinda hard when I'm locked up in solitary."

Klaus wrinkles his forehead. "For this long?"

I nod.

"Where's Skeele?" he asks.

"Down the hall from me but I haven't seen him much. They keep him away. Don't let us talk." I sigh. "Not that I want to talk to that liar."

Chel makes a face, and his eyes linger to where my hand is tucked into my pocket, scraping out dirt.

"We'll storm the Safe House," Klaus suggests. "We'll get you out. They can't do this in your own realm."

"I should be out soon," I promise. "Hey, have you ever seen any birds in the ground around here?"

The Hellions think for a moment before Chel says, "There are ground owls." He points to the edge of the Safe House. "The land is cleared, mostly dirt over there. I saw their burrows on the way in." His eyes roam to the pile of dirt that's under my seat. "What are you doing?"

"Don't speak of it," I warn. "Did you all know Skeele went to find me on the Earthen plane?"

All three Hellions close their mouths and look at each other. I guess they weren't preparing themselves for my question.

"You're a bunch of asshats," I say. "I didn't need him."

"He couldn't serve the throne without you in Hell," Klaus says. "It is our duty."

"Would someone have followed Lucifer?" I ask.

"You should talk to Skeele about it," Tukka says. "Don't bite his head off."

"Too late," I warn. "I brought it up when I noticed his matching scars." I hold up my arm with the fern-like pattern from the lightning strike. "That was a few weeks ago."

"Cool," Klaus says, stepping closer to get a better look. "Is that from lightning?"

"Yes." I rub my arm, remembering the tingle.

"You match." Klaus makes a face of satisfaction. "That's a sign."

"Of what?" I shake the rest of the dirt out of my pocket and brush my dusty hands off on my pants.

"A sign of something important." Klaus looks entirely too excited over the prospect that Skeele and me were struck by lightning at the same time.

"Deacons told me we were tossed out of the Earthen plane. That's all. Nothing special but battle scars," I say.

Klaus strokes his beard and narrows his eyes on my arm. "Sure."

———

JED AND SHAY VISIT. I contemplate hiding in my room, but I owe these two. Of all my visitors, I *have* to attend this visitation. I owe them too much to blow them off.

"Hey," Shay leans forward and moves to grip my fist. Her hand hovers over mine.

"It's okay," I lift my fist and let her touch me. "I'm glad to see you. Are you both doing okay?"

"No complaints from this department," Jed says, inspecting me. His fingers tap on the wooden table between us in a rapid beat.

"Are you nervous?" I ask.

He tips his head toward the Deacon. "You think they know what I am?"

"I'm sure. They tend to know everything. Or at least they think they do." I make quick action of emptying my pocket.

A few moments later, Skeele walks in the room. Jed stands and claps him on the shoulder. "Hey man, you alright in there?"

Skeele says, "As well as I can be."

There's a moment of awkwardness. Jed wants to ask Skeele something but as he casts hesitant glances in my direction, I get the sense he doesn't want me to hear.

"I already know," I finally say. "I know he glamoured himself and followed me."

"Hey, man, it worked." Jed smiles and slaps Skeele on the shoulder again. "You brought her back."

Skeele winces and holds up a hand. "Easy." He rolls his shoulders. "My assigned method of contrition has been physical."

"They couldn't give you some prayers to say?" Jed asks, lifting his hand and inspecting Skeele's back. "Dicks."

"I go back next week and they tell me if I'm forgiven." Skeele rubs his hands together and refuses to look in my direction. "My father was a Hellion. I've had worse."

"We have got to get you all out of there," Shay says, patting my hand.

"I have a plan–" I start to say.

"It will not work," Skeele argues.

"I've dug a hole. It's almost completed." I lower my voice. "I should be done by next week."

"Good," Skeele says. "At least you can get out of here."

"Wait, wait." Jed holds up his hands. "We can't leave Skeele in here." He presses fingertips to his head for a moment. "Tell me more."

"The hole is small," I say. "I can get out. He won't fit."

Shay turns to face Jed. "She can get out. I can go in. Then you all can storm the place and get out Skeele." She leaves her hand on mine. "Can you still poof from place to place?"

"Not since I was struck by lightning." I shake my head.

"Jed could do a glamour. We've been practicing." She touches Jed's arm. "Show her. She should know."

Jed's fingers dance in rhythmic spellcasting and Shay turns into a mirror image of me.

"Holy shit." I lean forward and touch her hair. "That's amazing."

"Jed's been practicing new spells from his book," Shay says.

"Have you been pretending to be me?" I ask.

"We had to," Jed says. "The Deacons showed up and the new Hellions were spreading rumors. She didn't do anything you wouldn't do." A mischievous smile lifts the corners of his mouth. "So next week. You get out. Shay can get in. Skeele, create a distraction. Maybe start a fight. Then we raid. Watch this." Jed's fingers move again, and he disappears then reappears a few minutes later. "We can get in, get the keys, get Skeele and Shay and get out. You know the layout. You can lead us while we are cloaked."

The plan sounds good. I think it could work. "Is there a backup plan?" I ask.

"I just thought of this like two minutes ago. I haven't thought of a backup plan," Jed says.

I nod. "Let's do it."

———

The next week, my tunnel is completed. The only problem is I'll have to displace the little burrowing owls while I crawl through.

During the day the Hellions visit, and we solidify the plan. The Deacons don't have security like a normal prison since this is more of a spiritual setting. Churches don't have security, neither do the Deacons.

After dinner, I crawl through the tunnel. My heart is steadily beating faster and faster as I follow the dim light in the distance. When I come to the little burrowing owls, I set them on my shoulder and take them along for the ride. When I finally get to the opening, I pause to take in my surroundings. The tunnel isn't far from the Safe House wall. The opening is in a dip in the land that looks like a retention pond. I scoot out, dirt covering my white scrubs and falling out of my hair.

I see motion in the tree line. The Hellions are there. So is Jed and Shay. She looks just like me. I scramble toward them. When I reach the shadows, Klaus grabs me and pulls me in for a tight hug. I let him hold on to me until he's ready to release me.

Noah and Nightingale aren't here. I wouldn't expect it. They have to watch Thrush. We have enough people.

"Ready?" I ask Shay.

She nods and walks away. I grab her arm to stop her. "Just wait for us. We'll get you out."

Shay pats my hand. "I know, Meg. I know you'll get me out."

The little owls hop around the entrance to the tunnel as Shay climbs inside.

"How long should we give her?" Jed asks.

"A few minutes, then we follow the next Deacon inside."

Jed casts his spells and we are all invisible, then we make our way to the front door.

———

Skeele

Skeele waited, pacing his cell, knowing what was transpiring down the hall. Meg was switching places with Shay, and then they'd be freed. Hopefully. It all sounded too easy. But Skeele no longer cared. If Meg was free, that's all he could ask for. She didn't belong in this Safe House prison. The Deacons had tormented them for long enough.

A metal door squealed. Shit. Skeele pressed his face to the bars hoping Meg and Shay had switched places in time. Footsteps echoed. Many footsteps.

A handful of Deacons stopped in front of Skeele's door. "Let's go." They readied their batons as one opened the door.

Skeele held up his hands in defeat. He just wanted to see if Shay was there.

"Kinda late for interrogation," Skeele said.

"Move," a Deacon ordered.

Skeele behaved. He left the cell without fighting and walked down the hall. His stomach sank when he saw Meg's cell door was also open and no one was inside.

Shit.

A Deacon shoves Skeele from behind. "Move."

They led him to the interrogation room.

Meg was there.

Skeele blinked. Meg didn't make it out. She turned to look at him, a hopeful smile spread across her face. Skeele nodded as he realized this wasn't Meg.

Meg would have greeted him with less excitement. It had been less and less since she found out he was Kal and he'd lied to her. She hadn't smiled in all the weeks they'd been imprisoned.

The man at the center of the desk-of-questioning tapped his gavel. "You're both here for some clarification. You're keeping secrets from each other."

Skeele and Shay looked at each other.

The door creaked and Skeele felt familiar energy enter the room. He sniffed the air and recognized the real Meg and the other Hellions.

"Skeele," the man on the left said. "You ate a family of Newcomers. This is forbidden."

"I was hungry." Skeele replied.

"An entire family, before they had time to reach us." The man at the desk was disgusted. "There are few rules in Hell. Surely you can follow the simplest one."

"It was an emergency." Skeele rolled his shoulders, wishing the others would hurry and get them out.

"What kind of an emergency?"

"Meg was dying," Skeele said.

"You killed to save the ruler of Hell?"

"Yes." Skeele cleared his throat. "And I'd do it again. I was born and bred to serve the throne."

One man tapped his fingers together. "You are like your father, so faithful to Hell."

"There is no other way to be." Skeele lifted his chin. Proud. He was a Hellion. Different than the previous ones, but a Hellion none the less. He'd studied and read and trained. And Sparrow had taught him to be better just before turning into a monster himself.

There is a long pause before the men turned their attention on Shay.

"We need to discuss your situation," the man to the left said.

Shay pressed her lips together.

"The Queen of Hell should not be trying to abort her fetus or be acting recklessly. You were doing drugs to harm your unborn child. God cast you out of the Earthen plane with force. What do you have to say?" the man said.

A feeling of dread combined with the need to be sick flooded Skeele.

Meg was pregnant.

Meg was pregnant. All the vomiting and strange behavior was

making sense. He wanted to slap himself. He should've known better. He should've done something. He could have helped her if he'd known.

The fake Meg never said a thing, but in the back of the room Skeele heard Meg's voice quietly say, "Break the glamour. This is not her sin to answer for."

MEG

Shame.

That's the only feeling I have. Complete and utter shame. It's bone deep. Tattooed on my soul. I have never felt more shame in my life.

Everyone in the room heard. I can't let Shay answer to my sins. Those are mine, not hers. And they are no longer secret.

Skeele's jaw is slack, like he can't believe it. I can't look at him. I keep my eyes on the men at the center of the desk of questioning and cross the room to stand next to Shay. Her glamour fades and blue hair returns.

Now I have a giant pile of shit to dig myself out of.

Dig Deep Down

I CAN KILL THEM ALL AND GO ON WITH MY LIFE. I CAN drain them dry. Every one. The Hellions, the Deacons, Skeele, Jed, and Shay. No one will know. No one but me. I can think up some lies to tell the others. It's not like I haven't killed to survive before. This would be... this would be... nothing.

A giant lump forms in my throat. My head hurts. My heart hurts. I can't kill them. I have to protect them. That's what I was trying to do by running away but the Deacons and God destroyed that plan for me. Dicks.

"What do you want from me?" I ask, walking to the front of the room to stand in front of Shay and protect her.

The men at the desk-of-questioning whisper to each other for a few moments before one raises his hand. "We propose a trial since you aren't telling us the truth."

I open my mouth to speak.

Brows rise, putting me in my place.

My mouth snaps shut.

"You sit on trial, Meg. And a jury will decide your fate. Not us. Deacons keep the balance." The man clears his throat.

"A jury of who?" I ask. "A jury of Deacons. I don't think so." I feel the rage gathering in the center of my chest.

"A jury of your peers. Your friends," the man says.

"I don't want to bring them into this mess. This is my mess, not theirs," I say.

The man at the center of the desk-of-questioning wrinkles his placid face. "The blood of the covenant is thicker than the water of the womb."

I control my blood rage. I don't kill everyone in the room. I suck it up and watch the Deacons as they bring in desks and chairs and set up the room like a courtroom.

It's been a long time since I was in a real courtroom. The last time was when me and Noah stole that car as teenagers and spent the weekend in juvie. This feels much different. I suppose because I'm an adult now and I've done a few things that are a lot worse than stealing a car and going for some joyrides on a Friday night.

Omens Between
the Veil

A gavel falls. I sit and look to my left. The Deacon who brought me back and forth from my cell is sitting there. It's all very dream-like.

The door opens and another Deacon ushers a line of people into the room and toward the jury seats.

Noah, Nightingale, Shay, Jed, Klaus, Tukka, Chel, Klaus, Teari, Gabriel, and Skeele; they are all sitting to the right of me, looking utterly surprised.

Deacon leans close to whisper to me. "I think we have enough evidence."

"For what? To lock me up for a lifetime in this place? I'll be here until the end of days."

He tries to pat my hand, but I jerk it away.

My Deacon stands and addresses the men from the desk-of-questioning. "I'd like to call our first witness, Nightingale."

Nightingale makes her way to the witness stand.

"How did you meet Meg?" Deacon asks, barely giving her time to sit.

"We met in the basement of my family home."

"Why were you in the basement?"

"That's where my father locked us up." Nightingale's face is placed, serious as shit.

"Can you talk more about that?"

"I was crazy. My family was cursed. Me and Sparrow got the worst of it. Remiel, my father, was embarrassed. He didn't want Meg with Sparrow and he didn't want anyone to see me. So, he locked us in the basement."

"How did Meg react to being locked up with you?"

"She told my father he was a dick then she stole Sparrow away in the night."

"And you eventually went with Meg also?" Deacon asks.

"Yup."

Deacon crosses his arms and taps his chin, narrowing his eyes on Nightingale. "Do you think Meg deserves your friendship? Or, even more, your alliance?"

"She deserves it more than she knows." Nightingale goes into stories of our adventures together. Her marriage, her birth, her death. "Meg saved my baby during the fast-Zombie War. She didn't have to take Thrush and hide him. She could have left him to the will of the Archangels. Meg is more than a friend. She's family. It might be hard for her to comprehend that feeling because she's never had any before. But I don't hold that against her because she never held my being batshit-crazy against me."

Nightingale whistles a light melodic trill that brings a tear to my eye.

"How did you meet Meg?" Deacon asks Noah.

"We went to school together. Same hometown."

"You've known her for years?"

"Most of our lives."

"But then you died."

Noah raises his hands in defeat. "Sure did. Dead as a doornail."

"Who found you in Hell?"

Noah points. "Meg did."

"I will not ask about this rap-sheet." Deacon waves a handful of papers. "Tell me, why did you friend Meg in childhood?"

"Because she was hot." He quips but then his smile fades, and he clears his throat. "Because she needed a friend. I used to bring her lunch. Her dad never fed her, she was tiny. So skinny. I watched her pick through the garbage after lunch. She would hide from the lunch ladies who tried to give her the leftovers from the lunch line. She was too proud for that."

Deacon nods and paces. "It seems you know a side of Meg that none of us have seen."

"Probably."

"Did you have a romantic relationship with her?"

"For a little bit but we were better as friends."

"I'd like to try something if you'd allow it." Deacon holds up a glass ball that's appeared out of thin air. "These are your memories. I'd like to play your memories of Meg throughout childhood."

"Sure." Noah agrees.

Deacon holds up the ball, and light from the window passes through. Above, memories play like a movie in the clouds.

They see it all. Things I'd forgotten, things I never wanted to remember. Noah watching me fight a dog on a chain for that peanut butter sandwich, digging in the trash for clothes, the towel full of holes, the dirty mattress on the floor of my filthy childhood bedroom.

When it finally stops, Deacon says, "Thank you, Noah. You are free to go back to your seat."

I feel a little bit like crying and a little bit like punching someone. I never wanted everyone to see all that shit. They didn't need to know John Lewis raised me like a dog in the backyard.

———

"How do you know Meg?" the Deacon asks Jed.

"I first met her in my shop. She came to me for a tattoo." He holds up his arms, showing off his ink.

"Did she know what you were?"

"She didn't know. I had to explain myself."

"You were comfortable explaining yourself to her? You've been in hiding for so long."

"She was in hiding at the time too. We were kindred. Plus, she needed a tattoo, and she could see my blue light." Jed wags a finger. "Only the safe ones can see blue."

"Any problems after meeting Meg?"

Jed rubs his neck. "She did bite me once." He laughs lightly. "It didn't hurt. It was kinda nice, kinda sexy." He clears his throat and sits up straight. "But then she ran off with Sparrow. Our paths crossed again when the zombies started taking over on the Earthen plane."

"And she brought you to Hell against your will?"

"Nope." Jed shakes his head with certainty. "Never against my will. She's never forced me to do anything." He pauses. "Well, besides tattooing Gabriel but that situation wasn't terrible."

———

Shay takes the stand and Deacon begins his questioning.

"Was that the first time you met Meg?"

"Yes, she rescued us from a house that was under siege with the dead. Jed and I were going to die. Then she showed up at the window and did that *poof* thing. And got us out of there."

"You're full human?" Deacon asks.

"Yes."

"How do you feel about being in Hell? You don't necessarily belong here."

"I hope to stay here." Shay tilts her head like no one is going to tell her what to do with her life. "I spent plenty of time on the

Earthen plane and Hell has been much nicer to me. I have freedom and safety here. I have people like I've never had before."

"Does Meg ever scare you?"

"Of course. I can tell she's struggling. But most of us are. I can't imagine the things she feels responsible for. But I can tell you when Nightingale and Sparrow were injured, she did *everything* in her power to get them to safety. And when Thrush was stolen by Demore, she never slept until he was home. Most humans care less about their own children than Meg cared for Thrush. Do you know how many missing children there are on the Earthen plane? How many kids are abused, stolen, left to raise themselves and given nothing?" Shay is shaking. She tucks a piece of blue hair behind her ear. "Meg isn't perfect. Neither am I. But Meg tries, even if she doesn't realize it."

———

Tukka looks uncomfortable in the hot seat. The Deacon asks questions about being a Hellion under my rule. Tukka's answers are neutral and straightforward.

"Did you ever see Meg hurt someone?"

Tukka glances at Skeele. "Hurt them how?"

"With her teeth. Her power." Deacon replies.

"It was always in self-defense." Tukka rubs his dark-red cheek. "Once I tried to train her how to fight. I was generous in my mocking."

"How does she fight?"

"Fair enough. Better when she's fed on fresh blood."

"Explain."

"She cut my leg and nearly ate me for dinner."

"How did you get out of that situation?"

Tukka chuckles. "I flew away."

Ouch. That burns.

Klaus and Chel each have a turn on the stand. They discuss our hunt for the basilisk.

"What did Lucifer do with the basilisk babies after he caught a mother?" Deacon asks.

Both Hellions looked uncomfortable when they replied. "Grilled them for dinner."

"What did Meg do with the basilisk babies?"

"Put them in a tank and took care of them."

I shiver recalling their slimy lips sucking the poison out of my arm. I never thought to eat them. That just seems kinda wrong.

"I MET Meg in Hell the first time," Teari says. "It was a rescue mission."

"Were you successful?" Deacon asks.

"Always." Can't beat Teari's confidence.

"You're close to Meg?"

"As close as she'll let me get. She has walls up."

"Tell me about the Zombie War on the Earthen plane." Deacon paces in front of our desk.

"I went to find Sparrow and Meg. No one had heard from them for a long time."

"How did you find Meg?"

"God led me to her. There were signs."

"You found Meg, then Sparrow, then you were bitten by the dead?"

Teari holds up her healed hands. "Chopped off both my arms. Meg helped."

My cheeks flame. It was not my proudest moment.

"She cut off your arms?" Deacon asks.

Teari makes a flippant motion. "I made her."

"And then she abandoned you on the Earthen plane?"

"She came back for me."

"And then she locked you up in the burning caves?"

"I was a danger to myself."

"What happened next?"

"She came back with a vial of my father's blood and healed me."

"I thought you were the healer?" Deacon asks. "You *are* the personal healer to King Gabriel."

"All of that is true. But Meg healed me. She saved me."

The Deacon nods as he moves closer and sets his hand on the box of the witness stand. "Strange how she keeps saving people. But she fights so hard against saving herself."

Ouch. What in the absolute hell is wrong with this guy? I slam my fist on the desk and stand. "Objection!"

The men from the desk-of-questioning focus on me.

"I want that comment scratched from the record," I say.

Deacon chuckles. "Sorry. I was out of line." He sits next to me as Teari moves across the room.

"I thought you were on my side?" I seethe.

"I am." The Deacon smiles. "Just making a point.

"You are the current Hellion Commander?" Deacon asks Skeele.

"Yes."

"Are you close to your Queen?" Deacon asks.

"As close as one can be."

"Would you say you're bonded to each other?"

"No." Skeele's voice is sharp. "To be bonded both parties would have to be agreeable to that."

"But she takes your blood?"

"Yes."

"You offer yourself to her. You kneel at her side?"

"Always."

"Your relationship should be more."

Skeele stares straight ahead at the wall. "It is what Meg allows. Nothing more."

"Were you aware that Meg was with child?" Deacon asks.

"No." Skeele shakes his head.

"Did she act sick around you? There have been no signs?"

"She vomited. I thought she was disgusted by me."

"Why would you think that?"

"She has said that she hates the Hellions, they disgust her."

Oh Christ, I am the biggest jackass in all of the realms. I want to hide in a hole.

"But you never left her side? You've been loyal all this time?" Deacon asks.

"I vowed to. It is my duty. I was born and bred to be a Hellion. There is nothing else."

"So much so that you tracked her down on the Earthen plane? You tricked her into thinking you were human."

Skeele shrugs, guilty. "It was the only way I could see."

"Actually, the others colluded with you to find her. Isn't that right?"

"Yes."

"Why would you all go after her?"

"She belongs with us. Life isn't the same without her. Hell is not the same without her."

I swallow the lump in my throat. What have I done to this Hellion? How could I never see it before?

"Do you know whose child she is pregnant with?" Deacon asks.

Oh fuck. No. No. No. No. This is not his information to tell. This is my secret to release. This is mine. No one knows but Teari. No one. Panic creeps up my chest, nearly choking me. I feel like a trapped animal in the smallest cage.

"No." Skeele says. "It's none of my business. It is only my business to serve Meg, to feed her when she allows." His leathery wings shiver and something flickers behind his dark eyes.

I stand, my chair falling over with the force of how quickly I move. "It's yours," I shout across the room to Skeele. "The baby is yours."

He looks shocked, troubled. I don't know how to read him because I've been so selfish. I never took much time to learn about him, I only took from him. I took his blood. I took his sex. And, now I see it, I took his love and stomped all over it. What the fuck is wrong with me?

No apology can make up for this. None.

Skeele's features are stone as he is released from the stand and returns to the jury.

———

"Our next witness, Sparrow," Deacon announces.

Oh shit. My body feels like it's on fire with warring emotions of hate and fear. What the fuck is Sparrow doing here? If they listen to him, I'll surely be in the slammer for eternity.

My Deacon refuses to look in my direction. It's better that way. If looks could kill he'd be ended.

The door slams open and Sparrow walks through. I can't take my eyes off him. His energy fills the room. His giant black wings drape on the floor like a king dragging an extravagant robe. This is a very different Sparrow than the one I traipsed across the northeast with. This is not the quirky Sparrow who was obsessed with collecting feathers. No, this Sparrow is power and anger and menace. I always wondered if I'd even like him once he was back to his normal self. It seems the answer is no. I don't like him. But we are close as family now with Nightingale living in Hell with us. So, I guess we can have mutual respect. As long as he doesn't stab me again.

The Raven King moves to the chair at the front of the room. His darkness is far reaching, and I can feel it inching toward me. The air becomes thick and hard to breathe. If this is a parlor trick, I need to learn how to do it. Energy like that could turn the tables in any argument.

"Please, keep yourself contained," my Deacon says. "We know your history with Meg is turbulent. This is a neutral zone."

Sparrow tips his head like a raven on the phone wire watching food in the middle of a busy road. There was a time that his birdlike mannerisms were comforting.

Deacon clears his throat. "Meg has stated on multiple occasions that you are her hallelujah, heroin, and reason to breathe. What changed?"

Sparrow tips his chin down. "It all started to go a little south when my father threatened her and then she killed him."

I could crawl into a hole right now with those green eyes boring into me. His father was an asshole and Sparrow knows it. Locking up Nightingale was a sin if I ever saw one.

I stand and shout. "How about when you stabbed me to death?"

My Deacon pulls on my arm, forcing me to sit and shushing me. "Stop."

I try to stand again, pointing with venom. "He tried to kill me." I pull at the neck of my shirt. "I have the scars to prove it!"

Ireland-grass green eyes singe my soul. "Remember when you stabbed me in the heart and took the last spec of my grace?" His voice is deep, solemn.

"The Scarecrow told me I had to do it. The Deacons hired the Scarecrow to fuck everything up," I say, my hands shaking. "I found you!" I shout. "I found you and saved you and healed you after the fast-Zombie War. We are even."

Sparrow presses his lips in a straight line and he nods, knowing.

The Deacon bends to make eye contact and grips both my shoulders. "Sit. Meg."

I suck in a weary breath and wrap my fingers around the arms of my chair. "You're a bunch of fucks." Air whistles as I breathe heavily through my nose, my mouth set in a grim line to hide sharp teeth that want nothing more than to rip out some necks.

Satisfied with my control, Deacon turns and addresses Sparrow again. I glance toward the men at the desk-of-questioning. They don't seem fazed by my outburst.

The Deacon asks, "You brought something to show the jury?"

Sparrow reaches in his pocket and pulls out the Argentavis feather Clea gave us. He passes it to the Deacon. "What is this?" the Deacon asks.

"An omen." Sparrow motions in my direction. "From her mother."

Deacon holds up the feather into the light passing through the room and the omen play for all to see.

Wars. Blood and death. Good and evil. A dead Sparrow. A motherless child and a fatherless child. Light and dark. The Earthen plane and the Ethereal realms. A burst of light. An explosion. Fear and pain. Emptiness. A dark, never-ending vat of emptiness that would suck every joyful moment right out of me.

I remember that moment I shuddered in his arms, soaking wet. "*Just remember, we are invincible together.*" I thought he was the one person who has ever shown me love and caring and truth.

"Your interpretation of the omen?" the Deacon asks, knocking his knuckles on the table in front of me. Somehow, he knew I was getting lost in my head.

"It all happened," Sparrow says matter-of-factly. "Just like Clea prophesized. Just not like we thought it would."

"Hm." Deacon rubs his chin. "Prophecy can be like that. Gray and malleable. None of us really know with absolute certainty what will happen. What did you think would happen?"

"That she was mine."

The way Sparrow says it sends a shiver up the back of my neck.

"But she isn't." Sparrow leans to the side and sets his elbow on the arm of the chair. "Especially now that she is with child. My Kingdom will yield in our desire for revenge. The Archangels yield as well. As long as my sister resides in Meg's realm, we will truce."

Sparrow tips his chin and whistles a light trill in Nightingale's direction.

———

"OUR NEXT WITNESS is going to be delayed," my Deacon says. "He has a long way to travel."

A gavel falls with a loud thud.

"We'll break for lunch." The man in the middle stands.

Deacon escorts me to my cell in solitary. I'm surprised they didn't search it after I switched places with Shay.

"You want something to eat?" Deacon asks. "I can have a tray delivered."

My stomach lurches at the thought of food but I'm hungry. "I want an orange soda and chicken fried steak and a side of curly fries with cheese dipping sauce."

"I'll see what I can do." Deacon walks away. "Don't get too nervous. Maybe take a nap."

Yeah right. Take a nap in the middle of this.

Deacon's footsteps echo as he walks away. Metal squeals as they slide the doors closed and lock me inside, twice.

I move the bed and find the tunnel is still there. They didn't fill it or put me in another cell. I sit, cross-legged. This is too easy. All I have to do is crawl through again and escape to freedom. I can be done with this crock of shit and move on. Running away would be better than killing everyone in the room. It would be better than eternity in this cell.

I tip my head and hear the gentle cooing of the burrowing owls. In the tunnel's darkness, the light from my cell reflects on their eyes. They walk closer, old friends in dark places. There isn't enough room for both of us in that tunnel. I'd have to push them out.

I can't crawl through that tunnel because I will never be free without my friends.

What would Andy Dufresne do? I move to the bed and sit, waiting for my food with my back against the wall. I could do well to believe in the power of hope. That's all we really have, after all.

Tip the Scales of Darkness

The person sitting on the witness stand doesn't look like a person at all. It is an opaque cloud that's struggling to take shape. It swells and ripples, the edges lighten to mist.

"Can you hear me?" my Deacon asks the cloud.

"Yes," the cloud replies with a voice too familiar to forget.

It's Jack!

I turn to look at Noah and Nightingale. They are both leaning forward in their seats. Noah rubs his mouth.

"Thank you." Deacon stands. "I'd like to present Jack Cooper, brother to Noah Cooper, husband to Nightingale, childhood friend of Meg."

I never thought I'd hear Jack's voice again. I can't stop looking at the cloud, trying to will it to take form so I remember him as more than a teether for the undead during the fast-Zombie War. I'd give a lot to see him whole and not covered in blood and bite marks.

"You met Meg in childhood?" Deacon asks.

"Yes," the cloud with Jack's voice replies.

"Then you died and went to Hell. Is that correct?"

"Sure is."

"Who helped you find your way to a Safe House to repent and find your place in the afterlife?"

"Meg."

"Was she alone?"

"No. She was with a Scarecrow. I guess she'd gotten in some trouble."

"You'd gotten in some trouble too. You committed the worst crime of humankind, correct?"

"I killed John Lewis, but it was well deserved." There is no remorse in Jack's voice.

"What would make you do such a thing? Commit your soul to Lucifer for a lower demon?"

"He hurt Meg. She didn't deserve it."

"So, you killed in defense of your friend?"

"I'd do it again. One million times over again. I'd end him for what he did to her." Jack's voice is dead-cold.

Deacon clears his throat. "She brought you to a Safe House but you didn't stay."

"I was worth 400 souls. You all were using me as leverage to pay for Remiel's death. If you ask me, he deserved it. I would have never survived repenting. I would have wasted away to nothing in the Safe House. You all knew it. The whole situation was a load of horse shit. You tried to play me."

"You went to Heaven though," Deacon clarifies.

"I did. I made a deal for the people I love."

"And you were a King." Deacon's voice has a hopeful lilt.

"Until the fast-Zombie War broke through our ceiling." The cloud ripples and heaves and swirls like a tornado. "Now I am nothing."

Nightingale makes a noise from the jury area. Noah wraps an arm around her shoulder and tucks her against him. I remember the chaos in which they died every time I look at Nightingale's scars on her face.

"I am sorry the tragedy occurred." Deacon looks solemn. "I have one last question." He inches closer to the cloud swirling. "In your opinion, does Meg deserve friends like you who would kill for her?"

"Of course."

"Why is that?"

"Because she'd do the same for one of us."

He's not wrong. I cross my arms over my chest feeling cold and empty from hearing Jack's voice.

The cloud slowly dissipates. Without a goodbye, Jack leaves us again.

———

GABRIEL IS LAST. He answers the Deacon's questions about our history together and the battles we've faced. He tells them about losing me. About Sparrow being assigned to watch me, losing me, then the curse taking over. Gabriel tells them about the fast-Zombie War and the safety I offered him when the Archangels turned against him.

"I would give anything to change the way things went with Meg," Gabriel says, "but we thought we were protecting her. If I can do better by my grandchild, I promise I'll do everything I can."

Gabriel's eyes bore into mine and I want to turn away as my cheeks flush with embarrassment. This is not John Lewis who hit me and kicked me and starved me as a child. This is not the lower Demon who raised me under a roof of abuse and hate. John Lewis would have kicked me to the curb if he'd found out I was pregnant. Not Gabriel.

"Could you tell me for the record, how many heartbeats do you hear from Meg's body? There's no room for error."

Gabriel holds up his fingers like a peace sign. "Two." His voice cracks and a single tear drips down his cheek to get lost in his white beard.

I have never known Gabriel to be so emotional, but there is something about this moment; the confession, the truth that's brought tears to his eyes. I've never seen Gabriel in this state before.

———

THERE ARE NO MORE witnesses called to the stand. Instead, the men at the desk-of-questioning release the jury to discuss my fate.

My Deacon sits thin-lipped and offers nothing to me in terms of what to expect. My stomach growls loudly and I'm sure everyone in the room hears it. I sink down in my chair wishing I could dig a hole and hide forever inside of it.

When the door finally opens again, everyone files in and sits, except for Nightingale.

Nightingale stands and clears her throat. "One who is never given love, does not know how to give love or receive it." Her hands are clasped across her middle and she is very still before she says, "We the jury have determined that the only way to decide Meg's fate is to weigh her heart against the feather of truth." Nightingale sits and waits.

The men at the desk nod their heads in agreement.

"What does that mean?" I ask my Deacon.

"An old law, not used for many millennia," he replies.

The feather of truth is white with brown stripes. It's brought into the room on an embellished glass platter along with a gold scale.

"Your heart," the man at the center of the desk-of-questioning says, expectantly.

Gruesome images fill my mind of someone ripping open my chest and taking my heart out.

"Go get your jar of feathers," my Deacon says.

I stare at him. My jar of feathers is on my nightstand.

"Go get it." He motions with his hand. "Poof."

I close my eyes since this hasn't worked in a while and I don't trust myself.

Poof.

I'm standing in my bedroom in the castle. Elise's feathers are where they've been for a while now. My heart. I walk forward, pick up the jar, and tip it to the side.

I could go. I could run. I could *poof* to anywhere. I could *poof* to the moon or the bottom of the ocean and they wouldn't be able to find me. "What should I do?" I ask the feathers.

The urge to return and face my fate is strong. Maybe this is what I deserve: a fresh start. Maybe I can finally accept what I've become. Maybe I can finally accept what grows in my belly. I settle my hand over my womb. I never thought I'd get another chance. I never thought I deserved another chance. I've never embraced my place in this existence or my throne or the people who surround me. I have hope that maybe, just maybe, I'm deserving of it all. I must face the music.

Poof.

I set the jar of feathers on the desk.

"Just one," my Deacon says. "And we're glad you came back."

I smile but just a tiny bit. I choke down the emotion filling my chest and the tears forming in the corner of my eyes. I open the jar and take out a feather. At the desk, one of the old men has moved the golden scale and set the feather of destiny in its place. He motions for me to add mine.

My heart beats in my ears as I take the single feather from the jar and walk to the front of the room. I set it on the open tray of the scale and hold my breath as the scale tilts from side to side.

"If your heart is heavy, you go elsewhere." The man at the center of the desk says.

I swallow the lump in my throat as the tilting of the scale slows. My feather, my heart, it tips up and down and I can't get an idea of where it will stop.

Finally, it slows. It sits even with the feather of destiny, then raises.

"What does that mean?" I ask the men at the desk.

"Your heart is true. You will make the right decisions." The gavel falls, hard and heavy and loud. "You are released," the man in the middle of the desk says.

"What about Skeele?"

"He can go. His contrition is enough."

I rub my eyes, afraid to turn around and face my friends who have become my family.

"One last thing." My Deacon motions for me to wait. "Your belongings." He passes me the bag I was carrying the day I was struck by lightning. He holds up my old I.D., inspecting. "You're going to need to replace this."

"I know. It doesn't really look like me anymore and I don't live in NY."

"No." The Deacon rubs his fingers over the card like he's polishing a fork. "This one will just get you entry into Canada." He hands it back to me. "This is more official for your current situation."

The license is covered in strange markings, something like the runes Jed uses, and my picture is replaced with one more up to date.

WHO SAYS YOU CAN'T GO HOME

We leave the Safe House together. The Hellions branch out and surround us, watching for danger on the crumbling road.

The surroundings look familiar. "Is this the Safe House in Auburn?"

"Yes," Klaus says.

"It's a distance from the castle," I say.

"We can get everyone back if we fly," Klaus says.

"I still can't fly," I say.

"Jed and Shay have to be carried. So would you." Klaus rubs his hands on his pants.

I say goodbye to Gabriel and Teari.

"That arm," Teari warns. "Get the basilisk on it. Then come see me."

"Sure," I promise.

Gabriel hugs me tightly and whispers in my ear. "Whoosh-whoosh-whoosh, that's what it sounds like. Faster than your heartbeat."

He takes Teari's hand and *poof*, they go back to his kingdom.

Nightingale fades to nothing waving to me as she travels back to Thrush.

Noah approaches me. "Why did you break the tether?" he asks.

"I wanted you to be with your family. I wanted you to have time with them and to keep Thrush safe. You didn't need to run all over creation just to find me sodas and Twinkies and waffles with fried chicken."

"Maybe I enjoyed it." He touches my hand. "I meant what I said on the stand. Put the tether back."

Noah has always been the best friend a girl could have, and I ache for every moment of laughter we've ever had to come back into our lives. I want to throw bird seed and talk in whistles and chirps and call each other ridiculous names. I've missed it all these months.

"Do it, Meg," he urges.

I nod and replace the tether to our souls.

"Now," Noah gives me a dashing smile, "What do you want to eat? I'll have it waiting in your room."

I opt for waffles and fried chicken with chocolate milk. "Enough for two," I say. "Please."

"Shit," Noah chuckles. "Manners and everything."

"What can I say? I'm turning a new leaf."

"Let's hope." Noah disappears.

Chel approaches Shay and offers to fly her back to the castle. Shay glances to Jed and he nods, pointing to Tukka. "You take me," he says.

The four of them take to the air.

I'm left alone with Skeele and Klaus.

They're giving me an option. It's easy to see. I get an option after all those times I shafted Skeele and chose Gabriel or the Argentavis or traveled on my own.

Do better, Meg. I tell myself.

I've been with Skeele and embraced it before. My time with Kal was great. No judgement, no horns or blood. It was Skeele all along. I don't have to push him away. I accepted his invitations to dates and other things. If this is going to work, I can't keep pushing him away.

"Will you take me back?" I ask Skeele.

He nods, solemn. And I get the feeling he's guarded and just following orders. He's probably used to doing that. Not getting attached just like I said. He was definitely attached as Kal and I get the feeling he's attached as Skeele; he's just great at hiding it.

Klaus launches himself into the air and flies away.

I'm finally alone with Skeele.

"I'm sorry," I say.

"You don't–"

I press my fingers against his heart. "I do. I was afraid. I was wrong." I slide my hands up his chest and round his neck.

"Don't be afraid. I'm here." Skeele steps closer, closing the distance between us until our bodies are flush.

"I told you not to get attached." My eyes burn.

"It was too late." Skeele wraps his arms round my shoulders and holds me close. He lifts me into his arms, takes a step, and launches us into the air. His leathery wings beat hard and strong as he flies us through Hellsky.

I close my eyes and raise my face to the ochre sun. I should have let him carry me all those other times, because this feels right and safe.

———

"Child," Clea calls as I enter the giant door of the burning caves. "You're back."

Her cool, Astral form hugs me.

"They didn't ask you to speak at the trial," I say.

Red lips stretch to a smile. "Can't put a mother on the witness stand for her child. We'd say whatever we needed to. It wouldn't be right."

"Are you saying you'd lie for me?" I ask.

Her image wavers. "There are things I'd do, and the Deacons knew better than to invite me." She walks toward the ballroom and motions for us to follow. "While you were gone, I had planning to do."

Creatures scurry in the shadows as we walk, our shoes echoing on the stone floor. Skeele's footsteps are not far behind mine.

Clea pushes open the ballroom doors and everyone is there.

"Congratulations on your parole!" Noah shouts.

There's a table laden with food. Pizza and slushies, cake and fried chicken, fondu and shrimp cocktail and deviled eggs. Nightingale is skating in circles while Thrush laughs in her arms. She stops near a record player to drop the arm down. *Wake me up Before You Go-Go* starts playing.

Skeele touches my shoulder.

"When I was little, I would sing 'wake me up before the cocoa,'" I say. "Not to anyone, just to myself. In my room. Alone."

Everyone hugs me. And I let them. I squeeze them tight: Chel, Tukka, Klaus, Noah, Jed, Shay, Nightingale, Thrush, and when Gabriel and Teari crash the party a few hours later, I hug them too. There's no Sparrow, or Archangels from the Seven Kingdoms of Heaven. I'm not saying I'd hug them, but right now I wouldn't stab them. Just for tonight, I won't stab them.

As we're eating and dancing, one of the new recruit Hellions enters the Ballroom with a black-dressed Deacon.

I walk over to meet them, Skeele at my shoulder.

"What do you want?" Skeele asks. "We were released, fair and square."

"You were." It's my Deacon, the one who sat next to me during the trial. "But you left this behind."

He holds up the jar of feathers and passes it to me.

I reach for the jar. "Thanks," I say.

My memories of Elise. I rotate the jar and watch the feathers float. When I look up again the Deacon is gone. I wasn't planning on inviting him to stay but a goodbye would have been nice.

"Are you okay?" Skeele asks, watching me warily.

"Yeah." I set the jar on the table with our food and plates.

"It won't be like last time," Skeele says, drawing me to the balcony. "I'm here."

I nod and hold back threatening tears.

"Are you hungry?" he asks, glancing to the shadows. "We don't have to leave the party if you are."

"Until the bloodlust hits at least," I remind him.

He tucks his wings tight against his back. I touch the fern-like scars on his arm.

"So, Kal, did you enjoy being a human?" I ask.

He rubs his neck. "It was an experience. I didn't like not being able to fly." His eyes focus on me. "I didn't like you not taking care of yourself." He touches the matching scars on my arm. "Did this hurt?"

I shake my head. "I don't remember."

He turns me and presses his fingers against two bony ridges on my back. "Did this hurt?"

"What is that?" I ask, trying to get a look over my shoulder.

He smirks, knowing. "Can you feel them?"

"I didn't notice before." It doesn't feel like he's touching my shoulder blades; there's something else there.

Skeele picks me up and launches us into Hellsky.

My stomach churns. "Careful big boy, or you're going to get a faceful of half-digested pizza."

We climb higher into the night sky as he flaps his powerful wings. "None of us came out of the womb with wings. They need an urge to sprout." He searches my face. "Our parents would drop us from the sky. It's the only method we know. Kick the baby bird out of the nest and teach it to fly."

"Don't drop me." I grip around his neck. "I can't." I squeeze my eyes closed. All those times I was flung into the air surge to the forefront of my mind.

"We'll go together. I'd never let you fall. I'd never let you hit the ground. Know that."

I open one eye, afraid.

"Ready?"

I nod. I swallow hard and take a few deep breaths.

Skeele holds me out and stops moving his wings. We drop like a roller-coaster descending that first giant hill. He doesn't let go. He stays. His hands warm under my arms, holding me like no one ever has before.

A warm feeling begins in my chest, radiates across my shoulders and neck, then my back. After it feels like we have been falling for too long, we stop. Gently. Not like that time I fell from the sky and broke every bone in my body.

"Night Owl," Skeele says. "Open your eyes."

I open them, feeling the strange heaviness on my back. Skeele is looking at me like I'm something special. Our feet are on the ground. Skeele releases my elbows.

My wings are dappled gray and white, soft and downy as I run my hands down the sides.

Blinking a few times, my eyes focus slowly and everything changes in the moonlight filtered through Hellsky. My vision is crisp, colors more vibrant, the swishing of the grass audible to my ears like it has never been. There is something more, something beating fast, *lubdub-lubdub-lubdub*. It's faster than most pulses I've heard. Softer too, gentler and pure. The light lilt of a tiny bell.

"Do you hear that?" I ask.

Skeele shakes his head.

I glance down, realizing it's the baby's heartbeat. The one I had tried to silence. The one I'd tried to rid myself of. The one I'd tried to hide and exterminate like it was nothing more than a bug. I am reminded of the day I heard Elise's heartbeat for the first time. I saw her tiny arms and legs moving on the ultrasound in the doctor's office. I loved her in that moment. And not long after she was taken from me.

She was innocent in the war between the Seven Kingdoms of Heaven and Hell and the Earthen plane. She was harmless. But sometimes, men with power must crush innocence to stay relevant.

The sound quickens, *lubdub-lubdub-lubdub.* I can't believe I wanted it gone. I can't believe I would leave it elsewhere. I understand why Gabriel's eyes leaked tears when he said he could hear it. *lubdub-lubdub-lubdub.* It is more, so much more. Hope and inspiration and... home.

Epilogue

Teari was right. It was eighteen months. Eighteen months of apologies, forgiveness, and getting my shit straight. I accepted the throne of Hell in all of its glory. I accepted the Hellions as my legion of warriors. We had law and order, and Hell wasn't all that bad for the Demons and the dead. Or at least, that's what they told me. My grandfather led by fear and death for eons. Newcomers rarely found a Safe House during Lucifer's time. Now they are escorted daily and as a result the dead that walk Hell are fewer in numbers. Their souls are not lost. They do not wake up a walking sack of flesh. The Hellions patrol and get them moving in time. The Deacons seem to appreciate the effort. Not once have they interrupted dinner since we left the Safe House the day of my trial-except to return my jar of feathers.

I stopped thinking of Sparrow. I no longer desired revenge for him stabbing me to death that one day. I try to focus on what he taught me-what the entire incident taught me. That it's okay to fall ass over teakettle in love and lust but people change, circumstances change. We can't go back in time and relive those days, but we can build a new home. Something like we've never had before.

Noah and Nightingale raised Thrush in their little corner of Hell. The cemetery has been their paradise. No one bothers them, not even me. Even though I replaced the tether, I do my best to give Noah his freedom and time with Nightingale. Since Jed brought her back, we're not sure how long she'll stay before her soul is whisked away back to death. My hope is she'll be like Clea and Noah, and her Astral form will stay with us forever.

Jed and Shay have stayed at the castle. They tag along with the Hellions, rescuing lost souls and practicing ancient magic. Jed is sure he will come across another Nephilim. But like he's said a thousand times before, they rarely make it past childhood. It doesn't stop him from looking.

We never rebuilt the portals. Each month the Hellions make the rounds to ensure they are nothing but rubble. If someone wants to sneak into Hell, they must use Demore's pond which is heavily warded thanks to Jed.

The basilisk babies grew too big for the castle. We kept two and released the others. One protects Noah and Nightingale's chapel. Two went to Demore's pond. The others went back to the dark waters of the black river in the Adirondacks of Hell.

When the birth finally came, there was no bloodbath like in the books she showed me. There was no gore or torn apart vaginas or vacant eyes. The birth was quiet. The parts of me that hurt during and after, Teari healed almost instantly. Skeele held me and fed me and brushed my hair out of my eyes when Teari set the naked baby on my chest.

"She has dark hair, like you," Skeele said.

I touched his horns and asked, "Not these?"

"No." He shook his head as the baby let out a blat. "She's mouthy like you too. Looks like she has your temper."

The Hellions made a bassinet out of dark stained wood. In the middle of the night, I sometimes woke to find Skeele rocking it with one foot while he sat reading in the leather club chair.

In the time that followed, I healed. I learned to love. I learned to accept what others gave me. I told Skeele to get attached. I got attached. I grew stronger. I became more than my hunger and blood-lust. Skeele kept my bed warm and my heart full. We had everything I never thought I deserved. For now.

A truce can only last for so long. One day, I know they'll come again. The fast-dead, the Archangels, God. Whoever it may be. Veils of shadows surround us in every realm, filled with secrets and silent wars. A veil of shadows once occluded my vision. It kept me small. It kept me weak. It kept me angry and afraid and filled with venom. It is no more.

-The End-

Veil of Shadows III (Preview)

Etched in Darkness

Running for your life wasn't a sport on the Earthen plane, but for Jed, it was survival. Jed had been on the run since he could walk on two legs and finally escape the creatures that came for him day and night. Since he was Nephilim, this was the way it would always be. He'd been around for a while. He'd been hunted for a while. He knew this from the few others he'd met that were like him. They didn't last long, but they traded stories and methods to stay alive. Jed tapped his pocket, feeling the notebook of spells that was left to him by the last Nephilim he'd come across decades ago. Declan wasn't much older that Jed, but he'd lasted by way of spells and runes carved into every flat surface of his house and belongings. Jed took it one step further and carved those runes into his skin. It was good practice since now he could make a living with the tattoo gun. But, every so often, a creature would walk through the doors of his shop that didn't belong. Like Meg did that one day. Meg, with her dark energy and light eyes. There was something about her he didn't understand. She paid in full and held conversation while he tattooed the watercolor sparrow over her heart. He revealed little about himself. It was when she came back again and brought that fallen-Angel Hellion Sparrow that she wound up ruining the pleasant spot he was at in life. Sparrow was all kinds of cursed. Jed could see it the moment he laid eyes on the guy. Worse was that Meg was head over heels in love. He helped them, tattooed them with runes of protection. And all it got him was noticed.

Jed touched the mark on his neck. He also lost a little blood when Meg bit him. Jed tried to shake away the feelings. Lust and heat had filled his body. He remembered touching her waist before he passed out. Whatever she was, he wanted more but he also wanted to never see her again. Meg was trouble. Trouble he didn't have time for if he wanted to stay alive.

Now here he was on the run again, making his way toward the rural towns of the Midwest, away from the crowded cities of the Northeast. With any hope, he'd avoid the dead until someone else took care of them and he'd avoid Angels and Demons and dead things as well. He'd find food and shelter and hunker down until it was safe again.

Jed stopped under the awning of an empty gas station. The dead hadn't been walking for long, a few months at least, but the destruction and abandon was rapid. Jed glanced through the glass of the gas station and auto shop to see if there was anything inside worth investigating. His pack was heavy with clothes and food, his water jug half-full. He focused on the shelves behind the counter. He could use a smoke. It had been a long time since he set a cancer stick to his lips. He gave up the dirty habit when New York State outlawed them. It surprised him Indiana hadn't outlawed them too.

The sound of shuffling feet broke the afternoon silence. On this daily trek from Walkerton to Kingsbury, Jed hadn't seen much life. He was sure the dead were making their way to nearby Chicago. They always seemed to move with purpose, clustering in small groups. Something drove them to move and follow as one.

A man's voice startled Jed. "A large herd of zombies are making their way through California."

Jed walked to the door of the gas station and found the television mounted in the far corner of the waiting area. A map of the U.S. replaces the reporter's image; the movement of the dead is illustrated with green blobs like weather radar. There's a large area of green over southern California, moving north. They color the area south of the green zone black. A dead zone. A universal warning. Do not go there.

"If you're still in northern California and you're hearing this message, evacuate. Evacuate now! The Coast Guard has abandoned the west coast. The National Guard has declared California a complete loss."

Jed focused on the spattering of green where he was traveling. The Midwest wasn't overly populated, it would be easier to hunker down. His gaze went to the west coast again. The green blob travelled along a main highway. He found that interesting. The dead didn't care about roads, they moved through forests just as haphazardly. It was almost like they were following something.

The news reporter rubbed his face and looked thoroughly terrified. There were loud thuds from the television and a light fell over and hit the desk where the reporter sat. The reporter stood. "Evacuate now!" he shouted one last time before picking up his chair and throwing it. A dead woman walked across the News set before the screen turned to static.

Jed glanced at the shelves and noticed some of the snack foods hadn't been completely pillaged. There was a handful of Slim Jims, Oreos, and a few tins of Spam. Jed went for the protein. The sugary cookies might taste good, but he knew he'd be feeling like crap the next day.

There was a change in the air. Something like mild electricity popping. Turning, he noticed a figure walking down the street.

Jed paused, crouched, and watched the tall man walking down the road. Angel wings were invisible on this plane, but he could see their transparent glimmer. He always knew when they were near; feathered or leathered, he could see the wings in the right light.

This was an Angel. Come to put an end to his life, since he was forbidden and all. They never stopped. Jed traced his footsteps in his mind and tried to think of any clues he could have left behind. He'd been careful on his travels. He was always careful. Never left a trail or a crumb or much of a memory. He was good at being invisible. He was beige in an ochre world, blending in with vacant faces and warm bodies. He tipped his hat lower to hide his face. A shuffling sound echoed.

Jed whispered a spell of glamour and his fingers tapped gently in spellcasting. He leaned to the side and didn't see his reflection in the glass window of the gas station. He scooted forward, careful not to step on any debris that would make the Angel walking down the road notice him. He made his way out the door, keeping to the shadows. He stopped once he got around the corner of the building.

The shuffling sound got louder. It didn't seem to bother the Angel walking down the street. He was tall, lithe with muscle, a blade drawn. His clothing was similar to what most wore on the Earthen plane; leathers and linen or jeans and a T-shirt. A Demon he'd be able to spot based on clothing alone. They were always in full leather. Dark leather, black or deep red like a kidney bean. The Angel gripped his blade and walked with purpose. Jed wiped sweat from his brow, worried the glamour wasn't doing its job.

The wind blew.

Jed sneezed.

Shit.

The Angel picked up his pace and began running in Jed's direction. The shuffling sound got even louder as five of the dead broke onto the street and went after the Angel.

Jed ran. He wasn't a coward; he just knew it was easier to avoid the creatures that came for him than expend the energy needed to kill them. He needed to save his energy for the important battles.

About Veil of Shadows III omnibus edition

A collection of the Veil of Shadows Series Books 7-10.

———

This omnibus edition begins with "Etched in Darkness", book 7 in the Veil of Shadows Series. You can start here if books 1-6 are not your jam. The next few books in this series will focus on Jed and Shay's relationship and can be read without books 1-6. We will go back in time and revisit old friends. Then catch up with Sparrow and Meg's timeline.

———

If you want to immerse yourself further in the Veil of Shadows, visit the blog for Veil of Shadows discussions, previews, and spoilers.

———

Etched in Darkness (Veil of Shadows 7)

When darkness beckons and love defies the unknown, destiny takes an unexpected turn.

Before Shay got her blowtorch blue hair, she was just an ordinary Montana cowgirl, raised by prepper parents on a remote ranch. But everything shifted one fateful day when a ranch hand struck a perilous bargain with a Crossroads Demon, unleashing chaos that forever altered Shay's existence.

Amidst the turmoil, Jed, a mysterious man with a past intertwined with the supernatural, arrives in town, becoming Shay's unexpected ally. As the eerie consequences of the unholy pact unfold, Shay finds herself at a crossroads, torn between the safety of her familiar ranch life and the allure of a journey into the unknown alongside Jed.

Haunted by newfound powers and grappling with the weight of an otherworldly destiny, Shay must navigate treacherous landscapes—both within and outside herself. Will she embrace the unknown, embarking on an adventure fraught with danger and desire, or choose the familiar comforts of her home despite the looming darkness?

In a tale woven with dark enchantment and the whispered promises of forbidden love, Shay must confront her deepest fears and make a choice that will alter not just her fate but the destiny of those entwined with her.

Embrace the Night (Veil of Shadows Book 8)

Haunted by shadows, Bound by fate.

As Jed and Shay embark on their journey to California, the path ahead is fraught with peril. Angels, hell-bent on Jed's demise, and Demons coveting Shay for their own sinister purposes, shadow their every step.

All seems to be progressing smoothly until a heartbroken ghost intervenes, diverting their course and leading to Shay's abduction. With each twist in the road, danger emerges anew, compelling Jed to contemplate the solitary and perilous route to ruin.

In a relentless pursuit against supernatural forces and unforeseen threats, Jed must navigate a treacherous landscape where allies are scarce, and the odds of survival grow slimmer. Will he defy the odds to rescue Shay, or will the Demons of their journey propel him toward a desolate path of self-destruction? The road to California unfolds as a haunting odyssey, where every turn unearths not only the perils of the present but also the ghosts of Jed's past.

Shadows of Destiny (Veil of Shadows Book 9)

A journey of darkness and despair: Will Jed defy fate to save Shay, or succumb to his own ruin?

If looks could kill, Alastor would raze all of Hell in retribution. He didn't appreciate being sent home in a blast of light with everything he'd built destroyed, and he's going to do everything in his power to hunt down the half-breed who did it.

For Jed and Shay, Hell is filled with challenges, from hiding a stolen Angel baby to being a body double for the Queen, these two have their work cut out for them. Yet, beneath the surface, Jed wrestles with the guilt of upending Shay's once-normal existence.

Jed and Shay must navigate a perilous path, where the line between savior and destroyer blurs, and the consequences of their choices echo through the infernal corridors.

———

Midnight Serenade (Veil of Shadows Book 10)

Trapped between Heaven and Hell, Jed faces his demons while Shay's fate hangs in the balance.

Jed finds himself ensnared in a perilous web of darkness and despair as he confronts his inner demons. Shay's fate teeters on the edge of oblivion, her very existence hanging in the balance.

Meanwhile, amidst the chaos of the infernal realm, Alastor, driven by a thirst for vengeance, searches for a means to infiltrate the castle and unleash his wrath upon those who have wronged him. But his path is fraught with danger, and the shadows of betrayal lurk around every corner.

As if the looming threat of Alastor's vengeance weren't enough, Nero's transformation into a monstrous entity sends shockwaves through the kingdom, casting a pall of fear and uncertainty over all who dwell within its walls. Outside the castle, a malevolent presence lurks, waiting to unleash its fury upon any who dare to cross its path.

In this dark and twisted tale of betrayal, redemption, and the struggle for survival, Jed and Shay must navigate a treacherous landscape where the line between friend and foe blurs and the consequences of their choices echo through the halls of Hell itself. Will they find the strength to overcome the darkness that threatens to consume them, or will they be lost to its unforgiving embrace?

About the Author

Thank you, thank you, thank you for sticking with the Veil of Shadows Series. It took a long time but we finally found an end to Sparrow and Meg's story. I know, it's different than what we wanted. I still love Sparrow. Who couldn't? There's SO much that he and Meg went through. I cried at the ending of Night Owl. I was so sad to see them go. BUT, they are two of my favorite characters and we revisit them in the near future. They are immortal after all :)

Veil of Shadows is not over. I will continue to write in this world. Up next is Etched in Darkness. Over the next few books we will dive into Jed and Shay's stories. Shay was an unexpected character who showed up in Raven King and she's been tethered in my brain, asking to get out. I'm loving her story of a badass Montana cowgirl who gets caught up in a world of Demons and Angels. You can start their adventure today, there's a preview included at the end of this book!

————

M. R. Pritchard writes about the elemental struggle between good and evil, and gods and monsters, and about people who turn into gods and monsters. Usually with a mix of apocalypse or post-apocalyptic setting. She also includes a spec of a love story because what is humanity without love?

M. R. Pritchard is a two-time Kindle Scout winning author, her short story "Glitch" has been featured in the 2017 winter edition of THE FIRST LINE literary journal. Her short story "Moon Lord" has been featured in Chronicle Worlds: Half Way Home (Part of the Future Chronicles) and will be time capsuled on the moon on the Lunar Codex in 2024. M. R. Pritchard holds degrees in Biochemistry and Nursing. She is a northern New Yorker transplanted to the Gulf Coast of Florida who enjoys coffee, mint chocolate, cloudy days, and reading on the lanai.

Visit her website MRPritchard.com or MRPritchardbooks.com and sign up for her newsletter. You'll get a monthly newsletter with updates, special previews of new projects, and book deals.

If you enjoyed *Veil of Shadows*, please leave a review, tell a friend, or gift to a friend. These small acts keep authors writing. Thank you.

Looking for Special Edition Hardcovers? Visit her website for signed and Special Edition versions of stories you love!

www.ingramcontent.com/pod-product-compliance
Lightning Source LLC
Chambersburg PA
CBHW061534190726
48289CB00004B/1035